For Mum, Dad, all my friends, my whole family and everyone in between.

'Do not be overcome by evil, but overcome evil with good.'
Romans 12:21

Dear Sammy and David,

Enjoy the book — I know you've been waiting to read it!

TAINTED BLOOD

Joseph Mead

Book 1 of the *Aleera* Series

Joseph Mead

Published in 2008 by YouWriteOn.com
Copyright © Joseph Mead
First Edition
The author asserts the moral right under the Copyright, Designs and Patents Act 1988 to be identified as
the author of this work.
All Rights reserved. No part of this publication may be reproduced, stored in a retrieval system, or
transmitted, in any form or by any means without the prior written consent of the author, nor be
otherwise circulated in any form of binding or cover other than that in which it is published and without a
similar condition being imposed on the subsequent purchaser.
Published by YouWriteOn.com

1

Midnight. Thin white curtains waved in the dull breeze that washed over Aleera's back and rustled strands of pure-black hair, the thick, heavy covers long since pushed back in the stifling heat of the summer night. Closed eyes and deep, slow breathing were of no help, and the window opened earlier to let the heat out succeeded only in letting *in* the infuriating noises of angry cab drives shouting over blaring horns and a pair of alley cats fighting somewhere. The old lady upstairs was shouting to whoever lived above her to 'turn down that god-awful noise', and Aleera could only agree with the sentiment. Whatever idiot lived up there apparently thought that the volume control on his stereo was there by a factory error. Turning over for what must have been the hundredth time, she gave a tired groan and pulled the pillow over her head, which only succeeded in making the itching heat even worse.

Finally giving up the futile effort, she turned over to see what time it was. It had been a long while since she last felt so strong an urge to blast a hole in the ceiling like the stressed seventeen-year-old demon she was, and tell the entire building to shut its collective mouth and let her sleep. And as her eyes attested, whatever threat she thought to make would likely be far from idle.

The eyes again, she realised. That was always annoying. Concentrating, she felt her irises relax slightly as their colour changed from the less-natural vivid red to their standard chocolate-brown. While there was no-one else there to actually see the small change in appearance, it had still become an irritant over the years that it happened without mercy every time something pestered her. It was hard enough keeping them normal at school all day.

The noise from upstairs was finally replaced with a cacophony of shouts exchanged between the old lady and the young man, who a few minutes later finally turned down the music and freed her from the temptation to deal with it herself.

If the long, *long* night hadn't thoroughly drained her sense of humour- for which Aleera was not best known on the cheeriest of occasions- she might have found the irony amusing on some level when she next opened her eyes five hours later and discovered that she was late for school.

Still, there was time- or rather, she made time- for a cold shower to wash away any remaining desire to sleep. Besides, it wouldn't do to spend the day feeling so infuriatingly hot and sticky. The company she was forced to spend her classes with, with all of two exceptions, was bad enough.

Honestly, if there was a God, human beings were all the proof needed that he, she or it had a sense of humour. And it appeared to be the sort to giggle like a lunatic at dead baby jokes. Then again, the main alternatives were Draconics or Demons; one that could do magic and thought it had the moral high ground over humans, and one that could also use magic, didn't have any moral high ground, and honestly didn't care about moral high grounds. Aleera had once heard a saying that, if a God did create this world, then it was a God in learning. Upon further consideration, she had decided that it was a D-student, speaking generously.

She stepped out of the shower; there would be time to wash her hair later, and now she felt awake and much cooler. After drying herself off, she picked out her preferred outfit, a black blouse and matching jeans. On the way out- and this seemed to be the main difference between herself and most other girls her age- she found the time to grab a slice of toast along with her book bag. Half of her school's female population would give her some kind of dirty look whenever she sat down in the cafeteria to a lunch that actually looked like it could sustain a growing seventeen-year-old, as if eating were some diabolical sin. Heaven forefend there should be a pretty face that wasn't bulimic as was, evidently, expected of her. God, normal people were twisted.

Aleera actually made it to school with a few minutes to spare, which was always nice. It never did to rush things, and she often liked to observe humanity in its natural state. It made her feel better about herself to know that it could always be worse. The school itself was a typical place of its kind, plucked from any education system that nobody in charge ever seemed to be paying much attention to. Old, square, grey building, sports field out back, clock on the front; generally, one of those 'nobody cares' places. Students who think black fingernails or hooded sweaters were somehow rebellious, were of course fitted as standard. Aleera was just there to try and get on with her education without school ruining it. It was a losing battle.

Still, it looked as though it would be a passable day; she even made it five feet past the gates before the catcalls started, and even managed to travel almost a full meter before having to twist one of the apes' arms for trying to grab a free handful of her backside. Once, she had taken her friends' advice and gone to see the Principal about the matter. The only good it did was that she learned to avoid the old pervert when he looked down her shirt and asked 'can you blame them'?

That was what being half-succubus did for you. A succubus was a sexual being, plain and simple, and a full-blooded one could quite easily sustain herself on the energy, ahem, exerted by her, *ahem*, partner. Even if Aleera was only one by her mother's side of the family, it apparently meant three things: the first was being bisexual, which she was used to; it was, after all, the norm for her- in fact, it was hard to understand sometimes why humans felt the need to limit themselves to only one choice. Second were the pheromones that, over time, led to idiotic behaviour like this, which she did not overly want to be used to. The third, if you didn't just put that down to the normal kind of genetics, was, however much it meant having to put up with some brain-dead human's eyes falling out of his head to stare at her, being among the most gorgeous young ladies anyone could hope to meet; a, midnight-black hair that reached down to her hips and perfectly framed her pale face, delicate cheekbones, deep, dark brown eyes and the type of figure that, even when fully clothed, never let anyone forget that she was naked underneath.

Luckily, being taken seriously wasn't too much of a problem. Ironic, really, that if someone heard of a half-succubus they would probably assume the other half to be human. That was, unfortunately, not the case; her father had been a demon, and not just *any* demon. It was that side of the family that caused most of the dirty looks she caught from draconics and even the occasional demon. She'd picked up enough from her father's side, though, that it was very easy for her to be very frightening with very little effort. She gave off the impression that trying anything with her was about as wise as placing one's arm in a car crusher.

She did get the occasional... *problem*... of course. But it really wasn't so much nature as nurture. Not every demon went on killing sprees and wanted to raise the fires of hell. Not that they were all good, certainly not. They we roughly the same in terms of morality as humans... wow, they were bad.

Stopping, Aleera took a quick drink from a leaky old water fountain on the side of the school building. Since when was she this reflective of a morning? It was probably the weather; it had been overcast, dull and dreary for about two days, and the muggy night and lack of sleep hadn't helped. The weather reports had given out a thunder storm about three days ago and it still hadn't come. Aleera didn't like storms. Bad memories. Or maybe it had just been a little too long since she last indulged.

It would be nice, though. Maybe after school, if she could find someone. Just for a few minutes.

Finishing her drink, she stepped away from the water fountain and intended to step away from the building, expecting to meet her friends in the usual place beside the bike racks. Were the world to come to a sudden end, there were about five people Aleera would miss whom she could name off the top of her head. Two of them went to school with her, and like her, they were considerably more than human. If someone could use magic, they could sense it in someone else without even trying. Any draconic or demon would know another just from a glance. But instead of the bike rack, filling her vision was a growing crowd of students, informing her that there was doubtlessly some form of juvenile altercation occurring. That, naturally, drew a crowd. All the precious little children yearning for the sight of blood and crowding around like a pack of hyenas.

Of course, if this was where she met her friends... Aleera pushed her way through the crowd to see what was happening. When she did, her blood boiled.

'My brother asked you a question,' a fifteen-year-old in a woollen cap- in the middle of summer, no less. Practicality didn't get a look-in next to conformity- was saying. His breath smelled strongly of marijuana.

'Why you bein' such a bitch?' The boy in the jacket with a smoking joint still in his hand repeated himself. 'I said-'

'I heard you,' the girl on the bike railing answered without being threatening. Maybe she was trying, but she obviously wasn't used to it. Her entire appearance, from her straight shoulder-length blonde hair, pale skin and shining blue eyes to her pink T-shirt and light-blue jeans, was too complementary to her bright voice to be intimidating.

Aleera didn't know what all of this about, but she had known Sara since the day she started at that school. Seeing this did not please her in the slightest.

'Then answer me,' the older boy said with the so-called authority of the street. Apparently it came from being stoned and owning a knife. 'Why won't you go out with me?'

Sara didn't want to repeat her answer. She wasn't used to being threatened. 'I don't want to,' she finally said, shining eyes wide open and hands behind her back.

'Well,' the boy took a drag from the joint and leaned in with yellow eyes. 'I do'. He stepped back and shoved the girl back, turning to the gathered students, waving his arms and giving an indignant shout of 'the hell you lookin at', as though nobody had any right to interrupt him. Idiots like this seemed to think they were God.

'She ain't gonna go for it, man', his brother laughed. Then laughed a little more. Probably the pot at work. 'She hangs round with that freakin psycho with the weird name, remember? The dyke.'

The older one took another drag, then put out the end of the joint with his thumb and finger. He stepped up to Sara, grinned with yellow teeth, and grabbed her, pulling her forward and grabbing her lips with his. Sara pulled back straight away and was shoved unceremoniously to the ground for her troubles.

Then a hand grabbed his wrist, pulling it up sharply behind his back at the right angle to cause the maximum pain. Unlike Sara, Aleera *was* used to being threatened. And she knew how to deal with it.

'It's time to stop now,' she said levelly.

'Fuck you,' the boy spat, 'you want summa this?'

Aleera struggled. Not with the boy. He was too blasted to even know where his arm was, much less how to free it. She was struggling with the desire to twist the arm the rest of the way so that it would pop out at the joint. Aleera had four friends in the world, and she wasn't about to let someone do this to one of them. Besides, it really *had* been too long since she last indulged, and hearing this pathetic animal scream was sounding more and more tempting by the second. 'Firstly, no, not particularly. You're not my type. That, and frankly some deodorant wouldn't kill you. Secondly, mind your language.'

'Dyke,' the younger one spat. Literally. Aleera wiped a spot of saliva from her cheek.

'Bisexual, actually. Though that might give you some trouble; it does have more than two syllables.' The ape stared at Aleera in a mix of confusion and disgust at the existence of a being of actual intelligence. The world really would be better off without idiots like this, and Aleera was more-than-willing to reduce the idiot population right this minute.

The boy trapped in the half-nelson struggled. Aleera kicked his legs out from under him, releasing his arm as he fell to the ground, then brought one foot up and used it to press down on his back, effectively pinning him to the ground. 'I said,' she repeated with the same external calmness, 'It's time to stop now.' This time, her voice was now level- though she didn't raise it either. It still managed to somehow drip with enough menace to make its owner's point. If he had anything resembling a brain- *if*- he would drop the matter straight away.

He didn't.

As soon as Aleera stepped away, he did what she had truly hoped he would do: pulled a knife out his jacket pocket and lunged at her with it. Sara's eyes widened. Everybody gasped. Aleera simply swung to the side, allowing the knife to bypass her, grabbed the ape's wrist in one hand and jabbed the other elbow into his face with the very-satisfying crunch of a breaking nose. For a split-second, her eyes lidded as the irises flooded with bright red. It was only a second, but it was still ever-so-pleasant to cut loose. The ape fell straight to the ground and dropped the knife onto the asphalt. Aleera glanced over at his brother, caught his angry glare, and silently mouthed the words 'don't try it'. The boy did the smart thing and ran for what little life he had.

Sara stood up. A small, silver cross dangled from her neck as she traced its edges with her thumb and finger.

'Are you alright?' Aleera asked as her eyes reverted to their normal colour. Sara nodded shakily. Aleera turned and gave the crowd her iciest glare. It began to drift apart almost at once, allowing Aleera and her friend some privacy.

'Thanks, Aleera,' Sara smiled weakly when just about everyone had drifted away. She looked away from Aleera, fidgeting awkwardly for a moment as she fished for something to say.

'Come on,' Aleera advised, leading Sara away from the human wretch who was beginning to hobble away, cradling his bleeding nose. 'You should get a drink of water.'

'I'm not the one who almost got knifed,' Sara answered, the words contrasting strangely with the lack of sternness in her voice. 'Sorry. But you should be more careful than that.'

'We can do magic,' Aleera answered dismissively. 'What could happen?'

'Draconics shouldn't tempt fate. Besides, imagine if the Guild found out you were using magic around here. You get into enough trouble as it is.'

'That doesn't stop you from using it,' Aleera lectured.

'Half-human, remember?' That was true. Sara, being half-human and half-draconic, was the closest thing to a likeable human Aleera had ever met. 'And anyway, I hate it when you or Michael gets in trouble because of me.' Sara half-smiled. 'I can't tell who's lecturing who here.'

Aleera smiled back. 'I'm not having that happen to my friend if I can help it, Sara. I mean it.'

'You do realise that half the school thinks we're a couple because you keep standing up for me, right?'

Aleera flinched slightly. 'Oh,' was all she could think to say at first. 'Sorry'. Truth be told, someone had asked her that once, but Sara wasn't *that* kind of friend to her.

The sound of a foot tapping against the ground started behind Aleera. When she turned, a tall, severe-looking woman with half-moon glasses, a suit and entirely too much make-up was standing there glaring at her.

'Yes?' Aleera asked impatiently. She had a friend to attend to.

'That's "yes, Ms. Wood",' the teacher said severely. 'And you can take your attitude to the Principal's office, young lady. I expect you can explain to him why you assaulted another student on school grounds?' Honestly, why did these people always feel the need to speak like a textbook? Aleera would have debated that parts about her 'attitude' and 'assault', but that would be a waste of time. People who talked like textbooks didn't listen to you unless the textbooks told them to.

It wasn't that Aleera hated school. She didn't even particularly dislike it. She just wished that it wasn't crammed full of students who were of slightly less value to society than her little finger. It would also be a bonus if the fat little man behind the desk could keep his eyes off her for all of twenty seconds. She'd been sat in the small, dusty office, whose prominent placement of various diplomas on the walls and school trophies on the desk and windowsill suggested that the office's owner was overcompensating for something, for around five minutes, and she was fairly sure that the man who called her there was using the paperwork as an excuse to take a few minutes to look her up and down.

The Principal finally finished signing the last of the list of papers and turned to Aleera. 'Aleera,' he began, 'This is the third incident we've had with you in as many weeks.' Aleera didn't respond. 'Do you know what that means?'

Aleera pretended to think for a moment. 'The other students just aren't getting it?' she hazarded.

'No,' the Principal answered sharply. 'It means you can expect two weeks of detention, you'll be expected to meet with the school counsellor tomorrow, and in addition to that you can consider yourself on probation. You're aware that this means that one more act of this nature will result in a suspension?"

Aleera turned and glared at him. Before she voiced what was on her mind, she needed to check something. 'And what about him?'

'I beg your pardon?'

'What about the waste of flesh that was harassing my friend and pulled a knife on me?'

'Can you prove that this happened?'

Aleera barely suppressed a very bitter laugh. 'You're telling me to bring you proof?' She raised her eyebrows. 'You're not a police officer. You're a fat little man behind a desk who doesn't have any idea what to do with someone who's actually trouble, so just puts someone else there on probation so that he looks like he's doing something about what's going on in school. So you put someone on probation for helping a friend, after they almost get stabbed *in your school*, as opposed to the knife-wielding piece of human filth out there, because you people, every last one of you-'

'One more word, Miss Maheste, and you will be suspended,' the Principal spat defensively. It was fun to do this to someone like him.

If only she had *only* been talking about the faculty.

'Fine,' Aleera finally answered. She would have very much liked to pursue the argument, if only to vent some of the anger so that she didn't find the ape and crack his skull open, but it would serve no further purpose. She turned, strode to the door and pulled it open. She'd have been worried about Sara, but the fat little man wouldn't try that. Too much danger of getting his own precious self in trouble. The bastard didn't even have the decency to stop staring as she walked out and slammed the door behind her. Stopping on the other side, she listened with a great deal of satisfaction as the diploma nearest to the door fell and the case smashed on the floor.

'How bad was it?' A voice asked from her left. A boy slightly taller than her, and Sudanese by descent, was leaning on the wall. His black hair was short almost to the point of being shaved, and his eyes were a vivid green.

'I was wondering when you'd get here,' Aleera said in as pleasant a tone as she could manage. It hadn't been a very good start to the day. Still, it was Michael, and therefore not a viable target for her frustrations. A draconic/demon and the one person in her school other than Sara whom she was willing to tolerate. 'Have you seen Sara?'

'She's next door. She just got sent to talk to the school counsellor. What happened?'

'One of those stoners that hangs out by the gates every day thought he had the right to plough her.'

'And?'

'I half-twisted his arm off and broke his nose,' Aleera explained matter-of-factly.

'I heard he pulled a knife.'

Aleera flexed her fingernails with a knowing smirk. 'As if I couldn't if I wanted to?' Another perk of her lineage.

'Jake's gonna kill you for this,' Michael pointed out.

'Jake doesn't need to know,' Aleera replied sharply.

'But he will, because he works for the Guild, and the Guild keeps tabs on us,' Michael replied in imitation of Aleera's own tone.

'And by "us", you mean "me". And Jake doesn't work *for* them. He's a freelancer.'

'Same difference.'

'I could never figure him out anyway,' Aleera admitted.

'Yeah, weird guy. I bet he's gay.'

Aleera arched one eyebrow. 'What?'

'You've seen the girl he rooms with. He lives with her, he's not going for that, and you think this is a straight man?' Michael caught himself as something clicked in his head. 'You just changed the subject,' he noted with a chuckle and a "you-sly-dog" tone. 'You could still get in a lot of trouble.'

'I *am* in trouble. The fat little man put me on probation.'

'What'd he do to that guy?'

'Nothing as far as I know.'

'What, seriously?' Michael pressed indignantly. 'Goddamn bullshit human,' he added under his breath. 'Seriously though, you're Ok, right?'

'Fine.'

'You're fine? A guy pulled a knife on you, and you're "fine"?'

'Not the worst I've had. It's Sara I'm worried about.'

'Yeah, and she told me that *she* was worried about *you*.'

'I know,' Aleera sighed distantly. 'Look, Michael, you don't have to be here. I know you've got that girlfriend of yours to-'

'We split', Michael answered sharply.

'Really?' Aleera was quite visibly taken aback.

'You know Jack from Chemistry?'

Aleera's face fell into one of realisation. 'Oh. …I'm sorry.'

'Why? Not your fault.' Michael let out a heavy groan and leaned back against the wall. 'Hell of a Monday morning, huh?'

'True,' Aleera noted. 'Doesn't look like this is going to be the best week.'

2

Aleera's life had changed a great deal in the last three years. Up until that point, she had lived a life that left her... well, the way she was. Perhaps not as bad as she could have turned out, but bad enough that she felt a routine need to go out and find someone's head to bust in. She took Tae Kwon Do on Saturdays just to vent, in case there weren't any drug-addled students to unleash herself on. That, and she was around socially active enough to have entirely two friends who hadn't met her through being involved with a supernatural police force. In hindsight, it probably wasn't a very good reflection on her that she looked back on the day her father died and silently thanked whatever higher power was out there that he was dead. But not many young demonesses had Kudra for a father. They were teaching about him in Draconic history now, and the supernatural side of the world was still recovering from the ten years of secret war.

So, when that part of her life was *finally* over, she actually looked forward to being able to go to a normal school for the first time. When it comes to hindsight, of course, everyone as 20-20 vision. If anything, the place just frustrated her more and more every day. She hadn't been able to properly cut loose in about a month, and she hadn't had a boyfriend or a girlfriend for the better part of a year. For a half-succubus, that was *not* healthy. And her school life, to bottom-line it, wasn't helping anything.

The day at school, and the walk back, had been equally uneventful; at least two teachers had made no great effort to keep their eyes away from her figure, and she'd had to put up with the captain of the football team trying to grab hold of her backside at lunch and earning himself a discreet punch to the stomach; the usual little annoyances. That was what happened when your mother was a Succubus; and it also meant that everyone 'noticed' her; and that meant *everyone*. It wasn't a choice of hers, it was simply a fact of her biology; something that evolved to give her species on her mother's side a wider spectrum of prey. It just also meant that when anybody looked at her, all they really saw was a pair of breasts with a girl attached.

But that had never been the worst of it.

The worst was the awkward silence that would crop up, just now and then, between her, Michael and Sara as one or both of them struggled to keep their eyes off of her. She cared for them both more than she cared to admit, and she truly, honestly hated what she did to them. And what she hated more was how much that wicked little part of her loved to see them both look at her that way. Michael and Sara were the only two people in that school that she even remotely cared about; even if- and she would never admit to it- there was a little thrill to be gained from having some fool stare at the back of her trousers as she walked away, she didn't want to do this to those two.

Grumbling to herself, she ducked into the alley to use it as a quick shortcut home past the overflowing dumpster, mounds of litter and on some days the occasional strung-out junkie.

That was the main reason she didn't keep much human company. Well, that and the coked-up animal sniffing to himself as he pulled out a switchblade. It dawned on her that, while wrapped up in her mental grumbling, she had paid worryingly little attention to where she was going, even though 'worried' would not be the word for her. More a mixture of irritation and hope for the lurching thing- it had apparently at some point in the last twenty or so years been a human being- to try something so that she could vent said frustration.

'Hey,' he called to her with an unshaven, germ-coated mouth, 'Where you off to in such a hurry, gorgeous?'

Aleera stopped, turning round, that dark little part of her speaking up with a message of "just to point it out, this is a perfect chance to vent".

'Nowhere,' She answered, trying to sound as clueless as she could. It must have worked, because the thug took another step forward before grabbing her and pushing her against the wall, pulling out the switchblade and holding the gleaming blade to her cheek.

'Got anythin' for me, babe?' He grinned in her face with stinking breath that smelled faintly of marijuana. Noteworthy, and helping to make it all the more tempting to carve him up right then and there, but not surprising in the least. Oh, please, *please*, just let her beat up one little stoned mugger.

Aleera turned her dark eyes down to the blade as it pressed softly against her face, inching its way down.

'Not much,' She answered simply.

'Shut up and gimme your money!'

'Mugging someone in broad daylight,' Aleera observed dryly. 'Inventive.'

Ignoring her, the coke-head turned his gaze down, greedily drinking in the sight of her breasts.

'While you're at it,' he smirked, 'How 'bout you be a real good girl and take that off for me, huh? Be a shame if a pretty girl like you had to lose those looks.'

In a way, Aleera was actually glad that this perverted, thieving, drug-addled piece of garbage was staring at her chest. Because that meant he wasn't looking at the rest of her. And her chest wasn't the dangerous part. And by now, she had all the justification she needed.

Oh, this would be fun.

Aleera turned her eyes straight up to him, and then gave a slight grin. The scum arched one eyebrow, his jaw hanging open slightly to show his rotten teeth. Much like those Aleera routinely encountered at school, he didn't seem too reassured by the fact that this teenage girl with a knife to her throat was not showing a single twitch of fear.

With a sudden jerk of motion, Aleera's knee was in his crotch, and he fell back with a painful wheeze as Aleera grabbed his shoulders and spun him round.

She pointed her index finger at the back of his head, and then the nail began to suddenly lengthen, turning from its natural colour to a dark, sleek black as its edge narrowed into a razor-sharp point that pressed lightly against the back of his neck. Conveniently, the idiot would naturally assume that it was a knife pressing against the base of his skull, ready to stab into him without notice. Judging by his quiet shaking and a momentary pathetic sob, it was having the desired effect.

'I've got a better idea,' She finally replied to his remark, 'Why don't I remove something of yours instead?'

'Wait!' The thug wailed pleadingly, 'Wait, wait, wait, hold on a…'

'Why?' Aleera demanded, her voice suddenly taking on a note of venom at such a request, 'Would you?' She tightened her grip on his shoulder, the tip of the claw pressing lightly into him.

'Oh God,' He whimpered pathetically, 'Please, just let me go, I didn't wanna hurt anyone, I swear! I just hadta make some money!'

'Tragic.' Aleera observed disinterestedly.

'I ain't got no job…' Or any knowledge of grammar, apparently, 'I got bad genes, y'know, bad parents…'

'*Don't* whine to me about parents," Aleera hissed, the man whimpering and squinting his eyes like some stupid, frightened child.

He thought he could get what he wanted just because he had a knife and he was full of drugs, but he was pathetic. Like so many of them, just weak and vicious. The sort of thing that the world would be a far nicer place without, and all it would take for what, frankly, would be a civic act, was a little bit of pressure from her index finger.

In that realisation, Aleera had the power of God in her hand, and just for a moment, such a possibility left her breathless...

Finally, she pulled back her finger as the claw shrank away.

Oh well, she'd had her fun.

The claw receded back into her finger, replaced with the ordinary nail as she gave the human filth a slight shove and let him fall to the ground, still quivering.

'Now get out of my sight,' she ordered flatly before turning away and walking back home. Somewhere in her mind it dawned on her that these were not the actions of a stable individual. Then again, define 'stable'. Pulling a knife on someone wasn't stable. Killing yourself in a very slow and drawn-out way wasn't stable. Letting people run round your school with drugs and knives wasn't stable. In that case, she was probably about as 'stable' as most people.

Yes, because it was perfectly stable to seek out a mugger so that she could break a few of his ribs.

Aleera shut the door into the apartment behind her, pressing back on it for a second to stare absent-mindedly up at the off-white plaster of the ceiling over the wooden walls and floor as she dropped her bag onto the floor and, passing the small wooden table with the lamp and phone, pressed the 'play' button on the latter as she moved across the back of the living room, disregarding the sofa and TV, and entered the kitchen. *"You have... no... new messages,"* the hollow voice of the machine recited.

Work had been no more engaging than school, but it was at least a small comfort to have a part-time job she enjoyed. She'd picked it for the most obvious reason: the only really fond memories she had were of herself and her sister in an old kitchen cooking. It was something she'd enjoyed for as long as she could remember. That, and every time she thought about it, it brought the smallest of wry smiles to the edge of her lips; she'd have loved to see the look on her mother's face if she'd ever told her she wanted to be a chef. She'd started work just as a Saturday morning job, conscious that she wanted to provide for herself, instead of the Guild only keeping her there so that they could keep an eye on her. But one weekend, by a twist of fate, a few of the chefs ironically caught food poisoning, and Aleera, in covering for them, had duly impressed the manager.

Aleera started to fish through the fridge in the small kitchenette, which contained a cooker, microwave, fridge-freezer and table. The apartment had all of the essentials and was simply laid out enough feel like home; the small living room with a TV, sofa and table, branching off into the small kitchenette and a modest bedroom that led to the bathroom that, while not spacious enough for a bath, held a decent-sized shower. If not for where it had come from, she might have liked it. 'Cosy' would probably be a good work to describe it, and something about the small apartment, with its mostly-wood walls and floors, and the rug that covered much of the living room floor, gave off an oddly inexplicable sensation of security.

She found what she was searching for, and decided that it had been a frustrating day, she'd been a good little demon by not splitting anyone's head open, and she'd earned herself a reward. Removing a jar of honey from the cupboard, she took a spoon from the drawer and helped herself to a few spoonfuls. Aleera was a young lady who liked to steer clear of any nasty habits. No drink except on special occasions, no smoking, no drugs, but she would allow herself one vice, and that was honey. She could sit and eat a jar of the stuff by itself- though she preferred it spooned over ice cream, sorbet or a consenting partner of her choice.

Making her way back out of the kitchen, she flexed her neck tiredly before entering the bedroom, slumping herself down onto the bed to look back at the dress mirror that sat on the wall above a dressing table opposite to the bed.

Focusing on the eyes of her reflection, she willed a familiar process into action and watched as the blood-red colour started to spread out from the edges of her pupils, filling up her irises for a few seconds before receding. Lying back on the bed, she let out a long, quiet sigh as the process of the colour-change arbitrarily repeated itself.

Three years had gone by more quickly than she'd ever have expected.

She lay back on the bed and, for at least five minutes, stared up at the ceiling, idly fiddling with her hair before coming to a decision. She'd been busy lately, and she had work that evening; in between that, school and homework, she didn't get much time to unwind, to be herself... and that was what she needed to do, even if just for a few minutes. Cut loose, just to be *her*.

Standing up, she checked that the curtains were drawn and, moving her hands down, she sat up and unbuttoned the blouse, slipping the garment off before removing the black, lacy bra that had been concealed beneath. Well, there was no sense in letting her favourite outfit get shredded. Standing topless in front of the mirror, her shapely body slightly jiggling in the right places, she relaxed and stretched out her arms.

Painlessly, the skin between her shoulder blades parted at two points, thick folds of midnight-black skin extending from beneath before unfolding into segmented, bat-like wings that extended down to her knees, before folding outwards to a full span of at least seven feet, the light glistening eerily through the black, gossamer-thin membrane. The nail of each finger extended, the end seeming to push forward as the surrounding part of the nail thinned, the entire nail-turned-claw turning dark black before they stopped, each one roughly the length of a steak knife.

Exhaling slowly, Aleera looked at her reflection in the mirror with an expression that was torn between relief and a frown of mild disdain. On the one hand, the sight of this form brought up, to say the least, some unpleasant memories. It was no secret to anyone around her that she took no pride in what she was. Then again, she was getting sick of having to look human all the time. It was suffocating to have to act 'normal' all the time, to pretend to be something she wasn't to placate the animals who would hunt her down with pitchforks and torches if they knew what she was. The small scar on her forehead would have been enough of a reminder. Even though she was only half-demon, she couldn't help wondering how different things might be if the other half was human.

Looking down at her hand, she easily retracted the claws back into normal nails, and started to change between the two every few seconds. She turned her 'normal' right hand over, running the tip of her left index finger over the smooth, pale skin. Then, extending the claws again, she flexed them in the air with a sort of macabre fascination.

Shaking her head and giving a slight shudder, she retracted both the claws and the wings, looking at her more human self with the same sense of apprehension, silently running a fingertip across the scar as her eyes changed back from their malevolent red to the former dark brown.

No, she finally decided, it wasn't going to help. Spreading her wings in the middle of an empty apartment wouldn't help any more than smashing some thug's nose to pieces. She just needed to really get *out* for a while, the way only she could. The truth of it was, she'd been cramped up in her little apartment and surrounded by humans for entirely too long.

Still, it didn't look like the chance was going to present itself tonight. Closing her eyes, she relaxed on top of the bed and did her utmost to try and fall asleep.

Turning over in bed for what must have been the hundredth time, Aleera pushed the sheets back, resting her head on the hot, clammy pillow in the middle of the hot, unmoving air. A thin layer of stickiness clung to her skin as the mugginess penetrated the entire room. Having the windows wide open didn't do any more good than the previous night; there was just too much smothering, dull humidity.

This was insane. She'd been lying there for two hours, ever since getting in from work, and she just couldn't get to sleep. The numbers '01:48' shone out in that sickly electronic green.

But it wasn't the humidity that was keeping her awake, and Aleera knew it all too well.

Turning over yet again, this time ending up on her front, she nuzzled her face into the pillow as if trying to wipe off the unwanted stress and irritability, but succeeded only adding to the itching heat of the sticky sweat on her face.

Finally, blessed distraction came in the form of her cell phone ringing on the bedside table next to the clock, with that irritating jingle of bleeps and bloops that she still hadn't bothered to learn how to change.

Pressing the answer button upon recognising the number she lifted to device to her ear, pushing her messed hair away from her ear.

'Jake' She answered groggily, 'It's two in the morning.' Of course, this was Jake, she reminded herself. If he was calling about something, then it was important.

'Aleera,' The male voice, noticeably older than her own, answered from the other end of line. 'Sorry for the late-night call, but we need to talk.'

'What, now?'

'Right now. How soon can you get to Central Park?'

'Why there?' Then it clicked. Jake worked with the Guild. The Guild enforced supernatural law. What didn't click was what Jake needed her there for.

'Well,' Jake started, and as he finished his sentence, the five words were spoken that would haunt Aleera for years to come.

The voice hesitated for a moment, and then said: '…You need to see this.'

3

Crime was something that turned up in any culture. No people in the world had ever been exempt from it, and that included draconics. Magic, after all, was a powerful and versatile tool; applied properly, it could make you invisible, blast through concrete, get someone in and out of somewhere in the blink of an eye. Any criminal's dream tool. So, just as much as humankind, draconics needed laws, and without someone to enforce them, laws are meaningless. That was the role of the Guild of Guardians; enforce the supernatural laws as set down by the Dragon High Council. The Guild had existed since the seventeenth century and had been operating ever since in the name of protecting all mystical castes. Or, to believe the more popular vote, to cover the High Council whenever something went wrong so that none of the higher-ups had to get their own hands dirty.

Three years ago, the Guild had become aware of Aleera after the death of her father. Her father's fate was not something she regretted. Meeting the Guild was. As far as they were concerned, the effect her father could have had on her made her "unpredictable" and "a potential danger". Roughly translated, they didn't like her because her father was the worst psychopath the supernatural world had ever known. If Jake hadn't been there, they would probably have locked her up instead of what they ended up doing: Aleera had spent the last three years under official Guild surveillance just in case she *did* turn out to be a bad apple like her dear departed dad.

Aleera had nothing against the Guild. Not at all. She just didn't like being grouped in with her father just because she shared half of her blood with him. That, and it would be nice to speak freely. Alas, they had long-since tapped her phone, and her cell phone, and even appropriated her apartment to better keep an eye on her. When she moved in, there had been bugs and cameras in every room, though she was fairly sure the one in the bathroom was there for less-than-professional purposes. Between them, Aleera and Jake had 'accidentally' destroyed the cameras, and the Guild still didn't know that Jake had given Aleera a second cell phone. One of the perks of being a freelancer, he always said, was that people didn't ask as many questions. That and you don't have to fill in as much paperwork. The most contact she ever really had with the Guild was with the occasional psychiatrist.

'Psychologically damaged', was what the report had said. Probably close enough, but Aleera had never really cared what most people thought of her. Half her school thought she was a psychopath, which was utterly ridiculous. She was borderline sociopath at the worst.

Of course, a 'stable' person would probably immediately start to question why they were woken up at one-forty-eight in the morning and called seven blocks away. But Aleera knew Jake, and she knew that he wouldn't call at all unless it was important. Besides the fact that he was good at magic, it was about all she *did* know about him, other than the fact that nobody else knew anything. Age, birthplace, family, Jake didn't seem to have any of the above. She had her doubts as to whether 'Jake' was even his real name; all she knew that he was older than he looked and he was quite stunningly good when it came to magic. From what she'd gleamed from his familiar, he kept things close to the chest. She couldn't really complain about that without being hypocritical.

The best thing about being called to Central Park in the middle of the night, though, was that she could finally cut loose for a few minutes. Cold midnight air blew strands of her dark hair over her pale face as the thin fabric of her wings grabbed onto what breeze they could. It was far too muggy to catch a breeze at street level, but at this altitude there was enough of one to keep her in the air. Now this was cutting loose- it was the one part of what she was that she considered a blessing. She could do what the humans below her- all of them- dreamed of. She could fly, and in doing so, she could be herself as only she could.

As the dark trees of the park and the occasional criss-cross pattern of lampposts on the pathways came into view below her, Aleera pulled her wings back towards her body, letting the cold winds whip at her skin as she entered freefall. A few seconds later, she folded the wings back out, and the resulting parachute effect let her glide down with all the unearthly grace in the world.

Settling among the trees, she allowed the wings to slip painlessly into her back. She'd changed to a halter top before leaving her apartment; it showed more skin than she'd have liked, but at least she didn't have to choose between getting her upper clothing ripped off and having to remove it. That got tedious. She then gave a quiet whisper of *'Tyasans'*, allowing the spell she had been using to deactivate. The invisibility spell was a must for keeping herself hidden- obviously- and had been one of the first spells she ever mastered. She wasn't in the habit of using magic every day, thanks to some memories that she preferred not to share, but practicality outweighed sentimentality. The wings were the fastest way of getting to the park, and the spell the best way to make sure that no blurry photographs appeared in the tabloids. Being more than human really did have its advantages.

'Nice of you to drop in,' a voice said as its owner stepped out of the trees and into the shadowy moonlight. Jake was a few inches taller than Aleera, with brown hair hanging loose around the sides of his face. The open, creased light-grey shirt over his sweater and slacks left him with a casual appearance that bordered on scruffy.

'That's either a dig at me for not being able to teleport, or an atrocious pun. Which is it?' Aleera asked of the young man who stepped out to greet her.

'And what I really like about you is your sunny disposition,' Jake said with mocking cheer.

'You didn't call me out here to make bad jokes, Jake.'

'And you're sociable, too. Ok, then, you're right. It's under the bridge.'

'What is?'

Jake looked back at the bridge for a moment, looking for the right way to say something, almost as if he was trying to put off saying it. There was the briefest glint in his eyes that it took Aleera a moment to recognise. Emotions weren't her strong suit.

'He's burned,' Jake finally said. 'And I mean badly. All over.'

Aleera froze. *Now* it was clear why he called her there. 'A body,' she confirmed.

'It turned up this afternoon. After a few shouting matches, Khazahn decided to let me inform you.' There was no joviality in his voice now. This was beyond anything resembling a joke.

'Can I see it?' Aleera asked. Even as she asked, she found herself hesitant. She didn't actually want to see this at all, not if it was what she thought it was.

'This way,' Jake nodded into the trees. Aleera followed silently even as her brain raced over and over itself. Jake could have called her to the Guild later, if this was the case. Or come to her apartment about it. So why bring her all the way out here?

She could voice those questions later, she decided. Jake was one of the few living people she actually cared about. More than that, he was someone she could trust. And he was one of two people that she actually did trust with almost anything. Well, there were some things she kept to herself.

The underside of the bridge was illuminated by floodlights and taped off with bright yellow tape. The black silhouettes of police officers bustled around the edges of the tape, making only the slightest contact with the white-garbed figures that hovered like ghosts over the tarp that rested on the gravel under the false light. As the spectres waved back-and-forth, Aleera turned her dark eyes onto the body and the unknown soul that rested beneath the veil.

One of them stepped away, the gravel crunching under his feet as he approached, pulling down the white hood of the bio-suit and the blue surgical mask. Curly brown hair surrounded his boyish face and green eyes. The I.D. pinned to his chest identified him as 'Dr. Harold Drake'.

'I miss anything?' Jake asked.

'Nothing to report,' Dr. Drake replied. 'We just need to get hold of the body; it would have to turn up in the middle of Central Park. Khazahn told them the usual 'special-ops' thing. Seems to satisfy them.' He looked over to Aleera, and she took a moment to decipher his expression. It appeared to be one of puzzlement, bordering on amusement. 'So this is Ms. Aleera Maheste.'

'Aleera,' she introduced herself.

'Dr. Drake,' the doctor said formally. 'Guild Eighth Division, D-Unit Forensics. Friends call me Harry.'

'Magical forensics,' Aleera surmised as the doctor led them towards the police tape. 'Modern.'

'Well, lord known this lot's changed since the Guild started up,' Jake pointed out. 'Besides, everything's forensics nowadays. Good old-fashioned magic barely gets a look-in, and we came across this one too late for a spirit-trace. Speaking of magic...' Jake waved his hand over himself and Aleera. '*ThraioPhouxSola*'. The air around them seemed to shimmer for a moment, then settled into normality- and, to the eyes of all present, so did Jake and Aleera. Into a normal image for the occasion.

'What do they think you are?' Harry asked.

'Forensics, same as you,' Jake answered. 'That way nobody gets suspicious when a nineteen-year-old and a seventeen-year-old stand next to a body.'

'Getting back to that,' Aleera said as they ducked under the tape, 'You said it was burned.'

'And badly. Just about the sickest thing you ever saw. I still don't see why we need to show anybody something like this,' Harry butted in. 'Christ, Jake, you saw it, and God knows why you'd wish that on her.'

'Well, you'd better have a strong stomach,' Harry warned Aleera. That might have disconcerted a lot of people. Not her. It took quite a lot to faze her. Un-faze-able.

Harry knelt down and pulled the tarp away, and Aleera was well and truly fazed.

The body wasn't so much burned as, well, cooked. The skin had been… there *was* no skin, only a twisted covering of raw, burned flesh. Its cheekbones hollow, the face was trapped in the mad, dead grin of a skull, every bleached and gritted tooth, every exposed sinew, gleaming out of its red surroundings, the bone of the scalp exposed in a handful of places. Ashen, lidless eyes stared out from sunken pits, dark green irises still frozen in shock and fear.

'Well,' was all that Aleera could say for a moment. This was unexpected. Painfully obvious, looking back, but still… even to her mind, this was unsavoury. She felt like vomiting, but the acidic, sickly smell from somewhere nearby attested that somebody had already taken that liberty. But this was…

Familiar.

What appeared to be revulsion and pity crossed Jake's face as he knelt by the other side of the body. He reached into his pocket, pulling out and old coin, and started to turn it over in his fingers. It had been a habit of his for as long as Aleera had known him.

She looked back down at the body with macabre curiosity as various realisations came flooding to mind; that this would take a lot of power. This was something that only dark magic would be capable of. And the worst part: that this was how *he* did it.

'You Ok?' Harry asked tentatively, ready to pull the sheet back up. None too wise, but considerate.

'Hold on,' Aleera waved back his hand, leaning further down toward the burned face.

'Don't touch it,' Harry hissed.

'I'm not going to,' Aleera replied quickly. Honestly, she couldn't remember a time when her age hadn't meant that she was unable to handle any kind of responsibility. Youth equals stupidity, at least as far as any authority was concerned. She just needed a closer look.

There. Black, runes in an arc over the corpse's forehead. Holding her palm over it, she could still feel the heat. The runes themselves were Draconic, and they spelled something very familiar.

Demon.

Aleera nodded to Harry, who pulled the sheet back up over the wretch's face.

'That's how he did it,' Aleera finally said. 'It's how he killed people. Right down to the runes.'

Harry fished for something to say. 'The victim's male- near as we can tell. There's not much left to go on until we can run a DNA test. God knows what did this to the poor bastard.'

'Dark magic,' Aleera hesitated to say it. 'This had to be dark magic.'

'You're sure? I mean, with enough power, a regular spell could-'

'Well, *he* always used dark magic,' Aleera answered, 'and this looks a lot like his work. Besides, I'd recognise this spell anywhere. *EiahFhieh.* Dark fire.'

This was worrying. It certainly did resemble her father's handiwork. And if this was to do with him, then it was very likely that…

Aleera turned to Jake, and it dawned on her that it had been a few minutes since he last said anything. 'Jake,' she called quietly. He turned up to her sharply. 'I need to talk to you for a moment,' she turned her eyes indicatively away from the crime scene. Jake nodded, standing up to follow her.

Once they were suitably out of sight, the air shimmered around them again for a second. Jake relaxed as he no longer had to put his efforts to use maintaining the illusion spell.

'You wouldn't call me here just for this,' Aleera declared, 'and I know when there's something you're not telling.' Well, more so than he normally was. 'There's something else, isn't there?'

'Don't miss a trick, do you?' Jake sighed.

'And this is something to do with me; specifically, with me.'

Jake's eyebrows rose. 'How'd you know that?'

'You just told me. Now what is it?'

Aleera noticed that he was still fiddling with the old coin. 'Follow me.'

Jake led her a short distance through the trees, ending up with the bridge a small way to their left. All that was in front of them was an old tree. Jake crouched down in front of it, lifted a hand and whispered '*Sola*'. His palm lit up immediately, bathing the base of the tree in light.

'This,' he said, 'is what I had to show you.'

There was a word written in draconic runes, burned into the bark by obvious magical means.

Aleera's eyes widened. Her breathing quickened.

The word *Aleera* was burned into the bark.

4

The law of conservation of energy states that energy cannot be created or destroyed; it can only be transferred from one form to another. The same applied to magic; the bodies of draconics, demons and other supernatural kinds contained ambient energy. All the potential for magic. A spell was, explained on the simplest level, a transistor, akin to the inner workings of a radio or a hairdryer. It took the energy and converted it into another form. The most basic attacking spell converted a portion of energy into a burst of kinetic energy. *Sola*, the light spell that Jake was currently using, converted it into light energy. The more powerful and complex the spell, the more energy it consumed.

Aleera could only guess at how much of that energy Jake had. She could sense it in any draconic or demon, as could any of those two kinds, but it poured from Jake like water from a broken tap. He was also one of the *very* few people she knew who could exercise two such transfers- two spells- at the same time. For a good few minutes now, he had been both keeping them cloaked and illuminating the base of the tree while Aleera intently studied the word burned into the bark.

Aleera.

The word stared back at her from its sunken hiding place in the tree bark, whispering its threat silently into her ear. Her name, next to a dead body. The clearest and most unmistakable threat possible.

No. Not just a threat. This was too big. If you wanted to threaten someone, you threw something on their window. Or, better yet, walked up to them and actually threatened them. This was something else. It was a strike at her, at the very deepest part of her. This *was* somebody saying "I'm out to get you, Aleera", but they were saying something else as well; "I know you. This is personal. I *challenge* you." Someone had gone to a great deal of effort to make sure that this message, this challenge, got through to her.

Message received and understood.

'Well?' Jake finally asked.

'Somebody wants to tell me something,' Aleera answered distantly.

'Any idea of who?'

'It would have to be a demon to do this. They're the best at dark magic. No idea who exactly, but I think we both know why.' She traced the burned lettering with her fingertip. It was still warm. 'So where do we go from here?'

'Hope the body turns up some clues,' Jake replied with a note of pessimism. 'You'd better be careful.'

'You don't think I will, do you?'

Jake's answer came in the form of a smirk, before his face became deadly serious again. 'We'll find whoever did this.'

'Whoever did this wants to talk to me more than the Guild,' Aleera observed.

'And they're not going to get to. Maybe you should head home,' Jake recommended.

'I'm fine.'

'It's two a.m. and you've got school in six hours. You should get some sleep.'

'I'll probably need to,' Aleera observed dryly. 'I'll need to be rested if this lunatic turns up.'

'Is that a vote of no-confidence I hear?'

'Not in you,' Aleera replied, glancing back over at the officers.

'Go on; Harry should be able to get the body to the soon anyway. I'll let you know as soon as something new turns up.'

Aleera nodded. 'Thanks for the warning, Jake.'

After one more worried nod from Jake, Aleera stepped back into the trees, whispered '*Tyasans*' and felt the air shimmer and bend around her. Her wings slipped silently out of her back, and like a great, graceful raven she rose into the dark sky.

When Aleera took off from Central Park, it had been in the hope that it would help her to clear her head of the various sentiments that were currently scrambling over each other.

Oddly enough, fear wasn't one of them. She was concerned, certainly. She had just been threatened in an incredibly clear and violent way. Anger was certainly there. The idea of having her past dragged up and thrown in her face for some childish threat was one that left her rather indignant. That one was there as well; she didn't much care for being threatened, for having her life invaded like this. No fear, though. Of course not. It wouldn't do to be afraid.

She found it rather worrying how little in the way of sadness or empathy there was, as well. Whatever had happened to the poor soul in the park would churn the sturdiest of stomachs. Maybe it was simply harder to feel human sympathy for something that no longer looked human, but judging by what was left of the expression on what remained of the face, the victim had still been alive when the burning occurred. She admitted to wincing a little at the thought of that kind of pain. She knew what burning felt like. Perhaps that was it. Perhaps it was too long ago that she used up the last of her fear and her empathy.

Upon returning to her apartment, Aleera had promptly removed her clothes and collapsed back into bed. Her little escapade to the park seemed to have done more than expected, for better or worse, and she fell almost straight to sleep. Finding out someone was sending a threat to you with a scorched body was a tiring experience.

The next time she opened her eyes, the sickly green numbers on the clock read '06:27'. Groaning, she turned back over as her mind started to wake itself up, bringing the events of the night with it. She'd have thought that the threats were the problem, but it was the body that came up first. Aleera enjoyed… unwinding, occasionally. The mugger in the alley had been a prime example of just how satisfying she found the breaking of the ribs of someone who was really, truly, begging for it. Never anyone who didn't deserve it. And never too far. She'd never killed anyone. She never wanted to. That would be entirely too much like her father.

The realisation was finally creeping up on her that it wasn't a charred husk, but a person living under that sheet. Someone with their own life, their own family, whose last thoughts would have been of the worst burning pain imaginable. And that had happened because of her, whether she put her hand to the man or not.

Aleera sat up in bed and realised that she was shaking. The thought of the blood in the cold heat of the sweat that coated her palms made her want to vomit. She shook some more, and what sounded like a faint sob came out of her mouth.

No, she told herself. This wasn't helping. Get a damn grip. Whoever did this, they wanted her to be like this. Shaking. Afraid. *No*, she wasn't afraid. Not again. It was just that there was this black pit in her stomach that seemed to be forcing its way up her throat… *No*. She'd been like this before. She'd spent too many years of her life with someone doing things like this to her.

A challenge, she reminded herself. That was what it was. "I'm coming to get you, Aleera".

She felt a dangerous little smile creep its way onto her face.

Bring it on.

The usual smell of grease and fat emanated from the other end of the cafeteria as the students crowded around to eat, while Aleera remained alone at her table, drumming her fingers on the wooden surface. The ape from yesterday wasn't far away, throwing her the occasional dirty look. Evidently he still hadn't learned his lesson. Standing next to him was, in addition to his younger brother, a boy just older than Aleera whose name she believed to be Gregory Smith. Apparently, a few years ago someone had been observant enough to take note of his significantly-portly physique and taken to labelling him "Gregzilla". Whoever had thought of this had no doubt praised themselves for their enormous creativity at the time. Gregzilla had now taken to associating with the pothead who had recently taken it upon himself to enlighten Aleera about the useful points of owning a knife.

A year ago, Aleera had an encounter with a demon who had been arrested by the Guild. She never learned his name, oddly enough, but he had been a lieutenant of her father and had held to the view that demons and draconics should unite and bring the "cleansing fires" that would wipe humankind from the planet. After each day at school, she understood the mentality a little better.

The latest idea to occur to Ryan Shane, as she had learned to be the ape's name, was to pick up a hot dog and throw it at her. No doubt he thought that this would be hilarious to someone other than himself, his brother and his overweight friend. He didn't appear to find it amusing when Aleera snatched the object out of its flight path. She fixed her dark eyes on him and, in her most venomous voice, said levelly 'I'm trying to eat'. A pleasing flicker of fear had crossed Ryan's face as she dropped the hot dog into a neighbouring trash can and returned to her own lunch, before he replaced it with a mask of feigned contempt and walked away with his brother and his overweight friend.

'That guy still bothering you?' Michael's voice asked from the other side of her. He and Sara both sat down opposite her with trays of food. 'He's got guts.'

'He's an idiot,' Aleera replied.

'Still. You do know that half this place is shit-scared of you, right?' Aleera shrugged.

'Are you alright after yesterday?' Sara asked worriedly.

'Why wouldn't I be?' Aleera lied. She didn't make a point of lying to what few friends she had, but there was no need to worry them. No sense in anyone else having to lose sleep over it.

'Ryan pulled a knife on you. Do you know what he's like?'

'Should I be worried?' Aleera replied.

'He tried to knife you just for embarrassing him. That isn't stable.'

'I keep larger blades than his inside my fingers.' Aleera flexed the fingers of one hand to accompany the statement. 'And even if I didn't, I could break every bone in his body from over here if I wanted to.'

'Besides, it was human enough of him,' Michael said with contempt. Aleera shot him a warning glare.

'They're not all bad,' Sara pointed out.

'Yeah? Name me one human in this place that isn't a total-' Michael stopped in mid-sentence when Aleera turned her gaze symbolically from him to Sara. '-Oh. Sorry.'

'It's alright,' Sara said without conviction.

'Anyway,' Aleera said to steer the conversation in another direction, 'How are you two since yesterday?' She just needed to check. Make sure that whoever was responsible for what happened in the park hadn't been anywhere near them.

'Not bad,' Michael said first.

'Same,' Sara spoke up. 'After I got out of the Principal's office.'

'What?' Aleera asked immediately, angrily and indignantly. 'What for?'

'About what happened yesterday. All I got was a warning.'

Aleera turned to look at Ryan, and saw that he was glancing at their table and laughing. *Laughing*.

'That piece of-'

Before she could put her sentiments into strong words, Aleera noticed something drop onto the table; a small, folded-up piece of paper. By the time she looked back up, whoever had dropped it had vanished into the crowd of students.

'Secret admirer?' Michael chuckled.

Ignoring the comment, Aleera unfolded the note. Scrawled across it, in poor handwriting typical of the writer, was:

Football field at 1:00. –Jake.

As soon as Aleera, Michael and Sara had arrived on the field, Jake had swiftly led them into the stands and handed them a photograph of what he had shown Aleera. The stands themselves cast a thick shadow around them as they stood under a gap in the shroud of seats above them, a thin crack of sunlight rendering the dirt beneath their feet an off-brown instead of the surrounding darkness. A small gathering of crows were perched on top of the stands, peering down into the shadows below with cold and hungry eyes. After that, Aleera had been forced to tell them about the name scorched into the wood, which was still burned so clearly into her memory. Once that was done, it was just a matter of their reactions.

'Son of a bitch!' Michael snarled under his breath, while Sara remained still and tried to keep her eyes off the photo Jake had dropped on the ground, until Jake considerately picked it up and pocketed it. 'So Aleera,' Michael asked harshly after a few seconds, 'when were you going to mention this to us?'

'What would that have done?' Aleera replied simply.

'Oh, so that's how useful we are?'

'Michael, you know I didn't mean that,' Aleera snapped. 'If someone wants to get to me, then involving you two would just be stupid.'

'We could be involved already,' Sara spoke up.

Aleera opened her mouth to reply, then said nothing.

'Are you done here yet?' A voice called, firm and authoritative, with an edge of confidence and just the very slightest cocky assuredness.

'Khazahn," Jake turned round on his heels, 'To what do I owe this enormous delight?' He asked sardonically.

The tall man, his black hair- greying slightly at the temples- combed back, his firm jaw line cropped with the thinnest layer of stubble and set squarely, dressed in a prim, finely-creased navy blue three-piece suit, took a few striding steps out from under the rafters, the thin strips of light floating over him between patches of darkness. 'I assume your errand's finished,' He repeated sharply.

'Apparently,' Jake replied dryly. 'Why?'

'We need to talk,' Khazahn replied, his voice now darker and more serious, 'Usual place.' He turned his head to Aleera. 'I haven't seen you in a long time, Aleera. At least *one* of you can stop causing me any trouble. Just a shame about the circumstances.'

Aleera gave the man a familiar nod.

'They put you in charge?' She asked. 'And I thought they only made you baby-sit Jake.'

'And he makes me regret it more than enough,' Khazahn glared daggers at Jake. Khazahn, as Aleera knew, had been Jake's contact with the Guild for quite some time. The two respected each other. They recognised the skills that the other possessed. That did not mean they were friends.

'I do my best,' Jake beamed.

'Yes, Chara put me on the case,' Khazahn explained.

'Who?' Michael mouthed silently to Sara.

'Guild officer,' Jake informed him in a voice that seemed to carry some bitter memories. 'Head of the Eighth Division.'

'Apparently he wants you involved as well.'

'What?' Jake, Aleera, Michael and Sara nigh-shouted, all for different reasons.

'Orders from above,' Khazahn recited, 'don't ask me. All I know is that he wants the both of you onboard.'

'No way,' Jake said authoritatively with a pair of sideways palm-swipes.

'Why not?' Aleera cut in. 'What we found in the park was a message, Jake.'

'One that means someone's after you," Jake hissed. 'We might as well tape a bulls-eye to your forehead.'

'Perfect.' Aleera answered simply, the slightest sinister ring creeping its way into her voice. It did look like it worked; she was, after all, hoping to meet the man responsible for that pit that was still gnawing in her stomach. Most people would probably see the flaw in risking her own life. And in the various extremely-violent things she intended to do upon locating that person.

'No,' Jake realised as it hit him, 'No way. Absolutely not.'

'Bait?' Khazahn realised, his only reaction being to slightly raise his eyebrows. 'That's not an option.'

'You're insane,' Michael spoke up, pointing at Aleera with a sudden concerned anger dancing across his face. Behind him, Sara looked on, her bright eyes shimmering with shock and sudden fear as her fingers folded around the cross dangling from her neck. 'Seriously, you're suicidal or something!'

'Whoever it was that did this, they sent me a message,' Aleera declared harshly, the sharp tone of her voice silencing all of them, 'and he killed a man to do it. So I'm sending him a message back.'

'What message?' Michael demanded? '"*Aim here*"?'

'We're not doing it,' Jake declared firmly. 'Discussion over. I don't know what's going through Chara's head that makes him think this is a good idea.'

'I'm in anyway,' Aleera said simply. 'You can't stop me, Jake.'

'Aleera-' Jake said, but he caught himself before he said something he might have regretted. 'Have you lost your mind?'

'Jake!' Aleera snapped, fixing her dark eyes on his with a sharp, deep gaze that stared into his soul, 'I'm doing this.'

Jake looked back at her for a moment, then nodded slowly, stepping back as his eyes blinked slowly with the small sign of understanding and acceptance.

'Alright.' He finally said.

'You are kidding me!' Michael shouted angrily. 'Jake, tell her, man.'

Jake didn't answer for a few seconds. A moment passed in which something strongly resembling frustration passed through his eyes. 'It's her choice,' he said finally.

'Why are you doing this?' Sara finally spoke up, looking straight at Aleera as she released the cross to let it dangle in front of her chest.

'I have to.' Aleera gave no more of an answer.

'Besides,' Khazahn pointed out with firm authority, 'This means we can keep more of an eye on her if they do try anything. Usual place," he repeated to Jake, finally shifting the conversation, before turning away and striding back into the patchy darkness beneath the stands. Aleera managed to hear him say '*Appiras*' as he left, before their suddenly seemed to swallow him in transparency from the outside-in, and in a second-long shake of air, Khazahn was gone, not a single trace left that he had ever touched the ground there.

'I'll tell you what I find out from him,' Jake said to Aleera as he similarly turned away. 'Just don't do anything more insane than this, alright?' With that, he walked away, leaving Aleera, Michael and Sara standing in the fractured darkness.

'Aleera,' Sara began timidly, 'Do you really think someone's…' She thinned her lips and looked away.

'It looks like it,' Aleera admitted.

'This was gonna happen eventually,' Michael muttered darkly, evidently doing his level best to keep a savage snarl out of his tone.

'You don't even know if it *was* a human,' Sara cut in. 'Jake said it was more likely to be *black* magic than anything else.'

'Think they're above that?' Michael shook his head.

'Michael,' Aleera warned, 'Leave it. Besides,' she confessed, folding her arms and turning her head down a little, "Not many humans can use magic, and even if they can, it's nothing like what was used on that body. If it's Dark Magic, then chances are that it's a demon.'

'Yeah,' Michael said bitterly and under his breath. 'Heard that before.'

'Michael, this isn't helping,' Aleera snapped. The crows above her took off as the school bell rang to announce the end of lunch. 'I'm going to class,' she declared, slinging her book bag over her shoulder. 'I'll see you two later.'

Aleera crossed the football field swiftly, ignoring the catcalls that reached her ears from the stands, before she heard footsteps running after her.

'Aleera, wait a second,' Sara called from behind her. After a second, Aleera relented and allowed her to catch up. 'You can't do this, Aleera,' Sara insisted. 'What if-'

'I'll be alright,' Aleera said in the most reassuring tone she could manage. It was another of those emotional things she'd never quite gotten the hang of.

'Just-' Sara bit her tongue. Her fingers returned to tracing the edges of her silver cross. '-Promise you won't-'

'I told you, I'll be fine.'

'I don't mean that,' Sara answered. 'Aleera…' she took a sharp breath; this obviously wasn't an easy subject for her. Her sparkling eyes seemed to fade as she avoided looking at her. 'Yesterday, the worst guy in school pulled a knife on you, and you're the one who nearly got suspended. Then on the same day, this happens. I don't know how anybody could cope with that, but you… you just don't seem like you're-'

Ah. That. Probably not how most people would react.

'Sara, I promise,' Aleera said softly, 'I'm fine. Just wait, the Guild will get hold of whoever did this and it'll be like it never happened.'

Hoping that Sara would believe that, she turned and walked towards the school building, leaving Sara standing in the empty football field and fumbling with the old silver cross.

The counsellor's office was on the ground next floor, a worn wooden door with the painted letters faded on the glass. Aleera noticed, but didn't overly care, that she had never been there before. Knocking the door, she heard a suspiciously peppy female voice call out 'Come in!' Inside the room with the drab, faded pink wallpaper behind the doily-covered desk was a gratuitously made-up woman who looked about twenty, though Aleera instantly realised she was probably much older. Her short dyed-blonde hair framed her face impeccably as the result of what must have been several hours in the hairdresser's, and her suit didn't have a single crease. Every pen on her desk was laid out to the millimetre.

'Aleera,' the woman said with a plastic smile. 'Take a seat.'

Aleera sat down in the chair without a word. Something told her that this would be vaguely amusing on some level, and highly irritating on several others.

'Aleera,' the woman repeated, 'that's a lovely name.' That was the thing about humans, and the biggest reason why draconics had been in hiding so long. Michael and Sara had often asked why, with a name like "Aleera", she had never been discovered. The reason was that, when a human came across a name like "Aleera Maheste", they didn't stop and think "my God, a secret society of supernatural beings", they thought "oh, that's an odd name. She must be foreign" and got on with whatever it was they were doing. 'I'm Ms. Candi.' The name seemed sickeningly appropriate. "The school has asked me to talk about the problems you've been having with one of your fellow students.'

'Problems?' Aleera repeated incredulously, folding her arms and making sure to give the woman her full and undivided attention. Nothing seemed to unnerve people like this more than a teenager who behaved like an adult.

'Yes, it's my understanding that there was an altercation on school grounds yesterday. Now, Aleera,' she leaned forward, 'I want you to know, we only have your own best interests at heart,' she lied, 'have you had any prior relationship with Mister...' she checked without needing to, anything to appear more human, '...Shane?'

'No,' Aleera replied levelly.

Ms. Candi checked the file again. 'I understand you had a loss in the family some three years ago. Were you close with your... father, wasn't it?' she knew full well that it was.

'Not particularly.' Aleera couldn't help wondering whether this woman had seen any kind of psychiatric evaluation on her. No, of course she hadn't. She wasn't nervous enough. At least she looked slightly taken aback by Aleera's response.

'I understand that you've been living with a non-parental family member for some time.'

'My sister. She moved away a while ago.'

'I see. And you're now living with...?'

'Myself.' Aleera felt an internal giggle as the woman blinked in open surprise.

'You live alone?'

'More or less. That's what the file says, isn't it?'

Ms. Candi gulped and turned her attention to the file. Ah, now she was getting nervous. Aleera was good at that. She wrote something down.

'What's this about, exactly?' Aleera asked in the tone that suggested that this was not a request for a reply, but a statement that she was going to get one.

'This is to help you after what happened yesterday.'

'Then why do you keep asking about my family?' Aleera demanded. She felt she had a fair-enough right to demand. This was, after all, supposed to be about the previous day's incident, not her private life. Emphasis on "private".

Ms. Candi cleared her throat in a failed attempt to be authoritative. 'You see, Aleera,' another fake smile, 'you're...' she pretended to check, 'almost eighteen years old now, and you're at the age where people come to realise who they are.' Any philosophy that the statement had was negated by the plastic smile on the face that delivered it. 'So what do you think you'll find?'

Aleera didn't reply. For once, she was dumbfounded. Honestly, what on earth kind of moronic question was that?

'Do I have to be here?' she asked levelly.

'Well, no,' Ms. Candi replied, 'but the school feels that it would be in your best interest.' Translation: the principal wanted to cover his own backside so that nobody sued him.

'Well,' Aleera said as she stood up, 'I think I'll go.'

'Of course, you can leave if you-'

She hadn't even finished the sentence before Aleera slammed the door behind her and left Ms. Candi to wonder how on earth a seventeen-year-old had managed to so unnerve her.

The shrill 'ding' of the elevator bell snapped Jake out of his thoughts as he lurched forward thanks to the jerky old mechanism. The rusty elevator doors, made of metal grates that had probably looked fairly presentable at some point in their long history, open with a crunch of dry paint giving way. An exposed light bulb flickered and cast shadows over corridor and the spider-web pattern of cracks on the walls. His footsteps were accompanied by the steady 'drip-drip-drip' of old, leaking pipes. There were sounds of a fight between a husband and wife behind one of the unpainted wooden doors that hung on rusty hinges.

Jake had acquired an apartment in this building because it was, as he called it at the time 'out of the way', which suited him just fine. Most draconics who could afford it went for some of Midtown Manhattan's slightly more upmarket residencies. 'Out of the way', of course, didn't necessarily mean 'nice'.

He pushed his key into the lock of his door with practiced precision and pushed the door open without a creak. Across the threshold, the apartment itself was markedly different; the walls were plastered smoothly and a small table with a telephone, a lamp and some sticky notes sat by the door. The hardwood floor of the corridor led into a surprisingly spacious living room that, by all rights, shouldn't fit, especially not as it branched off into a small kitchen. The whole place had been Jake's little experiment some time ago, when he first moved in; special displacement. Fitting something inside a space where it shouldn't fit. It wasn't that hard; not if you had a solid understanding of magic and a great amount of power. With the staircase leading up to another floor, the place looked more like a house, or certainly a much more expensive apartment. That said, the living room didn't look quite as spacious as it was, thanks to the various objects that cluttered the coffee table and much of the floor and sofa.

Jake slumped down onto the sofa, fishing the old coin back out of his pocket and turning it over in his hand and looking at it as if fascinated somehow. It was small, made of bronze and ridged around the edges. An image of an oriental dragon, curled up with its snout in the centre, was carved into the middle. Hmm. Dragons; Jake could still remember the last time he saw one of those. Five hundred years. Things had changed a bit since then, and so had he.

Still. Reflection was all well and good, but there were other matters pressing more heavily on his mind. There was all this business with the body and whatever Khazahn had found out about it. And then, of course, there was the *other* thing, which would definitely have to wait. It wouldn't be the best of ideas to make Aleera deal with that as well.

'Bad day at the rat race?' a female voice asked chirpily from behind him. 'Or bad day-and-a-half?' A hand gently slapped him on the back of the head.

'Ow,' Jake complained, rubbing the back of his skull. 'What was that for?'

'Where have you been?' the girl, probably a year younger than Jake at most, demanded, tapping her foot with both hands planted firmly on her wrists. Her slim figure was flattered by a sleeveless red top and low-cut jeans, and her wild red hair gave her an energetic air. The really striking thing about the young lady, though, was the pair of dark cat-like ears that replaced her normal ones. Her fingernails were sharpened into points, her canines were slightly more pronounced than most, and her eyes were a soft honey-colour with slit-like feline pupils. Katya had been Jake's familiar- simply put, a magical assistant- for around three years. She had not ceased to be eighteen years old for those three years. After some unknown misdemeanour- Jake, knowing better than most that some liked to keep things private, had never pried- that somehow resulted in her being rendered with cat-ears, claws and gold eyes, the Draconic High Council- largely on the suggestion of Khazahn- had decided to leave one unageing troublemaker with a number. And so, Jake found himself with a new familiar from that day onwards. Neither had been keen on the idea; Jake didn't want a familiar, and Katya didn't want to be one, but neither of them got much of a choice in the matter. Since then, they'd fortunately grown on each other.

'Work,' Jake answered, flipping the old coin as Katya, with effortless grace, flipped herself over the back of the sofa.

'So "work" made you run off in the middle of Breakfast yesterday?'

'We found a body,' Jake answered as he turned the coin over again. 'It wasn't pretty.'

'How "wasn't pretty"?'

'The whole thing was burned; head-to-toe. We still haven't been able to identify him.' Jake leaned forward and rested his chin on his hands.

Katya's golden eyes widened slightly. 'You mean like-'

'Something like that,' Jake answered bleakly. 'I think it was something to do with Aleera. I found her name burned into a tree about twelve feet from the body.'

'Someone wants to get at her?'

Jake nodded.

'With a body?' Katya paled slightly. 'How'd she take it?'

'Typical Aleera. Hardly batted an eyelid. We'll have to wait for the lab to turn something up, which looks like it'll take until at least tomorrow, but Khazahn says he's got something for me.'

'Since when does Khazahn give you anything? Besides grief.'

'Well, you never know. That's not until ten o'clock tonight, so there's nothing we can do until then.' Jake trailed off, staring at the coin as he turned it over in his fingers, until Katya's own fingers snapped in his ear.

'Wake up, Jake,' she waved.

'Sorry. Just thinking…' Jake trailed off again for a moment. 'I've been thinking about this all day. Something just doesn't quite make sense; why Aleera? Why now? Why this?' He clicked his tongue as he turned the coin over again. 'Whoever did this left nothing on that body. Harry told me there wasn't a single fingerprint.'

'So whoever did it was careful.'

'Careful, but they wanted to be heard. They went to all that trouble to- to do what? Send a message? Who goes to that much trouble getting a call through, and then doesn't leave a name on it?' He leaned back into the sofa. 'I don't know,' he finally sighed.

'Did you sleep last night?' Katya asked, moving to lean on his shoulder.

'I got an hour or two at the Guild.'

'Thought not. You worry too much, Jake. Aleera can take care of herself, and this stuff is exactly what the Guild's there for; and Khazahn might be a prick, but he knows what he's doing.'

'Point being?' Jake stifled a yawn.

'Point being that you need to relax,' Katya lectured. 'You're not gonna figure out much of anything in this state.' She wrapped an arm around Jake and nuzzled into his shoulder, a slight purr escaping from her throat. Jake shifted slightly; it was funny how an action perfectly innocent for a pet- or a familiar- took on a different implication when said familiar was human. Or close enough to it. 'So,' Katya suggested, 'Movie?'

Jake sighed and glanced at the clock on top of the T.V.

'If we get pizza,' he agreed.

The day at school had come and gone with little out of the ordinary. Aleera had stayed behind for detention and noticed that Ryan Shane was not in attendance, which hadn't left her best pleased. In retrospect, concerning the previous day's other significant development, one school thug shouldn't have bothered her, but it helped to keep perspective of the usual irritations, like humanity. Detention had been dull, but she'd had time to think.

After her discussion with Michael, she had contemplated the likelihood of a demon being responsible for the thing that turned up in the park. It made enough sense; black magic, the killing itself being in the style of that most infamous of demons, right down to the markings. But… there was definitely a "but" there somewhere. The more she thought about it, the more the obvious conclusion came to her: someone had gone to great pains to send a message, but from what she had gleamed there had been no evidence there to identify the killer. A great effort, but not an overly consistent one. If someone was that desperate to get their message across, why remain anonymous about it? If someone wanted to threaten someone so deeply, why not *show yourself, you coward*? The answer was a painfully obvious realisation of "because there will be more messages". And that meant that more would die.

So whoever was responsible, they were not finished invading her life. That was annoying to realise, though. More deaths, too. More people killed.

There was that pit in her stomach again…

Now stop that. Threats were something she was used to. They'd been part of her everyday life for a long time. Too long.

She would find whoever did this, she reminded herself. She would find whoever it was that killed someone to invade her life. And what a perfect opportunity that would be to *really* cut loose.

Still. The everyday needed to be attended to as well. That was why she was still hoping for the opportunity to teach Ryan a stern lesson about respect for his fellow man. And woman. And demon.

There was a little grocery store between her apartment building and her school that Aleera frequented. It was one of the few places nearby that sold fresh ingredients rather than the processed garbage that humans insisted on shovelling down their necks. Either that or something that had been genetically modified to the point that you couldn't even tell what you were eating anymore. Then again, half of them didn't even know that there was meat in a hamburger -in most cases, of course, there wasn't as much meat as meat by-products, but still. The owner of the place was a forty-something-year-old Austrian man named Kristoff, who always greeted her with a pleasant smile and asked how her friends were. He spoke fluent English and had spoke with a thick New York accent, but liked to adopt an Austrian one for some of the customers before switching to his normal one as they left, just to see their expressions.

Aleera had spent some time perusing the aisles and deciding what she was going to cook for herself. She'd had a love of cooking since she was a little girl, and she spent a few summer afternoons in the kitchen with her sister. It was something they'd always bonded over- actually, she hadn't seen Lilith in a while. She'd moved to Phoenix with her boyfriend a few months ago, but it wasn't working out. Maybe she should call her; tell her what was happening. No, that probably wouldn't be wise. She didn't want to burden her with this; Lilith was the only member of her family that approximated a halfway-decent person, and the only one she never had nightmares about. She'd tell her, though. Just as soon as whoever was responsible was dealt with nice and viciously.

There, decision made. It was nice to have that sorted out. Now, what to cook? Lasagne would be good, she decided, so she started to look for tomatoes, garlic, some oregano...

What if they knew about her sister?

Stop it. Now: she had mince and pasta at home... oh, and she could use some more honey. Maybe for a treat after dinner.

But what if they knew about her sister?

Shut up!

What if they'd already found her?

Alright. She'd call her. Just to make sure that she was alright, and that whoever was after her hadn't found her. She wouldn't tell her, just make sure she was Ok.

There, she told herself. I'll call her later; now don't bring it up again. Now, tomato paste…

She paid for her purchases, gave Kristoff a friendly smile and left the store with the bag of groceries in one arm. It didn't remain there for long, as when she stepped out of the store someone in a needlessly large coat for the time of year bumped into her and knocked the bag from her arms and sending the groceries falling out. Blowing some knocked-around hair out of her face in a moment of frustration, she knelt down to pick up the groceries before a strange hand reached them first and passed the oregano and tomato paste to her.

'Thanks,' she said offhand as she stuffed everything back into the bag and glanced up at the stranger.

She wasn't sure why it was that she froze when the tall, African-looking man turned his dark eyes on her and narrowed them slightly, or why a slight grin caught the edge of his mouth. He was looking at her. Normal enough on its own, but he was looking right at her. Right into her. A look that could only come from someone who knew her and whom she did not know. A look of cold, clear contempt.

'Any time,' he said in a deep, cold voice that sounded like a shovel being dragged across a shallow grave. 'See you soon, Aleera.'

Before Aleera could stand and turn to follow him, he was away, round the corner. When Aleera was there after him, he was gone, with nothing left but the words ringing behind him. It was him. He was here.

Another message. Another challenge. And this one came with the slightest bit of excitement pushing its way through her. Here he was, ready to close the distance and begin the game of hunter and prey.

At the same time, something else had presented itself, and after a long moment it finally stood up to be counted. And this one was as interesting as it was unexpected.

Even as the black pit started to force itself open in her stomach, Aleera felt herself grin.

Let the games begin.

5

The chain of command within the Guild was simple enough; starting at the lowest rank, the order was Private, Lieutenant, Captain, Sergeant, and Commander. Khazahn was a sergeant, answerable directly to the Commander, head of the Division of the Guild in which he worked. New York, along with the Eastern Seaboard of the United States, was under the jurisdiction of the Eighth Division. Each Sergeant was in command of a unit; A-Unit, B-Unit and so on, just to keep things manageable. The Commander answered to the Head of the Guild, who himself had a seat on the Dragon High Council and only answered to the High Chancellor herself. D-Unit, of which Khazahn was in control and with which Jake was affiliated, was a sizeable unit that oversaw New York City itself. Hence, Khazahn was in a position of quite some power, at which not much was classified from his knowledge.

Thusly, if he had some manner of information to impart to Jake, it was no doubt important. And, if the case to which it pertained affected Aleera as directly as this one, surely she would have a right to know.

It wasn't that she didn't trust Jake. On the contrary, she trusted him with her life. Her sister was the only other person to share that honour. Of course, Aleera liked to take care of her life herself as much as possible. No sense getting too many people's fingerprints on it. But yes, she trusted Jake. It was just that this would help her know something, and she was getting somewhat impatient to know anything at all about that was going on. She knew where Jake and Khazahn met and what time they would be there, and she had enough time to see to a few other things. First on the list had been to call Lilith, just to calm herself down about that.

Now, if she would just pick up…

Finally, the receiver clicked. 'What's the occasion, baby sister?' the soft voice asked from the other end of the line. She wasn't feeling too worried then, not if she was using that old nickname.

'I need an occasion to call my big sis?' Aleera replied, feigning normality as well as she could.

'First call in three weeks. What's up?'

'I just wondered how you were coping without me,' Aleera said in her sweetest voice. She hated using that one, but it softened her sister up.

'I'm missing my little sister, but I'm fine. Nice city. You gonna come and visit sometime?'

'Love to. So you're Ok, right?'

'Never better. You remember Steve?'

'The boy who stole my big sister from me?' Aleera pretended to pout. Just behave normally and be sure everything was fine. 'Yeah.'

'Well, I don't,' Lilith declared proudly. 'You'll never believe what happened.'

'What?' If somebody had hurt her sister- well, she was worried about physically right now, but in any sense- she might have to abandon her upcoming match with her unknown antagonist to pay a violent visit to Arizona.

'He was a god-damn crack head. I dropped him two weeks ago.'

'You didn't call?'

'Did you call me when you dumped Dante?' Lilith reminded her.

'I was still living with you then,' Aleera pointed out. 'And don't bring him up,' she added bitterly.

'I know, baby sis, I'm sorry.'

'So are you seeing anyone new?'

'Well, y'know, a couple of guys, a couple of girls...' There was the sound of a horn from the other end of the line. 'Sorry, Aleera, but I've gotta go; cab's here. Wish me luck.'

'Just-' Aleera said quickly, 'You're Ok, right? Nothing weird or anything?'

'Why?'

'Just tell me if you're Ok?'

'I'm fine, what's happened?' Lilith's voice changed pitch. Aleera knew Lilith well enough to know that it was worry.

'Nothing,' she lied.

'Aleera,' Lilith said urgently, 'What's wrong?'

'It's nothing,' Aleera insisted. 'I'm fine. I'll call you back, alright?'

Lilith sighed. 'Alright. Love you, baby sis.'

The line clicked and went dead.

Wonderful. She'd done the very thing that she was reluctant to call Lilith just to avoid. She didn't need to burden anyone else with this. Michael, Sara and Jake were exposed to this, and had more chance to become involved, because of it. Not her sister as well.

Someone was stalking and threatening her, she realised, and she was more worried about causing concern to her sister? Maybe there was something to those psyche evaluations.

Still, at least that was one thing sorted. Taking a deep breath to calm herself down, she set to work on making herself something to eat. It took up some time, and a decent meal would also help to calm her down slightly. She was just eager to get out and see what Khazahn had found out. Not afraid. Certainly not.

It turned out that she only had the appetite for about half of what she cooked. Thanks to the pit in her stomach she didn't feel like eating, and her mind was too elsewhere to focus on making her mouth consume anything. She wasn't aware of how long she spent pushing lasagne around the dish until she looked at the clock and saw that it was nine-forty. Leaving the remaining food in the refrigerator, she made her way to the bedroom and changed into her more-practical halter top. Opening the window, she whispered '*Tyasans*' and, once the spell was safely in place, she allowed the wings to expand from her back and flexed the tired, stiff membrane. The sickly green digital numbers of the alarm clock read: *21:50*. Finally.

She launched herself out of the window, caught the breeze and sailed upwards.

The Manhattan skyline was banked with a thick layer of cloud, stretching from one horizon to the other. There were no stars, no moon, just the sickly glow of the street lights and the occasional glow from the headlights of cars below. The inhabitants of the alleys scurried across steaming manholes and piles of trash that smelt even worse in the stifling heat.

Aleera brushed a strand of hair off her sticky forehead. Even at this height, it was still irritatingly muggy. She checked again to be sure that she was out of sight, and then checked her watch. It was just after 10 p.m.

The rooftop of the next, slightly shorter, building was cast with long shadows from what little moonlight forced its way through the clouds. Other then the dull, continual hum of the air conditioner, it was empty and silent.

Aleera was fairly sure Jake knew she would be there. He wasn't stupid.

And he was making it far too easy. Focusing her eyes on the empty spot of the roof, she whispered as quietly as she could, '*HthwailYeins*'. Third-eye. Another spell she'd mastered quite a while ago. Her vision flashed, and she could clearly see the image of a figure, immediately recognisable as Jake, standing near the edge of the rooftop, if slightly blurred. Further, the figure looked grainy, as though seen through a grey filter. There was no colour on it. The third-eye spell was the standard way to counter invisibility; the standard invisibility spell simply used the wielder's magical energy to redirect the light reflected from that person and speed or slow it to a spectrum where the naked eye could not detect it. Third-eye simply drew that light into the optic nerves as it should be, though it bypassed the cornea, which was why the invisible object appeared in black-and-white.

Jake definitely knew she was there, then. There were many much-more-advanced methods of avoiding detection that he was more than capable of using, and which Third-eye could not detect. Aleera couldn't help smirking. The whole scenario was almost like a game of chess between the two of them, with them both on the same side. Khazahn, with whatever information he had, would be in check the moment he opened his mouth. Finally, she would make her first move against her real opponent; at least, she would be on the board at long last.

Entirely too much time passed, which Jake eventually started to spend pacing impatiently around his rooftop. Aleera glanced down at her watch again. She'd been waiting for twenty-five minutes. Jake and Khazahn, she knew, always had always held to the arrangement that, if one of them didn't arrive within a half-hour, then they weren't going to.

Five more minutes passed, and Aleera gave a last look around. No Khazahn. So much for her first move in the game; an irritating realisation. Khazahn had never been the most pleasant of people, but she had hoped that, just this once, he might actually cooperate. Maybe that was naïve of her.

When she looked down at the other rooftop, Jake was gone. She relaxed and turned off the spell, and came to an immediate realisation that her head felt distinctly light, and her balance seemed a little off. Maintaining the spell for such a length of time had used up more energy than she would have liked.

'I don't suppose anybody's told *you* anything?' Katya's voice suddenly rang from behind her. Aleera's lips tugged into a wry smile as she turned round.

'Nice to see you too,' she said dryly. 'You knew I'd be here, then?' Katya was the final one of the few people she actually liked, and of course they'd met through Jake.

'Never doubted you,' Jake said from one side. Anyone not used to Jake would have been taken aback, but the remnant shimmer in the air around him betrayed the teleportation spell.

'Ok, now you're showing off,' Aleera commented. She turned back to Katya. 'And how long were you there?'

'A while,' Katya beamed. 'I was tempted to sneak up on you; just to see your face.' Well, she did have a little bit of cat about her, and cats were creatures of the night by nature. This was always the time of day that Katya was most... well, herself. 'By the way, I'm supposed to give you this. Just in case.' She handed Aleera a small vial of thick, red liquid.

Aleera turned the vial over in her hand. There was magic in it, she realised; she could sense it. Magic in the blood. The only creatures in history that had that were...

'This is dragon blood,' she realised, wide-eyed. She liked to maintain her self-control, but this was not an everyday sight. There hadn't been a dragon seen in five hundred years. Everything about them, she had heard told, was magic. Their very blood, in fact, possessed the power to heal.

There was, of course, nothing fantastic about it; dragon blood cells simply healed at a fantastic rate. In larger quantities, the effects of the substance were instantly fatal; barring that, they were reportedly still quite gruesome. In small doses, however, it did a better job of promoting regeneration than any healing spell or potion. But the question remained... 'where did Jake get dragon blood?'

'God knows,' Katya shrugged. 'He's got a few vials of the stuff, and he thought you'd better have some, just in case it comes down to it, considering what's been happening.'

Wow. Her, standing there with a vial of dragon blood. Just imagine.

Still, there was business to attend to, she reminded herself as she pocketed the vial.

'Well, either you set up a *very* clever distraction for me,' Aleera wouldn't put that past Jake. He was canny, if anything. 'Or Khazahn won't be joining us.'

'It's ten-thirty,' Jake confirmed, his brow creased into a worried frown. 'Why isn't he coming?'

Aleera thought for a moment. She might not have ever been good at working out people's emotions, but logic was simple enough to grasp when you didn't worry too much about the morality of it, and unpredictable people were easy enough to predict; just expect them to do what you wouldn't expect.

'He's the one who called you here,' she observed, 'But then he didn't show up. That means that he's got a good reason for not being here, if he missed his own appointment and didn't contact you about it.'

'A good reason like being ordered not to tell it to an untrustworthy freelancer,' Jake caught on quickly. 'You thinking what I'm thinking?'

'It's not for us to know,' Katya gave a wicked little grin.

'Important, though,' Jake pointed out. Aleera could see immediately where this train of conversation would lead.

'And if it's important,' Katya's honey-coloured eyes lit up.

'Nobody could get that upset if something slipped out,' Jake finished for her.

'Would we do that?' Katya asked, putting on her best innocent face.

'Katya,' Jake pretended to scold her, 'What an unthinkable thing to say.' That was Jake and Katya in a nutshell; a perfect pair of troublemakers if there ever was one. Almost everyone who met them instantly made assumptions of hanky-panky in that terminally-messy apartment, but Aleera knew them better than that. Jake and Katya were like Lennon and McCartney, maybe with a dash of Bonnie and Clyde. They could sleep naked in the same bed without sex rearing its ugly head.

'We'll let you know what we find out,' Katya said to Aleera.

Aleera grinned a little herself. 'Thanks, you two.'

Pieces in play. Her move at last.

After returning to her apartment, Aleera had certainly felt much hungrier, if only because of the amount of energy she'd used up in maintaining the third-eye spell for so long. Keeping herself cloaked there and backed hadn't been overly helpful either. Even though it was probably a little too late at night, she'd heated up and eaten the last of the lasagne.

While waiting for it to be ready, she allowed herself a minute to think while stealing a mouthful of honey. Consider her next move, as it were. The pieces were in play... only... she paused and chided herself. Get a handle on it, Aleera.

She shouldn't have thought about Jake and Katya like that. They weren't her pawns, and this wasn't a game. Well, at least not a game in the literal sense. But it was true that Jake and Katya could be bringing any amount of trouble upon themselves if they went snooping inside the Guild. The pit in her stomach opened a little more, and she felt a stab of guilt.

Stop that. Jake and Katya could handle themselves. Jake especially; he'd dealt with worse. Besides, he was good enough with magic to wipe the floor with the whole of Khazahn's unit at once. No problem. And besides, they'd offered their help. Anyway, it couldn't hurt to have someone on her side.

Before the lasagne finished heating up, she decided to check the answer machine to see if there were any calls from Lilith, which there probably would be if she had sensed something was wrong. It was a slight surprise to hear the empty voice of the machine inform her that *'you have... four... new messages.'*

The first one was from Michael; *"Hey, Aleera, it's me. You're probably busy but I was just checking everything was alright with... you know, what happened. Look, I think Sara's really worried about you, so if anything happens, just call one of us, Ok? See you tomorrow"*. The second turned out to be from Sara, and its content much the same, although Sara sounded a little bit shakier, a little bit less certain of what to say or how to feel. This was getting to Sara, Aleera realised, maybe more deeply than it was to her. The third was from Lilith: *"Aleera, it's me. Listen, if you're not there, call me back when you get this, alright? And don't say nothing's bothering you. Just tell me, Ok?"*. Ouch. No nickname. Lilith really was worried.

One last message. Probably a *"Caught you"* from Katya.

Or not. The voice that rang from the phone was cold, deep and carrying an echo of superiority. That same air of 'I know you, you don't know me'. That same voice from earlier. Him. And he said *"I know what you are"*.

Aleera stared at the machine for a moment, feeling her dark eyes turn red. So he knew where she lived. He did know about her; everything. And now, even if only in voice, he was invading her home. How *dare* he?

Then, she felt the naughty little thrill again.

Another move. He was making his play. Scare tactics designed to back her into a corner. Go ahead, she thought. He could back her into the corner as far as he wanted, and then, when he closed in…

Aleera switched off the answer machine and turned away.

Check.

My move.

6

Draconics had been in hiding for the better part of five hundred years. All record of their existence had been stricken from recorded human history in that time, and they had been in hiding ever since. The Dragon High Council of the time had of course known at the time that there would be no going back; there was a theory held by some more-intellectual humans that, if ever contact was made with alien life, some excuse would be found to declare war on it. Most reasoning determined that the consequences would be roughly the same if mankind knew that magic, demons and (once upon a time) dragons actually existed. Of course, some had leaked out, but no real magic, more arrangements of superstitions. Voodoo, Ouija boards and the like. Nothing of the real thing.

Of course, this meant that places to hide would be needed. For most draconics, this was not a problem, but such organisations as the Dragon High Council, and indeed the Guild, would require meeting places to function efficiently. Needless to say, no humans knew that the headquarters of the Eighth Division of the Guild, and one of the several worldwide offices of the High Council, were located directly underneath Times Square. The entrance was below the Flat Iron Building itself, and they had absolutely no idea.

The offices were not so much "offices" as labyrinth, ancient stone catacombs carved out centuries ago; the central hall, which branched off into all other areas of the offices, featured rows of pillars supporting the carved ceiling's depiction of a mighty dragon looking down sagely upon everything beneath it, with the pillars themselves ornately carved with serpentine dragons. Their prominent inclusion as a design aesthetic was not a surprising one; the dragon was a mystical creature that featured in some form in almost every culture around the world, and, more importantly, the reason for this was that every supernatural caste could trace its evolution back to the dragon.

Still, Jake reflected as he and Katya strode across the central hall, they were gone now. They had been for half a millennium. Jake remembered them, all their magnificent grandeur, from so long ago. Five hundred years. He'd been normal- more so than he was now- back then. He'd watched the supernatural world change along with the natural one, and not all of either one had been pleasant to see.

The sixteenth century had been an important one. The dragons left, the draconics went into hiding, that one important event in his life had happened... and he knew the connection. That was the darkest reflection. Aleera would have to as well. There was no telling how much time there was now. But that would come later. He would tell her, but not just yet. Let her enjoy her youth first. When the body had turned up, he'd thought for a moment that she would have to find out already, and part of him hadn't wanted to burden her with it- but if she was as closely connected to the situation as he suspected, she needed to be aware of it.

'You Ok?' Katya asked from his side. He'd been quiet since they arrived, having teleported straight there after speaking with Aleera.

'Yeah,' Jake answered quickly. 'Just thinking.'

'Well you can think later. Come on, we'd better make this quick.' They stopped outside of one of the stone doors, also carved with the face of a dragon. Katya knocked, and a voice from the other side called out 'Come in'.

The room certainly didn't have the splendour of the central hall, and certainly had more of an "office" feel. Hollowed-out pillars reached the low ceiling, stuffed with files and papers. Admittedly, on top of the carved stone desk, the computer looked slightly out of place. Sitting behind the desk, tapping a pen on the side of his head in boredom, was a young man of Indian descent with spiked black hair, his brown eyes creased as he frowned irritably at the stack of papers before looking up to the new arrivals.

'Oboy,' he sighed immediately. 'What'd you do now?'

'You're a ray of sunshine, Makian,' Jake gave a sardonic reply as he approached the desk and used the computer as an armrest. 'Look, I need a favour.' Makian was someone whom Jake knew to be trustworthy; in addition, he was a good source of information. If you wanted information, you didn't go to a high-ranking officer who wanted to keep you from finding things out. You went to the person who looked after the information. You went to the desk-jockey, and the one Jake knew best was the young lieutenant behind the desk.

'You know what happened last time I did you a favour, Jake?' Makian replied as he looked back down to the papers. 'I got six more months in this office. Piss off,' he said, looking up with arched eyebrows.

'That wasn't my fault,' Jake said defensively. 'Besides, this is just a small thing that nobody ever has to know about it.'

'Which means you don't want anyone to know about it, which means I'll get my balls broken again,' Makian said with sarcastic cheer.

'Come on, hear us out,' Katya pouted.

Makian sighed. 'For a friend. That's the only reason I'm doing this, and I'm not doing it if I don't like what it is.'

'The case that D-Unit's on,' Jake explained.

'The burned guy?'

Jake nodded affirmatively. 'I just need to see if you've got any new developments, that's all. Failing that, anything unusual.'

'We found a human barbeque in the middle of Central Park, Jake; *everything* about this shit is unusual. What am I looking for?'

'Not sure, just something that shouldn't be there.'

'No, that won't be a waste of my time,' Makian answered sarcastically. 'I'll dig up some dirt on the Virgin Mary while I'm at it. Dare I ask what brought this on?'

'Khazahn said he had something to tell me, but he didn't show up.'

'The phrase 'let it go' means nothing to you, does it, Jake?' Makian shook his head in dismay.

'It's for a friend.'

Makian looked up. 'Who?'

'Keep this under your hat,' Jake said in a hushed voice. 'You remember Aleera?'

Makian thought for a moment. 'Oh, yeah.' The slightest smirk started to creep outwards from his mouth. 'Demon girl, black hair, hell of an ass.'

'I think this is something to do with her. And with her dad.'

Makian looked up at him. 'Shit. Seriously?'

'Just keep this between us, alright?' Jake asked urgently. 'If Khazahn asks-'

'I barely even know you,' Makian finished for him. 'Now if only that were true.'

'So can you do this?'

Makian avoided his gaze for a second. 'You owe me.'

'You're the best, Mak,' Katya grinned, leaning over the desk and favouring Makian with a peck on the cheek.

'Yeah, I know,' Makian answered coolly. 'Oh, and you two might want to pay Harry and Tomoko a visit. Harry's been red-faced all day after what Tomo found out.'

Jake shut the door behind them and leaned back on it, taking a thoughtful breath.

''sup?' Katya asked.

'Aleera's protective detail,' Jake muttered. 'Something about it just strikes me as a little strange, I guess.'

'What about it?'

Jake looked worriedly at her. 'There doesn't seem to be one.'

Tomoko Shinju looked up from the microscope and used a gloved hand to pinch the bridge of her nose as she stepped back and mulled over the puzzle before her. Her dark hair was neatly and surgically tied back as her light-brown eyes squinted in frustration behind a pair of rectangular-frame glasses.

Magic brought a lot of things to mind, chief among them spells and old, dusty tomes of lore. Not so much the pristine autopsy lab in the middle of which lay the most perplexing thing Tomoko had come across in her career. The edge of the circular room was lined with computers, chemicals and surgical equipment, interrupted only by the door that led out into the rest of the Guild offices. Draconics had gone into hiding five centuries ago, but they could hardly be expected to stand still in all that time. Humans had moved along and evolved, and so had they. So had the Guild, which was just as up-to-date and well equipped in the more modern detective sciences as any agency of human law-enforcement. It had been just the thing for a budding twenty-three-year-old medical genius. Unfortunately, so far all of that had turned up absolutely nothing to help catch whoever had done... *that*. Studying forensics, Tomoko had been trained to deal with gruesome sights, but nothing like this.

Dr. Harry Drake stood leaning on the autopsy table, staring intently at the sheet that covered the body. Harry had been Tomoko's direct superior since she joined the Guild; she'd been snapped up shortly after graduating from Kawasaki Medical University. An IQ of 216 had definitely helped.

Harry looked up as the sound of a sharp knock came from the door. 'Come in,' he called to whoever was on the other side. His expression lit up slightly when Makian led Jake and Katya in.

'We were wondering when you two would turn up,' Tomoko greeted them with a smile.

'Well, it's not the nicest place to meet, is it?' Jake observed.

'Did Makian tell you, then?' Harry asked, stepping round the table.

'He said you've got something,' Jake replied. 'So…?'

'You won't believe this,' Tomoko said as she crossed the room and picked up a clipboard, handing it to Jake. 'We finally got the results of the dental records back this morning, and guess what?' She turned and gave a smug wink in Harry's direction.

'Lay it on us, eggheads,' Katya nodded.

'Dr. Drake was…' Tomoko prompted, looking back at Harry.

'I was wrong,' Harry sighed grudgingly. 'The victim's a woman.'

'A woman?' Katya repeated.

'A very manly woman,' Harry said defensively. 'Laurie Strode; she lived in a shared apartment in Midtown, and worked part-time as a waitress in Pentagram.'

Jake's brow creased. 'The killing,' he muttered, 'was like one of Kudra's.'

'Right.'

'But the victim was a demon,' Jake carried on thinking out loud, 'who worked at the biggest demon nightclub on this coast.'

'Could be a gang thing,' Makian offered up, 'a lot of that stuff happens around there.'

Jake shook his head. 'I wonder…' for a long moment, he remained quiet.

'The other thing we found out,' Tomoko went on, 'was that the burning isn't the cause of death.'

'You sure?' Makian asked levelly, 'Because I definitely smell barbeque.'

'There were two causes of death,' Harry began, 'There was the burning, and a stab wound to the lungs. The lungs were filled with blood, and something like that takes a few minutes to kill the victim. The…' he stammered for a second. 'The burning… would have taken place just before death.'

'Free cremation,' Makian observed grimly.

'Anything we can use?' Jake asked.

'Not a trace of foreign DNA on the body,' Harry replied. His voice carried a note of irritation. 'Whoever did this was careful. Not so much as an eyelash- and if there was, it went the same way as most of the victim.'

'In other words, we've got nothing,' Jake mused. 'Thanks, docs,' he nodded before turning back to the door with Katya.

Once they were outside, Jake leaned against the wall and drummed his fingertips on his forehead. 'Something's not right with this,' he finally said.

'What *is* right with it?' Katya retorted.

'Someone kills a demon in a demon way, and it's to do with Aleera,' Jake thought out loud, 'There's something about it that we're obviously not supposed to know, and whatever that is… something doesn't fit, that's the problem,' he breathed. 'We're missing something.'

The phone mounted on the adjacent wall rang. Harry answered it, listened for a moment, and then turned to Jake, his expression one of direst urgency. 'This, ladies and gentlemen, you won't believe.'

Everything was burning.

A sheet of darkness hung over what was left of the village, the light of the African sun blocked by acrid smoke from the burning huts. The only sound louder than the crackling of the flames that cast the ground and the edges of the jungle a sickly orange was the screams of the dying, the wails of children as they were torn from their mothers' arms.

He stood in the heart of it all. Bodies dropped around him, scorched or bleeding or beaten to a point that they could no longer be given the name human. Orange light from the flames danced across his form and glinted on the segmented metal claws of his gauntlets.

What had been the Maasai chief was on his back, his spear in pieces around him in and his clothing torn and burned to shreds. Where his right eye had been, there was nothing but a raw, bleeding hole, half his face covered in dark blood. He coughed on a mouthful of blood as he pleaded in Maa.

Kudra was six-and-a-half feet tall. In the glow of the flames and the dark of the smoke, smeared with human blood, he looked like a giant. The hooded cape draped over his shoulders was caked with red, and the gauntlet of his right hand was tightened around the dripping sword. His face was covered by a mask of welded bronze, fashioned into the image of a shape that was just barely human, crowned with horns and adorned with curved, jagged teeth pointing out from the mouth.

Behind him, a young man with a spear ran forward, thrusting the blade towards Kudra's back. At some point as he turned, Kudra laughed. His left hand opened, and the tribesman's body buckled before the impact of the wave of pure force. Bones cracked with a sickening crunch as the blast hurled him through the air. Kudra turned round to the sound of the man's screams as he landed in one of the burning huts.

He revelled in the sound.

To his side, there was another movement. Something swung at his midsection. With barely an effort, Kudra grabbed the offending spear and swatted its owner away. The eleven-year-old body hit the ground hard.

Aleera looked up at Kudra with red eyes that burned with hate. In a moment, the child's fear had given way to anger and sheer hate at the knowledge that this, this was what her father was. The man who had raised her was doing this. Her young face was coated in shining tears.

Kudra regarded her for a moment, then turned back to the chief. In a voice that sounded like cracking glass, he gave a mutter of 'disappointing'.

Aleera spat something bloody and disgusting out of her mouth. It had taken a moment to even notice that the impact had dislodged a tooth. She hadn't felt it. Maybe the rage boiling inside her numbed the physical pain, or maybe it was just shock setting in. She didn't care.

Another cluster of corpses fell at Kudra's feet, adding to the wretched pile that had formed in the middle of the village. Men, women, children, it was hard to even tell where one body ended and another began. Around it stood men, none as tall or as dark as Kudra, but all garbed in similar black robes.

'The last of them, lord,' one of them said.

Kudra nodded and turned to the chief. 'This,' he said in the broken-glass voice, 'is what awaits you all.'

'Lord,' one of the men asked, 'What about her?'

Kudra looked back to Aleera.

'Spare the rod, spoil the child,' he said coldly. 'She is a disappointment. She needs to be punished.'

Beneath the man's hood, Aleera saw a perverse grin of yellow teeth. 'Yes, lord.'

Aleera stared up as the men approached her, each grinning that perverse grin. Quivering fear started to worm its way up from a pit in her stomach as she managed to stand, backing into strong arms that wrapped round her and pulled her close, tugging at her clothing. She screamed, but a hand covered her mouth. Red eyes widened in fear of what was about to happen as she struggled and cried and let out muffled screams in the mass of hands and grins.

The last thing she saw before they enveloped her was him, picking up the chief. He managed to say, in English, 'why?'

Kudra grabbed him by the forearms. The claws of the gauntlets dug into his flesh.

'Because I can,' Kudra chuckled beneath the mask. 'Because we can, and you cannot. EiahFhieh." *The chief began to smoke as the last of Aleera's vision was obscured, and then came the deepest pain.*

Aleera woke with a scream.

Gone. He was gone. They were gone, she told herself immediately. Just a dream, she focused on that knowledge and its safety. Just a dream. Just a dream. Just a dream.

She was sobbing. When she woke up, her wings had erupted from her back without permission, and her claws were extended and clicking together as her hands shook. Her chest rose and fell as her breath came in ragged gasps. Just a dream. Just a memory. She breathed deeply and fell back on the pillow, rubbing tears from her eyes. She noticed that the expanding wings had torn through the bed sheets. Her body was covered in cold sweat. It was just a memory. It was over, long ago dead and buried.

Only it was coming back now, in this new way, what he did was coming back and… and…

Stop it, she scolded herself. Get a damned grip. It was not going to come back. She was not going to be that way, that afraid, that weak, again. She was in control of herself, and she would be in control of this.

She closed her eyes and covered them with one hand to wipe the last of the tears from her face. She relaxed in what little in the way of a breeze was coming in through the window. Her fingertip traced the shape of the scar on her forehead.

There. She was calm. Rationality returned.

Whoever he was that was doing this, he was going to pay.

She sat up in bed and reached out for the bedside lamp. She squinted as the painfully bright light flooded the room. The sickly letters of the alarm clock read "*03:22*". Taking another moment to steady herself, she turned and stood up out of bed. She'd need to change the sheets, and if nothing else she needed a quick shower to remove the layer of sweat. Maybe after that, if she could summon the enthusiasm, a spoonful of honey to help herself get back to sleep.

The hot water of the shower was warming and welcoming, and she allowed herself to relax a moment, feeling her pulse slow down. Once she was done, she quickly pulled off the damaged sheets, pulled some spares from the top shelf of the closet and replaced the damaged ones. It was only when she climbed back into bed that she noticed the cell phone on the bedside table and its message of "*You have -1- unread message. From -Jake-*"

Aleera picked up the phone and opened the message.

"*We've got another one*".

7

Pentagram certainly had something of a reputation among the draconic population of New York City. In only a few years, the nightclub had asserted itself as one of enormous popularity, almost entirely among demon clientele, and now there was no better- or worse, depending on one's perspective- hotspot for demon activity. Almost all of it was black market goods, sex or drugs, and none of it was legal. On most nights, the pounding bass rhythms and shouts of intoxicated revellers could be heard despite the club's heavy steel door and underground location. It wasn't the sort of place Aleera liked to frequent, given her views of what went on there; why so many people seemed to think that enjoyment was to be found only in sniffing, smoking, swallowing or injecting something was beyond her. But to be a supernatural being in Manhattan, and to be in any way connected to the Guild, was to have heard of it at the very least. The only reason the Guild hadn't shut the place down long ago was that most of the clientele tended to keep their activities to themselves-that and the politics of policing, which in layman's terms roughly translated to 'someone rich in Pentagram paid someone powerful in the Guild'.

The entrance to Pentagram, appropriately enough, was located in a small, dank back alley where the reeking piles of garbage undulated with rats and the occasional passed-out customer. Aleera imagined that the back entrance, wherever it was, was much the same. Should someone be foolish enough to bring an overdose upon themselves, practice within Pentagram, rather than risk involving the authorities was to toss them out with the rest of the trash. It was a mentality that Aleera had come to understand rather well, although if she ever should meet someone responsible for such a decision... well, she didn't like drugs on principle. She would probably take the opportunity to indulge her 'borderline' side and give a painful lecture to whoever took it upon themselves to enact such a waste of any more lives in addition to their own.

Tonight, however, the alley was silent. There were no groans from passed-out junkies among the trash heaps, and no pounding rhythm from inside. Instead, it was a different kind of activity that filled the cramped space between two walls. Black cloaks swept around the white shapes that knelt next to the unmoving form of the tarp, moving amongst themselves in a manner and space entirely indifferent to the outside world.

Illusion spells were funny things in the way they worked, and one of the most complex because their principle was a more abstract one: the energy given off by the spell had an effect on the brain and senses so that anyone looking in the direction saw the image that the spell implanted, rather than what was actually there. However, if someone already knew what was really there, the brain already contained that information and, on its unconscious levels, therefore rejected the false image. Aleera, already expecting to see the Guild soldiers and pathologists around the body, was consequently unaffected herself.

Jake and Katya were both milling near one of the less-pungent dumpsters. As Aleera approached, its smell became overpowered the stench of burned flesh. Lovely.

'What happened?' she asked.

'This one turned up a few hours ago,' Jake answered. 'They're searching the scene before they can move the body; we finally managed to get the normal cops out of the picture- actually, you'd best settle down, we've got a lot to tell you.'

'You found something?' Aleera asked.

Jake nodded. 'The body in Central Park turned out to be a woman. She was also a demon, and *now* I think we've got something, because she worked right here at Pentagram.'

Aleera nodded, soaking up the information. They'd been busy.

Immediately, her mind started to click as she processed what Jake had told her. Demon victim, demon *modus operandi*, demon nightclub, and the killer...

No... surely not. She forced her lips not to grin. If she was right about him, if she could confirm it... oh, now this was unexpected. It raised a great many questions, left her with a great many unknowns, this one impossible thought...

She would tell Jake. Of course she would. Just as she would tell him about the meeting in the street, and the message on her answer machine. But there was this to deal with first, and her realisation would have to wait until she was sure. It was far too huge an element to bring in on such a slight suspicion, but if she was right, oh how her mind buzzed.

'Come on,' Jake nodded to Katya and Aleera. 'I'm gonna try a spirit trace.'

'Any luck on what Khazahn had to say?' Aleera checked as she followed.

'No such,' Jake shook his head, 'I got Makian to look into it.'

Makian? Well, fair enough... even if Aleera did have cheese that had matured better.

One of the soldiers gave Aleera a cautious glance as she passed him. She brushed it off as the usual reaction; being the daughter of the worst madman in demon history was bound to bring some infamy.

The uniform of the Guild soldier had remained largely unchanged over the years, though it was certainly distinctive; supernatural crime brought its own risks. The torso, arms and legs were covered in Kevlar underneath a segmented layer of stronger armour. Built-in cowls covered the soldier's head, which was afforded additional protection by a metallic mask consisting of a basic helmet with holes for the eyes that reached down to the nose and a v-shaped plate covering the lower half of the face. Bronze-coloured metal staffs, adorned with three curved blades on each end, were also standard issue.

'Did I miss anything?' Jake asked as they stepped past the soldiers. Aleera noted that both Dr. Harry Drake and a young Asian woman, with whom she was not acquainted, were knelt next to the body. From what she could see, the body was much the same as the last one; red, raw and burned, still frozen into an insane grin of horror and pain. It brought back the Maasai chief's screams from her nightmare, which she immediately silenced by confirming with Harry that the body was the same as the last one. Jake introduced Aleera to Dr. Tomoko Shinju, and then set to work scattering a thin circle of dust around the body.

'Now that we know what we're looking for,' Tomoko explained, 'We found the stab wound in the chest.' Aleera glanced quizzically at her. A stab wound? So the burning...

'The cause of death in the last one was a stab to the lungs,' Harry enlightened her. 'But this one was to the heart.'

Interesting; a difference, however slight, held its own implications. Maybe her opponent was still developing his game plan.

Jake finished scattering the dust and squatted down, holding his palm out over the body. He took a deep breath, and the dust began to swirl. Aleera watched with a momentary, perhaps morbid, fascination. The spirit trace was officially designated as one of the most dangerous spells by the Guild, to be used only by those of exceptional skill. The dust itself was enchanted; not in the sense of childrens' tales of pixies and unicorns, but in the sense that an amount of magic had been stored in it. Emotions were powerful things, and they contributed towards magic a great deal; the angrier someone was when using a spell to attack, the more energy that anger would drive them to use. That gave it a very real connection, and in the case of extremely strong emotion, that could leave an imprint. A residual mental negative that, until it faded, could be developed with the right skill. The enchanted dust could soak up some of that magic and help whoever was searching to gather it; 'see' whatever was there to be seen.

There was the faintest shimmer of air, the slightest glow around the dust, and then that glow waved in the air towards Jake's palm, into his own magic, taking the echo of a memory, the trace of a spirit, with it. The hairs on the back of his hand stood up. His breathing became shallower. His closed eyes seemed to struggle behind their lids. He flinched.

With a shout of pain, Jake's eyes flashed open, flashing with light. His palm wavered as he fought the urge to instinctively pull it back and break the link. Katya held onto his shoulder, her own honey-coloured eyes wide with worry, as Jake's eyes creased shut again and he gritted his teeth, forcing himself to outlast the ordeal. Whatever he was picking up, Aleera observed, it was bad. She suddenly realised that he needed to stop; there wasn't enough to be gained to justify this, not for her sake.

The glow in the dust finally vanished. Jake snapped his hand back, taking a deep, sharp breath like a drowning man who had just broken the surface of the water and fell backwards, still gasping. He wiped a few beads of sweat from his forehead.

Jake grunted, forcing himself to sit up. 'Lots of fear,' he gasped painfully, through gritted teeth and as if he couldn't breath. 'Even more pain.' He took a desperate breath, shaking his head. 'She was alive,' he gasped. 'She was alive when he did this.'

Aleera glanced at Harry and Tomoko, who both sat and muttered to each other thoughtfully.

'Did she see who did it?' Tomoko asked after a moment.

Jake shook his head, his breathing now becoming more regular. 'No.'

'What about where he was?' Tomoko pressed. Katya gave her a whispered hiss to 'give him a minute'.

'She was inside somewhere,' Jake said shakily. 'Small, wet, salty smell; maybe a boat.'

'Or somewhere near water,' Aleera suggested thoughtfully. So the victim, whoever she was, had been moved there. Left for her to find. Next to Pentagram, to... to deliver the message. Two demon victims, and now a demon nightclub. Did that make sense? Maybe. If her suspicions were right. But there was something... something more. Something she couldn't put her finger on.

'I'll tell Khazahn,' Harry suggested. 'He'll have D-Unit check out the waterfront.'

'Good,' Jake said, standing up with what looked like a painful twinge in his shoulder. 'He can explain why he didn't turn up.'

'You Ok?' Katya asked from beside him.

'Yeah,' Jake nodded uncertainly. 'Just a lot of emotion in there. Something very, *very* bad happened to her.' There was something in his tone that belied his meaning. Something *bad*. Something deeply painful. The deepest pain. Something rose in her stomach as she thought back to what they had done to her. What her father had done to her. The pit in her stomach had opened at some point.

'So what now?' she asked, just to say something lest anyone notice her silence and draw her attention to the quivering feeling in her throat.

'We'll I.D. the victim,' Tomoko said with brisk authority.

'Just a thought,' Katya mentioned, 'Does anyone else feel like they're missing the party?' She gave Jake a conspiratorial grin. 'It's all going on in Pentagram.'

Jake caught on and nodded. 'Who feels like clubbing tomorrow night?'

8

The name Kudra was quite possibly the most despised one in the history of the mystical world. Up to three years ago, it had been a named mentioned in hushed voices in secret council rooms or by the few that managed to survive him, spoken then in broken voices and with nothing but raw, uncomprehending fear. And Aleera had the most reason to fear him.

Demons had split from the Draconic species a great number of centuries ago; the exact day, year or even century had been long-since lost to history. But there had always been a considerable degree of hostility between the two groups. There had been violence, wars... well; at most they were minor skirmishes. Especially compared to what would come later. At some point in the early-to-mid 20th century, there had been a demon organisation established in the United States dubbed the "Dark Circle". It had been, at best, a loose, squabbling gathering of a handful of demons devoted more to organised crime than anything else. It rose to its height of notoriety in late 1962 when they expanded their black market to Cuba, and hadn't helped the human political crisis of the time one iota. That heyday was well-and-truly over by the end of the sixties, however. In 1975, however, the organisation recruited a 13-year-old psychopath whose name was Kudra. He rose quickly through its ranks and by 1994 he was the head of the Dark Circle. Under Kudra, it rebuilt an enormous amount of its strength and began to recruit many, many more, including draconics and any other caste that could be coerced by the promise of the mystical no longer being in hiding, and Kudra's promise of victory over the oppressors. Most joined, though, because of the threats. Two years later, Kudra abolished the Dark Circle and replaced it with the Dark Council. The following year, the declaration of war came in the form of terrorist attacks on high-ranking draconics of the Guild and High Council.

Aleera spent that time, laughably, thinking her father was a kind and decent man, who raised her after she was rejected by her mother, even if she was a bastard child, the product of a one-night stand with a succubus.

When she was eleven, Kudra had sought to break her into the Dark Council. He took her with him to Kenya on what he told her was a business trip. She'd been excited, expecting to see grandeur and excitement as only an eleven-year-old's imagination could expect.

What awaited was not the man she thought she knew. It wasn't even war. It was genocide. There was no cause behind the atrocities she saw Kudra commit in his maddened search for the High Council as they convened somewhere in Nairobi. It was nothing but the slaughter of what he saw as vermin. Humans, draconics and anything in his way were butchered like pigs.

Kudra was not "evil" in the sense that humans thought of from the word demon. He wasn't the "bad guy" of a Saturday-morning cartoon who would get his comeuppance at the end and be back next week with a scheme whose flaw the hero would find some way to take advantage of. He was beyond that. He was beyond morality, beyond suffering, beyond feeling. This was not a man. This was not even a demon. This was the worst mass-murderer that the hidden world ever knew. This was a twisted, genocidal monster.

This was her father.

Kudra had died three years ago, after the secret war finally came to an end. The Dark Circle was abolished, and the Guild became aware of the worrying fact that the monster had sired an offspring, so they had placed her under careful supervision from that day forth. Anything to avoid the risk of it happening again.

Now, Kudra was just a faded memory, a name printed in the history books. Now he was just the thing that had left part of itself in that dark corner of her, the thing that kept her up at night and the thing that wanted her to, just once, truly cut loose like never before and become like him. He was that little thing inside her that was purely, totally, evil.

Aleera sat up in bed and pushed the thoughts of her father back where they belonged. There. Kudra was gone. He died, and was still dead. All that was coming back to her now was the memory of him. She would put a stop to this, and that memory would be gone. Just as soon as this man, whoever he was, had paid.

She jumped at the shrill noise of the alarm clock, before lashing out and silencing the wretched thing. Another day of this waiting game, and she had her move to prepare for.

Aleera found Michael near the basketball court, storming away from three students who apparently found five-to-six-letter words beginning with 'n' denoting dark-skinned people to be absolutely hilarious. As fate would have it, it turned out to be the three stooges themselves. Ryan himself was giggling like a lunatic with a still-smoking joint in his hand, and "Gregzilla was looking away with a touch of shame on his face.

Oh, of all the days for the poor idiot to try such a thing.

Mostly out of friendship, largely out of anger and partly because, as she was fully aware, her nightmare and lack of sleep had not left her in the most pleasant of moods, Aleera used the smallest claw she could manifest to tear two holes in a paper napkin that had contained a slice of cafeteria pizza that she didn't have the appetite for. She then strode brazenly up to Ryan, draped the makeshift hood over his head, which promptly set his contemporaries to giggling at his expense instead. Much more acceptable. That had been for Michael. When she curled her hand into a fist and punched Ryan in the stomach, it was for herself.

Kneeling down, she positioned one hand in front of Ryan's belly, allowing the claw of her index finger to extend just far enough to poke him slightly. He froze in fear as what he thought was a blade scraped across his soft gut. As Aleera regarded his panicked face, he reminded her of the junkie from two days prior, and how that would most likely be Ryan in a few years' time. Another predatory animal roaming the alleys of the concrete jungle; and what those animals really needed was a predatory check.

It was *very* tempting to truly lose herself in the heat of the moment, to allow the anger to slip that little bit further and push the claw that inch or two into him. To rid herself of the piece of nearly-human refuse that had taken it upon himself to hassle herself and her friends.

Instead, she decided a verbal reprimand would do for now, until she was less distracted by other problems. She didn't want to vent all her stress on so unworthy a target. So she leaned towards him, and whispered into his ear, in horrific detail, what would happen to Ryan if he was anything other than exceedingly pleasant to Aleera and her friends. Once he was shaking sufficiently- and his trousers were suspiciously damp- she left him to it and strode over to Michael on one of the benches.

She couldn't quite place his expression when he looked at her. It was something like ashamed gratitude.

'You didn't have to do that,' he finally said. He looked away awkwardly.

'You didn't have to take that,' Aleera replied matter-of-factly as she sat down next to him.

'Just like you don't have to put up with those catcalls,' Michael pointed out, turning back to her. Then he sighed heavily and looked away again. 'Thanks,' he finally said.

Aleera glanced back over to the basketball court. Ryan, his brother and Greg had evidently had the wisdom to depart. 'You know, you had a point the other day,' she said.

'What about?'

'It *is* tempting to put them in their place,' she answered darkly. And it was. It really, *really* was.

'Like I said, though,' Michael shifted awkwardly. 'You don't need to stick your neck out for me like that.'

'Michael, you and Sara are about the only two people in this school that I actually like, and you're the only people outside the Guild that I count as friends,' Aleera stated simply, 'And I don't like to see friends taking abuse from somebody with a room-temperature I.Q.' Michael chuckled slightly at her comment. 'Don't you ever get sick of it?' she asked.

'Just used to it, I guess,' Michael shrugged. He sighed again. 'Prick,' he muttered bitterly at the spot where Ryan had been.

Aleera took a moment to consider his response. It was true; eventually you learned to ignore the whispers behind your back, the insults and the discriminating stares. It was common ground for the two of them; perhaps the reason they got on as well as they did. It was painful. Humiliating. Enraging. Especially to know that, for the same reason as Michael, she had to remain quiet and take it her entire life, even though they were something so much higher and the rest of them were just a pack of rats. Except that packs of rats were better at cooperating. 'I suppose,' she finally said. A long, slow moment of silence followed in which neither of them spoke. Michael glanced over at her a few times as he steeled himself up.

'So how're you doing?' he finally asked. 'I mean about the-' he caught his tongue. 'The thing.'

Aleera thought back. 'More-or-less the same as yesterday,' she said levelly. Michael turned, and a flicker of suspicion filled his eyes. She took a deep breath, and suddenly it was so easy to simply say 'he knows I'm a demon'.

She caught herself. She'd just said that out loud. She hadn't even informed Jake of that yet. Since when could she blurt out things like that so easily? 'There was a message on my answer machine last night. I think that's why he's doing this.'

Michael's eyes widened. Aleera's lidded slightly. All of a sudden, she felt ashamed to have kept that to herself. God, where was this coming from?

'Shit,' he finally said. 'You told Jake about this?'

'I'll have to.'

'So you haven't?'

Aleera bit her bottom lip. 'No.' it had suddenly become extremely hard to lie.

'Have they done anything yet?' Michael asked.

'We've got something to go on,' Aleera replied.

'And when they catch this guy?'

'I hope to get five minutes alone with him. Just me, him...' Aleera turned her right hand over and extended the fingernail of her middle finger. It darkened and sharpened into a claw, '...and these.'

'More than they'll probably do,' Michael muttered.

'Jake's not like that,' Aleera answered defensively.

'Face it, Aleera; they hate us,' Michael said indignantly. 'It's a wonder they're even trying to catch this bastard.'

'Well at least *you* get to be half-draconic,' Aleera reminded him sharply. She chided herself, even if what Michael said hadn't been helpful.

Michael was silent for a moment. 'Yeah. Sorry.' He shook his head. 'It's just- you shouldn't have to deal with this. Nobody should.'

'I'm fine,' Aleera said in her best reassuring voice. 'Really.' She leaned back on the bench and looked up at the thick layer of cloud in the sky. That storm was still waiting, and she was getting impatient.

'Feel like talking about it?' Michael asked.

'I'm fine.' Aleera said it as softly as she could, but there was plenty of "end-of-conversation" in there.

'Look,' Michael said with baited breath, seemingly a little too conscious of how to articulate himself. 'I'm not as good at this talking shit as Sara. I know that, and this is probably gonna come out completely wrong, but… you don't have to do this on your own. I'm here for you, and so is Sara. Ok?'

Aleera sighed. It was true. They both were, whether she liked it or not. And at the end of the day, it was better to have someone on your side than not, and if anyone was going to be there for her, whether she liked it or not, it would be those two. And, she found herself thinking, she did like it. She didn't care what the whole world thought or said or felt, except for them.

She smiled. 'Thanks, Michael.'

Aleera was not proud of her heritage, and quite understandably so given her paternal lineage. Of course, the other side of her family had never been that much better. But it really could be a lot worse, as the usual clamour at the end of the school day attested. A gaggle of bimbos was saying something typically childish and shallow as she walked past. There were the usual catcalls from the group on one side of the school gate. One of them- a member of the football team, name of John McCarthy, if she recalled- was brave (or foolish) enough to walk up behind her, squeeze her backside, then put his arm around her just far to settle on her breast and say 'hey, babe' with all the arrogance in the world.

Aleera looked to the hand, then back to him, and said, coldly and clearly, 'remove it.' He did so immediately, and Aleera walked on as if nothing had happened.

Part of her nevertheless felt that little bit of a thrill at the idea of what had just transpired. She was a succubus, and therefore as much of a sexual being as a "psychologically damaged" demon. There was some excitement to be gained from the group staring at her like a group of monkeys. It was surprising to some that she didn't do more to enjoy it; perhaps that was the damage.

To the side of her, a circle of unwashed students were sticking something in their faces and lighting it to forget their troubles. Slow suicide as a pastime. What quaint ways these creatures called humans had.

Yes, it really could be worse.

'Hey,' Sara greeted her from one side. Aleera turned to see her approaching with a timid smile. 'Haven't seen you all day; Michael told me about what you said at lunch.'

Aleera forced herself to look at her. Suddenly, she somehow had to. Something was different in Sara's shining eyes.

'You don't need to worry,' she finally said. She looked for something, anything, to focus on. Suddenly there was very little to say, so she anxiously looked past Sara and waited for her to say something.

'It's a little late for that,' Sara said at last. She startled to fiddle with that silver cross again. Aleera focused on it. Time to talk, now, she reminded herself.

'I'm fine,' came the poor attempt at a reply. Sara didn't fall for it, not for a second.

'You look pale,' Sara finally said. A strange observation for her. Aleera couldn't quite fathom the meaning behind it.

'I'm just tired,' she finally said. 'I had a long night. They found another body.' The last sentence slipped out, again much too easily.

'Have you eaten anything?'

'Today?' Aleera tried to avoid answering. Honestly, Sara worried so much. What was a meal or two in the face of something like what had happened in the last two days? Then again, what was Ryan in the face of that? Although, really, she had an excuse. Sara was supposed to be a perfectly balanced young woman.

'I didn't think so,' Sara said folding her arms. 'Come on, let's grab a burger.'

'I'm fine,' Aleera repeated pathetically. Even if Sara had been convinced by that, it was undone when Aleera's stomach growled.

'Thought so. Come on, I'm buying.'

Aleera shook her head in defeat and allowed herself a smile.

Jake shifted frantically through the pile of knickknacks on his coffee table, brushing artefacts, scrolls and books aside before pausing to scratch his head, clicking his tongue in thought. It had definitely been here; he definitely left it on the coffee table. Definitely. Certainly. Absolutely.

Or maybe it was in the kitchen. Or upstairs, or in the study, or... yep, he'd lost it. Crap.

'Katya?' he shouted upstairs. "Did you see where I left my-'

He turned round to see Katya poking her head out from the staircase. 'Looking for this?' she asked teasingly, holding the cell phone between her thumb and index finger.

'Yes,' Jake answered elatedly as he made to take it. 'Don't know what I'd do without you, kitkat-' Unexpectedly, Katya held the object higher above her head.

'Jump for it,' she giggled, standing on tiptoe on the bottom step as Jake reached for the phone.

'Katya!'

'C'mon!'

'It's important!' Jake finally put an end to it by opening his hand, and the phone immediately flew out of Katya's grasp and into his.

'Spoilsport,' Katya pouted playfully as she followed Jake into the living room and dropped onto the sofa. 'I checked anyway; Makian hasn't called.' She moved over slightly as Jake sat down, and rested her head on his shoulder. 'You should get some rest; we've got another busy night.'

'*I* have,' Jake corrected her.

'Oh, c'mon. You know I'm good at hiding these,' Katya pouted as she demonstratively whispered '*ThraiPhouxSola*', and a second later her cat-like ears faded from view along with the honey-colour of her eyes, her sharp fingernails and the pronounced canines. 'You can set me up with enough magic, and I don't even need it. I'm not gonna be that much of an unusual sight at Pentagram.'

'You seriously want to go to the worst demon-crime spot in town?'

'I can handle myself. What've you been helping me practice for?' Katya put on a puppy-dog-eyes impression that Jake had often commented on as extremely ironic. 'Pleeeease?'

Jake sighed. 'You get out at the first sign of trouble.'

'Deal,' Katya beamed, deactivating the illusion spell and pressing her lips to Jake's cheek. 'Oh,' she remembered, fidgeting uncomfortably before removing something from beneath her, 'I thought you said you were gonna clean this place up.'

'And?'

'It's a total sty,' Katya said sternly. 'I cook, you clean.'

'Trade?' Jake shrugged.

'Oh, please. We both know you can't make ice.'

'Well for your information,' Jake folded his arms defiantly, 'I did clean the place up.'

Katya looked at the pile of clutter on the coffee table. 'Then why...?'

'I had to find something when I was done,' Jake answered sheepishly.

Both of them turned round as a series of sharp, angry knocks sounded from the door. Jake cursed under his breath and stood up to answer it, while Katya watched and chanted 'Jake's gonna get in trouble' in a sing-song voice. Jake pulled the door open, and on the other side stood a familiar tall, black-haired figure in a familiar three-piece suit, glaring at Jake with angry blue eyes.

'Khazahn,' Jake said with false cheer. 'You should've said you were coming,' he stepped aside to allow him in, and muttered 'I'd have been busy' as Khazahn stepped past him.

'Connolly,' Khazahn scowled. Jake immediately paid attention. Nobody ever called him by his last name unless it was a formal occasion or they were extremely angry. 'You had better have a *phenomenal* explanation for this.'

'Nice to see you too.'

'Quiet,' Khazahn barked.

'Ok,' Jake sighed, feigning ignorance; it was worth a try. 'What'd I do?' Khazahn continued to glare at him. So much for that. 'Fine, so I asked around a little. No biggie.'

'You've been looking into the Guild records,' Khazahn seethed.

Jake contemplated saying "No I haven't" or "Makian was", but he knew immediately that he wouldn't. It was hard being the good guy. 'Ok, fair enough, but can you blame me?' He made the most innocent expression possible.

'I intend to.'

'Well you're the one that never turned up,' Jake answered strongly. 'You tell me you know something and then drop off the damn map.'

'Take the hint,' Khazahn said through gritted teeth.

'You think that just because you're keeping quiet, I'm gonna walk away from a murder? One that involves a friend?' Jake demanded. Khazahn looked away. No, he didn't. He knew Jake too well to think that.

'If the Division Head catches you-'

'Let him try.'

'Jake,' Khazahn snapped, 'What you are doing is illegal in about five different ways. Now drop it, or I will take you off this case right this second.'

'And that won't stop me from working on it, and we both know it. Besides, so far your unit hasn't done a goddamn thing.'

'So you have a suggestion?' The volume of Khazahn's voice rose considerably. 'We've got no idea where to even *start* looking for this guy.'

'Pentagram. I told that to Harry in forensics to pass onto you.'

'And we'll look there as soon as the warrant's ready.'

'Twenty-four hours to get one warrant?'

'Jake, you may be a freelancer, but during the course of an investigation, you are under *my* command,' Khazahn shouted, 'and I am ordering you to stop what you are doing right. This. Minute.'

Jake glared back at him, saying nothing.

Leaning over the sofa to observe the argument, Katya muttered 'God, I can smell the testosterone from here.'

Jake took a warning step forward. 'What are you hiding, Khazahn?'

Khazahn didn't answer. He turned away from Jake and walked back to the door.

'Leave this alone, Jake,' he said gravely. 'Just think ahead for once and leave it.' He slammed the door shut behind him.

Jake stared at the door for a few seconds, slowly removing the old coin from his pocket.

'So,' Katya finally spoke up from the sofa, 'It's that bad?'

'Looks like it,' Jake nodded. His expression turned into a wicked grin. 'Well, it's no fun otherwise.'

At weekends, Aleera tended to meet Michael and/or Sara in a small diner she'd stumbled upon shortly after moving to Manhattan. It was close to each of their homes and, unlike the rest of her everyday surroundings, didn't seem to be crammed full of walking advertisements for forced sterilisation.

In retrospect, she'd been hungrier than she'd thought. She'd devoured a burger and fries in next to no time, along with a milkshake, and as she sat there she could almost feel her level of blood sugar rise back up. That was probably what had been wrong with her all day. Nothing emotional, certainly. That just wouldn't be sensible.

'Ok,' she said, throwing up her hands in mock surrender, 'I admit it.' Good lord, a sense of humour now! What next?

'So what's on your mind?' Sara asked with a smile that somehow wavered. Her shining blue eyes seemed to avoid looking at Aleera, and her hand had returned to the dangling silver cross.

'Nothing,' Aleera answered. Nothing much to focus on behind the clock. Three-fifty-five. And seventeen seconds. 'Honestly, nothing.' Eighteen seconds, nineteen.

'Aleera,' Sara said softly. This time she fixed her shining eyes on Aleera's dark ones. 'Please?'

Aleera sighed. 'I've been thinking,' she finally said, 'about... well, it's because of what's been happening lately. I was thinking about my-' It was hard to say. Everything else was so easy that she couldn't believe it was just pouring out like this. Where in the world was Aleera? But this part was still somehow difficult. 'My dad. He was a demon.' Naturally, Michael and Sara didn't know who her father was. It wasn't the sort of thing she broadcasted.

'I see,' Sara said in a near-whisper. 'Michael told me that you think the person doing this is doing it because of- because of that.'

Aleera nodded slowly. 'I'm just... I'm not sure,' she admitted with this disturbing newfound ease. 'I just need to stick this out on my own, really.' She did. She knew it. But why was she saying it so easily?

'You *don't*,' Sara insisted. 'You've got me. You've got Michael, you've got Jake, you've got Katya...'

'I know,' Aleera answered, 'but... humans can just go to the police about something like things. Draconics can go to the Guild. Me, I've just got you four and my sister. Let's face it, the Guild... they just don't want to know.' Wow. Where was this coming from? She hadn't even been thinking any of this, but here it was, pouring out of her, and every word a true one. When had she gotten so... *emotional*?

Sara sighed gently. Her hand moved across the table to Aleera's without either of them noticing. 'Some of us do,' she finally said. She smiled. Aleera smiled back. What else could she do? And besides, somehow... somehow the smile, and the shining eyes, made her feel like smiling.

'Thank you,' she said quietly.

Sara's gaze dropped. The shine in her eyes flickered, and her hand returned to the cross. Aleera followed their movements for a second.

'Can I ask you something?'

'Shoot,' Sara looked back up at her.

'Why do you hold that all the time?' Aleera continued to follow Sara's fingertips over the silver shape.

Sara looked down at it herself, as if having only just become aware of doing it. 'Habit, I guess,' she finally answered. My parents are pretty religious; we spend every Sunday morning in church, so... well, it just helps, you know?'

'...Not really,' Aleera confessed. She really didn't. She had a great many assets- claws, wings, eyes that changed colour, a sharp mind and quite the figure- but she had never listed faith as one of them. She found the idea of herself in a church to be quite ironic, considering.

'I suppose it's guidance, really,' Sara said distantly. 'If I'm nervous or confused or anything; it helps.'

It dawned on Aleera how much Sara fiddled with that cross. With it came something else that had somehow never occurred to her, and she felt a stab of guilt. She suddenly felt very selfish.

'I see,' she finally said. 'I guess it must be a little strange, considering... well, I'm a demon, and there's probably a commandment or something against that.' She felt slightly amused at the absurdity of her own statement.

Sara smiled, but it was a half-hearted one. 'It's not that.' Aleera almost asked what, but caught herself. Perhaps it wasn't entirely appropriate.

There was something hanging in the air that Aleera had picked up on at some point in the conversation. A hesitation, a quivering in her chest, a distance between the two of them. The moment, it dawned on her, was very much an awkward one.

'I should probably get home,' she said in an effort to end the heaviness in the air. 'Jake might have found something out.'

'Yeah,' Sara said with baited breath. 'I'll see you tomorrow.'

'Why don't you come over on Friday?' Aleera asked as they walked out of the diner. 'I was thinking of cooking something and... I could use some company.' Had she really just said that? *Her?*

Another oddly-weak smile. 'Sure,' Sara answered breathlessly.

'It's a date,' Aleera smiled. Sara smiled again, but somewhere behind it she blushed. Her eyes lidded uneasily. Aleera wasn't sure whether to ask her why, and when she turned and walked away down the street it was too late.

What in the name of all things sacred was wrong with her today? Had she broken a mirror and not noticed it? It was almost as if... as if...

Oh, no.

It suddenly hit home what that shining was in Sara's eyes, that uneasiness in her smile, that constant uncertain fiddling with the cross, what it all meant. Why Sara would sometimes become so quiet and so timid, why she always worried about her, even before all this... oh, no, no, no, *please* no...

Oh, God, and Michael as well, that same hint of awkwardness, that same heaviness in the air, it had been there as well. Please, please, no, she didn't want to do this to them...

'Another sin for your collection?' the cold voice came from the bus stop behind her. That same shallow grave of a voice.

Him.

Aleera grinned. Oh, at last.

She turned round. The man was probably about six-foot-five, and his toned physique made him look taller. Dark eyes turned down to her with a burning intensity.

'I was wondering when you'd get tired of leaving messages,' she finally said. Her heart pounded with excitement. Try something, she begged silently. Please, just give me my excuse.

'Consider this...' the man looked thoughtful for a moment. 'A warm-up.'

'A warm-up?' Aleera repeated. When she was sure it was safe to, she glanced down the street. Sara was safely out of sight, but of course there was no way to know how long he'd been there.

'I just thought it was time to introduce myself.' He stepped forward. 'Since I know you so well, it seems you should at least know my name.'

'And that would be?'

The man fixed her gaze with his. Aleera's eyes never faltered. She could see something, just a little something, deep in him that was surprised. No fear. Men like this would expect fear. Check.

He leaned forward and whispered: 'Azrael'.

The name was familiar. Aleera had heard of it before. Azrael; the angel of death.

'I like it,' she said levelly, 'memorable, nice and simple; good choice.'

"Azrael" stepped back. If he had taken notice of her lack of fear, it wasn't affecting him. Not as Aleera had thought. Check. Counter-move.

Aleera looked him up and down. She had longer this time. Enough time to confirm.

Well, well, well.

Azrael nodded slowly. 'Yes, your kind can tell, can't they? They're like rats; they can always smell their own.'

'So this *is* about that,' Aleera observed.

'You're an intelligent one, *demon*.' He spat the word out like poison on his tongue. 'It doesn't matter now, anyway. Justice is here.'

Azrael stepped past her, and in a rush of air, she turned to see nothing but an empty space.

The name rolled over in her mind, leaving her thinking of all its whispered implications and promises. And what else she had felt... or, as it were, not felt.

No magic. He was human.

Her lips curved into a dangerous little grin. This had certainly been a memorable afternoon. "Know thine enemy", it was said, and now, finally and at long last, she did.

Check.

9

The intervening time between the meeting at the diner and the scheduled visit to Pentagram had given Aleera time to think about a few things. First and foremost was this "Azrael", though she doubted this to be his given name. The first thing she did upon returning home was research the name; she didn't have any literature relating to the occult- her childhood, she had long-since decided, had given her more than enough exposure- or on religion, where if she remembered correctly the name was more likely to be found. She didn't own a bible; it wasn't that she didn't believe in God, but she didn't think it was appropriate. Jake, she knew, had a wealth of books on the like, but it was doubtful that he'd be home. Yes, that was a good reason for not contacting him about something this important, she thought with more than a hint of sarcasm. Not that she was trying to keep this to herself for the same reasons she'd been doing all along, mental problems seeming to be at the forefront.

With nothing else readily available on the subject, she turned to something she very rarely used: the laptop computer that she kept in the bedroom and hadn't used for several months. Technology had never really been a favourite of hers, mainly because it was a human invention and consequently when she was young her father would meet out severe physical punishments for its use. She flinched a little at the memory.

Here she was, then; a being of magic searching the internet. More irony. Not laughing at the idea definitely earned her the pot of honey that sat by the table.

As the sites, articles and blogs Aleera came across purported, "Azrael" got around. The name was of an archangel; an English version of the name Azra'il in Islam and Judaism. It was the same there as in Christianity. Spellings included "Izrail", "Ezraeil" and "Ozryel". Most interestingly, the name, as it turned out, translated to *"Whom God Helps."*

She thought back to what he had said in the street. He'd spat the word "demon" like the foulest five letters imaginable. Followed by saying "Justice is here". Justice, perhaps as in divine justice. As meted out by the Angel of Death. The name was a more appropriate one than she'd thought. It betrayed quite a lot. Bringing together the evidence with which she was confronted, the conclusion was obvious: this wasn't an everyday psychotic vendetta. She was dealing with a fanatic... which explained a lot, actually. Something with a hate that transcended the stifled rage of an everyday resentment and became all-consuming. Hatred, she realised, for demons. Well, that was hardly unheard of.

Needless to say, this was considerably offensive. That you were a wretched sinner for the way you were born was hardly the nicest thing to hear, and she had a few choice words of her own to say on the subject. Humans had far from the best of reputations amongst draconic society; they were killing the planet by degrees, choking the world to death, they nuked anything new or unexplained into oblivion, and they used whatever trivial reason was at hand to tear down anyone they could, even without a need for it. Most of the time, they couldn't even stop killing each other over which of their religions was the best one or what the right skin colour was- when you were of a different species, they were both considered to be moot points. It did beg the question, though: if being a demon made her evil, then what did being human make them?

Anyway, back to the matter at hand. Right from the first body, something hadn't sat right. Now, however, it was all falling into place. This explained the choice of victims, leaving the second body at Pentagram, and even the choice of, ahem, weapon. A symbolic gesture for the daughter of the worst demon there had ever been. This was a mind that was far from stable; Aleera had the experience of living with one to know one when she saw it. If he had done his homework like a good little fanatic well enough to know where she lived, went to school and what her unlisted phone number was, the first thing he would find out would be whose offspring she was.

She felt quite clever. Look at her, sitting there psychoanalysing and working things out like a proper little detective. It would seem that, after a day of being significantly off her best performance, she was back in intellectual shape.

Her mood brightened by that thought, she set to work on the second problem; the one she really didn't want to think about. But something was going to have to be done. Now, if only she had some idea *what*. Michael and Sara weren't supposed to be a problem, they were her friends. The only ones outside of the Guild she had, and therefore not ones she wished to lose.

There were times when it was very easy to damn herself and what she was, and they tended to be like this. She didn't get into many relationships, because not many feelings toward her weren't caused by succubus pheromones.

Sara, she knew, was straight. Hence, this was the doing of the pheromones, and if anything, this was what she felt the most guilty about. She couldn't imagine how confused the poor girl must have been feeling in the heavy moment of awkwardness in the diner. Aleera, of course, appreciated a pretty girl as much as any succubus, but this was not what she wanted to do to Sara. It was bad enough for her that half their school already thought they were a couple.

And Michael; he was a friend, not a boyfriend. A nice one, though, she found herself thinking. He was loyal, passionate if a little short-tempered...

Stop that.

What? She was just thinking, hypothetically, perhaps that could work. They'd known each other for a long time, and if there was something there...

No. What was she thinking? What was wrong with her lately? The only difference between those pheromones and a vial of rohypnol was that the pheromones didn't come in liquid form. It would be taking advantage of someone, plain and simple, and that was not going to happen.

She should call them, she thought. Talk this through. No, not over the phone. She would sort this out, but it was something that needed to be done face-to-face.

The phone...

Wait a minute, that pit in her stomach spoke up. If her phone number was unlisted, then where did he get it from? It could have been from her school, true; if he was careful enough to barbeque two young women and leave no trace, he could probably break in there. But for that, he need to know where she went to school in the first place, and that information was only held by the Guild.

She sat back and thought. Yes, it was definitely time to tell Jake.

The alley that led into Pentagram wasn't silent this time. The vibrations of the pounding rhythm from inside the club could be felt underfoot as Aleera, Jake, Katya and Makian made their way towards the heavy steel door. It still reeked, though. Makian had been waiting at the end of the alley to talk to Jake. From what Aleera could gather, they had both been on the receiving end of some strongly-worded warnings by Khazahn.

Aleera still hadn't discussed with Jake the events since their rooftop meeting. She would, definitely, but for now this needed to be the area of focus. She was not best pleased to be about to visit Pentagram, but she was a big girl; she'd cope. She'd changed to her halter top before coming, just in case the wings should be needed. They could give a lot of thrust, and the intimidation factor would probably help.

'So, Aleera,' Makian asked as his gaze travelled up and down her figure, stopping in a few choice places. 'Ever done much dancing?'

'Not much,' Aleera replied curtly. Crowds of junkies, overpowering noise and sweaty "legitimate businessmen" negotiating affection with young ladies did not add up to her idea of enjoyment. She preferred to be able to hear her own thoughts and spend her time in more intelligent company.

'Shame,' Makian shrugged. He stole another discreet glance and moved to the side of Jake, who was stood in front of the door fiddling with his old coin. 'You waiting for an invitation?' he asked sarcastically.

Wait, Aleera realised. Something hit her.

Jake held the coin up between his fingers. 'Listen.'

Aleera took note. There was the pounding rhythm from below, the occasional movement of a scurrying rat... and nothing else.

Nothing.

'I don't hear it,' Makian declared, having quite missed the point.

'Exactly,' Aleera told him. 'Jake's got something. This is Pentagram.'

'Yeah?'

'The worst, loudest supernatural club in New York.'

Makian nodded dumbly.

Aleera sighed and decided to just be blunt. 'Do you hear anything from inside apart from the music? Any shouting? Any arguments? Any sign of anyone whatsoever being inside that club? There isn't even a doorman out here.' She should perhaps have noticed that sooner, although in defence there was a lot clouding her mind lately.

Makian made to reply, then paused and took a deep breath as he realised. Bravo.

'You think?' Katya asked, but she didn't name her suspicions. Jake nodded slowly. He stepped forward and took hold of the door. It wasn't locked. The alley suddenly seemed deathly quiet. All present noted how dark it suddenly seemed to be. The sound of clanging metal echoed as Jake pulled the door open. The hinges creaked.

First, there was the stench. That was bad. Then there was the sight. That was worse.

Jake froze and looked down at the body in what didn't look like disgust. More indignation and pity for whomever it had been. Katya gagged. Makian froze in a moment of shock and said what sounded like 'oh, sweet mother of shit.' Aleera stepped forward and tried not to look at what was left of its expression.

Body Number Three was lying against the wall in a cloud of the pungent stench of seared flesh and hair. The expression was the same as the last one. A patch of dried blood on the wall trickled down to merge with the dry red stain on the floor.

'Makian,' Jake finally said, 'call Khazahn.'

Aleera held her palm forward. There was a definite difference in temperature close to the body. 'It's still warm.' She silently noted the macabre nature of her statement. But that meant that "Azrael" was still close. Maybe even still...

She took of like a rocket. Her wings erupted and folded behind her back, streamlining her by instinct. If he was still here, just maybe, please... the claws extended. Her eyes turned red. She turned the corner as Jake shouted after her.

Blood-red lights flooded the sunken, tiled pit of the dance floor and the small booths on either side of the club, casting everything in long shadows of black and red. Chairs were knocked over. Suspicious-looking drinks were spilled over the tables and floor. Glasses and bottles were smashed on and around the bar, and there was a general sense that there had been a great deal of movement towards the back exit. But what had moved was gone now. There was nothing but the empty nightclub and the dull thudding that evidently nobody had bothered to switch off in their hurry.

Movement. A sudden, rustling movement on the other side of the floor. A white movement, stained red by the lights. A tall figure, wrapped in a white robe that covered his head, flowing around it as the ethereal shape turned to face her. A hand wrapped in a white glove gripped the handle of a dagger whose blade became a slit of red as it caught the light.

Aleera didn't even need to see the face. Azrael turned slowly. The robe draped around him as the dagger turned in his hand.

'Ceremonial,' she observed. As soon as the word was out there, its echo brought the realisation to her. Ceremonial; a ceremony to be followed. A ceremony set down by someone. Just a hunch, a nagging possibility, but one that would bear thought.

Azrael placed the blade back within a sheath on his belt and straightened up. 'Perceptive of you,' he said in his cut-glass voice from beneath his hood. 'I was wondering when you'd be here.'

Aleera froze as her brain clicked over again. Now that, *that* had implications upon implications. Later, she reminded herself; she could worry about that later. Her heartbeat quickened. She smiled. Her claws twitched.

Finally, that chance to cut loose. Finally, here they were.

There was a sudden commotion moving into the room behind her. 'Aleera!' Jake shouted breathlessly. Makian and Katya stopped abruptly aside him. Jake stepped forward and surveyed Azrael with intrigued caution. 'Well, then,' he finally said. 'Who might you be?'

Azrael let out a low chuckle. 'You've not told him.'

Jake turned sharply to Aleera. 'Aleera,' his speech came out stifled.

'Is this the time?' Aleera said quickly and defensively. 'Right now, we deal with him.'

'Is someone gonna tell me who the frickin' hell this guy is?' Makian spoke up.

'Azrael,' Aleera replied, not taking her blood-red eyes off the spectral figure before her. 'He's called Azrael. He's your killer.' There, that should do for the moment.

Azrael stepped back. 'Not tonight, *demon*,' he spat the word out again. 'Not tonight.'

'Oh, I think tonight,' Aleera hissed. The wings unfolded and, in one massive motion, launched her across the floor. She struck Azrael, tackling him to the ground as the claws of her right hand slashed through the flailing cloak. Everything tumbled over everything else as they both vanished into the dark at the edge of the floor.

Aleera, in her childhood, had been forced to study various forms of self-defence, and had ended up considerably adept at Tae Kwon Do. Even in the most recent three years, she had maintained the practice, and she was long-since at the level of a black belt. Add wings, claws, magic and a red-hot temper, and the result was potentially an extremely dangerous young lady.

Azrael lashed out with his left fist. Aleera caught it, twisted the forearm and brought her own knee swiftly into his chest. He grunted in pain, and she was fairly sure she heard a rib snap. She grinned in satisfaction. Oh, *finally*. She stood, pulling him with her as the fabric of the robe tore against her claws. She spun round, and Azrael's head struck the corner of the nearest booth.

'Aleera!' Jake shouted over the drumming bass rhythm. 'Aleera, that's enough!'

The words didn't register. The blood pounding in Aleera's ears was too loud. The need to finally indulge that wicked darkness inside her was great enough that she wouldn't release her grip for the world. Too much anger. Too much excitement. Too much *glee*.

Azrael's foot caught her midsection, knocking the wind out of her and replacing it was a solid ache in her stomach. She staggered. Azrael rolled past her.

Oh, no you don't. Aleera turned, clutching her stomach and holding one palm open. The other form of defence she could use well was, of course, that which was innate to any demon. Basic offensive and defensive spells were standard.

But the impact that struck Azrael was not from her. The shockwave that slammed into him like a crashing car, shaking the air with its passing and hurling him through the air, came from the other side of the floor and sent Azrael falling into the bar with a painful grunt and the sound of breaking glass, before he half-rolled, half-fell to the other side.

Still buzzing, Jake's hand returned to his side as he glared coldly at the bar. Nothing moved.

Aleera stood slowly, with deep breaths, and caught Jake's angry glare. She felt a brief flash of shame. She'd wanted to cut loose, be herself, but not in front of Jake. She hadn't wanted him to see her in her darker side, however much she enjoyed it... truth be told, she felt like a teenager caught with porn by her father.

What, was that how she thought of Jake now? Somehow paternal? Get a grip, woman.

And *focus* on what's happening here, for God's sake! What was the matter with her?

Makian pulled something out of his jacket pocket. The small, bronze tube extended, sharper points emerging and finally a triangle of blades extending from each end. The end of the Guild Standard-Issue Staff gave a low buzz of energy. He approached the bar, hands taught around the staff. Jake stepped forward alongside him, sparks of magic dancing across his fingers. Aleera watched from across the floor with baited breath.

Makian thrust his staff in a downwards motion behind the bar as it buzzed with power.

Then his face turned into one of shock.

'Nothing!'

Aleera and Katya both approached the bar. It was true. There was nothing behind it but broken glass reflecting scattered red light.

The Guild had arrived within the hour. From what Aleera had heard, the club was indeed vacant; presumably, the patrons had seen through their drug-induced hazes enough to notice the corpse. Fear plus a room full of junkies: panic. There was, of course, no sign of Azrael.

Aleera was seated on a bench out on the sidewalk, partly to think and partly to clear her head. It had been embarrassing, losing her self-control like that. Frustrating, too, and that wasn't good, though more so because he got away. She'd read once that those with sociopathy had a less-than-exemplary tolerance for frustration, which certainly explained how irritated she was that he'd gotten away.

'*Xiaol*,' she whispered absently, tracing her fingers across the pain in her side where she'd been struck. It felt like a broken rib. Tiny, blue sparks danced over the spit, and she winced at the momentary sting before the pain subsided altogether. A healing spell was, for obvious reasons, always a good one to know- it focused the body's energy on healing, enormously speeding up the process, although it had, of course, its limitations depending on the size and severity of the injury.

It had been a long day; a long, frustrating day, and more than anything else she felt tired. She was tempted to go home straight away and get a decent night's sleep, but she knew Jake would want to talk to her. She looked up to see him finish speaking to Harry and Tomoko, before he walked sharply over to her. He didn't look happy. Aleera didn't say a word as he sat down next to her and started fiddling with that old coin. She didn't want to have this conversation.

'What the hell was that?' Jake demanded. Aleera looked away down the street. She didn't answer. Her tongue swelled up and there was nothing to be said. 'Right,' Jake breathed harshly. 'You could have killed that guy.'

This time, Aleera replied. 'Would that be such a bad thing?'

Jake looked at her cautiously, like a parent who had caught his child on a dirty website. 'How long?' he asked.

'How long what?'

'Don't give me that.'

'You've read the report they have on me, Jake. You can decide for yourself whether it's true.'

'Aleera, we've talked about this,' Jake said strongly. 'We agreed that you'd tell me whenever you got like this again.'

'And do what?'

Jake was speechless, but only for a moment. 'Do you even know what you were about to do?'

'Cause him an enormous amount of pain, and enjoy it quite a lot.' Aleera replied matter-of-factly. She didn't want to talk about this. Her face was flushed. It was like having to talk about sex.

'Would you have killed him?'

'No,' she said, and it was the truth. She didn't want to kill him; she never wanted to kill someone. The only person she had ever wanted dead was her father, which when you stepped back and looked at it was quite understandable. Christ, she was only "borderline".

'How long have you been wanting to...' Jake bit his tongue. 'Do this?'

'A few days; this hasn't helped.'

Jake sighed and rested his head in his hands. Neither of them wanted to talk about this, why did they suddenly have to?

'You're supposed to be finding an outlet,' he said at last.

'It's just been a bad week. Once this is over, I'll be fine.'

'Yeah, and that's gonna happen when you don't tell me anything,' Jake snapped. Ok, this she could talk about. This she could explain. 'God damnit, Aleera, I'm trying to help you. If you don't tell me what's happening, then I can't. Now-' he sat upright. 'Are you going to tell me?'

Aleera nodded. 'Ok.'

She explained it, starting with how, after talking to Jake on the rooftop, she'd returned home to find the message on her answer machine. Then had come that first meeting in the street, and her first suspicions about what was happening. Finally the meeting outside the diner when she had learned his name and finally managed to piece everything together. The last thing she did was tell Jake how she'd worked it out and, if she was right, exactly what they were dealing with.

Jake sat there agape. He honestly looked dumbfounded for a moment. The moment passed slowly; Aleera somehow felt embarrassed again, as if she'd done something very stupid without realising. It seemed like an age before Jake finally spoke.

'You didn't tell me when you first thought he might be human.'

'No.'

There was that dumbfounded look again. 'What in God's name could possibly make you think that was a good idea?' he nearly shouted.

'I couldn't be sure until I saw him again,' Aleera answered, sounding somewhat stubborn even to herself. 'Imagine if I'd told you, we'd carried on with that idea, and I'd turned out to be wrong.'

Jake sat still for a moment. Aleera could tell that he knew she had a point.

'You're certain that he's human?' he checked.

'A hundred percent.'

Jake turned the old coin over in his hands. 'Do me a favour,' he said, 'never do that again.'

'Deal.' Aleera smiled despite herself.

'There's only one way he could have gotten out of there,' Jake mused.

'Teleporting,' Aleera nodded.

'That's magic. Powerful magic. Complicated magic. And the burning...'

'Dark magic,' Aleera confirmed. 'You're right; nobody human could do that on their own. Humans can't even use magic...' she trailed off, much like Jake himself. Maybe he was rubbing off on her. When the thought struck her, it was like a freight train made of glass: big, loud, clear, and so conspicuous that she felt amazingly stupid for not realising it much earlier. 'Unless he's got something enchanted,' she gave the thought voice.

Jake's own brain shifted into high gear. 'If he has,' he rambled, 'we can check the Guild records. Other than that, there's only one place he could get it.'

'Black market.'

'Could he get something that powerful?' Aleera thought out loud. 'If he's done all this *and* he can teleport-'

'It could be something powerful,' Jake mused. He seemed to trail off on some disturbing line of thought, as though something felt dreadfully familiar to him 'Anyway,' he said, snapping back quickly, 'we know what to look for, and where's the only place in New York with enough black market connections to get something like that?'

They both turned and looked over at the entrance to Pentagram.

'Tomorrow night?' Aleera suggested.

Jake nodded excitedly. 'Tomorrow night.'

Perfect. Find the item, find the seller. Find the seller, find the buyer. Check.

Jake's smile faltered as he looked across at the gathering of Guild soldiers. He let out an exasperated groan of what sounded like 'oh, shit' under his breath.

The approaching Guild Soldier, his silver shoulder patch marking him as a Sergeant, and as D-Unit was assigned to this investigation, Aleera knew exactly which Sergeant it was. Khazahn pulled back his hood, removed his helmet and stopped a few feet in front of Jake.

'Well?' he said coldly.

'Nice to see you too,' Jake returned the greeting.

'I told you to wait for the warrant,' Khazahn stated.

'You're welcome. I was happy to find the body for you.'

Khazahn opened his mouth to reply, but froze immediately as a severe voice addressed him from behind.

'Sergeant.'

Jake and Khazahn both turned to regard the figure that approached with clear, rigid authority in every step. His shoulder patch was clear gold in colour, polished enough to almost look like the real thing. The man who removed the helmet was in his late fifties, with sharp, grey eyes and thinning hair of the same colour. His worn features turned to survey the party before him as if peering over a pair of spectacles. He sharpened the crease of one cuff.

Aleera had only met Commander Chara, the head of the Eighth Division of the Guild, once. She didn't like him. It was nothing specific that she could put her finger on, but he did not have the appearance or mannerisms of someone who was pleasant to be around. He looked too self-satisfied when noticing Khazahn's salute.

'Can someone here please tell me,' Chara said levelly, hands behind his back, 'why I was not informed of this development?' He was somehow looking downwards at Khazahn despite the latter being taller.

'Sir,' Khazahn replied, not looking him in the eye, 'we organised a sweep of the area as soon as possible. I was about to contact you.'

Chara gave him a cold, dismissive glance. 'I expect to be informed immediately of all future developments in this case,' he said without emotion. 'I assume that you are aware of the interest that the High Council has taken in this case?' Jake looked up. Chara glanced at him as if Jake was trespassing in his home.

'Understood, sir,' Khazahn said.

'Very good.' Chara turned to regard Aleera. She had been observing him through the short exchange of sentences masquerading as a conversation. Something in his eyes told her he didn't like it. 'Ms. Maheste. It's been a while since we met. I'll trust you to keep your associate appropriately informed, young Master Connolly,' he said to Jake, suddenly as if she wasn't there. 'As you know, we run a very tight ship.' He gave them a knowing glance. 'That will be all, Sergeant.' He turned and walked away, back toward the gathering in the alley.

Jake waited until he was out of earshot. 'The High Council's sticking their noses in?'

'We've had three bodies turn up in as many days,' Khazahn reminded him, 'and in *that* condition. 'We're lucky the offices haven't turned into a circus already.' He muttered something under his breath as he turned back towards the alley.

'This is bad,' Jake muttered. 'Chances are, if we're going to find what we're looking for in the offices, we'll have to do it fast.'

'There's another problem,' Aleera pointed out, turning her dark eyes toward Commander Chara. 'He's poking his head in, and from what he said about a "tight ship"...' she let Jake figure out the rest. Chara obviously didn't want Jake snooping around below decks.

Which meant Khazahn wasn't the only one who wanted Jake kept out of something. Therefore something, quite certainly, was being hidden.

10

Aleera woke up slightly earlier than normal. The weather was no less overcast, but she still felt much more rested. The first thing she'd done upon returning to the apartment after the Pentagram visit was collapse into bed and try not to think about the things that had been plaguing her for the past three days. She decidedly failed to do so.

It had truthfully never occurred to her how worried Jake had been about her... less stable tendencies. She'd never even told Michael and Sara, but then again, half the school thought she was a psycho, and they weren't that wrong. It didn't seem that far-fetched for them to have noticed something was... off about her, even if it hadn't impeded the effect of her pheromones that led to the *other* thing nagging at the back of her mind.

It dawned on her that, while the preceding two days had been considerably difficult, the past twenty-four hours had somehow led to things becoming a great deal more complicated than they were before, or at least than she'd ever noticed. When had everything become a problem like this?

Fortunately, she was more tired than she had expected, and sleep overcame her within a few minutes. The next thing she knew, she was blinking in the painfully bright light and checking the sickly numbers of the alarm clock. *"06:45"*. It was convenient enough; she had time for a shower and a decent breakfast. A decent night of rest, on reflection, had helped quite a bit.

As she picked up her bag for school, she noticed that the light was blinking on her answer machine.

She froze. Another move, a counter of some kind? Her pulse quickened. There was that pit in her stomach again and her breathing became shallow.

She reached out. She pressed "play".

An unexpectedly heavy sigh escaped her when the voice turned out to be Lilith's. *"Hey, Aleera, it's me again. Look, if something's wrong, just tell me, Ok? And if it's not, just- just let me know, alright? Come on, you're my baby sister. I'm supposed to worry about you. Just let me know, Ok?"*

There was that pit again. She snapped at it to go away. It refused. She never did call Lilith back, and about that she would admit to feeling a guilty. She was worried about her, and she hadn't told her anything.

And however complicated things had become recently, she wasn't going to let it extend to the one living person in her family who actually gave two shits that she was alive. On the way to school, she dialled Lilith's number on her cell phone. It rang for a minute, and Lilith picked up.

'Finally,' she heard her sister say when she picked up. 'What'd I do to get the silent treatment?'

'Hey,' Aleera said. She noticed that she might sound a little distance. 'I just wanted to say "sorry" about the other day.'

'Don't,' Lilith replied seriously. 'Look, Aleera, just tell me one thing: is something wrong.'

This was it. Performance time. Break a leg, Aleera.

'No,' she did her best to sound honest, as if she was looking back on it and laughing. 'I'd just had a rough day. There was this guy at school hassling a friend, and I guess I was still kind of in a mood.' Good. The "I was wrong" approach. Always a winner.

'Is this guy still a problem?'

'No, no. It's all sorted out now. I'm sorry if I worried you, Ok?'

Lilith sighed. 'Ok. Just don't do it again.'

'Deal. Gotta go.'

'Alright. Love you.'

'You too.'

She hung up. There. Problem solved. No more burden on her sister.

So why was that pit still there?

Okay, so maybe lying to her sister about this was in the grey area. But if she told her what was going on, all it would do was worry her, and it wouldn't help the situation one bit. If it wasn't the "right" thing to do, it was certainly the lesser of two evils.

Now, would that damned pit in her stomach *please* go away?

She tried to ignore it and carry on walking. It worked well enough. When she was heading into school, her phone rang again. Jake this time.

'What's up?' She asked.

'Change of plans,' Jake informed her. 'Turns out, we're not going to be able to go anywhere near Pentagram.'

Not good. This could mean any number of things that were all not, decidedly, good. 'Why?'

'Nobody is. The Guild's closed the place off for forensics to carry out a thorough sweep of the entire area. It'll probably take all night.'

'So what do we do now?'

'Well, Makian checked all the available Guild records, and there's nothing that could have supplied this Azrael guy with the magic to do what he's been doing. So he's been looking into any black market places he can. I'll let you know if he turns anything up.'

'Right. Good luck.'

'And you. Watch yourself.'

She hung up again.

Katya drummed her fingers absent-mindedly on the bookshelf as she idly paced around the study, occasionally glancing at Jake, who sat a million miles away in thought as he continued to fiddle with the old coin.

Three of the four walls of the study were covered with bookshelves, leaving only a space for the door, reaching from the floor to the ceiling and being stacked with, in addition to all manner of books, scriptures and tomes, various beakers, bottles, small chests and other various knickknacks commonly associated with the supernatural. The last wall had a desk that stretched from one side of the wooden wall to the other and held a personal computer, a test-tube rack, and more often than not several books and papers strewn over the surface. Sets of drawers were filled with much the same things as the bookshelves. Jake was sat at the desk with an expression that was at once intense and far away.

The study was always where Jake went to think, surrounded by old texts and normally just fiddling with that old coin until he came to a decision. She'd known it of him to shut himself in there for whole days, and as it happened, that morning she'd had to remind him to eat something. He'd had a slice of bacon and returned to the study.

She didn't know why she bothered sometimes.

'Did you even sleep last night?' she asked.

'I told you, I've had plenty of sleep.' The credibility of Jake's statement was somewhat rebuked when he yawned halfway through the sentence.

'I saw you sleep for about a half-hour yesterday afternoon.'

Katya's honey-coloured eyes softened. The cat-ears drooped slightly. 'Just take your mind off this for a while.'

'I told you, I'm fine.' Jake returned to fiddling with the coin.

'The hell you are,' Katya said, now much more forcefully. 'You've hardly slept in the last four days, *and* you still haven't cleaned the place.'

'I told you, I did.'

'There's a newspaper under the sofa from 1977! You didn't even live here in 1977!'

Jake thought on this for a moment. 'Was there anything else?' he asked curiously.

'A whole mess of paper, some hairy pieces of candy, about three dollars- and half a euro- in change, and a James Bond movie.'

'Which one?'

'I don't know, but we can watch it *tomorrow*. Now go to bed!'

'I'm-'

'You're running on empty, Jake. You're not gonna be of any help to anyone like that. Just go to bed for a few hours.'

Jake let out a stifled breath. He turned the coin over again. Katya softened, sitting down in his lap and wrapping her arms round him, resting her head on his shoulder as she so often did. 'You worry about her, don't you?' she asked gently.

'I guess I just feel responsible for her,' Jake admitted. 'Considering.'

'Well, I don't see how this is ever gonna be your fault,' Katya lectured. 'Now go and get some sleep; I don't care if you *are* a ghost-'

'I'm not a ghost.'

'You might as well be. You don't tell me any damn thing.' Katya's tone carried a great deal of indignation and resentment of that truth.

'Do we have to bring this up now?' Jake sighed tiredly.

'Actually, I wasn't trying to,' Katya confessed, 'I was hoping you'd leave the room like you always do and get some damn sleep.'

Jake gave a quiet chuckle. 'You should be a doctor, kitkat,' he sighed as he made to stand up.

'Nah,' Katya smiled as she stood up herself.

'Yeah, you're right,' Jake gave a tired grunt as he stood up. 'Terrible beside manner.' Katya poked her tongue out as he walked out of the library and across the hall to his room.

Before he was halfway across, however, the cell phone half-buried under books and papers started to ring. 'Go to bed,' Katya ordered, 'I'll get it.' She lifted the phone up to her ear. 'Jake's house of disasters,' she said as she answered it.

'Katya,' Makian's voice said with an audible grin of triumph from the other end of the line. 'Tell Jake that I am very, *very* good.'

Aleera tried to barricade herself against a tide of frustration as she tapped the end of her pencil on the side of her head. Fifteen minutes to lunch. She hadn't seen Michael and Sara all day. Not that she was avoiding having to talk to them about something. Heaven forefend.

'Ms. Maheste?'

Ms. Wood crossed her arms and glared at her in a manner that begged for the re-institution of the cane.

'Yes, Ms. Wood?' she tried to keep her voice nice and civil.

'I take it you can answer the question?' the teacher gestured to the trigonometry problem on the chalkboard. 'Or were you too busy staring at the clock?'

Both, actually, but it was clear that this was a woman a lot like her employer; eager to exercise power where she could. Ms. Wood was quite certain whe could make her feel embarrassed for daring to allow her gaze to wander for half a second.

She examined the problem for a second, took a moment to think, and said 'x equals fourteen-point-three-five.' Ms. Wood's face changed to an amusing shade of red.

'And your sarcasm isn't appreciated,' Ms. Wood took whatever excuse was at hand before turning to the class. Aleera tried to avoid smirking and failed.

The classroom door opened. The principal half-walked, half-waddled in. 'Sorry to disturb you, Ms. Wood. There's someone here to talk to Aleera Maheste.'

Aleera looked up quizzically. Was it Jake? No, he'd have dropped her a note by now. Khazahn? The only person who'd ever surprised her with a visit like this was... Lilith. Had she worked out that something was wrong? Maybe she'd just decided to surprise her- while it was a nice thought, the timing left a lot to be desired.

The principal led her down the hallway. 'I take it there'll be no more incidents between you and Ryan Shane?'

'No, sir,' Aleera said briskly. Other than that, the principal didn't say a word. He seemed to be restraining himself, and with quite some effort.

She saw who was outside the principal's office. Well, it wasn't Lilith; the only time she'd been glad not to see her sister. Sadly, it was worse.

'Thank you,' Commander Chara addressed the principal. 'I'll just be a moment with Ms. Maheste.'

The principal nodded and returned to his office. That explained the apparent temper: "police officer" was the classic Guild cover story.

'Can I help you?' Aleera asked dryly.

Chara motioned to the door. 'Walk with me.'

She followed silently. She didn't trust Chara. She didn't trust anybody, but if she had to pick someone to trust Chara would not be it. Whenever he looked at her, he seemed to be looking down, not at any body part as a lot of people did, but generally down at something stuck to his shoe.

'Are you going to tell me what this is about?' she asked as they entered the school parking lot.

Chara glared at her briefly. It seemed he didn't like being spoken to in sentences that didn't end in "sir". He wasn't married- no wedding ring- but if he were, he would probably prefer it if his wife and children were to call him "sir". This was a man to whom informality was tantamount to a personal insult.

'Very well. As you may be aware, the ongoing investigation has been somewhat slow in pace.'

'I've noticed,' Aleera replied in an "infer what you will from this tone" tone.

'During such circumstances,' Chara went on as if reading from a script, 'It is necessary to ensure that all those associated with the investigation are trustworthy.'

That pit in her stomach started to open again. *Jake*, was her first thought. He knew someone was looking through the Archives, and he knew it couldn't be her; she couldn't get in if she tried. He wanted information on Jake. He wanted her to inform on him.

There went the eyes.

'Since you're a part of this investigation,' he continued in a robotic tone, 'your input is as valid as any.' Wow, even from him, she could be sure that was a lie. 'So I would simply like to ask: has any irregular activity reached your notice?'

'None at all.' Well, he lied about not knowing what was going on, and she wasn't exactly about to betray one of the five trustworthy people she knew.

'You're sure?' the question sounded like a bear trap closing.

'Completely. I haven't even been inside the Guild so far.' Well, it wasn't technically a lie.

'Ms. Maheste,' Chara said like a spitting cat, 'any information you withhold could potentially compromise a high-priority Guild investigation.'

'I'm not withholding anything.'

Chara took a deep breath. The pigmentation of his skin seemed to change, and he put an unruly hair back in its proper place. He composed himself immediately and deliberately.

'Ms. Maheste-'

'I've answered the question,' Aleera answered simply. 'Now can I go back to my class, *sir*?'

Chara set his jaw grimly. Oh, how dare she misuse that sacred word?

'Very well.'

Aleera turned away from him and walked back to the school, around to the door that would lead most immediately to the classroom; when she was almost there, however, the bell chimed to signal the start of lunch.

Her stomach flipped. Well, time to get on with it. She wasn't worried. Certainly not.

It shouldn't be too hard. All she needed to do was find Michael, talk to him, explain *that* side of her nature, be gentle about it, and above all, make everything clear… which would be uncomfortable. And then do the same again with Sara, which would be even more uncomfortable. Easy.

But first, it appeared that another familiar face wanted to exchange a few words with her next to the wall of the gym.

Ryan was marching towards her with the look of death in his eyes. His brother was grinning madly on one side of him. Greg was looking around nervously on the other.

'You think you're pretty funny, don't you, bitch?' Ryan snarled. The snarl turned to a smirk as he plunged his hand into his bag.

'Well, I'd find *you* rather amusing, but I've never liked clowns,' Aleera replied levelly. She couldn't help herself; it was much like the temptation to poke an angry animal with a stick, just because it was amusing to watch it bark. Except, of course, that she wouldn't do such a thing. She had much more fondness for animals.

'Yeah?' Ryan spat as he dropped the bag to reveal the object in her hand. Aleera indifferently eyed the chunk of marble clutched in his fingers.

Oh, that brainless little ape.

'Laugh at this, you little skank!' Ryan spat. He made to lift the chunk, before- unexpectedly to all parties- Greg grabbed his arm.

'C'mon, man,' he insisted, 'this ain't cool.'

'Leggo my arm,' Ryan spat, sharply pulling his arm free of Greg's grip. Greg stepped back, looking very much ashamed.

'Now,' Ryan sneered, lifting the chunk of marble above his head. 'This is what you get-'

Through her life, Aleera had read a few fantasy novels and seen a number of television programmes with scenarios rather like this one. The hero or heroine would say "you don't want to do this" or "I don't want to fight you". That was where any resemblance between them and Aleera ended; because she *did* want to beat some sense into this barely-sentient sack of stupidity.

Ryan brought the chunk of marble swinging down towards her head. Aleera swung to the side on one leg, and Ryan, largely missing his mark, fell forward from the unexpected lack of anything to absorb the momentum. Aleera grabbed the back of his clothing, pulled him back and slammed him face-first into the gym wall, followed by a sharp punch to the kidneys that, judging by Ryan's reaction, was also rather painful.

Letting him cradle his side for a moment, she knelt down and, fully aware of how carried away she was getting, picked up the chunk of marble, turning it over in her hands. That, she knew, would be a step too far. This frustration, this anger, was reserved for Azrael. It wasn't Ryan she was so angry about.

Although he really was asking for it this time.

A wicked grin started to spread across her face as she lifted up the chunk of marble. Ryan looked up, his eyes widening in horror. He whimpered and began to babble like an idiot before shutting his eyes tight shut and letting out a pathetic sob.

When he opened his eyes, Aleera was gone. His brother and Greg were looking around with embarrassed and bemused faces as Aleera walked away as though nothing had happened and dropped the chunk of marble into a nearby trashcan.

Honestly. Pathetic.

Now, where to find Michael and Sara? Although, of course, there was that essay that her English teacher wanted to talk to her about. Not that she was avoiding talking to them. No, certainly not. Never.

She gave silent thanks when her phone rang again. Again, it was Jake; his number, at least.

'Jake?' she answered.

'Close,' Katya's voice chirped. 'Good news…'

Makian may not have been one of Aleera's favourite people, but credit had to be given where due: he knew what he was doing. According to what Katya had told her, he had managed to dig up the name of one of the biggest black marketers operating in the state, and unsurprisingly his favourite base of operations was in Pentagram. Makian had, shortly after, discovered where else he liked to operate from.

Aleera met up with Jake in the evening and was soon shown to the place. It turned out to be slightly less upmarket than Pentagram, though she hadn't previously thought it possible; an old apartment building that, by the look of its barely-intact edifice, should have been long-since condemned.

The gentleman, who went by the name of "Skinny Jack", was primarily in the business of trading enchanted- or the much-more-impressive-sounding "supernaturally augmented" items. Sources of magic should their owner ever be low on the real thing. Civilian possession of such things had been outlawed by the Guild around two hundred years ago, and their usage was restricted solely to members of the Guild, and even then only under exceptional circumstances. Aleera didn't bother asking why "Skinny Jack" hadn't been arrested by now; money, drugs and women probably had a lot to do with it. The advantage, however, of enchanted objects was that their active ability to supply magic could be "switched off", but they would still retain the ambient magical energy while remaining undetectable to draconic and demon senses. They tended to be activated exclusively by a pre-selected word, meaning that there was no actual way of determining whether an object was enchanted. That was probably the other reason why "Skinny Jack" was still a free man. Nonetheless, Makian was one hundred percent certain that he was the only individual in the Tri-State area who could have provided Azrael with an enchanted item of sufficient power for what he had been doing.

Aleera's first realisation upon being faced with "Skinny Jack" was that his moniker was definitely one of those ironic nicknames. The portly man in the three-hundred-dollar suit, glistening with sweat, showed herself, Jake, Katya and Makian into his "office", a dingy room at the back of the building. They waited while he took care of some "business" in the private bathroom into which the room branched off.

'So,' Skinny Jack began as he seated himself on the chair. It creaked audibly under his weight. 'What can I do for you nice young people?'

'Does the name "Azrael" mean anything to you?' Jake asked in an offhand tone.

'Isn't that from that *Dogma* flick?' Skinny Jack asked innocently. 'I'm not a very religious man, my friend. Nothing about him seemed to change.

'A friend of mine,' Jake started, 'bought something from you recently.' There was no sense in letting the gentleman know that they were with the Guild. He'd probably never talk then. 'He recommended you, but he didn't say exactly what it was that he bought. One that had a lot of power, actually.'

'This friend of yours,' Skinny Jack queried, 'is called "Azrael"?'

'He's a little strange,' Jake answered. 'Religious guy.'

Skinny Jack let out a scoff of amusement. 'And you think this guy's one of my customers? The hell are you smokin?'

'Can you tell me what you sold him, anyway?' Jake continued. 'I'd be interested to see what you have to offer.'

'Sorry, friend,' Skinny Jack wheezed, 'but it's been a whole lotta years since I sold something of that cal-e-br.' His eyes shifted. He was sweating a little more. Aleera's dark eyes narrowed slightly. This was going nowhere. Here came that low-frustration-threshold again.

'Jake,' she spoke up, 'do you think I could speak with... Mr. Jack... in private?'

Jake eyed her suspiciously. He stepped up to her and said in a whisper, 'don't you dare.'

'Do you want to get something out of him or not?' Aleera whispered back.

Jake glanced back at Skinny Jack. 'Excuse us,' he said, stepping out. Aleera followed. Jake closed the door behind them.

'Aleera-'

'He'll still be in one piece. We're short of time.'

Jake looked around with frantic movements as he struggled to find something to say. 'What are you going to do?' he demanded.

'I do know how to control myself, Jake,' Aleera said dryly. 'You know I can make him talk.'

'I can't just let you-'

'He'll have a few bruises at worst. Besides, what do you plan to do?'

Jake's silence spoke volumes.

'If I hear anything,' he hissed, 'I'm coming in there.'

Aleera nodded. 'Deal.'

Jake opened the door. Aleera stepped in, and at a nod from Jake, Katya and Makian stepped out. Jake shot Aleera a final warning glare and closed the door.

'So,' Skinny Jack asked from behind the desk. 'What can I do for you?'

Without saying a thing, Aleera grabbed a chair and positioned it strategically against the doorknob. There. Nice and private. No embarrassing interruptions.

Time to cut loose.

He was, she reasoned, a criminal. Someone who had knowingly aided and abided thieves, murderers and rapists. She'd seen the list of suspected offences on his part. And she wasn't planning to do anything *that* bad to him.

She removed her top without a word. Skinny Jack's eyes focused immediately on her impressive cleavage and the bra that barely contained it.

Aleera walked purposefully up to him. Her face held nothing of suggestiveness, but it was only when she grabbed hold of the front of Skinny Jack's suit and stuffed the garment into his mouth that he realised what he was in for. He gave a muffled cry of protest as Aleera dragged him into the en-suite bathroom, which she hadn't been able to see without getting an idea.

Skinny Jack was as heavy as he looked, but the claws that emerged from Aleera's fingers served as a suitable deterrent to keep him in place next to the sink as the she turned on the hot tap. She waited a few seconds until she could see visible steam coming out.

'You sold something powerful,' she said. It was a statement, not a question. She removed her top from his mouth.

'I didn't freaking sell-' Skinny Jack was cut off when Aleera's knee struck his stomach. He doubled over and wheezed.

'Who did you sell it to?' Aleera asked in the tone someone would use when inquiring about the weather on the phone to a relative. That should help the effect. 'I won't ask this politely again.'

'Fuck you,' Skinny Jack spat. For a moment, she saw a little something of Ryan in his face. 'What are you gonna do?'

Aleera stuffed the top back into Skinny Jack's mouth, pulled in front of the sink and pushed his face under the running, scalding hot water. He screamed, muffled by the top but still, unfortunately, audible. In Aleera's moral defence, she pulled him out straight away. Didn't want to cause any permanent damage. The banging against the door started immediately. Jake shouted to her. She simply turned back to Skinny Jack.

On the surface of it, this would probably look reprehensible at best, but Aleera knew exactly what she was doing. Jake, she knew, was as much an expert at healing spells as any other kind. The burns caused by this would be easy for him to heal. Nothing permanent, nothing broken, and it looked effective.

'You're quite capable of making me stop,' she pointed out innocently. 'Just answer my question.'

Jake's shouts continued. 'Okay!' Skinny Jack wailed. 'Okay, okay, okay!' Satisfied, Aleera released him. He sobbed and clutched the side of his face.

'Well?' Aleera pressed as she shook the soaked top and started to soak it under the cold tap. No sense burning herself when she put it on; it had certainly looked painful.

'I only sold one thing like that lately,' Jack gasped. 'He only gave me his account number. The ledger's in the second draw down of the desk, look for yourself.'

The door flew open before a wave of magic-induced force. Jake ran in just in time to see the nearly-topless Aleera step out of the bathroom, wringing out a soaked top.

'He'll be fine,' Aleera reassured him. 'Just as long as he puts some ice on it; he was only under there for a second.'

Jake immediately ran past her to the bathroom. Skinny Jack was cradling one side of his face. 'She's crazy,' he gasped painfully, 'that bitch's freakin crazy!'

Aleera had to take a moment to compose herself after that. Hearing a scream like that was certainly far from pleasant, and she knew how painful burning could be. Still, Jake could fix the damage in a heartbeat, and it had the desired effect. Makian, meanwhile, had found the ledger and was currently leafing through it.

She suddenly felt shaky. Skinny Jack's scream was still cutting into her, almost as if it was still happening.

It was wrong, she realised somehow. That pit was back again, and at its deepest.

Jake, having attended to Skinny Jack, stepped out into the corridor. Judging by how hard he slammed the door, he was at least as angry as he had been at Pentagram.

'You-'

'I knew you could fix the damage,' Aleera replied defensively without turning to look at him. She'd had enough lectures recently. 'There was nothing permanent, and it worked. I knew exactly what I was doing.'

'That was *torture*,' Jake snapped.

'And he hasn't done worse?'

'That doesn't give you the-'

'Necessary evil,' Aleera declared flatly. This time, she turned.

Jake was silent for a moment. He looked taken aback.

'You didn't like doing that, did you?' he asked.

Aleera shook her head. She felt suddenly breathless. She felt hollow, and she felt very, very tired. 'No.' And she hadn't. Not like almost cutting into Azrael, or landing a solid blow to Ryan's kidneys.

Jake sighed heavily. Neither one of them spoke for a while.

'I'm sorry, Jake.' Aleera finally said. Oh, God, not this again. First the guilt over interrogating scum like Skinny Jack, now this sudden pouring out of truth? 'About last night. About that just now.' Something caught in her throat. It was suddenly hard to speak.

'It's alright,' Jake said quietly, putting an arm around her.

For a long moment, they both simply stood there. Neither of them moved or spoke. What Aleera had just done, she realised was indeed torture. It made her feel cold. Dirty. Suddenly she just wanted to go home and crawl into bed. And maybe eat a million jars of honey to get over this one.

On top of that, it was an awkward moment she didn't want to carry on with.

She stepped back and asked 'I don't suppose your friends in forensics dug anything up?'

'Actually,' Jake recalled, remembering what he'd forgotten to tell her as his face took on a flash of reserved excitement, 'it turns out that all three of the victims were regulars at Pentagram. Harry and Tomoko manage to identify all three, and-' he paused, as if chiding himself for almost recklessly blurting something out. 'They all disappeared about a day before their bodies turned up.'

Aleera nodded thoughtfully. Her mind immediately set to work: if they went missing, he presumably did something with them in that time. All women, she recalled, and killed in the manner of Kudra. She shuddered at the memory that came with the realisation of what he had very probably done to those women.

The door suddenly opened, and there was Makian, Katya behind him, and the open ledger in his hand.

'Jake,' he said urgently, 'you are not gonna believe this shit.' He handed over the ledger and pointed to one of the many numbers on the list.

Jake looked at the number, read it and recollected. His expression became one of concentration, followed by disbelief. What followed was shock. And finally, realisation. The kind of realisation that brings with it a shade of dread, of disbelief, of feeling that "this can't be true".

'What is it?' Aleera voiced her curiosity.

'The account,' Jake said breathlessly. He hesitated, as if checking hopefully to see if he was wrong. 'It's the Guild,' he stated disbelievingly. 'This item- it's the only thing on here powerful enough to let Azrael do what he can do- it's a Guild account.'

Well. Now, *this* was an interesting development.

'Which means,' Makian pointed out, 'That the Guild- well-' he struggled to name it.

'The item that Azrael is using,' Jake declared, 'was supplied by the Guild.' He held the ledger under his arm and looked fearfully around at the group.

'Someone in the Guild is working with Azrael.'

11

By nine o'clock, the rain was beginning to pour heavily. It formed streaked patterns on the windows and soon began to fall in a thick, steady surge. The size of the raindrops left blurred outlines over whatever they landed on. The thunder echoed over the city, and the rooftops were lit up by the occasional flash of sheet lightning.

Michael took another glance out of the window of Sara's apartment and muttered irritably to himself about having to walk home in that kind of weather. Sara had mentioned that it looked like it would probably be in for a day or two. He'd visited in the afternoon, when Sara had called him sounding worried and saying she hadn't seen Aleera all day. Michael had seen her once, wandering around school. He'd heard somewhere that she'd finally kicked the shit into Ryan, and heard somewhere else that she nearly busted his head in with a chunk of marble. That didn't sound like her. When he'd spotted her, he'd thought of going up and making sure she was alright, but remembering the awkwardness from yesterday he'd stopped himself.

Sara, apparently, had left a message with Aleera making sure she was alright. She'd eventually replied with a short text message saying that "*I'm fine, will talk tomorrow*". Sara was still uneasy, though, and the afternoon and evening had been awkward. Michael had reassured her that Aleera was more than capable of taking care of herself, and that whoever had been messing with her would probably be locked up by the end of the week. But that wasn't what either of them was worried about.

Aleera was... she hadn't been herself lately. She was always quiet, and she'd always had a temper, but lately, especially today, she seemed to have become more withdrawn than ever. Sara had confided in Michael, just once, that she thought Aleera's childhood (neither of them really knew any details) had a worse effect on her than anyone thought, and it was just possible that what had happened over the past four days wasn't helping. Thinking about it, it made sense: considering what she was going through, there really was no telling what it was doing to her. Michael had finally noticed the time and decided to head home- just as it started raining.

'See you tomorrow,' he said as Sara opened the door for him.

'Are you sure you don't want a coat? There's a spare one,' Sara offered.

'Nah,' Michael shook his head, 'I'll just run; it's not far. Seeya tomorrow.'

By the time he'd run to the first corner, he was already soaked. His clothes were already sodden and he had to blink to keep the water out of his eyes. But his focus was still on the events of the last few days and the bitingly short text message.

Damnit, Aleera, what was going on in the head of yours?

He was so focused on the thought that he never even noticed he was passing an alley- until strong arms grabbed hold of him and tugged backwards, pulling him from his feet and throwing him across the soaked concrete. The world spun for a second until he slammed to a stop against something hard, sending a jolt of pain through his side. It was suddenly hard to move, probably thanks to the impact.

'What the hell?' he wiped a layer of dirty water from the alley floor out of his face and made to stand. A strong fist caught him across the face and knocked him sideways with another burst of pain. There was the sharp, stabbing ache of something dislodging in his mouth. He spat out the bloody tooth. As soon as his limbs started to move, the booted foot struck him in his side. He gritted his teeth to keep himself from crying out as two ribs snapped.

The figure moved. Michael took a deep breath to nurse his winded side and saw the moving shape of the white robe as it stepped around him, further into the alley. Gloved hands grabbed the back of his shirt and painfully pulled him to his feet. A fist immediately caught his face, and his nose cracked and gave way to a spurt of blood.

'You,' the voice snarled beneath the hood, 'are going to deliver a message.'

Message? Like Aleera had said? Then-

The hand pulled a gleaming dagger from the belt and turned it over in the rain. The blade glistened with droplets of water.

'The hell I am,' Michael hissed. One of the first things taught to young Draconics under the Eighth Division of the Guild was basic offensive and defensive magic. Michael had been a quick student. He thrust his palm forward with a shout of '*ThuraiShiahl*'. The adrenaline gave the spell all the power it needed; the shimmering wave of solid force struck the white shape, carrying it down the alley at an angle until he struck the brick wall. He fell to the ground in a trickling shower of dust.

Michael never thought of himself as a coward. But he already had a broken nose and ribs, and his entire left side felt half-dead. Staying there to fight would go from "brave" to "stupid". And he'd never thought of himself as stupid either.

He turned and ran back for the end of the alley. Then from behind him there was the shout of '*Sliahozai*', and myriad sharp, burning pains cut into his back. The last of the tiny, shimmering, burning sparks vanished just as the figure in white reached him, pulling him up even as he stifled another painful howl, the rain falling onto the raw, stinging burns. The figure's elbow smashed into his chest. More ribs snapped. Michael fell back as the blade turned in the gloved hand.

Michael struggled as strong hands gripped his forearm and elbow. As the pressure on the limb started to build, realisation struck him, survival instinct kicked in and his struggling became desperate.

He screamed an animal howl of agony as the skin tore and the bone snapped at the elbow, filling the entire arm with pain and a revolting, ripping, tearing noise. He collapsed, the arms releasing him and allowing him to fall to the floor. For too long, he couldn't move, couldn't think, couldn't do anything in the all-consuming pain.

He was pulled to his feet again. The blade of the dagger glinted in front of his face, and he froze in fear as he realised what was coming.

'May God have mercy on your soul,' the voice beneath the hood spat, 'though the path you chose to follow leads not to him.'

The blade stabbed into his side, one more white-hot pain laid into the endless hurt. He screamed again as the knife plunged and tore through skin and blood and muscle.

He fell to his side. He couldn't move. The pain kept him still.

The last thing Michael was aware of was the solid tip of Azrael's boot colliding with his temple. Everything reeled, there was one last explosion of pain, and finally the world was dark.

12

It was dark. Everything wrapped in cold darkness. The door into the tiny room was locked. The windows were boarded up, the edges allowing the only thin shafts of light in the room. She stayed away from the light, backed into a single corner.

The room was empty and silent. All she could even see were the slits of light that kept her backed into the corner. She looked at them and shook with rage. The painted mark on her forehead stung.

She didn't know how long she had been there. A day, two days, three? Her stomach growled. She couldn't see, but her skin felt pale. She shook with cold induced by tiredness and hunger.

There were footsteps from outside. Quiet but approaching. She shuddered and buried her head in her hands, sobbing quietly. Not again, please don't let him come in again...

The door opened. She backed away as most of the room was filled with light, its brightness stinging her eyes. Her forehead stung her again as she remembered.

He closed the door again. She looked up at him, pain and fear forgotten before a tide of boiling hatred. Her fists clenched. Her eyes turned the colour of blood.

Kudra took a step towards her and looked down at the shivering, naked child, her face coated in tears. She was a disappointment; her... misbehaviour... in Kenya had demonstrated that much. If he was to have what he wanted from the girl, then more severe measures had to be taken.

She needed to learn what he had taught himself; to embrace the dark, and what it had to offer. But she was an unruly child indeed.

As her father approached, Aleera's fear welled up again. She moved back as far as the wall would allow. He stopped, looming over her.

'You will have to do it some time,' the dark voice told her.

Aleera glared up at him. Her eyes remained red.

Kudra reached a hand down towards her. 'Take my hand.'

She said nothing.

'Do it.'

Aleera shook as her rage built up again.

'Either do it, or face the light again.'

A flicker of fear crossed the young face. She looked from him, to the door. Where he had turned on the light outside, there were thin white slivers on its edges. A pit of fear opened in her stomach.

No. Stop it. That was what he wanted her to feel, to be afraid of the light. She would not. She would refuse.

'*No,*' *she said.* '*I won't do it.*' *Kudra's hand returned to his side.*

She swallowed her fear and ran for the door. Kudra made no effort to stop her. It was, they both knew, a useless effort. But Aleera was too overcome with hate and defiance to think as she grabbed the doorknob and pulled the door open. The room flooded with light.

Aleera screamed as the enchantment Kudra had placed upon her reacted to the presence of the light. Every inch of her skin that was exposed to the light felt as though it were on fire. She collapsed as the door swung shut, leaving her in the darkness again. The soft, painless darkness.

No. Don't think about it like that. He wanted her to choose it like that. Don't. Fight him.

She spent a moment there, curled up on the floor and sobbing.

'*You can go to the light as many times as you chose,*' *Kudra said coldly. He had shown no reaction to her pain; she was certain that in whatever sick way, he enjoyed her screams.*

'*Stop it!*' *Aleera sobbed.* '*Stop it! Why are you doing this?*'

'*I am teaching you,*' *Kudra's tone did not change.* '*This is what happens when you go into the light. This is what it brings. This is all it will ever offer you. Choose the dark, Aleera. It will set you free. It will give you the strength that should be yours. It can make the light go away forever, if you will only use it. Its power is greater than any of them know. You could be more than they can ever imagine.*'

'*I won't do it!*' *Aleera shouted.*

'*You will. In time, you-*' *Kudra paused as Aleera spat in his face. A metal gauntlet wiped the saliva off, and then returned to his side. It didn't look like he was going to move, but Aleera still trembled, knowing what she had brought on herself.*

In a blur of motion, the cold, hard gauntlet struck her. The side of her face exploded with pain, and her world was a blur of confusion as she fell sideways. She cried out in pain as Kudra lifted her by the hair, a million tugging stabs in her scalp.

'*You stupid child!*' *Kudra roared. He turned, shifting his weight into the throw, and hurled Aleera into the wall. She hit it hard, fell and* came to rest on the floor. Everything was pain. The sharp metal jabbed into her skin as he grabbed the back of her throat and lifted her up. Her breathing was stifled and the dull ache of the pressure started in her throat and the base of her skull.

Kudra pulled open the door and held her in the blinding, burning light. Aleera screamed. The pain consumed every inch of her, set her every fibre on fire.

'You force me to this, Aleera,' Kudra shouted over her screams. 'You brought this on yourself.'

Aleera screamed. She begged for him to stop. He did not. 'Let me go!' she managed to howl through the screams. He held her forward, and the burning continued.

And then it happened. Her eyes opened, their tears suddenly gone. For a fraction of a second, everything was numb. Somewhere, deep inside the frightened little girl, something snapped. Suddenly, fear was gone. Pain was gone. They left the rage to fill her in a heartbeat, pure and unbridled, total and all-consuming.

'Let! Me! Go!'

Without thinking, she screamed and lashed out with all her rage, and what came forth was just that. No thought, no fear, no doubt, no power, no magic- rage, pure, burning and all consuming, a wave of dark light powerful and unstoppable, something dark awakened and lashing out for the first time. The mark on her forehead burned away in a blink. In a second, the room was more of a crater, floorboards and walls splintering and buckling before the outward force. The coverings on the windows were smashed apart, flooding the room with light. The force struck Kudra with the force of fury itself, burning the edges of the cloak, cracking the gauntlets and mask as he was hurled away.

The next thing Aleera knew, she was running, her legs racing as if by themselves as her heart pounded against the inside of her chest. She was out, out of his grip, out of the dark, into the light. She would never go back. She would never be as he wanted her to be. She would never let herself become like him.

Behind her, Kudra rose to his feet, surveying what remained of the room and the sight of the running child. He extended a hand, watched it buzz with energy and felt what remained in the air of that which had been so furiously unleashed at long, long last. And beneath the mask, he smiled to himself.

Again, Aleera woke screaming. By a small mercy, this time her wings didn't tear into the sheets when they erupted from her back. Like before, she shook, her eyes wide open and the covers clutched tight in her clawed hands. Freezing sweat covered her body as she tried to slow her breathing and her pounding heartbeat, telling herself again that it was 'just a dream'.

Only…

There was something in the back of her mind. Something that tugged at her consciousness as the pit in her stomach refused to close. A dark feeling; a simple *knowing* of something that was wrong.

It was odd; she couldn't shake that feeling. She told herself to be calm, that nothing was wrong, that between them, herself, Jake and Makian would find Azrael in next to no time, Guild or no Guild. All the same, she'd seen Jake's face. Learning this changed everything; made everything questionable. Made no-one trustworthy.

Azrael, you cunning dog. The playing field changed again, and again it turned out that she had been playing without even knowing the rules. Check. And it dawned on her that she didn't quite know what her next move would be.

The problem was that this wasn't what worried her so. There was something else, and she had no idea what. As if she somehow knew without knowing that something was wrong. What was this feeling, and where was the knowing, self-composed young woman she had been before?

As she arrived at school, she pushed these thoughts to the back of her mind. There were other matters to attend to first, and there was no sense in putting this one off and letting it grow any worse.

It looked as though the rainy weather would be in for a while, and so she looked for Michael and Sara inside, leaving her coat in her locker while a pair of bimbos whined about their hair frizzing in the rain. The nightmare, she reflected, was curious in its timing; she normally slept well during storms. She found the patter of rain on the windows curiously soothing, but during the night she had tossed and turned and generally had trouble falling asleep. That damned stomach-pit had refused to take its leave again.

Focus, Aleera. Time to focus on the matter at hand.

Sara was sitting by herself in the cafeteria. Michael was nowhere in sight; he was probably either running behind schedule or grabbing a late breakfast. Sara looked up and gave her a much-heartier smile as she sat down. Well, well, a proper smile again. Hopefully that was in some way a good sign.

'Hey,' Sara greeted her.

'Hi,' Aleera smiled back, but it was a little bit weak.

'I didn't see you yesterday.'

This was it. 'I...' she should have thought of what she was going to say. She'd had time hadn't she? What the hell had she spent all of yesterday doing? Oh, yes: the demon-slaying serial killer. Quite distracting, that. 'Bad day,' she half-lied.

'Right,' Sara said. There was something in her voice that, try though she might, Aleera was unable to identity. 'Are we still on for tonight?'

'Yeah.' There; a conversation, at last. 'I'm still not sure what to cook.'

'Well, it should be fun.'

Aleera nodded slowly. Get on with it, woman! She took a deep breath. Her stomach was in knots and her heart was doing backflips. 'Can I ask you something?' she eventually managed to force the words out.

'Sure.'

Another deep breath. Now how to bring this up? Her throat seemed to close. '...Actually, never mind. It's not important.' Oh, you stupid, *stupid* demon, she immediately cursed herself. She noticed that the blush creeping its way into her cheeks. Change the subject. Now. Anything. 'So have you seen Michael?'

Aleera shook her head. 'He's probably late.'

Aleera's phone suddenly began to chime its usual stream of noise from her pocket. 'That's probably him,' she said. A quick glance confirmed that it was indeed Michael's home phone number.

'Hello?' she answered it. To her surprise, it was not Michael's voice on the line.

'Aleera?' the stern, female voice asked briskly. She realised that it was Michael's mother.

'Yes.'

'I thought so.' There was something accusatory in her tone. 'Could you tell me where my son is, please?'

'Michael?' Well, obviously Michael. It was Michael's mother, and Michael's only sibling, he had told her, was attending college in Philadelphia. 'He hasn't come to school yet.'

'And last night?' Yes, definitely an accusation of some kind there, though of what she couldn't be sure.

'Pardon?'

'Michael didn't tell me that he was staying out last night.'

Aleera's brow furrowed quizzically. 'Mrs. Prince, I haven't seen Michael since Wednesday,' she replied. She suddenly remembered that they indeed had not seen each other since just after her "discussion" with Ryan on the basketball court.

Mrs. Prince didn't reply for a moment. 'Do you know where he is?'

Aleera felt a growing sense of dread start to belatedly creep up on her. 'No,' she answered.

The voice sounded suddenly stifled. '…Michael didn't come home last night.'

Aleera felt herself go pale. Oh, no… oh, no, no, no, please, *please* not this.

'I'll let you know if I see him,' she said shakily before hanging up. She turned to Sara and saw that her shining blue eyes held the same dread.

She looked down again. There was a text from a number she didn't recognise.

"*Now it begins*".

Aleera called Jake straight away. He met her and Sara at the same spot under the stands on the football field within the hour along with Katya, Makian and Tomoko. Aleera and Sara had stood waiting in the crisscross pattern of shadows, sheltering from the rain as well as they could as she tried to console her friend and reassured her that they would find Michael.

And they would. Without question, they would. This wasn't the stuff of games any longer. This was no longer moves and countermoves. This was a friend who had vanished in the hands of a madman, and she was going to find him before anything happened to him.

She felt almost guilty, ashamed of herself for having thought of it as some almost-trivial battle of wits between herself and Azrael. But she was damned if Michael was going to pay the price for that.

'We checked everything we could think of,' she said when everyone was there and started asking questions. She didn't bother to try and disguise the guilt. 'Azrael's got him. I'm sure of it.' She handed her phone to Jake. 'Take a look at this.' Jake took it and examined the message.

'Not to rub salt in anything,' Makian spoke up hesitantly, 'but if this Azrael guy's got the kid-'

'He's *not* a "kid",' Aleera snapped.

'Yeah, but going by what Tomoko here and Harry already worked out,' Makian said anxiously, 'we've only got a day to find him.' Thunder rolled in the distance.

Aleera silenced as the awful realisation of the full implications of what was happening sank in.

'The thing is,' Tomoko spoke up, 'this doesn't fit into what's happened so far.' All eyes turned to her. 'The last three victims were all women, and all regulars at Pentagram. Michael is neither.'

'So far as we know,' Makian piped up in a failed effort to be helpful. Katya sharply elbowed him in the ribs.

'Michael's also half-draconic,' Tomoko continued. 'The last three were all full demons. This doesn't quite fit.

'No,' Aleera spoke up, thinking out loud. No sense in hiding anything now, not if it could help. 'This entire thing has been about me, right from the start. Every detail. Everything he did so far was a message; one big threat.' She shuddered again. 'This could just be the next one.'

'So what does that tell us?' came Makian's clueless response. 'Besides that this guy never heard of the post office.'

'Shut it,' Katya hissed angrily.

'It means that he'll do to Michael what he did to those women,' Aleera replied. That pit in her stomach had worked its way up to her voice box, apparently.

'He won't get the chance,' Jake finally spoke up. Aleera realised how silent he'd been. 'Because, if we're lucky, if we're very, *very* lucky, Azrael just made his first mistake.' He passed the phone to Makian.

Makian stared blankly at the screen. 'I don't get it.'

'It's a phone number,' Jake said urgently. 'The Guild has access to the database.'

'Trace it,' Aleera realised. 'Find the owner. Find Azrael.'

'Fingers crossed,' Jake nodded as Makian pocketed the phone. 'Can you trace it?'

'Does my ass point down? I can find out who owns it by lunchtime.'

'I'll see if Harry and I can find anything more from the bodies,' Tomoko offered.

'I'll get hold of Khazahn,' Jake declared. 'Get him to help, and I mean right this minute.' Quite literally. He started walking away, Katya following.

'Given his feelings toward you right now, are you sure he will?' Makian asked after him.

'If he doesn't, I'll bust his damn head in,' Jake answered matter-of-factly. In passing, he turned to Aleera. 'We'll find him,' he promised quietly.'

Just as long as they did it before she found Azrael.

No more games. He had raised the stakes, and now he would see who he was dealing with.

Oh, Azrael would *pay*.

Once everyone had left, Aleera and Sara had been left standing alone in the crisscross shadows. Aleera stood still and took a moment to calm herself down.

Already, this was affecting her. She should have worked that out about the phone number much more quickly. She was too worried, too shocked, to think properly. Understandable, maybe, but also unacceptable. Michael had to be found, and if she yielded to the situation like that, it wouldn't particularly be helpful to such a cause.

Calm down. Think. Work with them. Find him. You can do it.

Sara was still standing in front of her. Raindrops fell through the hands to drip patterns over her head as she fiddled with the silver cross.

'Sara,' she said gently. 'We'll find Michael. I promise.'

Sara looked up at her. The raindrops on her face mixed with thick, salty tears. She bit her lip. 'Aleera-'

'I *promise*.'

'I know,' Sara said shakily. Her breathing was ragged. 'I know, but-' her face crumpled before a wave of tears. 'Aleera-' she broke down as Aleera wrapped her arms round her as comfortingly as she could. 'I'm scared,' she sobbed quietly.

'It's alright,' Aleera told her gently. 'I swear to you, I will find Michael, and I- *we*- will stop this man. I swear.'

'I believe you,' Sara sniffed, pulling back. 'But... Aleera... I'm scared for *you*.' This, admittedly, caught Aleera off-guard, which probably wasn't a good sign. 'I'm scared of what you'll have to do to stop someone like him.' Aleera knew exactly what Sara was talking about before she even said it.

She nodded slowly. 'It'll be Ok,' she finally said even as she searched for the right words. 'I promise it'll be Ok.'

As far as Aleera was concerned, the end of the school day couldn't come soon enough. Her mind had spent the whole day whirring and clicking as it desperately tried to tear its way to an answer. Every little possibility forced its way into her head until they tripped and stumbled over each other, but she was clutching at straws and she knew it.

Think, she told herself. She needed to get her old brain back, start figuring things out like she had been doing since the beginning. God damn it, Aleera, *think*. For heaven's sake, she could practically hear the wind whistling between her ears.

No- not wind; that was someone whistling at her, from beside the school gates. Oh, of all the days.

And of all the people to see when she glanced angrily behind herself, it would have to Ryan Shane, his brother on one side of him and Greg on the other.

'We still screwin with this bitch?' the brother sneered.

'Jamie, shut up for two freakin minutes,' Ryan spat, his breath reeking of pot. That was the brother's name, evidently. She'd never learned it. At the minute, she didn't much care.

'Seriously, man-' Greg spoke up. Ryan glared at him, and he looked away, shame-faced again.

Ryan stepped toward Aleera. 'So where d'you think you're goin', you little-'

The sentence never reached its end, as Aleera grabbed Ryan by the front of his shirt and swung him into the gate. She wrapped one hand around his neck and tightened her newfound grip on his windpipe. 'I,' she hissed, her face inches from his, 'am in no mood.'

For a second, before she released her hand and allowed him to breathe again, Ryan could have almost sworn that her eyes turned blood-red.

'...Hell was that?' Jamie gaped as he watched the departing young lady.

'Said we shoulda left her alone,' Greg pointed out.

'I said *you* should shut your scrawny face,' Ryan snarled.

Aleera left the three stooges behind and carried on her way out of school and down the street, ignoring the rain that poured down on her and still trying to force herself to think, to no end.

There was too much going on in there, she finally realised; too much frustration, too much anger, too much confusion. So, let some of it out; that was the obvious conclusion. Find an outlet, like Jake had always said. And for Michael's sake, do it *fast*.

No. Now was not the time. Focus. Find Michael. Put that damn brain to some use!

There was a shout. A frightened, angry shout from up the street behind her. The door to a small café was wide open, and a fat, stubbly man in a stained apron with a thick moustache was pointing and yelling at something. Next to him, a young woman with red hair whose attire marked her as a waitress was kneeling on the floor, sobbing in pain and clutching the red stain that spread from her stomach and mixed with the spilled soup that had been knocked from her hands.

Aleera's eyes turned to follow the thing to which the man pointed. The figure, its head covered by a scraggly grey hooded sweater, was stuffing something into its pockets. The coward running with his gains, leaving the cook to tend to the young woman with the gushing wound in her stomach.

She shouldn't go after him. She should find a police officer, do something less conspicuous. On the other hand, she had already started running, and was solely focused on getting hold of the filth and violently teaching him the error of his ways. She would probably have found some way to rationalise the decision to herself, but reason was not one of her primary concerns.

As she gained on him, she felt the anger fill her. Her eyes flooded with red as her fingernails erupted into claws, and she fought to keep her wings inside her back. The head beneath the hood turned to see her approach, her legs pumping and heart pounding as she discarded every rational thought. He ducked round a corner and into the alley, and Aleera followed him, grabbing the back of his hood and pulling. He fell, feet flailing in the air and gagging. Aleera felt her blood surge with glee as he hit the ground with a dull 'thud'. She pinned him with her weight and thrust her claws down on either side of his neck.

'Get off me!' the thug hollered as he thrashed wildly, like a trapped animal. His fist caught Aleera's cheek, knocking her face sideways. She disregarded the blow and drove her knee into his crotch, before pulling him up with her and throwing him against the wall. Even as he bounced off the surface, a curled fist caught his face, splintering his nose before she backhanded him and sent him falling to the ground. She pulled back and drove her foot into his side as he gave a sharp wheeze of pain.

Here we go. Now vent. Let it all out. And then, think. *Now*, something inside her screamed. Finish him. Let it out. Finally, at long last, let it all out, *all* of it.

'Having fun?'

Aleera whirled round. Jake stood in the middle of the alley, hands in pockets, looking warningly at her in the "don't do it" manner a parent would use on a child tempted to throw a stone through a neighbour's window. Aleera looked back from him to the semi-conscious thief, her claws receding and her eyes reverting to their normal dark colour as the raging storm in her chest quietened itself, and that screaming thing became quiet again.

'What's going on?' Jake pressed as he approached, eyeing the sprawled-out thug.

'He deserved it,' Aleera replied defensively, breathing slowly in her practiced exercise to calm herself whenever she got... over-excited. 'He hurt someone; we should call an ambulance.'

Jake turned his attention from Aleera's near-victim to Aleera herself. He looked at her incredulously. 'Was this meant to help?'

'Blowing off steam, I guess,' Aleera admitted. As rational thought returned, she looked up at Jake with a rush of hope. 'Has anything happened?'

'Khazahn already got in touch with the police liaisons; they're going door-to-door. Makian managed to trace the phone number.'

'And?'

Jake hesitated guiltily. 'The phone was bought yesterday, and all that was left was the account number; it was the same one that made the other purchase. He managed to triangulate the signal...' he gave a heavy sigh of defeat, 'to a trashcan about a block from Pentagram. Harry took a look at it, but he couldn't find a thing. Tomoko hasn't had any more luck with the bodies.'

Aleera looked down as the surge of hope dissipated as suddenly as it had swelled. That was everything. 'So why did you come here?'

'To make sure you were alright,' Jake replied. 'And... to see if anything had happened with you. I'd hoped you'd met Azrael again, maybe gleamed something.'

'I'm not feeling my best today,' Aleera admitted. 'Of all the days,' she added bitterly. 'I've got nothing.'

Jake sighed and placed a comforting hand on her shoulder. 'There's still time,' he promised. 'We'll figure this out.'

Figure it out indeed. She'd been trying all day without success. Nothing but murders and bodies and messages and Pentagram...

Pentagram.

Pentagram!

Oh, *yes*. She was back. Her mind clicked, whirring over itself.

'Pentagram!'

Jake looked at her in confusion. 'Pentagram?'

'Pentagram,' Aleera nodded urgently. Of *course*! Pentagram; his hunting ground. Still closed off, still empty of any interference. Everything so far had been a message, and a demon nightclub had been the perfect way to send a message to a demon. Maybe, just maybe, it still was. And he would want to be sure the message got through.

It was a challenge, taking Michael, the thought exploded in her head. Try and find him. Figure it out. Make your move. He'd left the clues for her; all the bodies had their connection to the place, so why not this one? It fit, it made sense, and in an almost-euphoric burst of epiphany, she knew it was true, because this was exactly the sort of thing that he- that Kudra- would have done.

'Pentagram,' she confirmed, 'think about it- all the other bodies were found there. It's still closed off. Everything else so far has led back there.'

Jake looked bemused, then thoughtful, and then his face lit up.

'Aleera,' he grinned, 'I confess myself impressed.'

And then they were both tearing through the alleys and streets, one block blurring into another. Aleera felt and heard her heart pounding like a jackhammer. Street after street passed indeterminately, as Aleera replayed her thoughts; it was perfect. Kudra's crimes had been the basis for every move Azrael had made. This was it. This *had* to be it.

Oh, please, let this be it...

As everything became a blur of rushing hope and tightening anxiety, Aleera felt herself snapped back to the world when, passing through an alley a few blocks from Pentagram, Jake thrust his palm forward and gave a shout of '*Appiras*'. The world suddenly became a spinning blur, and Aleera ceased to run with a sickening lurch. It suddenly felt as though she was falling uncontrollably, everything around her ceasing to be anything other than a blur as they warped into and through the place between places.

It happened in the time it took Aleera to blink, and when it ended, the sight and repugnant smells of the alley outside Pentagram were all around her. Her stomach still felt like it was rolling.

'You Ok?' Jake asked from beside her. She nodded groggily. She felt as though she had just stepped off a rollercoaster. 'Sorry about that. It's trickier to carry more than one.'

Not to interrupt, Aleera's mind piped up, but we're here.

She didn't waste another second before racing down the alley. A pair of Guild soldiers stood by the door; presumably stationed to make sure nobody got in. Evidently nobody had told them that Azrael was able to teleport. Ironically enough, it was on seeing her that they raised their spears and ordered her to stop, before Jake barked 'Silver clearance, Archimedes Eight-Seven-One. Now move!'

The soldiers obediently moved to the side as Aleera grabbed the door and pulled it open, not even registering the dull creak or one of the soldiers' protesting shout, before Jake shoved his way past, followed her in and told them to 'take it up with Khazahn.' She shot down the dank corridor and onto the blood-red dance floor, gasping for breath and, for the first time in her life, hoping, begging and praying…

Nothing.

The dance floor was empty. Every chair and table was still in the exact same position as when she had last been there. No Azrael, no Michael, no sign. She started to feel sick. The pit in her stomach opened up again and started crawling it way up her throat. Her stomach tightened in awful realisation.

Of course, she realised; it wouldn't be in here. Too obvious, too much chance of getting caught, there would have to be somewhere else around here.

'Where else is there in here?' she asked of Jake. 'Bathroom? Cellar?'

'Cellar,' Jake half-shouted immediately, bounding across the dance floor and around the bar. Aleera was right behind him as he pulled open the trapdoor that revealed a rickety set of wooden steps leading down into the cellar. Far enough underground that, as long as you had some way of keeping someone quiet, you could do whatever the hell you wanted and nobody would hear a thing.

She descended the steps at such as speed that it was a small miracle she didn't fall. As she urgently scanned her surroundings she noticed only the barest things: it was quiet, dusty, old kegs and vats, crates...

Nothing.

No, he was here. She was sure of it. Just think, think of what was there, where would he have hidden him? Come on, *think*...

Oh, yes.

One of the crates was against the opposite wall, its far end cracked and splintered as if it had been opened. As if something had been placed inside.

She reached the crate and didn't bother to try and pull it away; this was where claws were really useful. She extended the fingernails of her right hand and sliced through the wood at the top of the crate, before pulling sharply on the splintered planks until the nearest side was torn away.

'Michael,' she found herself gasping as she kneeled and fixed her vision on the shape inside the crate.

At least, the thing slumped against the inside of the crate appeared to be Michael. Any part of his skin not coated in dried blood was covered in multicoloured bruises, raw weeping puss or red, blistering wounds, their edges black and ashen. At the elbow of his right arm, the bone had broken through the skin, a dirty white spear jutting out of a bed of ripped flesh filling the crate with its gagging stench.

Aleera retched. For a second, black, hopeless doubt crossed her mind. Behind her, Jake stood frozen, his hands gripped tight around the old coin. Then, there came the dull, painful groan, the stifled cough in Michael's raw throat.

'He's alive,' Aleera breathed as her eyes started to pour of their own accord. 'Jake, he's alive!'

Jake shouted for the two men by the door to get a medic, while Aleera clambered into the crate and knelt down next to Michael and breathed a heavy sigh that held all the relief in the world.

13

Aleera had never liked hospitals; along with a few things she didn't like, she associated some rather unsavoury memories with them, but the main reason was that, generally speaking, a hospital was not a nice place to be, considering why people were normally there. The place was full of the smell of disinfectant and the faint noises of disease. But today, Aleera thought, there was nowhere she was more thankful for.

On reflection, while for a couple of days she hadn't quite felt herself, Aleera had been rather emotional during the past day; then again, considering the events of said day, she could probably be excused her indiscretions.

Michael was found. That was the important thing. Now, there was just Azrael to deal with- oh, and his little friend inside the Guild, whosoever that may be. Whoever had aided this in happening would definitely answer to her, especially now that she had finally managed to get a handle on herself.

She realised that she was trembling. Something sickly and fearful had taken a grip on her. Ok, so she *would* get a handle on herself as soon as she was certain that Michael would be fine. Her friend was in the hospital, she realised, and she wasn't even thinking about it. Good God, what was the matter with her?

Well, it helped to find things to focus on. It stopped her from-

Yes, go on, from what?

-From thinking about Michael; from falling into that pit in her stomach; from thinking about what she knew already. Her friend was in the hospital, and he was there because he was her friend. She turned her hands over in her lap. It felt like there was blood on them.

A set of doors further down the corridor opened. Sara ran through, bright eyes wide with panic. 'Aleera-'

'We found him,' Aleera told her breathlessly. 'He's alive.'

Sara almost collapsed. Her hand covered her mouth and she blurted out a burst of tears. 'Oh, thank God…' she nearly fell forward. Aleera caught her and she shook lightly in her arms. After a moment, she stepped back and wiped her eyes.

'Is he alright?' she asked desperately. The fear was still there in her shining eyes.

'I think so. He's still in there.'

Sara nodded slowly and dreadfully. She needed to know more, Aleera saw. She needed to put her mind to rest. So, what to tell her? She didn't know much... not much that would settle her, at least. Saying "the bone's sticking out of his arm and he's been carved up" wouldn't help. There was, of course, the most reassuring thing to her.

'Jake says he'll be alright,' she said. 'He's talking with the doctor about something.'

That seemed to help. They both sat down as Sara sniffed quietly.

'We didn't get Azrael,' she said guiltily. She realised that she hadn't thought about him until well after arriving at the hospital.

They sat in the hospital corridor for what seemed like a year, trying to talk and pass the time until they heard something. It was four a.m. when Jake finally emerged.

'He's fine,' he said before Aleera or Sara could say anything. 'The doctors are saying he'll make a full recovery, and we're going to transfer him to sickbay at the Guild as soon as he's well enough to be moved; it'll be more secure in case Azrael tries anything again.'

'Can we see him?' Sara asked.

Jake shook his head. 'He's still under anaesthetic. You two should head home.'

'I'm not-' Aleera started, but Jake interrupted.

'You're not going to get anything done sitting here. He's Ok, now go and get some sleep. I've arranged for the hospital to let you know as soon as he's ready for visitors.'

Something, Aleera could tell, was wrong. He wasn't looking at her; it was as if he felt guilty about something. There was something, she realised, that Jake didn't want her to see.

Something kept Aleera awake all night. That pit in her stomach, she realised, was still being singularly stubborn and refusing to budge. Michael was alive, she knew that, and he would recover, but Jake didn't want her to know something, at least not yet. It was certainly something bad; that was the only reason Jake would hide anything, especially about this of all things. By the time she woke up, she had realised what it was, and that pit was only widening.

Around midday, Jake had called her. Michael was still in the hospital; apparently Khazahn was arguing with some higher-ups who didn't see the call to move a civilian into the Guild's medical facilities, but hopefully it would be done soon. Michael was now awake, and in "surprising condition"- no doubt Jake's doing, she smirked- and had been deemed well enough to receive visitors.

She arrived at the hospital by half-twelve and met up with Sara again. The doctor, a tall, slim man with blonde hair and the hollow pleasantry of a practiced bedside manner, had told them that they could talk to Michael at last.

Aleera's heart was again beating too quickly for her liking, and her breath was shallow. Well, here it was, the moment of truth.

The doctor pulled back the curtain that surrounded the bed and allowed them in.

Aleera froze. Sara covered her mouth again and gave a shaking sob. There was that pit again. The sight in front of her was… unsettling… but, she realised, that wasn't why she wanted to retch.

'Oh, God…' Sara whispered, muffled by her hand.

Michael's right arm was held up by a frame, wrapped in a thick cast, and there was a ring of bandage around his forehead. That was far from the worst. A patch of skin on his left cheek was simply gone, replaced by raw, red flesh and gleaming white burns. A dull, stony patch of bone was visible somewhere near the chin. On the right side of his chin, a stringy scar reached from under his mouth to the side of his temple.

But somehow, it brought the tiniest smile that he still had enough energy to give a groaning reply of 'yeah, thanks for the compliment.'

'God, Michael,' Sara breathed as she stepped slowly toward the bed. 'What did he do to you?' she whimpered quietly.

''s not as bad as it looks,' Michael's voice sounded like a grating groan. 'Most of the burns, Jake says he can deal with, and I can get skin grafts for the bigger ones. It's just…' his eyes turned briefly to the right cheek. 'Well, never mind, huh? Jake says I should be fine.'

Michael gave a smile that was somehow made all the brighter by what surrounded it. Aleera discovered that she couldn't bring herself to return it; she could only look away as something tightened in her chest and made her want to throw up.

Aleera sat in the hospital corridor alone and silent. The rain was dying down outside, but the sky was still a sheet of overcast grey. She felt tired. The noise around her consisted not so much of voices as one low, monotonous buzz. The door of Michael's room was next to her. She couldn't go in. Once or twice, she'd tried, but her stomach would clench and something in her chest would stop her hand from taking hold of the door handle.

He wouldn't want to see her, she reasoned, not after she brought this on him. He wouldn't forgive her of that, and she didn't expect him to. She couldn't ask to be absolved after being responsible for this. She should probably have left a long time ago, but she couldn't quite bring herself to do that either.

Someone sat down next to her. She hadn't even heard the door open. 'Penny for your thoughts?' It was Katya, albeit minus her more unique features: the eyes were a soft green, and there were no traces of the cat-like ears, fingernails and canines. She always had to use that disguise in public. Aleera wondered how she coped with it.

'Just thinking,' she replied distantly. 'How's the disguise?' She wasn't quite sure why she said it.

'Same as ever,' Katya seemed unsure of just what response to give. 'Why?'

'Don't you ever get tired of it?'

'Why, does it look that bad?' Katya smiled.

'I mean having to use it,' Aleera explained.

Katya looked down at herself. 'Well, it's either this, or I walk around looking part-Garfield. I don't really go out much, anyway, except to the Guild.'

'Should you really have to use it?'

'If I didn't, everyone in here would be screaming and calling the cops. Or animal control,' Katya shrugged. Aleera found herself smiling slightly at the comment. 'Besides, it's nice to look human sometimes. At least you guys look the part.'

Aleera nodded, with another little touch of guilt. Well, it certainly put things in perspective.

'I know why you asked me that,' Katya said. Aleera looked quizzically at her? Did she? Well, that was convenient, because *she* didn't. 'Before you ask: no, being human wasn't much different.'

'I wonder sometimes,' Aleera confessed. 'You know, how "the other half" lives.' Hold on... hadn't she said... 'You said "being human".'

'I was. Back before I got this makeover and they stuck me with Jake... well, I say "human", it was only half. My dad was human, and he brought me up before...' she caught herself. 'Yeah. But... I'm in no hurry to change back,' she confessed. 'That's the thing about... well, after a while there's just not much to go back to. Besides,' she glanced back through the open doorway, 'He's all I've got nowadays.' She immediately turned back to Aleera. 'Of course, if you ever tell him that-'

'Naturally,' Aleera smiled. 'Thanks, Kat.' Katya was surprisingly good at cheering her up.

'No problem. Now if you're done "thinking", someone wants to talk to you.' She indicated inside the room.

Aleera hesitated. Her breath caught in her throat. 'I can't,' she declared.

Katya regarded her and sighed, 'Don't tell me you think-'

'Don't say it,' Aleera interrupted. 'Just don't.' She didn't want to hear it. She couldn't.'

'Aleera,' Katya started gently, and then became stronger in tone, 'that's just stupid.'

'I-'

'I don't blame you, Jake doesn't blame you, Sara doesn't blame you, and Michael doesn't blame you; if he did, he wouldn't want to talk to you. Now get in there.'

Aleera sighed in defeat. Jake, she believed, had once told her that he'd never had an argument with Katya and won.

She stood up and approached the door. Her chest quivered, and she took a deep breath to steel herself. She forced herself to enter the room. She became again aware of the steady, shrill beeping of heart monitors, the choked wheezing of respirators and the acrid smell of disinfectant.

Inside the curtain, Jake saw her approach and said something quietly to Sara. They both stood up and left, passing by her silently.

Inside, there was Michael, the same as before, like a bad dream, his arm held up in the cast and his face burned and carved. With her fingerprints all over it. Michael was leaned back on the pillow, eyes closed. He opened them as she sat down. He smiled. A flesh-coloured patch now covered the burn on his cheek.

'Hey, you.'

Aleera hesitated. 'Hi.' It was hard to find anything to say.

'Jake says I'll be transferred to Guild Medical by tonight. You should've seen the doctors,' he chuckled lightly. 'Couldn't believe how much better I got by this morning. Can't have anything to eat yet, which really sucks, but Jake says he can fix most of this. Most of what he can't do is because it's been too long since it happened, or something like that, but skin grafts can take care of it.'

Aleera's lips suddenly felt dry. 'That... that's good.'

'It's just the big stuff that...' Michael stopped, as if holding his breath. 'Well, that's why it's the big stuff.'

Aleera's eyes fixed on the scar that lined the side of his face. The pit in her stomach consumed everything. The compression inside her chest forced its way out. 'I'm sorry,' she finally managed to say.

'And don't start with that,' Michael lectured, turning his head to her. 'Jake said you'd probably start blaming yourself for this.'

'Don't say it,' Aleera said, even though it was too late. Before she could stop herself, it call just came pouring out. 'God, Michael, I'm so sorry,' she gasped. Her eyes started leaking.

'Stop that,' Michael said sternly. She couldn't quite recognise the look in his eyes, but for a second he looked pained. 'This wasn't your fault, alright? You didn't do this, so-' he fixed his clear green eyes on her. 'Don't think you did. Don't.'

Aleera opened her mouth to protest, but she didn't have time to say anything before Michael stopped her. 'I mean it. I don't give a shit how much time you spend beating yourself up because of the way you were born, because that's as much a pile of shit as this. Aleera, you're a good friend. You're loyal. And none of us gives a flying shit about the way you were born; if you hadn't found me, I'd still be in that crate with that sick bastard- hell, by now I'd be dead!'

'He did that because of-'

'He goes after demons. He'd have gotten to me before long. Now stop being stupid and tell me one thing.' He looked at her seriously.

'What is it?'

'Have you kicked the shit out of Ryan yet?'

Aleera paused for a moment. Then she couldn't quite help it; she burst out laughing. Michael laughed with her, and then winced painfully. 'Shit. "Laughter's the best medicine" my ass.'

'Should I call the doctor?' Aleera asked worriedly.

'Nah, I'll be fine.' Michael turned his head back. 'Jake tells me you did pretty good when I was missing; managed to figure out where I was.'

'I got lucky,' Aleera answered. The previous day was something she wouldn't want to talk about for a very long time.

'Y'know,' Michael admitted, 'I figured it'd be you that found me. You're a smart girl.'

Aleera sighed heavily. 'Thanks.'

'Look...' Michael made to turn to her, but then clearly decided otherwise. 'It's just-' he hesitated breathlessly. Suddenly, he looked anxious. 'When I was- I mean- well... it makes you think. So I was thinking, after I got here, well... thing is...' again he stopped, 'ah, forget it.'

'You can tell me,' Aleera insisted.

'It's fine, just- just this- thing. It's not important.'

'Whatever it is-'

'No, really; don't worry about it,' Michael repeated. He took another breath. 'No. Aleera, I- I wanted to just-' He seemed to hold his breath for a second.

Then, finally, Aleera realised. Being the attractive half-succubus she was, she'd seen it in any number of boys, and a surprising number of girls. 'Oh.' She bit her bottom lip. The fact of it was that she had almost completely forgotten about this; it really did pale in comparison to what had happened in between then and now, but now that it had been dealt with, it looks like she would have to face the music.

'Yeah, like I said, we don't need to talk about that, it-'

'Michael.' Aleera interrupted. She needed to clear the air, just get this dealt with and focus on other things. At least, hopefully, she could make matters that little bit less complicated. 'I-'

'No,' Michael insisted, 'look, you're a friend, Aleera; you're a good friend. I've known you for a long time. I'm not gonna throw that away, because- because that's what you are, and I know, it just sounds stupid, but after this, after what happened,' he stammered unevenly, 'I'm not gonna say "we should date" or shit like that, but- I just wanted to set things straight.'

Aleera straightened up. 'I'm sorry,' she sighed, 'look- I should explain something...'

'I know, I know, it's not gonna happen-'

'Not that,' Aleera said insistently, 'It's... I should tell you something,' she said. It really hadn't ever come up, now that she thought of it. So far she'd been lucky, but her luck did seem to be running awfully dry lately.

'What?' Michael asked, finally turning to her. His eyes widened a little. 'You really are-'

'I really am what?'

'Well, a couple of people around school said that- well- to be honest, they were saying you were gay.'

Aleera chuckled despite herself. 'God, that is so human.' Honestly, they loved their quaint little categories, didn't they?

'What is?' Michael asked.

Aleera stopped her bout of humour. 'The thing is- well actually, I am-' well, she might as well tell him, 'I'm actually bisexual.' She may have sounded like she said that too easily, but she was a sex demon, after all. She could listen to the most lewd of stories, and while anyone else would turn bright red, she wouldn't bat an eyelid. The bisexuality, specifically, was natural to her- it was hard to imagine confining herself to a single sex. So little choice.

Michael's eyes were like saucers. 'Seriously?'

'Yes.'

'So you like-'

'Yes.'

'As well as-'

'Yes.'

'Wow.'

'Is that a problem?' Aleera asked. She did her level best to keep her apprehension out of her tone. As she often reflected, there were exceedingly few people whose opinions she cared for, but Michael was one of them.

'No,' Michael said hastily, 'No, it's just- hell of an image,' he said under his breath with a slight chuckle.

'What is?'

'Y'know… you and Sara.' Michael almost seemed to struggle to say it.

'What?'

'Well, a lot of people said-'

'No,' Aleera said quickly- maybe a little too quickly, actually, 'no, we're not.'

'Oh.' Michael paused. Neither of them, it seemed, was entirely sure of what to say next. 'So, uh…'

'The thing I wanted to tell you,' Aleera continued, 'is that…' she hesitated. 'I'm half-succubus.'

Michael's eyes, if it were possible, widened even further.

'That's why I'm bi,' Aleera explained. 'And... with the pheromones... it also explains...'

'Yeah,' Michael admitted, shame-faced. 'But...'

Aleera looked at him curiously.

'...what do those things- the pheromones- actually do.'

'Oh.' Aleera's eyes lidded slightly and proceeded with caution. 'They cause attraction in people over long-term exposure.'

Michael took a nervous breath. 'How long-term?'

Aleera paused to think. 'Well, I'm only half-succubus, so probably a couple of months.'

'Oh,' Michael said, suddenly tense again. 'It's just that- well- you remember when you moved here?' Aleera nodded slowly. 'A few weeks after that...'

This time, Aleera was genuinely surprised. If it had only been a few weeks, then maybe...'

'I mean, I just thought you were...' Michael gave a nervous chuckle, 'kinda hot... but after a while.. I- I mean- like I said, you're a good friend. You're loyal, you're kind, you stand up for people...'

For a second, Aleera stopped hearing him. She realised that, *now*, she was starting to blush. If what he was saying was true, then maybe... she needed to think. Needed to calm herself down.

'Well,' she said breathlessly, 'I guess I should- I should go.' She didn't even wait to see Michael's reaction before she stood up and made for the door, everything he'd said already rolling over in her mind- but she already knew that, however she thought of it, the truth of it was...

'Oh, what the hell,' she finally said out loud. She couldn't stop the excited grin from spreading across her face as she walked brazenly up the hospital bed, leaned over, flicked her hair back and grabbed Michael's lips with her own in a fierce, hungry kiss. Eyes closed, she listened pleasantly to his stunned gasp as his lips slackened, running her hand through his short hair as their tongues danced over each other. It must have been at least a minute before they came apart, both gasping for breath. They each smiled, and Aleera gave Michael another quick peck on the lips before leaning over to his ear. 'Just wait until you get out of here,' she whispered heatedly into his ear. She stood back up, flashed Michael a coy smile, and walked out with her most seductive sway in her hips and enjoyed the stunned look on his face as she left.

As she walked out of the ward and back into the corridor, she allowed herself a moment to catch her breath. Wow. Had that really just happened? It had been almost surreal, so long after her last relationship, to throw caution to the wind and finally... well, french somebody's brains out. She licked her lips; yes, it was certainly going to be fun, having a boyfriend again. Maybe she'd treat herself to a spoonful of honey to celebrate... although, of course, now she had something far more satisfying.

Then, she cringed, remembering what still had to be done. She needed to talk to Sara, and with this added to her thoughts, that would, if anything, be even more awkward.

'Aleera.' The female voice that addressed her was sharp, prim and decidedly angry. Rising from the chair was a Sudanese woman in a sharp-cut black suit and half-moon glasses, with her hair tied back tight.

'Yes?' Aleera replied, noticing how angry the woman looked.

'I should have known,' the woman hissed venomously. 'Well, I hope you're proud of yourself.'

'Pardon?'

'Do you have any idea what you've done to my son?' the woman spat.

Ah. Michael's mother. That explained her mood.

'Let me make this clear,' the woman said viciously, but with tears in her eyes, 'I have seen what has happened to my son because of you people-'

'Excuse me?' Aleera interrupted.

'Michael has had enough problems with *that* side of his family, and now this. Do you think this is fun? Do you think it's alright to do this to people?'

Something inside Aleera flashed with rage. 'I did not-' she was cut off when Michael's mother slapped her round the face. Her cheek stung.

'Don't you dare,' Mrs. Prince hissed. 'Don't you dare try to justify yourself after this. After what you sick-creatures-'

'I'm half-demon,' Aleera replied sharply, changing her eyes back after realising that they had turned vivid red.

'Excuse me?' The woman looked perplexed.

'I'm half-demon,' Aleera repeated. 'The same as Michael.'

'This would never have happened,' Mrs. Prince seethed hysterically, 'if you hadn't been around Michael.'

'*Mrs. Prince,*' Aleera kept a savage snarl out of her voice as best she could, 'I think you should go and see how your son's recovery is going.' She stepped past the woman, with no interest in listening to the remainder of her rant. The woman's frustration, and certainly her anger, was understandable, given the situation.

For all its thrills, her… discussion… with Michael had distracted her from that issue. Now, though, the rage and shame were pushing their way back into her mind, and the greatest, most sickening rage was reserved for herself. She had always known, in some way, that her bloodline was going to come back to haunt her, but she had never quite *known*, never prepared herself; never been prepared for something like this. Michael had been made to pay just for being around her, and if him, then it could be Jake, or Sara, or Katya, or Lilith… how many more would Azrael hunt down?

The answer, she swore to herself, was "none". She was going to find Azrael, and he was going to pay for this. Oh, just wait.

The young woman fell shaking to the side of the dumpster, cold and painful, her hands trembling as she pulled the needle out of her handbag and cursed the moment she'd ever touched the stuff. When she tried hard enough, she could almost remember what it felt like to feel the high instead of just this, just the low all the time, the desperation, the need to know when the next fix would come and the fear that it might never be there.

She made the preparations as best she could, listening to the pounding rhythm coming from inside the nightclub as something to focus on besides the shakes, and was finally holding the needle above her arm…

'*Fhoa!*'

She felt herself be pulled back, screaming like a child as the needle fell from her fingers and she felt the fingers around her throat.

'Was it you?' the man snarled as he wrapped strong hands around her throat. 'You did it, you little skank! You narced on me, you-'

'I didn't, Jack,' she sobbed, choking, 'I swear, please, I swear to God I didn't-'

Her hands found the lid of the trashcan. It struck his head hard and fast. Then again. And again. She howled like an animal and struck until all that was left as a twisted metal lump.

Finally the man scrambled away, snarling like a wounded rat, and she collapsed into a sobbing mess, scrambling for the needle she needed.

Her hand was on it.

A boot was on her hand.

A pair of gauntlets pulled a white hood over a bald head, and plucked a gleaming dagger from a belt.

'Please,' she whimpered, 'please...'

Hands reached down toward her.

'May God have mercy on your soul,' the voice snarled, 'though the path you chose to follow leads not to him.'

14

The medical room of the Guild's New York City headquarters was, of course, a necessity. For a law enforcement employee, mundane or supernatural, an injury in the line of duty was a risk that came with the job. In exceptional circumstances, however, they were also available for use by civilians whose personal safety was threatened. Consequently, Michael had recently found himself to be on the list of patients. The only downside was that the local division of the Guild was noticeably understaffed, and so the secondary forensic analyst of D-Unit was, by way of her certified medical genius, also the Chief Medical Officer of the unit. And so Tomoko Shinju was seated next to the prone Michael, checking over the charts. Her forensics experience also allowed her to gauge his injuries, and she had prepared a report on what had been done to him and when, since in this case the evidence was more… fresh.

She popped the lid back on her pen and gave Michael a brief smile; the uncertain kind of smile that came from a woman not used to dealing with young people, even though it wasn't so many years since she had been one herself.

'You'd make a good nurse, y'know that?' Michael chuckled weakly. Tomoko glanced up. 'You'd look good in the uniform.'

'Watch it,' Tomoko warned jokingly, 'you'd better not let your ladyfriend overhear that.'

'Well, I gotta do something in here. S'pose I should be glad this isn't an autopsy,' Michael confessed a little more darkly.

'Well, we're done here for now,' Tomoko declared, putting the chart back. 'You'll be fine.'

'Got lucky, huh?' Michael sighed. 'Good thing Aleera knows Jake, I guess.'

'He knows what he's doing,' Tomoko admitted. She'd never had that much to do with Jake, only enough to know that he was what those working in the Guild referred to as an 'occasional employ'. He could be trusted, she knew that, but he wasn't exactly a professional. He'd always seemed a little too easy-going around authority, including Khazahn and all the way up to the High Council, and had always appeared to enjoy bending- or outright breaking- the rules a little too much. 'Anyway, you just get some rest,' she told Michael.

Michael nodded back, wincing at a slight pain on the side of his face. Tomoko picked up her things, closed the curtain and walked away. The rest of the medical station was surprisingly empty; it had been slow lately, other than the matter that D-Unit was presently assigned to.

'You finished with the kid?' Harry was near the door.

'Just now,' Tomoko affirmed.

'Brave kid,' Harry sighed, crossing his arms and glancing ruefully at the curtain. 'I heard him just as you were finishing up; he's been through God-knows-what, and he's still dropping bad pickup lines and catching dates.'

'Well, they only think with one body part at that age,' Tomoko pointed out shrewdly, 'and that was still attached.'

'Lucky for him,' Harry winced.

'Professionalism, doctor,' Tomoko smirked. 'What brings you down here?'

'I could use you in the lab; something turned up, and I need you to check the Central Park victim to see if it's a constant.'

'You've got something?' Tomoko asked with raised eyebrows. 'You're kidding.'

'Pray I'm not.' Five days in, they needed whatever they could get.

'Define "something",' Tomoko pressed as they both set off for the lab. 'Should we be telling Khazahn?'

'Depends how lucky we get. Fingers crossed that we're about to bust this thing wide open. Bet you dinner?'

Tomoko paused for a moment as he opened the lab doors. 'Come again?'

'If we get this right,' Harry explained as he rounded the autopsy table, 'I'll buy you dinner to celebrate.'

Tomoko found a smile creeping its way onto her lips. What the hell... 'If we don't find anything,' she replied, 'I'll buy *you* dinner to make up for it.'

Harry chuckled. 'Works for me; now let's see what we've got here.'

Aleera found Sara in their usual meeting place of a weekend, the oft-visited diner, and though she'd never described herself as superstitious, hoped to make of this a sign that the lunacy of the past few days was winding down. Sara had just finished a small lunch, and apparently hadn't expected to see her there.

'I didn't see much of you today,' Sara said quietly.

'I went straight home after the hospital,' Aleera answered as she sat down. 'I heard you'd gone.' After leaving Michael, she'd looked briefly for Sara, but Jake had told her that she'd already left. Once she was home herself, she'd decided to see if Sara was in the usual place. That was at about five p.m. 'I thought you might be here.'

'So how's Michael doing?'

'Good. They moved him to the Guild an hour or two after I left.'

'Good.' Sara's expression became distant and her hand moved to the silver cross. At some point that heaviness had returned to the air. 'I, uh… I heard you two talking.' She bit her tongue and tightened her grip on the cross.

'Oh.' Aleera closed her hands over each other and looked down at the table. Her mouth suddenly felt dry. 'How much?'

Sara took a second to answer. 'Not much.'

Aleera sighed. 'Sorry.'

'For what? It's not like you're doing anything wrong.' Sara still hadn't looked at her.

'Sara,' Aleera said with more urgency than she'd have liked, 'if Michael and I are a couple…'

'You're going to say we're still friends.'

'More or less,' Aleera admitted. 'The thing is…' well, the subject was essentially brought up already. Might as well. 'Sara…' she swallowed a lump in her throat. 'Listen- are you…'

Sara appeared to take a sharp breath and hold it. Her cheeks darkened. Her right hand was wrapped tight around the cross.

'I'm sorry,' Aleera said quietly. It was almost a whisper.

'It's not your fault,' Sara said quickly.

Aleera bit her lip. 'Actually… it is.'

Sara looked up at her with the closest her shining eyes ever came to incredulity. 'How is it your fault?'

'How much did you hear?' Aleera asked. That tight feeling inside her chest was back. She felt breathless.

'Just that you two are a couple now.'

'Did you hear what I told Michael?'

'No.' Sara sounded just a tiny bit hurt.

'I was going to tell you as well.' Aleera tried to reassure her. 'The thing is, Sara… I know you don't… I know that you're straight.'

'Except when it comes to you,' Sara said quietly and guiltily.

'There's a reason for that,' Aleera said softly. 'I don't tell anyone about this, because…' well, this was it. 'Because people don't like succubae.'

Sara's mouth opened slightly. Her bright eyes widened. 'You're-'

'Half,' Aleera explained. 'So that's why…'

'Oh.' Sara blushed hotly. 'Well… I fell pretty stupid,' she half-laughed.

'It's not your fault. Pheromones.'

'Can you-' Sara paused. 'Can you turn it off?'

'No,' Aleera sighed apologetically. 'I wish I could. It'd make school a lot more bearable.'

'So you and Michael-' Sara caught herself. 'No. Sorry. I shouldn't have said that.'

'It's alright.' And it was; the poor girl had been worried sick for a week, followed by this. A slip of the tongue was perfectly understandable. 'But no… there's more than…' she stopped herself. 'I sound like something out of a bad movie, don't I?'

'So,' Sara asked, 'are we Ok?'

Aleera took a deep breath. 'I don't know. Are we?'

Sara released the cross. 'Yeah. At least- I hope so,' she smiled weakly.

Aleera smiled back. Well, that wasn't so bad.

'So,' Sara said after a while, 'you're not part-dragon as well, are you?'

Aleera smiled slightly. 'No, just that.'

Sara sighed. 'You know…' she took a sip from a milkshake that still sat on the table. 'I don't know that much about you.'

Aleera pursed her lips thoughtfully. 'I suppose not,' she confessed.

Sara steeled herself up for a long moment. 'You don't talk about it much.'

'I don't,' Aleera replied distantly. It was true; she didn't overly want to. It wasn't exactly a pleasant topic of conversation.

'If you want to talk about it,' Sara said awkwardly.

Aleera sighed. She didn't. She *really* didn't. She never talked about her life. The only person who knew all of it was Lilith, and that's wasn't because she'd been told; she'd just been there for it.

Then again, things had been changing for her lately. She'd admitted one side of her heritage, so why not the other? Maybe it would even do her some good.

Wait, was she seriously considering this? Just blurting things out like she'd been doing recently?

'How long do you have?' her mouth asked without her permission. 'It's a long story.'

Sara glanced at the clock. 'I have to be home in ten minutes.'

'How much do you want me to tell you?'

Sara lidded her eyes. 'Everything?'

'Then I'll have to tell you another day,' Aleera admitted. Sara looked a little disappointed. 'It's just… not easy,' she said. Not more of this spitting things out so easily?

'I see.' Sara said.

'I can meet you back here tomorrow,' Aleera offered. Wait, what? What was she thinking?

'Promise?'

'Promise.'

Sara smiled. 'Ok. Well, I should get home.' She stood up. 'See you tomorrow. And…' Aleera looked up at her. She faltered. 'Thanks.'

'For what?'

'For… still being friends.' Sara gave one more smile before walking out of the diner.

Aleera sighed and leaned back. What in hell's name had she gotten herself into now? There's a reason you don't tell people this, you foolish girl, she snapped at herself. Who in their right mind was going to willingly associate with the closest thing the real world had to the devil's daughter?

Her phone suddenly rang in her pocket. She answered it, and on the other end of the line was Jake, sounding the most ecstatic he had done all week.

'Aleera,' Jake near-cheered, 'do I have news for you!'

Considering that the forensics department of the Guild's New York headquarters were strictly "employees only", Aleera could be forgiven for not having spent much time there- she'd hardly ever been in the building except for meetings with a psychiatrist, and of course a few days after her father's death.

Jake had only told her that Harry and Tomoko had found something helpful- very helpful, judging by his voice. And Harry and Tomoko, being D-Unit's forensic specialists, were of course working on what the unit had apparently termed the "Azrael killings". The thought of such a thing, of course, was a very exciting one; it meant a move against Azrael, rather than reacting to his moves so constantly.

On the directions Jake had given her, she arrived at the forensic lab, where she found the two doctors, Jake, Katya and Makian waiting for her.

'We were wondering when you'd get here,' Jake smiled.

'You said you found something,' Aleera said. Probably not that courteous, she reminded herself, but curiosity outweighed social mores for the time being.

'Oh, and find something we did,' Harry beamed. 'Take a look.' Tomoko handed her a small plastic bag labelled "evidence".

Aleera inspected the contents. Tiny, yellow-brown flakes of... 'Dust?'

'Dust,' Tomoko confirmed. 'Harry found it on- of all places- Michael's wounds.'

'He *was* in a nightclub cellar,' Aleera pointed out.

'But none of the others were attacked there,' Jake pointed out sagely. 'Probably, like the others, Michael was just left there for you to find.'

'The sawdust is contaminated with something else,' Harry explained. 'See how it's a little discoloured?'

'So what was in it?'

'Well, once we knew what we were looking for, we found traces on the other bodies,' Harry continued. 'First, after what Jake found out from the Spirit-Trace, we found traces of salt- as in, salt water. But what we found in the sawdust, we then found in the other bodies. Only tiny traces, but when we knew what to look for, we found it: ink. The kind of ink used to print playing cards.'

Aleera saw where this led. 'Can you trace it?'

'Already did. There's an old factory on the Hudson, not too far upriver from Pentagram.'

'You think that's where it is?'

'The place is disused,' Tomoko explained, 'and according to our police liaisons, someone fitting this Azrael guy's description was seeing around there the nights before our bodies turned up. Which means…'

'…We've found the bastard,' Harry grinned.

'Makian talked Khazahn into bringing D-Unit down on the place,' Jake beamed. 'You in?'

11 p.m. Aleera glanced at her watch as her dark eyes squinted through the darkness.

'Status?' Khazahn hissed to the air. Aleera couldn't hear the reply. The helmet of the Guild Soldier was certainly a useful invention; communication devices were installed that allowed for quiet, completely-concealed communication between officers.

Aleera, Makian, Khazahn and Jake were stood to the side of the old, rusty gate that led into the dilapidated old factory, complete with crumbling walls, a semi-intact roof and smashed windows. A dull breeze blew in over the waterfront, and the moon barely managed to break through the thick lumps of cloud. Again, there were no stars.

'Everybody's in position,' Khazahn affirmed. There's only one other exit, and we've got two men on it. Some of my best.'

Aleera glanced down at herself. She didn't overly like the Guild uniform she was currently garbed in. It provided protection, true enough, but she could take care of herself, courtesy of a lifetime of self-defence lessons. The trade-off, of course, was that her back was completely covered. No wings, then; a shame, as that would be a considerable advantage. She'd excused herself from the gloves, as her claws were an undeniable boon in close quarters.

'We're just going to walk in through the front door,' Aleera observed.

'Something like that,' Jake nodded. Sparks danced reflexively across his hands.

'Should she be here?' Makian asked uncertainly, referring to Aleera.

'You said you wanted her in,' Jake replied harshly. 'Let's just do this.'

'All hands, engage radio contact,' Khazahn whispered. The side of Aleera's own helmet crackled, followed by affirmative responses from herself, Jake- the only one not wearing a helmet- Makian and two others that weren't familiar.

'Alpha,' Khazahn motioned to Jake and Aleera, 'move in.'

As she, Jake, Makian and Khazahn dashed toward the front exit, Aleera tightened her grip around the Guild staff in her hand and thought over the situation, just once. Unfamiliar territory; Azrael had that advantage. They, on the other hand, had Jake and a demon very eager to stab her claws into Azrael's chest after what he'd done to

Michael. She felt the anticipation buzz in her chest, tempered with excitement. She was tired of reacting to Azrael's moves. Time to make him dance to her tune.

Jake approached the door first, inching his way in. He stopped and raised his hand. 'Listen.'

There were voices inside. Shouts, conversation, someone shouting loudest... voices, Aleera realised. Dreadful realisation began to creep up on her. Voic*es*. Plural. Well, this was certainly an unexpected obstacle. Oh, Azrael, you clever bastard, he just kept on changing the rules of the game.

Khazahn cursed under his breath. 'How many?'

Jake set his jaw. 'About two-dozen. How many do we have again?'

'Five.'

'Well, this got buttholled pretty quick,' Makian observed. 'Now what?'

'Call backup,' Khazahn instructed.

'Do you know how long it'll take to get enough for *this*?' Jake hissed. 'They could leave any second.'

'They'll come back.'

Jake paused, lifting a finger to his lips. 'Listen.'

The one, strong voice echoed from inside the factory. The others fell silent.

'Tonight, brothers, our faith is tested,' it shouted. 'Tonight, we are discovered!'

Jake paled. 'Wow,' Makian commented, '"shit" just doesn't cover this, huh?'

'They will hound us for our holy work!' the voice boomed. 'They will persecute us for doing what they are only too afraid to do themselves! But we are close now, brothers! Closer than we may ever be again to burning the devil's seed!' Herself, Aleera noted. Seemed she was right with her fanatic idea. They were talking about *her*. About killing her for the way she was born... not exactly a new idea, but this still wasn't a pleasant thing to hear. 'She will burn in hell with the other sinners, she will curse herself for eternity and drown in unsatisfied, foul succubus lust!' Yup. Definitely her. Shame about the "unsatisfied" part, but now that she and Michael were a couple...

Focus, Aleera.

'Hunt,' Khazahn's voice buzzed in her ear, 'This is Hound-One. Request back up to collect point; numerous targets. Repeat, numerous targets. Request at least thirty, over.'

The voice buzzed back: 'Hound-One, please repeat.'

'Request at least thirty men, back-up. Over.'

There was a second or two of static. 'Confirmed.'

'E.T.A.?'

'11:35 hours.'

'Half an hour?' Makian hissed.

'They'll be long gone by then,' Jake whispered.

'Can you teleport them?'

'Not that many,' Jake shook his head. 'Not unless you want them unconscious. Or inside-out.'

'Ideas?' Aleera whispered.

'Not one,' Jake shook his head.

Khazahn stepped back, stroking his chin in thought. 'Jake, you can teleport two, right?'

Jake looked up at him, realisation crossing his face.

'Undercover,' Khazahn recommended. 'Can you do it?'

'I can manage a disguise well enough,' Jake nodded.

'Same,' Khazahn confirmed.

'I can handle invisibility,' Aleera offered.

'And there's your familiar,' Khazahn addressed Jake.

'Don't even think about it,' Jake barked. 'She's not a soldier.' He turned toward Aleera. 'Neither is she.'

'We need everyone we can get,' Khazahn reminded him.

'The two of us will do undercover,' Jake replied. 'Aleera and Makian, you two keep an eye out for the backup.'

'I'm coming in,' Aleera declared.

'*Don't* argue,' Jake snapped. 'Just do it. *ThraioPhouxSola*.' The air around himself and Khazahn warped, and was in a heartbeat replaced by the appearance of two figures draped in white robes that resembled Azrael's. 'I mean it,' one of the hoods said. 'Stay here.' The white spectres turned and moved into the darkness.

A slow moment passed. A chilling breeze washed over from the river.

'So,' Makian started, looking away at the street. 'Here we are, then…' he trailed off as he turned round and saw an empty space. He hadn't even heard Aleera whisper the incantation.

Stay behind, Jake said. Don't argue, he said. Honestly, it was as though he didn't know her at all.

Invisibility was a wonderful thing, she reflected as she passed silently through the open doorway and crouched soundlessly behind an old piece of machinery.

And then she saw what was there.

There were definitely at least twenty of them, all gathered around the figure that stood in the centre on top of a crate, arms outstretched. She was put oddly in mind of the self-appointed preachers she'd seen on television.

She was behind enemy lines now, she suddenly realised. So many of them, dozens all baying for her blood. If they knew she was there, they'd drag her in there and do what they'd done to those women. And yet, they didn't know. They had no idea that their quarry observed them, silent and unseen. Rather exciting, really.

'Soon, my children,' he bellowed, 'the tainted blood will be spilled!' He turned to something that hung on a thick rope from the rafters. In the low light, she could make out the shapes of straw-filled limbs, as a pair of white figures raised themselves up and shook thick, square cans. What she could only take to be gasoline was thrown over the figure. 'And the devil child...' he pulled something out of his robe. The spark of the flame flashed in the darkness. '...will burn.'

The effigy was engulfed in flame, spreading across the entire body as the limbs and torso crackled and sparked. 'And now...' he descended from the crate. As he pulled down his hood, Aleera focused her vision on his face.

It was him. Oh, of *course* it was him. Just as the voice had suggested, now she was sure.

Her fingertips twitched of their own accord. The claws begged to be let out. Her eyes flashed red.

One of the white shapes handed him a crowbar. He lifted it, slamming it into the crate and prying away one side.

The shape that fell out gave a muffled scream. Aleera's eyes widened as she craned her head out to get a better view. Cast orange by the burning effigy, the naked female figure was dragged out by the hair as Azrael threw her to the other spectres.

'Another,' Azrael snarled, climbing back up onto the crate. 'Do with her what you will, brothers. Purge the sin! Force out the soul of the devil!'

Aleera's blood boiled. The red mist descended. Oh, she knew, she knew *exactly* what was about to happen to the young woman. The tiniest bit of fear crept up as she recalled that she also knew exactly what it was going to be like for her.

No. No, she couldn't just stand here. Not while, whoever that was, the young woman suffered the very deepest pain.

The white figures crowded round and closed in. The muffled screams only became louder as they descended. Aleera gritted her teeth.

There was suddenly a hand on her shoulder. She spun round to see the hood that hissed 'what the hell are you doing in here?' Khazahn, as she recognised the voice instantly. Of course: it was Jake maintaining both disguises. That left Khazahn free to make use of Third-Eye.

'Do you know what they're going to do?' Aleera whispered sharply. 'Where's Jake?'

Khazahn looked over his shoulder at the empty space behind him. '…God damnit!'

As the figures gathered, there was a sudden shout. One figure, apart from the others, shimmered and vanished, replaced by Jake's true shape as the wave of power shot through the air. Every figure in its line was sent reeling through the air as Azrael from his elevated position gave a shout of furious indignation. At least a dozen were sent flying into the opposite wall with bone-breaking force.

Azrael, above, pulled out the dagger and turned it in his hand.

Well, that was it for subtlety, Aleera decided. Abandoning the invisibility spell and, with a shout of "*ThuraiShiahl*", sent the wave of force slamming into Azrael and hurling him from his makeshift podium.

"Damnit, Jake," Khazahn seethed, before shouting "Get us out of here! Now!"

Jake cast a last glance at the recuperating figures, then grabbed hold of the girl, shouted 'Go for the exit!' to Khazahn, and finally shouted '*Appiras*'. He and the girl both vanished into the collapsing air. Khazahn's disguise vanished instantly.

'Come on,' he hissed to Aleera, immediately making for the door. Aleera's main reason for ignoring him was that Azrael was making his way across the factory floor toward her.

'Children of the sword!' he howled over the shouting hoods, 'the devil-child profanes our holy place with her presence!' he approached, turning the dagger in his hand and tightening his grip.

'Oh, shut up,' Aleera sighed as he made to grab her. She hoisted herself up the side of the old piece of machinery and round the corner; even if she did have a solid grasp of offensive and defensive magic, there was nothing quite like a good size-eight to the side of someone's head. Azrael fell as the tip of her shoe caught his temple, a flail of white cloak as Aleera grabbed his wrist and squeezed, the dagger dropping from his fingers.

There were furious howls from the white-draped figures as they tore towards Aleera, shouting 'slay it' among other such sentiments. For a second, Aleera found herself ignoring them as she pulled Azrael to his feet and kneed him in the stomach. Azrael was a problem that she had spent several days trying to find a way of eliminating. Her claws sounded ideal right now.

Unfortunately, the rest of the howling humans running at her seemed to take a dim view to that solution.

The air behind Aleera rushed as she kicked Azrael, sending him flailing back into the crowd like a white bowling ball.

'Aleera!' Jake shouted from behind her, 'what the hell are you doing?'

'There are six of these idiots close enough to try anything,' Aleera replied as her fingernails lengthened and darkened into the familiar claws. Beyond that, it was just a question of whether the back of the Guild uniform could hold back rapidly-spreading demon wings (it couldn't). 'I was hitting those numbers when I was thirteen.' Demonstratively, she expertly parried a blow from the nearest one, swinging him into the path of another's clawing hands before another grabbed her only to receive a sharp blow to his nose from Aleera's forehead.

Aleera, by her own admission, thought of herself as a rational person; when you weren't stable, you had to settle for rational. Rationality would normally cause her to take heed of the number of white cloaks presently baying for her blood, but the satisfying sound of the breaking nose, and the scream that came from a set of claws stabbing through the soft flesh of an arm, spoke to that dark place inside her far too loudly to be ignored. Here, at last, was that chance to really cut loose, and she was loving every second of it. A perfect way to vent those "borderline" tendencies without hurting anyone who didn't deserve it.

Azrael rose again. The blade glinted in the air. Not really a fair fight, Aleera thought as she flexed her claw-tipped fingers. He only had *one* weapon.

Typically, just as she was beginning to enjoy herself, Jake shouted '*Appiras,*' the teleportation spell kicked in, the world whirled and tumbled, and the next thing she knew they were on a rooftop a block away and her stomach felt like it was ready to empty itself via her oesophagus.

'Did you have to do that?' she muttered. The adrenaline was still rushing in her bloodstream, her heart was still pounding, and overall she hadn't felt ready to cease her stress-relief just yet. Irritating, to say the least.

'There were *twenty* of them,' Jake barked.

'I could have reduced it to at least fourteen, if you'd given me a few minutes.

'Yeah- before they ripped you to pieces.'

'You sent at least twelve of them flying with one spell.'

'*Aleera, will you calm the fuck down!*' Jake shouted. Wow. She hadn't known Jake swear much- if at all. She consciously withdrew her claws and wings and returned her eyes to their usual colour. She noticed that she once again felt like a child being lectured by her father, and once again that was a confusing realisation.

'Sorry,' she found herself saying meekly.

'This,' Jake sighed angrily, 'was a nightmare. Khazahn's gonna go insane once he finds me.'

'He doesn't know where we are?'

'Considering how badly this went, and that he was already tempted to tie me to an anchor and go fishing, I'm giving him some time to calm down. Preferably a year or two.'

'So what now?' Aleera asked bitterly, turning her eyes back in the direction of the waterfront.

'They'll have long-since cleared out by the time the backup gets here,' Jake muttered. 'Since they've got someone in the Guild on their side, and they've been smart enough to keep out of our way so far, they're not gonna be stupid enough to come back.'

In short, on a colossal disaster scale of one-to-ten, this had been somewhere in the vicinity of eleven.

Still, at least she'd finally made a move against Azrael- even if it had been a failed one. Then again, she suddenly realised...

'What about the girl?'

'Dropped her off at Guild Medical. Hopefully, we can find out something new on these bastards. Now,' he looked out over Manhattan, 'we know Khazahn's pissed, but we still have his boss.'

Oh yes. Chara. Maybe a twelve, then.

Aleera took a last glance in the direction of the warehouse. Azrael would probably have teleported himself out already. Again, the odds were tipped in his favour, and with this matter involving the Guild, she still didn't know what the rules of the game were.

Check.

16

'I'll say it if nobody else will,' Makian announced, 'epic clusterfuck.'

'Not the time, Makian,' Tomoko observed dryly as she emerged from the forensic lab, Harry in tow. She seemed to be trying to avoid looking at anybody. She shuddered.

'The girl's in Medical,' Harry informed them. His skin was pale, ashen. He seemed breathless. 'I.D.'d as Sharon Cooper; Pentagram call girl. We had to sedate her. Looks like he meant for us to find her some time tomorrow morning.'

'Think she can tell us anything?' Khazahn asked. He, Makian, Jake and Aleera had assembled at the Guild Headquarters shortly after the botched (mildly speaking) raid. Katya had also joined them, as arranged with Jake.

Harry shook his head grimly. 'She won't be in a condition to much of anything for a while- physically, maybe, but not-' he shook and bit his tongue. 'She won't talk.' He turned his gaze up to meet the group's. '*Ever.*'

Aleera felt a quiver in her stomach. It was Makian who piped up with 'why?'

Harry took a deep breath, but seemed to have trouble saying anything. 'Does anyone here know,' he began tensely, 'what Kudra did to stop his victims talking if they were ever found?' Aleera felt the colour drain from her cheeks.

'Shit,' Katya shivered.

Tomoko nodded grimly. 'H-he cut out her tongue.' She bit her shaking bottom lip. 'She was just lying there,' she whispered under her breath, 'just-just screaming.'

'Shit,' Makian mumbled. 'Shit, we know what else those psychos were about to do.'

Aleera tried not to think about it. First that, then what came after was worse. She knew what her father would do, especially to women. Only a few survived him. They always wished they hadn't.

'Will she live?' Jake asked.

'If you can call that living,' Harry shuddered. 'Wasn't just the tongue- they carved up her breasts, one of her eyes...' he covered his mouth and retched.

'So, could this've gone much worse?' Makian asked dryly.

'One way,' Jake answered. To one side, the door opened and Eighth Division Commander Chara stepped through. 'Thank you and goodnight.'

'*Someone*,' Chara stressed only that single word, leaving the rest of the sentence level, 'owes me a phenomenally good explanation of what happened tonight.'

'We didn't have sufficient forces for the number of hostiles in that building,' Khazahn claimed. 'There wasn't time to wait for backup. We did manage four arrests.'

'So you undertook an unauthorised undercover job,' Chara declared icily. 'And according to the two other men who were stationed with you, somebody fired off a spell, and you all know the rest. My question,' his pitch still hadn't changed a bit, 'is this: who cast the spell?'

There was a moment of heavy silence. Jake stepped forward.

'Young master Connolly,' Chara observed. 'I can hardly say I'm surprised. I trust you can explain yourself?'

'This was the scene of a kidnapping and torture,' Jake answered simply. 'Another minute and it would have been a scene of rape and murder on top of that.'

Chara stepped back. He almost looked shaken or a moment. 'I'll thank you to control yourself. I also see that there was a civilian present.' He turned to Aleera.

'You brought me onto this,' Aleera reminded him sharply. Chara looked sharply at her again. He didn't expect that; didn't expect resistance. He looked an awful lot like Ryan Shane for a moment.

'I think I've heard enough,' Chara declared, turning away. 'Master Connolly, you may consider yourself suspended from this case for the duration,' he spat with a great deal of vindication. If he came with subtitles, they would have read "*do not stand up to me again*". 'Sergeant Khazahn,' he immediately turned his frustrations to the nearest target, 'I expect an *excruciatingly* thorough report of this incident on my desk within twenty-four hours, as this unit's performance on this case so far has been frankly abysmal.' He strode toward the door. 'Carry on, Sergeant.'

The door grinded shut behind him.

'You think he knows?' Katya whispered to Jake. He nodded grimly.

'You heard him, Jake,' Khazahn declared flatly.

'So you're just gonna let this go?' Makian near-shouted.

'It's not my decision,' Khazahn answered without emotion. 'Anyone who isn't actively studying a body, get out of here.' He left without another word.

'Makian,' Jake said quietly, 'tell me you've got something.'

'Been a little distracted,' Makian reminded him. 'But somebody round here's hiding something, I can promise.'

'Keep going,' Jake instructed.

'I thought you just got suspended.'

'*You* didn't,' Jake smirked. 'Aleera, you need a lift back?'

Aleera looked up sharply. She hadn't been listening; too busy remembering what it felt like, as it would have felt in those last few moments for that sobbing girl in the middle of a circle of lunatics.'

'Sure,' she finally said. 'I should be going anyway.'

'Aleera,' came the impossibly gentle whisper, 'Please, honey, just tell me.'

The thirteen-year-old girl's hair was midnight black, with streaks of shining gold surrounding her flawless face and piercing blue eyes. Despite her young age, she was already developed, a clearly-defined hourglass shape beneath her clothes, one arm wrapped gently around her younger sister as the eleven-year-old clung to her side, shaking and sobbing quietly.

Lilith's beautiful features were long overtaken by a frown of concern as she subconsciously ran her fingers through her sibling's hair and gently wiped the tears from one of her eyes. What could have done this to Aleera, to the same girl who kept everything so bottled up, who never showed her emotions, who never seemed to be bothered by anything? At first Lilith had assumed that Aleera just kept too much of it inside- she'd thought so, after all, for years- and now something had tipped the proverbial balance, but soon she realised that this was not the case.

There was that look in Aleera's eyes, her silent shaking, and the emptiness in her expression that bore the telltale signs that the child was in shock. All she had to do was put two and two together; something terrible had happened, something that not even Aleera could just take in her usual stoic silence.

And Lilith knew exactly who was responsible. The knowledge made her shudder with rage, not for the vile, evil thing in a man's skin that she knew to be responsible, but for the woman who right now sat in the living room below them while her own daughter was traumatised by some insane monster. How could she? How could any mother be so utterly disregarding, so callous, so uncaring about her own daughter? Worse, how could any mother just sit and drink wine while her child was raised by a mass murderer?

'H... h...' Aleera gasped out faint puffs of air between sobs, 'H... he k...killed them...'

'It's OK,' Lilith whispered softly, lowering her face down to her sister's forehead. 'It's OK.'

'He killed all of them...' Aleera shuddered, clinging to Lilith, 'There was a baby, and he... he just...' At that, she broke down in tears again as Lilith whispered soothingly to her.

At that moment, Lilith's mind was made up. Her little sister was not *going back to that man.*

Three days later, the frightened little girl who bore the same name and face as Aleera was huddled against the headboard of her bed, arms around her knees as she sat quietly, her dark eyes glossed over, their light gone as she stared into empty space.

Nothing tasted right anymore. Nothing had any light or definition. She felt numb, shaking for reasons she didn't understand as she tried to stare past the images of the smoke and flames, the desperate, begging screams of the burning people burned into the back of her eyes. Faintly, on the fringe of her hearing, she could hear the voices from downstairs, her sister's angry shouts and her mother's cold, contemptuous replies.

'Who do you think you're talking to, young lady?' Aysha demanded.

'Don't you fucking talk to me like I'm a child!' Lilith shouted.

'You are,' Her mother reminded her, 'and you will respect your mother.'

'Mother?' Lilith spat, 'You call yourself a mother? What kind of a mother leaves her daughter with that psycho?'

'What kind of daughter is she?' Aysha sneered. 'She's a half-breed; tainted blood. Do you know much you damage your reputation just by being seen with her?'

'I don't care,' Lilith replied harshly.

'You should. Our family happens to have an image to maintain, and it's tarnished by that little ball of thrown-together filth upstairs. You're forgetting where you come from, Lilith. You're forgetting your place. You're betraying your own family for that little…'

'What the hell do you know about family?' Lilith screamed, 'Do you even know how many men have you spread your legs for in the past week? You even slept with Kudra! Kudra! And at least Aleera knows who her father is! You're a damn whore, and that's what you're trying to turn me and Aleera into!'

The sound of a hard slap followed, ringing through the house as Aleera squinted her eyes at the awful sound. She whimpered quietly, holding her eyes shut and covering her ears to keep out the sounds that followed, blocking the pain along with them.

It didn't work.

Almost a full minute went by before the door opened and Lilith stepped in slowly, shutting the door behind her while nursing one side of her face with her hand, leaning back on the door as her hair was left free to hang messily around her head, her breath coming in short, wet, ragged gasps.

'Lilith,' *Aleera managed to say softly, looking up at her sister with eyes full of tears and regret,* 'I'm sorry...'

Lilith kneeled down on the bed, pulling Aleera into her arms as she whispered into her ear:

'This isn't your fault Aleera. There's nothing wrong with you. It doesn't matter what you are, you're my baby sister and I love you. Don't you ever forget that. You understand me?'

Aleera nodded slowly.

'I just hurt people,' *she cried softly.* 'They hate me. All of them. Just like they hate him. Even Mom...'

'She's a monster. So is he.' *Lilith answered, her voice ringing with certainty.* 'You're not like him, Aleera,' *she whispered softly.* 'You're not.'

Aleera was for just a moment overcome by the sudden shock of the world crashing into her mind as she woke. Well, at least there was no scream this time.

Considering how much her bloodline on her father's side had been crawling out of the woodwork recently, she hadn't been giving much thought to the other side. Unfortunately, it hadn't been much better. She and her mother hadn't spoken for several years, and she liked that relationship perfectly fine as it was.

Her father had beaten, twisted and raped her. Her mother was better only in that she didn't try to do any twisting, and worse in the fact that she cast her illegitimate daughter off to be raised by a madman. Lilith was probably the only reason she hadn't gone on a killing spree. Yet.

Still. Hatred or no hatred, she'd promised to tell Sara about herself. Although it would probably be best to tone some- or most- of it down. No need to blurt out everything.

She got out of bed, checked the time, and decided that she still had time to pay Michael a quick visit.

'You really want to get your ass thrown in a cell, don't you?' Makian observed as he and Jake wandered through the stone forest of dragon-carved pillars that branched off to form the Guild's headquarters. Jake walked beside him, absently scanning the mural that formed the ceiling, looking up reflectively into the blazing eyes of the dragon. 'Hey! Jake? Anybody home?'

Makian had called Jake to the Guild about ten minutes ago. Apparently, he'd finally come across something in, of all places, financial. What was unusual was that it was classified *above* top-secret.

'If Khazahn wants to arrest me,' Jake replied simply, 'he'll have to prove that I did something illegal.'

'He did kick you off the case last night.'

'That he did.'

'Which means he could arrest you for this.'

'Only if he finds me. I miss anything?'

'If only,' Makian sighed. 'Everyone in Pentagram's so scarred shitless we'd have more luck getting the bodies to talk, and nobody's seen hide nor hair of your favourite psycho and mine since that bust we completely blew out. As for the guys we arrested, all we get out of 'em is that shit about being "children of the sword". Freakin' lunatics, the bunch of 'em. Chara, of course, can't wait to pin this whole thing on the Pentagram crowd.'

'Why's that?' Jake asked quizzically.

'C'mon, man, they told me you were smart; Chara's been against demons in the Guild from the get-go, and besides that, the High Council's been breaking his balls to do something about Pentagram for months.'

'This hasn't been going well,' Jake noted bleakly.

'So what're we doing out here?'

The carved-stone double door behind them slid open with a low grate. Khazahn stepped through, fists clenched and about ready to start spitting teeth.

'Jake Connolly, what in God's name is wrong with you?' he barked as the doors slid back shut. The last name again, Jake noted.

'Jake,' Khazahn snarled, 'You were removed from the damn case!'

'You did,' Jake answered, hands in pockets and idly looking around at the carvings, 'but I'm still a Guild associate, and therefore not restricted from Guild premises, as long as I don't go into any restricted areas; which I'm not.'

'Don't get smart with me,' Khazahn snapped, 'do you have any idea of just how far you have crossed the line?'

'I start looking around and he tries to stop me. A blind man could see he's hiding something.'

'Jake, this is the *Guild of Guardians*, and Chara answers directly to the head of the entire organisation, who has a seat on the High Council. So if you're supposed to be so smart, remind yourself that there is information contained in here ten levels above top-secret, and remind yourself of one of the fifty reasons that it can't be disclosed to a civilian!'

'Someone told you to keep something from me,' Jake snapped. 'I have a friend whose life is in danger. *She* has a friend who was kidnapped, tortured and almost murdered. You know what that means to me? *It means you can take your regulations and shove them up your-*'

'*Get out of here before I arrest you on the spot!*' Khazahn roared. 'I don't care what you're capable of, you are *not* above the law. Now get out!'

'Try it,' Jake said darkly. His eyes flashed. 'See what happens.'

'You have five minutes,' Khazahn glowered, 'to get out of here, or your contract with the Guild is terminated and you can consider yourself a target.' With that, he turned back to the door.

'Um,' Makian spoke up meekly, 'what about me?'

'You can count yourself lucky that you still have a job,' Khazahn snapped as the doors grinded shut behind him.

Makian gave a heavy, relieved sigh. 'Wow. I haven't seen him this mad since he found what I was using my internet activity for.'

He literally jumped when a female voice said 'thank you for that intimate look into your computer habits.' The air shimmered and parted to reveal a familiar, slim redhead with cat-ears and golden eyes, one hand on her hip and a folder full of papers in another. 'You can say it,' Katya winked as she handed Jake the folder, 'we're good.'

'Shit,' Makian wheezed as he gasped for breath, 'how'd you do that? Whole place has a suppression field.'

'You're right,' Jake grinned as he opened the folder, 'performing an invisibility spell in here would take someone of incredible skill disrupting the field.'

'Of course, you'd never do such a thing,' Katya smirked.

'Oh, never. Now,' Jake turned his attention to the folder, 'let's see what we've got here…' he flicked a few papers over, scanning the pages. 'Here we go, so…' he turned another page. His face became quizzical. 'Wait…' he continued to leaf through. He gulped. His face paled. 'Oboy… oh, this is bad…' he breathed, looking as though he was going to be sick. 'Oh, shit… shit, shit, *shit*, this is bad.'

'How bad?' Makian asked in a voice that suggested he didn't want to know.

'Think of how bad it could be,' Jake answered, 'and it's worse than that.' With a grim face, he handed the file to Makian, who similarly scanned the pages.

'Oh, shit,' Makian gulped, 'what the hell do we do now? Oh, *fuck*, this is not good…'

'Somebody gonna fill me in so I can shit myself too?' Katya chimed in.

'We know who it is that's been backing these guys.'

'And?'

Jake took a deep, dreadful breath. 'Chara,' he finally said dreadfully. 'It's Chara.'

As it turned out, Aleera didn't have time to see Michael for long; visiting hours were, quite understandably, much tighter within Guild Medical, and she only had about half-an-hour with him. Still, it allowed enough time for a few more kisses and some naughty promises whispered into Michael's ear. It really had been too long since her last relationship, considering that, being half-succubus, she could quite realistically sustain herself through nothing but sex, and she hadn't indulged *that* dark side in even longer than the other one. She was definitely going to enjoy having a boyfriend again at last.

After leaving, she'd killed some time at home, making some soup that she'd eat later in the afternoon, then made her way to the diner where she was going to meet Sara. No turning back now, she thought just a little bit ruefully as she pushed the door open.

Of course, she could just go straight home…

No. She owed Sara some honesty after three years.

And if that time ends right now?

What the hell was that supposed to mean?

Was Sara going to want to be within a hundred miles of her once she found out what her life had been? Would anybody?

Stop that!

She wouldn't be a friend to someone like her.

Stop it!

Anyone in their right mine would get as far away from her as possible.

Stop it!

God, there was that damned pit in her stomach again. Big as ever. Her breath became shaky, and there was a very powerful urge to turn away immediately.

Did everyone get so worked up about things? Why did she have to get so emotional lately?

Sara was waiting for her at their usual table. She smiled softly when she saw Aleera. 'Hi.'

Aleera smiled back and sit down. 'Have you eaten?'

'Not yet,' Sara answered. That heaviness was creeping back into the air. 'Wanna get a milkshake?'

'Deal,' Aleera smiled back.

Well, that was pointless, unless the point was to put off telling the truth about herself for all of thirty seconds.

'So,' Aleera bit her lip nervously- wait, nervous? Her? What the hell? 'Where do you want me to start?'

Sara gave a slight shrug. 'The beginning?'

Well, here we go. End-of-friendship express, please make sure all baggage is stored safely in the overhead compartments.

'Ok,' Aleera said. She was breathing heavily. She took her phone out and made sure it was switched off; if she had any excuse to get out of this, she'd probably end up taking it. 'Well…' might as well get on with it, she finally resigned herself to her fate. No sense in stalling any longer.

'My father…' she started. The following words caught in her throat. Sara's shining eyes became curious. Before she could stop herself, she blurted out 'look, I really don't want to say this.'

'Is it that bad?'

'Yes,' Aleera answered levelly. 'Yes, it *is* that bad.'

'You can tell me.'

Aleera paused. 'Promise you won't run a mile?'

'You're my best friend. Now come on.'

'Alright. My father…' again, she paused, but this time she managed to force it out. 'My father was Kudra.'

Sara paled, eyes widening.

'What?'

'Kudra,' Aleera repeated, her tone betraying her pessimism. '*The* Kudra.'

Sara's jaw dropped a little. 'The…' she stammered.

'Yeah.'

'Wow.' Sara looked down. She took a deep breath and pursed her lips. 'This explains a few things.'

'Like what?'

'Like why you never talk about your dad, for one thing.'

'And why I end up punching faces in whenever I meet someone like Ryan Shane?'

Sara looked up. 'I wasn't going to say that.'

'Were you thinking it?' Sara's shining eyes darkened with guilt. 'I'm sorry,' Aleera said quickly, 'that wasn't fair.'

'You don't seem like it,' Sara said quickly. It was Aleera's turn to look surprised, if only slightly. 'You don't- you don't seem like someone whose father was… your father.'

'…You mean that?'

'Yeah.' Sara traced the very edge of the cross, then released it.

Aleera allowed herself a tiny smile. 'Thanks.'

'It'd make parents' night interesting.'

This time, Aleera actually laughed. 'That's true,' she snickered.

'So,' Sara asked, 'Kudra's daughter. That's…'

'Do you want to hear the rest?'

'Do you want to tell me?'

'I'd have to tell someone eventually.'

'I'll listen,' Sara promised. 'I won't run a mile.'

'You don't know what I'm going to tell you.'

'You wouldn't do anything terrible. Not like he did.' Sara looked at her honestly. 'You can tell me, Aleera.'

Aleera took a deep breath. 'Ok. I'll tell you. Everything.'

Sara nodded slowly. Her hand returned to the cross.

'Like I said, Kudra was my father,' Aleera started. God, she'd never told anyone this. 'My mother was a succubus named Aysha. I'm not really sure how they met, or even… even how I got here. I honestly couldn't say if she wanted it or not. All I know is that I was Kudra's bastard daughter. The court decided- this was seven years before the secret war- that I would spend most of the time with my father and one weekend of each month with my mother- mainly because Aysha didn't want a half-breed around and she was doing some "favours" for the judge. It sounded stupid, but when I was growing up, I didn't know what Kudra was like. Back then, nobody did. I didn't even know for the first four years of the war, but I started to get an idea eventually.

'Kudra was... violent,' she went on, fighting to keep herself talking. 'He started hitting me since before I can remember. When I was five, he split the roof of my mouth. I ended up in the hospital with broken ribs when I was nine. When I got over, he... there's not really a nice way of saying this... he was violent in... *other* ways.' She shuddered at the memory, an icy chill down her spine as she recalled the deepest pain she'd felt. 'I didn't lose my virginity by choice. I was ten. There was Kudra and five of his men.'

Sara shook. She covered her mouth and gave a sickened sob. 'Oh my God,' she breathed, 'that... Jesus, that's...'

'Are you sure you want to hear the rest?'

Sara nodded uncertainly. They owed this to each other, Aleera realised.

That, and in some way, this was actually quite a weight lifted from her. This was possibly the first time since the psychiatrists that she'd talked about this at length.

'Aysha wasn't much better. To be honest, the only person who was remotely decent to me was Lilith. My sister, remember her?' Sara nodded. 'Well, actually, she's my half-sister. She's not sure who her father is- what comes of having a whore for a mother- but she's a full succubus and she's two years older than I am. See, when a succubus and an incubus... mate... the child's either an incubus or a succubus, depending on the gender. Like I said, she was the one good person around me when I was a kid. She got Aysha to back off, taught me to cook, played with me when I was small, and generally didn't treat me like shit.

'I found out what Kudra really was during the war. When he committed the genocide in Kenya. I saw him massacre a Maasai village. It wasn't pretty.' No need to elaborate on that. 'Kudra tried to... he tried to mould me into what he wanted, and that was a successor. Kudra the second. He put me through some... some real shit.'

Sara wiped a tear out of her eye. 'God, Aleera, I'm so sorry-'

'It's not your fault. Besides, I got out of there when I was eleven. Ran away and ended up with the only person who was ever decent to me.'

'Lilith?' Sara hazarded.

'Yeah. Aysha wasn't happy about it; she took it out on Lilith more than me. About a year after that, she started doing... what Kudra had done to me... to both of us. Lilith tried to go to the Guild, but Aysha just slept with the investigator. Lilith eventually got out when she was sixteen and I was fourteen. Same year Kudra died, and I can't say I was sad to hear he was dead.

'After that, things actually started to look up. I kept on living with Lilith; met Jake for the first time; moved to New York; met you and Michael; of course, the Guild started keeping an eye on me as soon as they knew I existed, but it was a lot better than Kudra or Aysha. I moved into the apartment I've got now when I was sixteen. Lilith moved to Phoenix about half a year ago.

And the rest, you were there for.'

Aleera gave a heavy sigh and drank some of her milkshake. Wow. That had actually felt pretty good, getting it all off her chest after a lifetime of what, on reflection, had been absolute shit.

Now there was just the reason she didn't want to tell anyone in the first place.

Oh, yes. That.

Sara looked down and folded her hands. 'Oh,' she finally said.

'Yeah.'

'I'm sorry,' Sara said gently.

'You didn't do any of it.'

'Suppose so,' Sara smiled weakly. 'It just seemed like the right thing to say.'

'That's it, then,' Aleera said. Sounded a little anticlimactic. 'That's all of it.'

'It's... a hell of a story,' Sara confessed.

'I know.'

'It doesn't change everything,' Sara declared firmly. 'If that was what you were thinking.'

'Nothing?' Aleera asked dumbly. This was certainly unforeseen.

'You're the same person you were two weeks ago. To be honest...' Sara gave a weak half-laugh. 'It's amazing.'

'What is?'

'Aleera... you've been through hell. What's happened to you shouldn't happen to anyone. Where you came from, those people, they're just… it makes me sick just to think about doing what they did. But you… you're here, now, as this… this *good* person.'

Wow. Good? Aleera? That was… unexpected. Imagine that. Aleera, good. She'd be singing in heavenly choirs next.

'Thank you,' she finally said.

'You thought I was going to shout and scream and tell you to stay away from me, didn't you?'

'Nothing personal. It's just how people react in my experience,' Aleera replied with a bitter touch to her tone. 'So… we're Ok?'

'Of course we are,' Sara smiled softly.

Aleera smiled back.

She really had been getting more emotional lately, and things had undeniably been changing between her and her friends, but this was the first time she honestly didn't mind a bit.

18

The penthouse apartment was one of those typically reserved for politicians and police commissioners; the latter usually being those who have used personal fortune, and usually the ill-gained personal fortunes of others, as a stair lift on the ladder to success. The fact that being the head of supernatural law enforcement for the Easter Seaboard helped, of course, as it came with a salary that provided greater quantities of green, paper leverage in a month than most earned in a year. Big, modern, meticulously clean, expensive, situated in one of the wealthiest parts of New York, and most significantly, almost entirely empty, the penthouse was exactly what one would expect a man like Commander Chara to spend his time away from the office in, however hard it might be to imagine him away from the office. It was early in the evening and his suit still lacked a single unruly crease.

Chara sat within his study, the door firmly closed behind him and his fist tight enough around his pen to betray frustration. It had been a week so far, and the results attained had been nonexistent. The job had not been to take frustrations out on street walkers and drug addicts. He began to doubt whether his associate would ever take the time to get the job done and let him put this entire mess behind him.

It was with regret that he penned his signature on a dotted line and placed the pen down, perfectly parallel to the others, and with a heavy sigh that leaned back in the chair. It was out of his hands now, he thought bitterly. This was the only course of action left. It was like putting down an uncontrollable dog; it was regrettable, but ultimately a necessity. Once it was done, he could dispose of the gun whenever he wished.

The door clicked. Chara half turned round, expecting it to be Manson; his butler was getting on in years, and usually retired early in the evening.

'Good evening, Manson,' he said without turning round.

'Guess again,' Azrael's voice said coldly.

Chara's heart convulsed. He spun up and round, but not fast enough to avoid being grabbed and slammed against the wall, sending papers and pens strewn over the desk as a PC fell to the floor.

'What are you doing here?' Chara hissed.

'They know something,' Azrael snarled viciously. 'They found the factory.' He released Chara by throwing him back into the wall.

'Jake Connolly,' Chara glowered. 'He's been suspended. It's done with.'

'That doesn't seem like the right tone of voice,' Azrael said. 'You doubt it as much as I do. What do they know?'

'Nothing. They couldn't.'

'Your Sergeant found out.'

'And he'll keep his mouth shut.'

'For how long?' Azrael demanded. 'Until this is done with? And then what?' he glared at Chara and fingered the handle of the dagger. He pulled it out and ran his finger along the blade. 'Did you think that I didn't know?'

'What?'

Azrael's foot lashed out into his stomach. 'We are not here to serve your purposes,' he seethed, turning the dagger over in his hand. 'You, Commander, are only alive because you have a purpose to serve; and at least *I* am honest about that.'

'I don't know what you're talking about!' Chara wheezed, clutching his stomach.

'We stand to lose every bit as much as you,' Azrael warned, 'and if that happens, you will fall with us. Bear that in mind, Commander. You've committed yourself to this. There is no turning back, and there is no betrayal.' He pulled Chara up and turned the glinting blade over in front of his face. 'We are not your men. We do not take your orders. Do not forget that.' He released Chara and pocketed the blade.

'I'll deal with it,' Chara gasped weakly. 'You have my word.'

'Which doesn't seem to mean much,' Azrael observed as he sheathed his weapon and checked that his hood was in place. 'Good evening, Commander,' he said levelly as he turned to the door. 'Your butler will be fine, by the way; though at his age you may want to call a doctor. And incidentally, you need a new lock.'

He stepped out, leaving Chara to catch his breath and lick his wounds.

Aleera returned to her apartment by seven, had a dinner of home-made soup and spent the remainder of the evening curled up with one of her favourite books. Considering the conversation she'd had with Sara, she forgave herself for feeling a little relieved; all in all, things really seemed to be looking up. Michael was safe, she was- or would soon be- dating again, and she'd salvaged the other of her very few friendships. The Azrael matter would hopefully be resolved soon, and two of his moves- Michael and the young woman in Pentagram- had been nicely countered. Additionally, even if the raid had failed, Azrael would be on the run, hopefully thrown off.

Overall, a productive weekend.

As she leafed through the book, though, she began to think. The young woman at Pentagram would be safe. Even if... if they'd nearly...

She shuddered. No, get it together, Aleera. Control herself. There we go. Deep, calm breaths. Calm down. That's better.

She snapped the book shut as something pounded on the door. She stood up as she recognised the muttering voice on the other side of the door.

'Aleera,' Jake gasped as she opened the door, 'where the hell have you been?'

'What?'

'I've been trying to get hold of you all day,' Jake insisted. Ah: she never did turn her cell phone back on.

'What happened? I didn't have any messages.'

'The Guild monitors your phone and your other cell, remember?' Aleera immediately realised what he was implying: he'd found something that couldn't be overheard.

She felt a little thrill along with the anxiousness of the situation. Oh, now this should be helpful. Or very interesting, at the absolute least.

'What is it?' she asked breathlessly.

'There's something you need to see,' Jake said hurriedly. '*Appiras*!'

The world warped around them, tipping and churning as Aleera's apartment whirled away out of view and was replaced by the inside of Jake's front door. The teleportation completed itself with a lurch, and Aleera gagged, tasting her dinner again for a second.

'You could have warned me,' she said as she gasped for breath. God, she hated teleporting.

'Sorry, but you really do have to see this,' Jake rambled as he nigh-dragged her into the living room and the jumble of papers and other god-knows-what that covered most of the coffee table.

'She here?' Katya asked as she emerged from the stairs. She looked at least as worried as Jake. Maybe more. It began to dawn on Aleera that she wasn't going to like what they'd found. More bad news. Wonderful.

'Jake says he's found something,' Aleera recited. 'I don't suppose someone's going to tell me what?'

'You need to see this for yourself,' Jake replied as he leaned over the coffee table and picked up a folder. He moved to hand it to her, then checked what it actually said, held his breath and frantically looked round.

'Please tell me you know where it is,' Katya sighed, pinching the bridge of her nose.

'I know where it is,' Jake said autonomously, picking up another file. 'Here.'

Aleera took the file, opened it and scanned over the pages. The first page was just a list of numbers, and the second was a list of account details. It took a moment for the fact to sink in that the account number was one she'd seen before. The very same account that had financed Azrael's purchase of the enchanted item from which he derived his capabilities. And it had the name in which the account was registered.

Chara, M. M? Well, well, Commander Chara did have a first name.

'Chara?' The knowledge dawned of why this had worried Jake so. This was certainly a… troubling… development. Were Aleera the sort to yield to panic, it could prove terrifying, even. The implications were problematic, at the least. 'Chara's the one backing Azrael,' she thought out loud.

'I wish,' Jake replied gravely, 'it wouldn't be half as bad if it was just Azrael. He's using Guild funds to finance Sword of Heaven.'

Aleera regarded him curiously. She recalled Azrael and the others in the warehouse referring to themselves as "the sword". As in, apparently, "Sword of Heaven". A little detachment really did help when it came to stepping back and thinking about things like this, even if she had been growing more attached to people lately.

'So they're some kind of cult?'

Jake nodded. His set his jaw gravely. He pulled his old coin out of his pocket and started to turn it over in his fingers.

'Sword of Heaven,' he began, 'can be traced back to about 1520. This was back when everybody thought the earth was flat, and there were imaginary witches in every village and real ones keeping their heads down. Angry mobs got together on a weekly basis to go and burn somebody, but most of them were just gangs of angry idiots that felt like "casting out witches and devils".

'But then comes a smarter mob. Some gang of bible bashers gets together and decide they're agents of the "sword of the angel of death". All it takes is a few angry priests good at rallying people around the idea of "purifying" their town- in other words; they lynched anyone who looked remotely shifty. The sad thing is, most of the people they went after were good men and women, but people like that just need something to hate. So when there are no "devils" to hunt down, what do they do? They move onto the next town, and then the next town after that, and so on and so on, and they recruit more people- and as they do that, they get themselves a reputation. Before long, they've got a leader and they start spreading a "holy message". Next thing you know, this mob's become a great big cult.'

'So they *are* fanatics,' Aleera mused.

'The worst kind,' Jake said grimly. 'They were the main reason the High Council took us into hiding. Of course, that didn't please Sword of Heaven one bit. They just went after whoever they could, because by now they'd been going strong for at least a hundred years, and they had power- and they didn't feel like giving it up.'

'And these guys are still going?' Katya asked, her golden eyes shaking with horror. 'All this time?'

'Not a chance. Eventually they had the nuts to try and start a war. Most they had was a few people, mainly their heads, with enchanted objects. Their appointed Demon-Slayers.'

'Like Azrael,' Aleera realised. 'That's what he is; some kind of slayer?'

'More or less. Of course, they just had a few guys like that; the Guild- well, back then they were called the Dragon Keepers- was an army. It was a pretty one-sided war, but it still wasn't pretty. Sword of Heaven was shattered in a couple of months. That was the first real Human-Draconic war.'

'So if they got rid of those guys, who were those lunatics at the factory?' Katya queried.

'People like that don't stay down. There's always someone who holds onto those old ideas and finds someone to hate- gays, blacks, and the way this went, us. Not just demons, because as far as these guys are concerned, there's no difference. They're just a glorified lynch mob. So they hang on, just a little, while, until eight years ago.'

'Two years into the Secret War,' Aleera recalled, though she wasn't quite sure what they had to do with it.

Unless…

Oh.

Oh, dear.

'All through the war,' Jake reflected darkly, 'I knew there was something going on behind the scenes. Things were desperate; Kudra was the kind of threat we never had to deal with, before or since. Desperate times and all that. So Chara- back, then if memory serves, he had the job Khazahn's got now- he decides that what's needed for this war is someone with experience against demons.'

'He brought back Sword of Heaven,' Aleera realised, feeling her stomach tighten all the while, 'to fight my father.'

'And I'm guessing,' Jake muttered, 'that they didn't feel like going back into obscurity.'

'And they're still going? Eight years later?'

'Chara knows it,' Katya realised. 'That's why he's been blocking us.'

It did explain a few things; why they would target her of all demons, why Azrael's methods were as such, why Chara had continually blocked Jake, perhaps… 'this is why Khazahn never turned up,' she realised.

'If he found out about this,' Jake muttered, 'and then Chara pulled rank on him.'

'You think Khazahn's involved in this?' Aleera suggested. She never did trust him; the Guild had kept their keen eyes on her for most of her life, and Khazahn was in charge of doing so. That and she wasn't really the trusting type. Not really sensible to put one's trust in many people, especially if they had those condemning psychiatric reports.

Jake shook his head firmly. 'No. I don't like him, but he wouldn't do this.'

'So… this is a *conspiracy*?' Katya squeaked. 'Chara's just letting them butcher people?'

'We don't know if this stops with him,' Aleera pointed out darkly.

'No, the head the High Council's got now would shut this down at a whisper,' Jake shook his head. 'Even so…'

'Who do we go to?'

Jake shrugged. 'Makian. Harry. Tomoko. We need to tell someone else before we take this higher- a freelancer, a familiar, and a teenager- we'd be thrown out of the offices.'

Aleera hardly registered the conversation, instead sitting still, folding her arms and closing her eyes as she thought. She understood- not in the sense that it was morally understandable, but she got her head around it when she distanced herself from worrying about the morality- why they were after her. The other women too. But Michael...

Michael...

He hadn't been killed. He was alive, and he was left in a place where he'd be found.

'Azrael's been playing games this whole week,' she thought out loud. 'He let Michael live. If they go after demons, why risk it all on a mind-game?'

Jake looked confused for a second, then his eyes became fearful. 'Unless they're still planning to kill him,' he finally forced the words out.

The realisation struck Aleera's brain with burning force. Of course! He wouldn't chance everything on this! Not if he had contacts within the Guild!

Not unless he still had access to Michael.

Her stomach contracted. She felt herself heave at the sickening thought. Without another word, she hurled rationality aside and ran to the door.

19

By the time she reached Times Square, Aleera had tried at least five times, without success, to calm herself down and start thinking rationally. The main problem was that, every time she did, it led to her realising that, if Chara was supporting Azrael, then Azrael had access to Guild, including the medical facilities, including Michael. And that gave way to the river of red that flooded her mind with a single thought: if Azrael was anywhere near her boyfriend, she was going to rip him to bloody pieces.

Calm down, Aleera. If Michael was in trouble, she just had to… get hold of Azrael and rip him to bloody pieces. Yes, that was a good enough solution.

Her heart pounded, hot blood boiling with fury and desperation surging through every corner of her. Now was not the time for calmness or clarity. Now was the time to be the barely-stable demon she was.

Without disrupting the invisibility spell that she had fortunately remembered to apply out of practice, she descended on the Flat Iron Building itself, ignoring the pointless chatter and honking cars from below and the dull buzz of screens of the building itself. Normally, whenever she was there, the first thing that came to mind was the surreal fact of an actual secret headquarters existing beneath a major landmark. Right now, she couldn't care less. She kicked in the door that led to the staircase and, racing down to the top floor, approached the wall and recited the password she recalled Jake uttering back at Pentagram: 'Silver clearance, Archimedes Eight-Seven-One'. Now, please work, please, please, please, she really should have thought this through, please…

The wall slid open soundlessly. The silvery sheen of the elevator's interior greeted her emptily as she entered and pushed the button for the floor that was not contained on any schematic of the building. The elevator lurched, and she barely felt the up thrust as it shot downwards. All she could register was the pounding blood in her ears and the claws itching to be let out and taste hot blood…

Soon. Soon she would find Azrael, save Michael, finally put this insane week to rest, and really, really cut loose… wow. This really would be a package deal.

Assuming Michael was still alive.

What?

What if she was too late?

She wasn't. She wouldn't let this happen.

But what if it already had?

Shut up! Just shut up and let me go back to normal!

The elevator lurched and stopped. The doors slid open. The stone corridor leading to a double-door sat in front of her, dull and calm. She took a slow breath to steady herself. Behind the desk to her right was a woman in a prim suit, her blonde hair tied back in a tight bun. She peered up at Aleera from behind. The spell was off, Aleera realised on some level; the suppression field. No magic could be used in here.

'Yes?' she asked levelly, in a sharp "this-is-not-how-things-are-done-young-madam" manner. 'Oh and... your clothing appears to be ripped.'

Aleera half-heartedly checked. The front of her shirt was just about hanging from her shoulders thanks to her wings ripping out of her back. She hadn't bothered to retract them. The bra strap was snapped too. She didn't care.

'Silver clearance,' she recited, 'Archimedes Eight-Seven-One.'

The receptionist arched her eyebrows. 'Pass?'

'Excuse me?'

'You should have a pass.'

Oh. Aleera had to bite her lip to keep from cursing.

'I need to get in.'

'Without a pass, I can't allow-'

'Open the door,' Aleera hissed, 'because somebody in Guild Medical is about to die.'

The woman looked at her incredulously.

'I'm with Jake Connolly,' Aleera insisted, 'I need you to get either Dr. Tomoko Shinju or Dr. Harry Drake.'

'I can't just-'

'Just get me Dr. Tomoko Shinju!'

The receptionist finally relented and punched something into the computer. Only one eyebrow rose this time. 'It says here,' she muttered, 'that Dr. Shinju has been signed off for the night- in fact, we don't' appear to have anyone on duty.'

'What?'

'This can't be right-'

Aleera glanced at something that protruded under the desk. Before the receptionist could react, she leapfrogged over the desk, twisted the key that had been left in the lock, pulled down the cover and flipped the switch. Without a word, she cleared the desk again and raced inside.

She reached the medical division in less than a minute. She slammed her weight against the door and it swung open. Not a good sign; near-murder victims were covered in the protocol of the Guild Medical Facility. The door was supposed to be locked and password-protected, and this door was neither one nor the other. On reflection, Aleera wasn't sure what she had planned to do upon arriving.

Forget that for now. Michael's bed was at the end, by the window. She ignored the smell of disinfectant as it came rushing to her- then realised that disinfectant wasn't what she could smell.

It was flesh and hair. Burning flesh and hair.

She reached Michael's bed and pulled back the curtain.

For the first time in years, she screamed.

The skin on Michael's face was almost completely gone, burned away to reveal weeping flesh splattered with charred blood, the look of sudden shock and horror still frozen into his glossed-over, lightless green eyes that looked as hard and cold as emeralds. On the patches of skin still there to be seen, the runes burned with wisps of smoke and fresh heat.

For a long, awful moment, Aleera couldn't speak, couldn't move, or even look away from the burned remains of a face frozen in burned flesh with its jaw still set defiantly. She felt the bile start to rise in her throat as her vision blurred with thick tears.

'Michael...' She finally whispered, finally allowing a single thick tear to slide unhindered down her cheek. 'Please... please God, no...' She blurted out, her face crumpling in abject misery as her cheeks were soaked with a flood of tears.

Everything, all the pain and rage and loss, welled up inside her in a second as she gritted her teeth, able to articulate her horror only with an animalistic howl, gripping the side of the hospital bed as tears covered her face before she turned and slammed her fist into the plaster wall, in raging, bereaved frustration allowing a single, heartbroken sob as her face collapsed into a tearful mess.

Not this, was all she could think. She'd worked it out, gotten there as fast as she could, gone there to save him, and now she was too late, too late to do anything, too late to save Michael, and all that was waiting for her when she arrived too late was another charred, indiscernible corpse. God, no, this wasn't how it should go. She knew what was happening; she should have been there in time...

She gagged. There was no detached thought now, no cold rationality, just this horrible, awful realisation.

'Pitiful,' the voice rang behind her. 'I could say he brought this on himself... but we both know why this happened, don't we? What do you make of your handiwork, then?'

Aleera felt her eyes burn with red. The claws extended of their own free will. He was approaching behind her. Five feet now. Four, maybe three-and-a-half. 'This is not my sin, demon,' Azrael's voice snarled. 'The boy was as much a filthy demon-lover as the rest of you. It was you that damned his soul to-'

There. Close enough. All that filled Aleera's mind was the pain and the rage that it fuelled, and there was no reason not to pour it onto Azrael right now.

She howled like an animal as she spun round, thrusting the claws forward in a thoughtless explosion of fury. Azrael, prepared, swung to the side and struck his knee into her side, letting her fall sideways as her ribcage exploded in pain and his elbow jabbed in-between her shoulder blades.

Idiot. He'd moved right into the path of the wings that folded outwards and... missed completely as Azrael leapt nimbly back.

'Pathetic,' he scoffed. 'As pitiful as you deserve to be. You can't even touch me, you-'

'*Shut! Up!*' Aleera howled as she swung at him. Azrael dodged sideways with another mocking laugh, and then jerked back, gagging as Aleera grabbed the flailing cloak and pulled, curling up one clawed hand and slamming a fist of solid keratin into his face. She gave another mad shout of blind rage as she threw him to the floor, grabbed him by the collar and, pulling the white hood back, slammed the tip of his bald, gleaming head into the wall.

'No magic now!' she shouted madly. 'Just you and me, you murdering piece of shit!' She brought her fist slamming into his face, and when it was pulled back the knuckles were coated in blood.

'I killed no-one,' Azrael spat. 'I was just the right hand of God. It was their own blood, and the boy... the boy *you* killed by being-'

'Shut up!' Aleera shouted again. As she swung for him, Azrael's foot lashed out and struck her stomach, knocking the wind from her as Azrael leapt up and carried her with him to the floor. Her head slammed hard against the polished floor.

'You dare!' Azrael roared. 'You dare accuse a holy man of murder! You are filth! You are-'

Aleera's knee drove into his stomach. A rib snapped. She smashed her forehead into mouth.

The door into the medical room suddenly exploded inward. Five black-draped Guild Soldiers, staffs extending and buzzing, with Jake, Katya and Makian among them.

'So this is how your filthy kind defends itself?' Azrael spat. 'Waiting for someone else to attack a man of G-'

Something swung and struck the side of his head. He fell, and didn't rise again. Aleera looked up through a blurry curtain of tears as Jake handed the staff back to its owner.

'What the hell just happened here?' Khazahn bellowed from the doorway.

'See for yourself,' Jake stated flatly as he looked up from Azrael's unconscious body.

'God,' Khazahn breathed, 'Get me a cell for this lunatic. Now! Someone contact the Commander.'

'For all the good that'll do,' Jake spat. Khazahn turned to him on the spot.

'What's that supposed to mean?'

'You know exactly what I mean,' Jake replied venomously. 'I know, Khazahn.'

'What?'

'I know. Don't even pretend you don't know what I'm talking about.'

'What the hell just happened here?'

'*Shut up!*' Aleera shouted through her tears. No restraint now. No reservedness. 'Just *shut up*! This happened because of you, you-'

'Aleera,' Katya said quietly from besides her, putting an arm around her to comfort her as best she could in the moment of abject nightmare. 'C'mon, honey, let's get you out of here.'

'What the hell is this place doing empty?' Jake hissed to Khazahn.

'How do I know?' Khazahn snapped back. 'What about the kid?'

'She's crying,' Jake replied through gritted teeth.

'I mean the boy.'

'I know. And she's crying. Just ask yourself why.'

Khazahn looked over at the hospital bed. For the first time Jake could remember, his eyes filled with guilt.

Aleera finally collapsed into tears. There was no point holding it in now. She couldn't. Not this. Not this much. She ignored the sting as she applied the healing spell to herself.

'I'm sorry, Aleera,' Katya said soothingly as she led her away. 'I'm so sorry.'

20

Grief is a personal thing. It is that rare thing to which everyone reacts differently, and yet it had always seemed to Aleera, in some morbid fashion, to be a great equaliser, a reaction to something that was, for everyone, inevitable. But somehow she had never really known it; she had never known the suffering it brought, or the horrible sickness that felt like she'd lost a limb. The only person close to her to have ever died before, she realised, was a monster. Maybe the lack of bereavement she felt then was part of what set her apart; ironically, the damage that had caused her only reaction to her father's death to be the word "good" had been caused by the same life that led to this. To the worst grief, the worst pain, she ever knew.

Everyone reacted differently. Aleera had volunteered to deliver the news to Michael's mother. She didn't know what she was going to say. There was none of her distance of cold logic now. Just this all-consuming emptiness; a black hole inside her. It turned out that she didn't need to say anything. Her eyes said it all as soon as the door was opened. Mrs. Prince's reaction had been one of hostility. She'd slapped Aleera in the face, screamed at her, told her that it was her fault, called her several indescribable names and slammed the door. Aleera made no effort to interrupt her. The woman's anger was a hundred times as justified as it had been in the hospital, and she couldn't bring herself to defend herself. The deepest, most horrible thought was that she honestly deserved it, because just by being around Michael she had brought this upon him.

Everyone reacted differently. Sara had cried when Aleera told her. Telling her was the single hardest thing she had ever had to do in her life. Aleera could think of nothing to say or do while Sara clung to her like a child and her face was covered in thick tears. What amazed her was that Sara hadn't shouted. She hadn't blamed her. In fact, as soon as she was actually able to say anything instead of just sobbing, the first thing she'd said was "it wasn't your fault". She'd said that no matter what, Aleera shouldn't blame herself, and that Michael wouldn't have wanted her to. The notion had seemed impossible, insane, but it was Sara that really amazed her. It was as though the girl didn't know how to think of herself for a second.

Everyone reacted differently. Aleera knew exactly what she was going to do and how she was going to react.

Come hell or high water, she was going to put Azrael in the ground for this.

Did that make sense? Was that rational? Yes, she decided. She wasn't like her father. She already honestly believed that, held to it as her mantra. But just this once, she felt justified in a slight moral lapse. A great many people had killed for a great deal less than what Azrael had done to her. If the Guild wanted any information on Sword of Heaven, they could get it from any one of the four that had been arrested during the raid on the factory.

That was the argument she would have made if she bothered to think. Instead, the most logic she applied was in working out how to get her hands on him. First, of course, there was Jake's reaction when she asked to be let into an interview room with Azrael.

'No.'

'Jake-'

'I don't want to hear it,' Jake answered sharply as he snapped the file shut. 'I'm up to my butt trying to get some solid proof about what we found out about Chara; I do not have time for this.'

'So let me eliminate the problem,' Aleera offered levelly. She didn't bother changing her eyes back when the flooded with red. 'He's got it coming.'

Jake slammed the file down on the Guild desk. Aleera had been there since getting back from seeing Sara; under the circumstances, the school had readily allowed them the day off. Apparently her principal did have some decency to him.

'Damnit, Aleera!' Jake shouted, 'I am not having you kill this guy!'

'He deserves it,' Aleera hissed. She stormed out without exchanging another word, knocking her elbow against Jake's side.

There, as her hand "flailed". Got it.

She left the room quickly and slammed the door behind her. Then she ran for the holding cells. Azrael was being interviewed right now, and Jake would soon discover that his pass was missing.

Aleera found the interview room easily enough; she'd been asked to look at her fair share of inkblots in there. And there was Azrael, arms folded and leaning back on the chair. He appeared to be praying. Fair enough. In a few minutes, he'd have plenty to pray about. Thick, hexagonal metal handcuffs were attached to his wrist; standard Guild equipment. They held the body's magical energy in its current form, effectively preventing the use of any spells. There was nobody in there with him, she realised. Probably on a coffee break; now was her best chance. She could already hear Jake running in after her.

Chara became the obstacle, unsurprisingly enough. He looked up at her as he would at a spider on his ceiling. 'Do you have clearance to be here?' he asked in a voice that was at the same time condescending and completely flat, the type of voice it took years to master.

Before any of the assembled officers could stop her, she swiped Jake's pass in the electronic lock, opened the door, slammed it beside her and shoved one of the small, dingy room's chairs under the handle.

Azrael turned his attention to her immediately. 'Here already?' he sneered. Aleera didn't bother to compose herself. She simply turned from the door and walked over to Azrael. 'What?' Azrael scoffed. 'You're going to hit me? Will that make you feel better?' He drummed his fingers on the desk.

Aleera's claws erupted from her fingers as the thrust her hand down. There was no way Azrael could move his hand fast enough; the claws stabbed through skin and flesh, grating against bone as he howled on instinct. Yes, actually, it did make her feel a little better.

But not enough. The blood still pounded in her ears. Her heart still surged with sadistic rage and boiling hate. There were angry, desperate shouts from outside. The door started to shake against the chair. She ignored it, pulling up her hand to the sounds of ripping flesh and smashing her elbow into the side of Azrael's face. He hit the floor hard.

He didn't stop sneering.

'You see?' he spat. 'No, you don't, do you? This is what we *say*. This is what we say about you. All of you.' His smirk grew ever-wider. 'And we were right.'

The bloodlust howled louder than ever. Aleera lifted Azrael to his feet and slammed him into the two-way mirror. The glass splintered, and still he smirked.

'You're a religious man,' she spat, her eyes turning blood-red. 'Ok: an eye for an eye. You think I'm doing this because I'm a demon? Because I care about what you think?' she drove her knee into his crotch, a perfect way to knock the wind out of him. Still smirking.

'Go ahead,' Azrael chuckled. 'Prove to me that you're a killer.'

Aleera threw him to the floor. For a second, thought gave way to rage. She stepped back and took a deep breath. 'There are two of us in here,' she said levelly. 'And I'm the only one who's never killed anyone.'

'Oh, but that's different. That was your kind. That was a service to the world. If *you* kill *me*, then it's one more sin on your own black soul. Your little boyfriend was a devil, and he was about ready to lay with a devil and a whore. He deserved every second of what I did to him.'

And then she snapped.

Aleera was on Azrael in a second, pulling him up by his collar and smashing her fist into his face. 'Don't!' her knee into his ribcage, 'You!' her elbow into his neck, 'Talk!' her knee into his face, 'About!' her heel into his skull, 'Michael!' she pulled him back to his feet, wrapped her fingers round the back of his head and slammed his face onto the top of the table. She released him, and he fell listlessly to the floor.

The smirk grew wider. 'He is burning in hell,' Azrael spat, 'cursing your name forever. And you... you are the worst. Whatever you do to me, I will always be better than you, *demon*.'

God damn it, shut and up and wipe that smirk off your face, you-

The door exploded inward, splintering the wooden chair even as it slammed against the wall. The soldiers swarmed in immediately. Aleera barely noticed the hands that grabbed hold of her and pulled her from the room.

'They will protect me,' Azrael chuckled darkly. 'And they'd turn you over in a second.'

The door slammed. Aleera shrugged off the hands that held her. Azrael was right. They'd hand her over if they could. Perfect way for them to end it. They were *against* her. They were as bad as him...

No. Get a grip. That wasn't *her* talking. Calm down. Rational. Calm. Stable. There we go.

The soldiers parted. Jake stepped forward, and immediately Aleera felt ashamed. It was like the incident at Pentagram or with Skinny Jack all over again. She felt like a five-year-old fumbling her hands behind her back and staring at the floor.

'I'll take her,' Jake said to the soldiers. He led Aleera out silently. She felt more like a child in trouble with every passing moment. Her stomach started to tie itself in knots. She felt guilty. She felt embarrassed that he'd seen her like that *again*.

Jake slammed the door shut behind them. He leaned against it and steadied himself for a second, then he turned round sharply and held his hand forward. 'Pass.'

Aleera bit her lip like a teenager caught with her father's wallet. Damnit, where was all this "father" garbage coming from? Well, wherever, she couldn't stop herself handing over the pass. Jake stuffed it into his pocket.

'So what the hell was that?' he demanded. Oh, God, don't make her explain herself. She felt herself turn red.

'Temporary insanity?' Well, it made enough sense. She was certainly entitled to it at the moment.

'*Don't* even joke about that,' Jake glowered. 'Do you have any idea what you were about to do?' Aleera didn't reply. She doubted Jake would find it funny were she to say "kill him". Jake let out a stifled breath, leaned back on the door and rested his head in his hands, before turning back to her. 'Aleera,' he finally said warningly, 'you remember what it says on your psyche report. "Psychologically damaged. Borderline-sociopath tendencies". You know what that means?'

Aleera froze. She took a deep breath as her blood boiled. Ouch. That hurt. Honest and true, coming from Jake. 'You don't trust me.' She tried not to sound hurt.

Jake softened a little. '*I* do. *They* don't. The second they catch you laying a hand on someone, even someone like Azrael, it goes to court. A high-profile case like this gets brought up in front of the High Council. They see the psyche report, and all you can look forward to is a padded cell, a straightjacket and daily injections. Hell, you have no idea how many favours I had to call in just so that you didn't get certified the minute they filed the report.'

Aleera found herself dumbfounded. A rare experience. 'Really?'

Jake turned away and stifled another breath. 'Just go home,' he finally said. 'Just go home. Now. I don't have time for this right now.'

He walked back through the door and slammed it shut. Aleera stood there, alone and honestly never more… ashamed? Yes, that was it, amazingly enough: she felt ashamed. She'd let Jake, one of five people who'd ever believed in her, down in the most shaming way, and she hadn't even avenged Michael for the trouble. And she realised just how far she'd crossed the line when the thought occurred to her that *this* was how she would think of Michael: a cause to kill something.

That pit opened up in her stomach again, and she couldn't bring herself to stop it. She just wanted to crawl away somewhere, curl up and not come out.

So Aleera did what she always did when it became too much. And just this once, it really had. It wasn't Jake being angry with her. It wasn't Azrael. It was Michael.

God, he was *dead*. Lying there without even his face left, on some cold mortuary slab or on an autopsy table with Harry or Tomoko poking and prodding at what used to be him. God damn it, he was dead, and…

And she'd loved him.

It felt like something had been torn out of her chest. It made her feel so hollow, so empty… she didn't think about it. She couldn't. She'd always been strong, cold, and now… she couldn't take this. She just couldn't.

So she did was she had always done: she'd gone to the one person around whom she could always show, weakness, or feeling, or… *this*… without hesitation. What any frightened little girl would do: she went to her big sister.

God, Lilith had no idea, she thought as she picked up the phone. She'd always been great with Michael and Sara; what would this do to her? She had no idea how to tell her, or how she'd react; well, she'd probably jump on the next plane to New York, knowing her…

God, what was she thinking? Lilith would come here, and if Aleera tried to stop her, she'd know in a heartbeat that something was wrong. And then how long before she was lying on a cold metal slab, with her face replaced by a mass of burned meat?

She slammed the phone back down. No. She couldn't. She needed to see her older sister, but she couldn't. Not now.

All she could do was sit and cry and remember that everything she and Michael had- their friendship, their trust, their smiles, that kiss, that- that *love*- was gone, ended, and might as well have never been.

Jake irritably tapped a pen on the desk. He'd been at this all day; after the failed raid, followed by a murder within the Guild's own infirmary, there had been a considerable amount of paperwork to deal with: insurance, statements, more statements, reports, wavers, more insurance… good thing he got paid for this.

Then, of course, there had been even more after the latest development, as if the problem itself weren't bad enough. He wasn't remotely looking forward to having to tell Aleera about that one.

He looked up as the door clicked, expecting it to be Katya back from the coffee machine. Instead, it was Aleera, looking surprisingly shameful, who entered and closed the door behind her.

'Hey,' he greeted her. 'I thought you went home.'

'I did,' Aleera answered quietly. Jake noticed her red eyes and wet cheeks. Had she been crying? Aleera? 'Look, I- I'm sorry about this morning.'

Jake sighed heavily. 'Yeah. Me too. I probably shouldn't have talked to you like that after what happened.'

'It's alright,' Aleera replied. 'If it's alright, I need to talk to somebody about this.'

Jake appeared mildly confused. 'You normally call Lilith, don't you?'

'I'm just not sure if it's... well, about how she'd react.'

'You haven't told her about any of this,' Jake realised.

'If I do, she'll jump on the next plane to New York.'

Jake removed the old coin from his pocket and turned it over thoughtfully. He set his jaw and tried to think of what he was going to say.

'Is Azrael still in one piece?'

He inhaled sharply.

'Is he dead?' Aleera checked. That pit started to open up in her stomach again.

'Well, no,' Jake cringed as he spoke, 'he... well... thing is...'

'Jake?'

'He's gone.'

Aleera sat completely still for a moment. 'Come again?'

'Azrael's gone. He escaped.

Aleera's jaw dropped. 'What?'

'He got out.'

'He what?'

'He's-'

'He's *gone*?'

And Aleera thought she was angry when she arrived back at the Guild offices.

'Found out from Makian,' Jake answered venomously. 'Apparently when they were putting him in the cell, he bludgeoned two soldiers, put a dagger to one of them and made a third open the door. They're in Medical right now.'

'He's just gone?' Aleera seethed. 'How the hell did he get out of here?'

'Somebody messed up,' Jake stated the brutally-obvious. 'I don't believe this,' he spat, 'we finally get this bastard, and then he gets away?'

'Or gets let out,' Aleera pointed out bitterly. Oh, Azrael, you resourceful devil, you. Check.

'You think?'

'Considering what's been happening lately? There's no way the Guild honestly underperformed like this, so that doesn't leave many options. Anything else turn to crap while I was gone?'

'You have no idea. Chara's threatening to have me arrested if this keeps up.'

'So it really is him,' Aleera noted darkly. 'Now what?'

Jake checked his watch. 'I've got a screaming match booked with Khazahn in an hour. By the way, you might want to go and see Sara.'

'So, Jake,' Khazahn started as Jake and Katya stood in the middle of his office. 'What exactly do you know?'

'That Chara, or someone at that level, has been aware of Sword of Heaven's actions for ten years, and he formed them while Kudra was active.' Jake answered darkly. 'And that makes him responsible for what happened to Michael just as much as this Azrael lunatic.'

'You're angry,' Khazahn talked down the comment.

'Angry?' Jake repeated in mock surprise, gripping tightly on the coin, 'Now why would I be angry? What could *possibly* be making me angry? Well, let's think: A close friend of mine is being stalked and threatened, a top-level Guild officer is condoning Genocide and sending you to threaten to have me arrested for finding out about it, and to top it all off, an innocent boy is lying on a mortuary slab with a tag on his toe along with four other people. So yes, I am considerably angrier than usual, Khazahn!'

Khazahn said nothing.

'You knew,' Jake realised, his anger now mixing with shock and just a touch of fear at such a betrayal, the weight of it sinking crushingly down onto his shoulders as his eyes widened in dread. 'You knew about this, didn't you?' He spat accusingly.

Knowing exactly where the conversation was going, Katya took a large backward step towards the door. If there was one thing Jake placed value in, it was loyalty. Knowing him as she did, putting two and two together and seeing where this would end up was an easy task.

'Any organisation has its secrets, Jake,' Khazahn replied simply.

'You knew that they were doing this,' Jake seethed, fists clenched and eyes burning, 'He's been allowing murder, and you let him get away with it!' He took a stop back, looking at the man in front of him with disgust, 'Jesus, Khazahn, I always thought you were an asshole, but I didn't think you were capable of *that!!*'

'And what would you have me do?' Khazahn snapped, 'Get this through your head, Jake: this isn't just some gang of idiots getting together to beat someone up; this is the Guild we're talking about. You might think you can poke your nose in anywhere because you think you're playing the hero role, but the rest of us have rules to follow, and so do you- it's high time you realised that!'

Jake simply stood still, glaring at Khazahn now with equal parts anger and disgust.

'That's it?' He demanded. 'That's your excuse? If there's anyone around here not obeying the law you care about so much more than you do about people, then it's your boss! Why doesn't he have to follow those rules? But no, he's your boss, and you have to be a good boy scout and do whatever he says instead of exposing him as the corrupt piece of shit that he is, and that's why an innocent person is *dead*, and you're just as responsible as Chara is, so how do you justify letting that happen, when we both know that all of this could have been avoided if you'd just told me the truth?'

Khazahn remained silent once again.

'The choice isn't mine to make,' He said finally. 'Face it, Jake. There's nothing you can do.'

'Wanna bet?' Jake smirked dangerously. 'I'm going to the High Council with this.'

'The High Council can't stand you, Jake. And even if they could it's your word- and you've been in the deep end as much as anyone I know who isn't currently dead or in a cell- against the Head of the Eighth Division. *And* disregarding that, you're a Guild employee, which means you can't just go around throwing accusations against your commanding officer like this!'

Jake didn't say another word; he gave Chara a final, cold glare, then turned, walked through the door and slammed it behind him, Katya following silently.

When they were gone, Khazahn gave a heavy sigh, turned and leaned on his desk.

'Damn it,' he seethed through gritted teeth. 'God damn it, when did this job get so-'

The door boomed. 'Jake, get out of here,' he snapped without turning around. The door grated open behind him.

'As you were, Sergeant.' Khazahn spun round immediately as Chara entered, each step meticulous and deliberate, arms behind his back. 'I see that your appointment with young Master Connolly just ended.'

'He might be off this case, but he's still an employee.'

'Indeed,' Chara noted disdainfully. 'A troublesome one.'

'We can't cut him loose. He's too much of a risk.'

'Indeed; besides, the High Council wouldn't be best pleased. Lord knows it's best to keep an eye on him,' Chara declared. 'It's my understanding that you wished to speak to me, Sergeant?'

'That's right,' Khazahn said, standing up straight now, having completely composed himself. 'Commander, this has gone too far,' he said fiercely.

'Really?' Chara asked disinterestedly, walking around the desk and glancing at Khazahn's papers, 'and what would "this" be?'

'You know exactly what I mean,' Khazahn scowled, slamming his hands down onto the table. 'A teenage boy was killed in our infirmary, and three other people have died inside of a week!'

Chara glared icily at him and raised his head slightly. 'I remind you, Sergeant,' he said warningly, 'of why this is a necessity. Sacrifices must be made. You know as well as I do that this profession is far from spotless. In short: this is the Guild, Sergeant.' He walked around the desk until they were less than a foot apart. 'Not the boy scouts.'

'Before, it was... excusable,' that last word was like admitting almost-total defeat, 'but it's out of control!'

'Enough,' Chara said definitively.

'We can't-'

'Enough!' Chara's face twisted as it never seemed to have done before and flushed hot with indignity.

'Chara!'

'*Enough*, Sergeant!' Chara snapped. 'There is only one course of action open to us now; this must be seen through to its end; otherwise, as you are already aware, it will become far too unpredictable.'

Khazahn swallowed a lump in his throat. 'My God... it really was you. The whole thing?'

'I can hardly be blamed for the fact that you never made it a point to find out who you were working for,' Chara sated haughtily. 'I'll see you later for your report on last night.' With that, he walked back to the door.

'Jake knows,' Khazahn said to his back; his weapon of last-resort in the argument.

'Does he know?' Chara stopped. 'Ah, yes: your friend who has secured classified information illegally.'

Khazahn froze. His eyes widened. 'You were waiting,' he realised. 'Waiting for him to-'

'You'll have the arrest warrant this afternoon, and Desk Sergeant Makian is suspended from duty until further notice.' The edge of Chara's mouth curved upwards.

'You're insane' Khazahn snarled. 'You can't throw rank on this and make it go away!'

Chara appeared not to have heard him. 'How much does he know?'

'What?'

Chara turned to give Khazahn his unnervingly full attention. 'Does he know the most important fact? The reason it's still there? The reason this has to be seen through to the end now?'

Khazahn felt an anger and indignation well up in him as it rarely did. 'No, sir. He doesn't,' he said, filled with regret. 'He has no idea.'

Aleera did feel a little guilty; she'd needed to talk to someone, but she hadn't even considered Sara as a potential candidate. She could have told herself that Sara wouldn't want to see her, or that she would probably blame her for what had happened to Michael, but in truth, the fact that she knew Sara would never blame her made the thought of facing her and her shining blue eyes seem impossible.

Sara was in the old diner again, drying a fresh layer of tears. She looked up and tried to manage a smile.

'How's Jake?' she asked as Aleera sat down. Wow. She really did think of everyone but herself.

'As good as anyone could expect, considering,' Aleera replied.

'I don't suppose…' Sara fumbled with the old cross. '…they're anywhere close to catching him?'

Ah. That was right. She never did mention to Sara that Azrael was- past tense, she remembered bitterly- in captivity. The thought was still irritating, not only because it lost her a chance for vindication, but because he was still out there somewhere, and the thought of him being anywhere near Sara opened that pit in her stomach right back up again.

'I hope they do,' she answered, looking out of the window. 'For his sake.'

Sara gave a quiet sigh and took hold of Aleera's hand. 'I understand,' she said quietly.

'About what?'

'You're angry.'

'Of course I am.' Well, it was obvious. Looking back, her file was rather accurate in saying she had some anger issues; Ryan Shane and the two petty criminals she'd bumped into during the past week could attest to that. And, really, she was entirely justified in wanting to crack Azrael's skull open.

'Would you really hurt him?' Sara asked quietly. 'If you could?'

Aleera made to say "I did", but caught herself. No knowing how Sara would react to that. 'I would.' Oh, bravo, Aleera. That was a much better response.

Sara gave a half-laugh. 'You wouldn't.'

Aleera looked incredulously at her. 'You are aware of what's happened with that guy at school- must be three times now- right?'

'Yeah, but you'd never *hurt*-hurt anyone,' Sara smiled.

No, she would. And had done. Did Sara really have such a wrong impression of her? She felt a stab of guilt. Or… did she mean *hurt-hurt*? As in, the last hurting the recipient would ever feel.

And, she realised, she would. In fact, she'd tried. Repeatedly. She'd very much enjoyed trying.

'I'm going to kill him,' she blurted out before she could think. Sara's jaw dropped as her fingers tightened around the cross.

'No,' she shook her head. 'I know- I mean, I hear you get into a lot of fights, but… no. You'd never kill anybody.'

'I never have,' Aleera suddenly realised that she said it reassure Sara. 'But if I had the chance… I would. After what he did, I would.'

Sara, for the first time Aleera could remember, looked horrified. Not nervous, not uneasy, but genuinely struck with fear. 'You can't,' she whispered.

'He killed Michael,' Aleera answered defensively. 'He's got a cult worked up just against me.'

'You can't- a cult?' Sara sat back. 'A cult?'

'White robes, daggers, burning effigies, definitely cult material,' Aleera replied grimly.

'The Guild can stop that.'

'Yeah, because they've done a shining job so far,' Aleera answered bitingly. For a moment, she was about to let slip about just how dire her situation was; a Guild Commander was supporting a cult that wanted nothing more than to cut her to ribbons and then burn the ribbons. But no, Sara didn't need to know that. She was worried enough.

'You can't just kill someone,' Sara insisted desperately.

'He did.'

'If you kill him,' Sara urged, 'what would it change? It wouldn't bring Michael back. It wouldn't change anything except that you'd be a murderer as well.'

'I-'

'Aleera,' Sara said pleadingly. 'Listen to me, Ok?' Aleera nodded. 'I love you. Not- not like we talked about the other day, but- you're my best friend. In fact, you're the only friend I've got. And I'm asking you as your friend,' she took Aleera's hand again and looked into her eyes, 'please,' she breathed, 'don't make me see someone I love turn into a murderer. Don't make me lose you because the Guild hunts you down.'

Aleera sighed. A smile curled the edges of her mouth. Wow. This was the most someone outside of Lilith, Jake or Michael had ever actually said that they cared about her. It was nice, she had to admit. It was something she did care about, if one of the few things.

'Ok,' she said quietly. 'Ok.'

Sara smiled and let go of her hand.

21

Any residual hopes Aleera had that she might feel better by school the next morning had by now been thoroughly dashed. She fished through the contents of her locker half-heartedly, trying to avoid reliving the moment where she'd pulled back the curtain to find…

She retrieved the textbook she needed and, about to close the locker, saw the one sentimental keepsake she had at school: she'd taken the old photograph shortly after moving to New York, before Lilith moved away: the two sisters had accompanied Michael and Sara on a trip to Coney Island, and somehow talked Jake and Katya into going as well. She'd held onto the memory ever since; she'd managed to forget everything for that few hours and replace it with cotton candy and cheer. The picture had the six of them together on the Ferris wheel, nothing behind them but the glistening sea on a flawless day in July.

She should get rid of the photo. It would just depress her every time she looked at it. She reached to take it down, but something stopped her hand. Without knowing precisely why, she let it remain and closed the locker, keeping the memory safe inside.

'Well look who's back,' the slurred voice giggled. Aleera immediately gritted her teeth as her eyes started to turn red, and her knuckles turned white against the surface of the locker. 'Whassamatter?' Ryan scoffed, 'huh? Where you been, bitch?' he took a brave- or rather stupid- step forward as the other students in the hallway turned to watch. Hyenas for the kill.

Greg looked around awkwardly as he made to say something to Jamie and was fiercely shrugged off.

Ryan's face twisted in contempt and satisfaction as he stepped forward and lightly shoved her. 'That right?' he smirked, 'you missing somebody?' he shoved her again. Aleera took a deep breath as a wave of anger swelled up inside her, and whatever might normally have kept it at bay was long-since warn down. That, and the poor dumb fool had no idea what he'd just stuck his foot into. 'Yeah, thought so. Least now the negro's outta the way there's more room for the frigid bitch, huh?'

Aleera exploded at that moment; she grabbed Ryan's arm as he went to shove her again, pulling him round and twisting the arm as he snarled in pain, then jabbed her free fist into his kidneys and slammed him face-first into the lockers. As the clang echoed down the hallway, she honestly hoped she'd brain-damaged the sack of filth.

'Shut your filthy mouth,' she snarled, pulling him round and punching him in the face. She wasn't thinking at all now, and this wasn't even venting any other rage. This was what he deserved for what he had just done. To say that about her friend? To her face? Two days after he died? How *dare* he! As soon as he hit the floor, she pulled back her foot and half the hallway screamed as she delivered a soccer-style kick to his face.

Jamie moved to grab her. No glared threats this time, no warning, just a sharp punch to his mouth that, judging by the way he spat at the floor, dislodged a tooth. She proceeded to grab his hair, push his head down and drive her knee into it. Ignoring him, she pulled the groaning Ryan to his feet and, grabbing the sides of his head, pressed her thumbs into his eyes. She felt herself grin as he screamed; that dark part of her was awake again, and it loved this.

'Now,' she hissed into his ear, 'listen to me, you worthless piece of filth. Stay away from me. Stay away from Sara. Or I will kill you. I will take this…' she extended a claw and, in her favoured method of intimidation, pressed it to his chest like a blade. 'and I will carve you like the pig you are. And I will do it slowly.'

She released the clamping grip on his eyes and let him fall to the floor and, making sure to change her eyes back to their normal brown and retract the claw, took a calming breath and turned away from him. A gathered crowd of students huddled with wide-eyed stares- until a bustling body moved the students to one side.

'What is this?' Ah: Ms. Wood, the textbook-talking-teacher. Lovely. 'Well?' she straightened herself and took a haughty breath. 'Ms. Maheste. Principal's office. Now.'

Aleera didn't bother to avoid glaring daggers at her. 'And him?' she nodded to Ryan.

'Go,' Ms. Wood snapped.

Aleera shot a final, piercing glare at Ryan before turning to walk silently down the corridor. Oh, wonderful: this again. She'd probably be expelled or suspended this time; it was hard to bring herself to care.

The door into the principal's office was already open, but she was still made to sit outside while Ms. Wood informed the principal of the skirmish. After a minute, she was ordered in.

'Well, I didn't think I'd see you back in here again this soon,' the principal said while stealing a few glances as Aleera sat down. 'I understand you assaulted the same student again.' Dear lord, he made it sound as if Ryan Shane was some kind of victim.

'I was retaliating,' she said bitingly.

'I am not going to put up with bullying in this school,' the principal started indignantly, as ever so full of his own self-importance.

'Tell that to Ryan Shane,' she answered sharply, 'because I really don't see how you could have missed what he's been doing for a week.'

The principal glared back at her. 'If you have a problem with this student-'

'I did say so,' Aleera pre-empted him. 'Did you even do a thing to him after he attacked my friend?' The following silence spoke volumes.

'Ryan Shane is a troubled student,' the principal answered defensively.

'He's a drug-addled thug with a room-temperature IQ,' Aleera spat. 'And you're coddling him because you know who his father is.'

The principal's pencil snapped in his hand. He took a deep breath, as if he had the right to be angry. 'I know,' he said patronisingly- something Aleera hated, of course- 'that you've been... affected... by what happed recently, but this behaviour has persisted for a week.'

'So that's what self-defence begets now? He tried to hit me in the head with a chunk of marble!'

'And you have evidence of that?'

'Evidence?' Aleera raised her eyebrows incredulously. 'You're not a cop. You're a school principal. You're a pathetic, pompous fat man too busy trying to cover his own backside to do his job,' well, at least she could be thankful that now the anger was coming out through words. 'Half your students could run a school better than you.' Oh, now that was satisfying.

'Three weeks suspension,' the principal seethed, face flushed with blood from his wounded ego. 'One more word, Ms. Maheste- one more word- and you can consider yourself expelled. Anything else to say?'

Aleera bit her tongue, stood up and walked out. The diploma smashed again.

A while after she left, the principal found himself looking down at the chair in perplexity. It almost looked as if a blade had been scraping on the end of the armrest.

'That *bastard!*' Jake yelled as he spun round, throwing the cell phone clear across the room and into the wall before leaning against the back of the sofa, venting angrily through gritted teeth as the fabric of the furniture bent under his grasp.

'So I can assume that wasn't a sales call?' Katya piped up from the kitchen.

'That was Khazahn,' Jake answered bitterly.

'Hence the stirring cry of "that bastard"?' Katya observed.

'Not him,' Jake said angrily. 'Chara. He's bringing us up on charges,' he seethed.

Katya stood perfectly still for a moment blurting out 'that *bastard!*'

'"Illegally obtaining information from the Guild archives without authorisation",' Jake quoted, tapping the old coin on the sofa behind him and gripping it hard enough for his knuckles to turn white.

'He's charging us?' Katya near-shouted in outrage, 'after what he did?'

'That's exactly why he's charging us,' Jake said through gritted teeth. 'Think about it: What better way does he have to keep us quiet?' he asked with venom on his tongue.

'So he's prosecuting us for finding out about his financing a bunch of murdering lunatics,' Katya hissed. 'He can't do that, Jake!'

'He can," came Jake's bleak rely. "He *is*.'

'But…' Katya spluttered, 'He… that's *insane!*'

'I feel sick,' Jake groaned, shutting his eyes and turning his head down. 'Shit, I probably just got us locked up and lost Makian his job!'

'This is nuts,' Katya insisted, 'He can't do this! Khazahn's just letting him get away with it?'

'Chain of command,' Jake answered spitefully. 'Khazahn can't do anything; he wouldn't know insubordination if it bit his head off.'

'What's happened to Makian?'

'Confined to quarters. By the time Chara's done, he'll probably end up losing his job because of me. Damn it,' He leaned down and buried his head in his hands. A few seconds passed as Jake took a deep breath, leaning back and glaring in frustration at the ceiling as he came to a very unpleasant conclusion about himself that he rarely allowed himself to face. 'When am I going to learn, Katya?' He finally asked in despair. 'When am I going to stop acting like I can get away with anything?'

'Hey,' Katya scolded, pointing her finger at him, 'You're not doing this; Chara is. Now stop blaming yourself, because Aleera does enough of that for both of you, and put that supercomputer of a brain of yours into thinking of how we can take this out of Chara's ass!'

Jake stood back up, breaking into a slight chuckle.

'I don't know *what* I'd do without you sometimes, kitkat,' he smiled. 'You know that?'

'Just don't forget it,' Katya grinned as she pulled him into a tight hug. 'So: Plan?'

Jake glanced around the room, clicking his tongue as he pulled the old coin out of his pocket, flipping it across his fingers as he put his mind to work racing for a suggestion.

'Right,' he announced, flipping himself over the sofa, narrowly missing the table from which he grabbed the papers, and kneeling down to pick up the phone. 'We take these to the High Council.'

'Right now?'

'Right now.'

Beaming, Katya stepped next to Jake as he waved his hand and announced '*Appiras*!'

The air shifting around them, the sight of the living room shooting away from them as earthy stonework, murals and pillars replaced them, everything blurring past as though they had been suddenly, sharply pulled from one place to another.

In a second, they were standing in the front of the temple, great carved dragons looking at down from them with wise eyes flanked by magnificent wings, the emblem of a great serpent carved in shining gold above the great door stone before them, its frame etched with runes that translated as *Truth-Justice-Honour*. Jake found himself bitterly reminded of how little he'd seen of those things lately.

'Still not used to that,' Katya groaned, shaking her head from the lurching feeling of the teleportation spell.

They stepped forward toward the door, on one side of which sat the polished wooden desk. The woman behind it, dressed in a crisp black dress with her hair tied back in a bun and half-moon glasses suspended on the end of her nose, looked up at Jake as he approached.

'Yes?' She asked.

'I'm here to see the High Council,' Jake answered. 'It's important.'
'Do you have a pass?'
Jake quickly dug his hands into his pockets, checked the ones in his shirt, and turned to Katya, receiving a Gallic shrug in response. Total lack of organisation strikes again.
'Not with me,' he answered sheepishly.
'Do you have an appointment?'
'Mmmmmnope.'
'Should've made an appointment,' Katya sighed exasperatedly. 'What, you expected to just waltz into the High Council's offices?'
'Look,' Jake said to the secretary, 'just tell them that it's Jake Connolly, and it's very important.'
'And this would be?' The woman asked, referring to Katya.
'My roommate,' Jake shrugged. The woman shot him a glance that, without a word, communicated a message of "Do-you-expect-me-to-let-a-teeage-boy-into-the-High-Council-Offices-*and*-his-roommate-without-a-pass-or-an-appointment?" 'Assistant? he changed tactics.
'Familiar,' the woman realised with a look of slight disdain and awkwardness.
'Yeah,' Jake nodded.
'I can ask them,' the woman shook her head, standing up and walking through a smaller door behind her desk, muttering something that started with 'Don't know what the world is coming to…'
'You could have just said "familiar",' Katya pointed out. 'I keep telling you, it's not a problem.'
'I don't like it,' Jake replied simply. 'Might as well call you a house pet.'
Katya shrugged. 'Just thinking,' Katya mentioned hesitantly, 'we found documents,' she pointed out incredulously.
'Evidently.'
'Why did we manage to find documents?'
Jake looked at her expectantly.
'If I was doing something as illegal as this,' Katya explained, 'I'd probably avoid writing it down and then storing it where I worked, especially if I worked at the Guild.'
'I've given it some thought,' Jake answered.
'And?' Katya prompted.
Jake turned his old coin over a few times. 'I don't know,' he finally said breathlessly.

Katya's eyes widened slightly. 'It's been a while since the last time you said that.'

'It's just… it shouldn't have been so easy for us to find out. Chara's been getting away with this for years, but you just walked in and fished out the papers…'

'Should I be offended by that?' Katya cocked an eyebrow.

Jake shook his head absently, probably having not heard a word she'd said. 'Weird. It's like it's staring me in the face,' his voice trailed off, but Katya managed to catch something that sounded like 'and I can't see it.' He took a sharp breath, as if rejuvenating himself. 'Anyway,' he said quickly, 'we can worry about that later,'' he smiled faintly, his concern now thoroughly covered up as usual.

'Well, while we're on the subject of ideas,' Katya pointed out, 'why don't we just teleport straight in there?' There was no point in trying to get Jake to tell her what he was thinking about, as she knew from experience.

'And do something even more illegal than what we've been doing for the last four days?'

'Point taken.'

The door behind the desk opened again, the secretary stepping back out.

'I've been instructed not to let you in,' she declared, before sitting down as if they were no longer there, and if they were there, certainly not of any consequence.

'…Any particular reason?' Jake inquired.

'Apparently,' The secretary replied, 'Jake Connolly… that is right, isn't it?' Jake nodded. '…You are currently pending possible legal charges by the Guild, and until that time, you have apparently been banned from all Guild offices and other offices of administration.'

'Ah.'

'Were you aware of this?'

Jake bit his lip. 'Yeah. Basically, I was just hoping you weren't. Worth a try. Thanks anyway.' He turned round on the spot before the secretary could reply, Katya following him angrily.

'You knew we weren't allowed in here?' Katya hissed.

'Relax, I know what I'm doing. First we go back and get our pass, and then we go to plan B.'

Katya looked stupefied. '"Plan B"?' she asked incredulously, 'we have a plan B now? So this was plan A? This by you is a plan?'

'Plan B's better,' Jake argued.

'How can it not be?'

'Oh, very funny. Now let's just go and find the pass. I think it's on the coffee table,' Jake trailed off, 'although I might have left it in the study. Or the kitchen this morning. Or it could be behind the sofa...' Katya sighed and rubbed her temples. It was moments like this that made her stop and think "dear God, I actually live with this guy".

'Let's go, then,' Jake declared, 'Hold on-' he pulled the jingling cell phone out of his pocket. 'Shit,' he grimaced, 'it's Aleera's school. Hello? ...what? ...she did *what*?' Katya winced. Seemed she'd stepped in it again. 'Hell... alright, thanks for calling.' He switched the phone back off. 'She got herself suspended,' he seethed, 'hospitalised some guy at school.'

'You're kidding.'

'God, why does she do these things?' Jake sighed. 'The way things are going round here, Chara can't get a whiff of this,' he said warningly.

'Think she's just... y'know,' Katya offered, 'stressed out? I mean, she's had some problems for a while.'

'You're telling me,' Jake muttered. He took the old coin out of his pocket and flipped it over.

Katya made to speak, then caught herself, and then finally managed to say it. 'Are you still going to tell her?'

'Not now,' Jake answered.

'Of course not now, the poor girl's got enough to deal with. But she'll have to know some day.'

Jake clutched the coin tight and gritted his teeth, and his eyes darkened with something unbearable, something old and forgotten and awful. 'She'll find out eventually,' he said flatly and pocketed the coin.

'That doesn't sound like you,' Katya half-smiled, her expression faltering as Jake failed to reply. 'Would you?' she asked nervously. 'Come on, Jake, you wouldn't let her find out that way,' she denied, 'you wouldn't do that to her.'

Jake flashed a look of anger, not at her, but of directionless frustration. 'You know what I wouldn't do,' he finally seethed as the anger projected itself with the deepest conflict and longest-buried remorse, 'I wouldn't make her deal with it, along with everything else she's suffered through. I wouldn't leave her knowing what's going to happen, what's already happened, what she really is, and all that's depending on her, because that… there just wouldn't be a word for something that cruel.'

Katya's eyes lidded shamefully.

'I'm sorry,' Jake sighed. 'I really am, to you and to her.'

'Do you wish you hadn't told me?'

'Young Master Connolly,' an unfortunately familiar voice, its tone unmistakable sharp, addressed him, 'I hear you've been rather busy since our last conversation.' Jake turned as Chara took a few confident strides forward.

'Chara, there's a train leaving in thirty minutes,' Jake answered dismissively, 'make sure you're under it.'

'You might want to show a bit more respect for authority,' Chara said dismissively, 'unless you'd like another charge to be added to your ever-growing list.'

'Add as many as you want,' Katya answered him, placing a hand on her hip and jerking her thumb towards Jake, 'just wait; Jake here's gonna hang you!'

'…And you be sure to keep your pet in line,' Chara continued with a contemptuous sneer towards Katya, who scowled back with an angry show of gleaming fangs.

'What do you want, Chara?' Jake demanded.

'Well,' Chara replied disinterestedly, 'I've decided to take some action regarding the situation with Kudra's daughter.'

Jake glared back at him, clenching his fist as he set his jaw in sudden, sharp outrage. 'What the hell have you done now?'

'Just making sure that the situation is properly contained,' Chara answered as haughtily as ever, turning sharply away. 'Good day.'

'You seriously think you can do this?' Jake shouted after him. 'You-' he froze. 'You said "contained",' he breathed. 'As in, it's out in the open?'

'The current situation simply needs to be dealt with before it gets out of hand,' Chara answered, perhaps a little hastily.

'What's to get out of hand if you're in control?' Jake challenged.

'Unless…' the most mixed of expression covered his face. 'It's already out of hand.'

'This conversation is over,' Chara snapped like a wounded jackal. 'I expect that I can trust you both to leave before I call security.' He turned and limped out of the room to nurse his wounds.

Well, at least Aleera could get home early. In fact, she'd been thinking that being suspended from school was something she could turn into a positive; it would certainly give her more free time in which to find Azrael and... and not kill him, she reminded herself. She'd made a promise, which meant that however badly she wanted to tear Azrael's heart out and show it to him, she wouldn't.

It was still hard to be pleased about it, though. God, that man was pathetic, and it really would be nice if he was the only one. He couldn't control the problem so he just left her to cope with it herself- and when she did, what did he do? It wasn't even as if Shane hadn't deserved it, and she hadn't done anything serious to him, or his idiot brother and friend. Although, that said, Greg had not, as she recalled, done anything. Most people would be irate enough to condemn him by association, but life had taught Aleera better. She'd been raised by a madman, but was perfectly stable- oh, yes. Not a good example. But still, it was probably her own emotional distance that allowed her to step back and look at things objectively.

And objectively, Ryan thoroughly deserved to have his face pulped.

There were no calls to her cell phone from Jake, which in all optimism she could take to mean there were no new developments. Of course, that would mean something actually going right, which lately didn't seem to be in the cards.

She approached her apartment building, passing by the old bus stop and bench that sat on the other side of the street.

She stopped.

No. Surely it wasn't...

Oh, *hell-o*.

'I thought you were a religious man,' she said without turning to Azrael.

'Really?' Azrael chuckled that goading chuckle and stood up. 'And what do you think is my sin?'

'Suicide.' She spun round, backhanding him with lightning speed before whirling back and driving her foot into his stomach. Azrael caught her foot and flipped to the side, and she landed on all fours.

'I see we're breaking our little promise, then,' Azrael observed.

The pit was back. 'What promise?'

'Oh, I was there. This…' he pulled a pendant out from beneath his shirt, 'is quite the resource. Word reached me that you found the supplier, as well- and that you scalded his face.'

'What do you want?' Aleera demanded. 'You're not here to fight; it's broad daylight.'

'Clever. No, I just felt it was time for another chat. I imagine you still have some questions.'

Aleera straightened up. That was true.

'Then answer this,' she said. 'Why?'

'Why go after you?' Azrael asked as though he were justifying a choice from a menu. 'Well… it's *you*. You know I did my homework on you; why I killed them all the way your own filthy flesh and blood did.'

'So it's because of him.'

'Kudra's seed must be pruned,' Azrael snarled, 'it's an infection. It spread to the boy, and look what happened.' Aleera fought to control herself. 'It has to be killed now.' He gave a mocking glance. 'Nothing personal.'

There. There it was, that flicker in his eye. To go to this length? To drag it out this long?

'You're lying,' she accused. 'This is personal, isn't it?'

'I was chosen to carry out heaven's justice,' Azrael replied coldly. 'I know what the devil was capable of.'

'Because it affected you,' Aleera realised. Ah, now she was getting somewhere. 'He did something to you.'

Azrael nodded darkly. 'Kenya,' he recited. 'Six years ago. You were there.'

Aleera felt her heart drop. Oh, good God. It couldn't… it couldn't be. No. No, it was impossible.

'He killed everyone in that village,' she breathed, feeling herself quiver. God, this was someone else like… dear heaven, like her. Someone else whose soul had been ripped out that awful day.

'Almost.' Azrael lifted his shirt. The skin beneath was strained and stretched; grafts, unmistakably. 'He tortured my father in the middle of the village. I tried to stop him, and he tossed me into a burning hut and left me for dead,' he snarled venomously.

'And you survived that?'

'By divine intervention. I alone survived that I might bring justice to the evil that unleashed itself.'

'Did you miss something?' Aleera challenged him coldly, 'Kudra's been dead for three years.'

'An eye for an eye,' Azrael stepped forward. 'The evil must be made to pay by those it wronged. And it still lives. The same flesh and blood still walks the earth.'

Dear God. Aleera's stomach tightened. That was it? That was his reason? Of all the things, of all the ways for it all to come back...

'You're going to kill me for what he did?' she snarled, feeling the colour of her eyes shift. 'I didn't kill anyone!'

'Did you stop him?'

'I was eleven years old!' Aleera hissed.

'You are the same evil!' Azrael growled. 'You know it. It runs through you as it did him. He passed it on, and now it is simply waiting for the right call. You are a child of evil, and you *are* evil. Think,' he glared, 'what have you done this past week? You tortured a man. You hospitalised a boy. You almost killed a petty thief.'

'Shut up.'

'You will pay for your sins,' Azrael declared, 'yours and his.'

'You *idiot*,' Aleera said through gritted teeth. Before she could stop it, the fury and outrage poured out. 'Do you think you're the only one who suffered because of him?' she shouted as she grabbed him and slammed him backwards into a lamppost. 'Do you have any idea- *any idea*- what he did to me?'

Azrael rose his forearms between hers, pushing them apart and freeing himself.

'Shall I tell you something?' he glowered. 'What I'm doing right here... it's nothing special. Nothing special at all. Any of them out there- if it was a choice between you, and someone they've never met, they wouldn't choose you. It's not just them. It's not just you. This is a world that's full of hate, to the point that it becomes trivial. The kind of hate that your father had for me and my kind. The kind of hate that they have for you. Believe me... you're no more of a victim than myself, or anyone else. Next time, demon,' he said, 'next time we meet, God's justice will be served. I promise you that.'

He stepped past Aleera. With the street empty, Aleera knew that by the time she turned round, he would be long gone.

22

Aleera rinsed the sink out, still tasting the hot bile in the back of her throat. After Azrael turned up, the thought of what he'd done to Michael came back and forced its way up. She collapsed back against the bathroom wall and wiped away some vomit, still tasting it inside her mouth.

Damn it. Damn it, damn it, God damn it, why had this happened? Why now, why Michael, why all this? She felt her claws scrape against the surface of the wall as she leaned her head back. Damn it. She wiped a fresh wave of tears away and bit her lip to keep herself from crying.

God, it was her fault. It really was because of her. Whether Sara or Jake or Azrael said it was or wasn't made no difference; Michael had died because of her.

The worst, the very worst, was that however she looked at it, there was truth in everything Azrael had said; there was something dark in her, ever since that day when it crawled inside her. She'd beaten half the life out of two people- even if they were only people in the same sense that a street-vendor hotdog could be considered food- in a little over a week, and that was discounting the at-least-two sets of bones she'd probably broken at the factory.

It had sat inside her heart the exact same day as Azrael. They'd both witnessed that hell, and both been left with such burning hate.

God, they were the same. Just two twisted killers, the only difference being that she was a killer that hadn't killed yet. It was still in her, and it wouldn't always stay there. Soon enough the claws would have the blood they craved.

No. No, stop it. She was just shaken. The thought of what happened had come back up. She was just shaken, that was all. Just a little shaken. Calm down. She wasn't like Azrael; Azrael was like her father, and she would never be like him. She may have been far from perfect, but she was a far cry from being what he had been. There we go. Much better. Nice and calm. Very nice to have that sorted.

She took a calming breath and tried to think rationally again. Azrael had appeared again, so…

So he was going to do something. Make his next move? Almost definitely. So the "game" was still on. And Chara, of course, was on the playing field as well. She was certain that Jake would have found proof by now; she'd been able to see it in Chara's face from the beginning, filled with the same contempt she'd seen before and senselessly over inflated authority- and who else was in a position to accomplish something like this? And of course, that conclusion brought problems of its own.

Knuckles rapped on the front door. Aleera retracted her claws as she quickly arrived to open it. For a moment, she considered that it could well be Azrael, and her stomach tightened; no, he wouldn't be stupid enough to try and enter her apartment, especially not right through the front door. He knew as well as she did that, even if she had made a promise not to kill him, that wouldn't stop her from taking him apart.

As it turned out, she had the pleasant surprise of seeing Jake on the other side of the door.

'Please tell me you've got some good news,' she sighed as she let him in.

'I wish.' Jake cringed jokingly. This would have offset the sudden heaviness in the room, if not for the fact that he was turning the old coin over in one hand.

'What is it?' Aleera asked urgently, dreading the prospect in the back of her mind. It wasn't... *that*, she told herself as if it helped. Jake had just done that cringe of his; if the news was that bad, he wouldn't have. He always had a point of staying serious about something like that.

'I tried to go to the High Council with what we found out,' Jake explained, 'nut Chara's had the idea to press charges after we went skulking through the archives. And... he's placing you in "protective custody".' He finished.

'In other words...?' Aleera prompted. That pit was back.

'You're under house arrest,' Jake answered bleakly.

Aleera stared back at him for a second.

'Are you serious?'

'I really wish I wasn't.' Jake said honestly.

'I can't leave my apartment?'

'Not without giving Chara an excuse to set his whole division on you. And of course...' Jake bit his tongue. It didn't really need saying. A few things could use saying under the emotional circumstances, many of them obscene.

'This means I'm an easy target,' Aleera finished for him. 'Chara might as well have just marched me up to Azrael.'

'I'll fix this,' Jake swore. His tone begged for the sentence to be gifted with an additional "somehow".

An unexpected sob caught her off-guard. She covered her mouth as everything, Michael, Azrael, Chara, everything, overwhelmed her. All of this, this nightmare, who was supposed to take all of that?

'It's alright,' Jake said gently, holding her as she fell forward. 'Easy.'

'I'm fine,' Aleera sniffed. Get a hold of yourself, girl, she chided herself. 'Sorry for that.'

'Don't be ridiculous, you don't have to apologise for-'

'It's fine,' Aleera said hastily. 'So now what?'

'Hopefully, I can fix the whole Chara mess by morning,' Jake hesitated, 'but I should tell you about something else.'

'There's something else?' She wasn't sure why she was still surprised.

'Yeah, and it's a big problem: from the looks of it, Sword of Heaven isn't taking orders from Chara anymore.'

Aleera took this in a word at a time. Part of her wanted to savour each syllable. 'He's lost control.' Well, she had to take gratifications where she found them at times like this. Of course, she knew the kind of man Chara was. If he was taken aback by a teenager standing up to him, he wouldn't take this lying down. He'd be desperate. Hence, giving them what they wanted in order to get them off his back and give himself some breathing room.

'You're sure?'

'I think so. Not that I can be certain,' Jake admitted, 'but Chara's running scared, and he's desperate. That and his butler was admitted to hospital the other night.'

Aleera nodded thoughtfully. It sounded reasonable, and Jake was seldom wrong about those matters.

'Anyway,' Jake said quickly, breaking the heaviness, 'I should be able to get you out of here tomorrow.' His voice became sombre again. 'So you can go,' he said hesitantly.

Aleera understood. The event she'd been dreading, that she hadn't even though about, had been arranged for tomorrow. 'Thanks.'

Tomorrow was to be Michael's funeral. Most of Michael's family was nearby, and his mother could hardly be blamed for wanting to get burying her son over with as quickly as possible.

'Oh, and one more thing,' Jake remembered before he left. '*Phoux Tyasans Blaish.*' The apartment seemed to spasm and shudder, then settled instantly back into place, trace sparks of magic dancing over Jake's fingertips. 'Protective invisibility seal,' he explained, 'nobody can see in from outside, even if they've got a Third-Eye working. So among other things you can get showered in privacy.'

'Thanks, Jake,' Aleera said honestly. Considering everything, it was a welcome gesture; it was standard Guild procedure to have someone stationed outside; in fact there had been a few there for her first six months of living in the apartment. 'You don't miss a trick, do you?'

'Just the big ones, I guess,' Jake answered regretfully. 'Before I forget: you still got that Dragon blood?'

Aleera nodded and pulled the vial from her pocket. 'Where'd you get this stuff?'

'Trade secret,' Jake answered knowingly. 'Gotta get to work; see you tomorrow. *Appiras.*' With a convulsion of air, he vanished and left the apartment empty save for its tenant.

The Guild soldier crouched on the edge of the rooftop and whispered what had just transpired into the radio of his helmet.

'Beater-One, please repeat. Over.' Chara's voice seemed to be barely held back from shouting.

'Looks like a protective spell,' the second soldier repeated for him. 'We can't see in. Over.'

'Third-Eye?'

'Useless.'

The soldiers heard Chara's teeth scraping. 'Maintain position. Hunt out.' The line went dead.

'I hate this, man,' one of the soldiers sighed when he decided it was safe to do so. 'Got a wife I could be home with right now, instead we get picked to baby sit some psycho demon.'

'Dollar's a dollar,' the other replied. 'Know what I heard? This kid and that freelancer, the Connolly guy- both looking at the cells; leaked information about the demon-killer investigation.'

'Heard it was a cult doing that shit,' the other soldier muttered. 'Nobody's safe these days, man. Things haven't been good with the demons ever since the war.'

Above them, on another rooftop, a figure in white crouched and earnestly fingered the handle of his dagger.

Bait, he scoffed. They thought they could draw him out this easily? They sought to manipulate him, to control him; that he was their pawn to move as they saw fit.

'Brother Azrael.' The voice from the white spectre behind him was sharp and commanding. 'We're running out of time. We need something done about her.'

'It will be,' Azrael said grimly. 'Just as soon as everything is ready.'

'This is personal for you, I know. But-'

'She will die,' Azrael snarled, 'once she has suffered as she has never suffered before.'

'You have to return.'

'The hunt must continue,' Azrael replied simply.

'You've been gone since the Guild raid. You are the leader; you have responsibilities to the cause.'

'This is the cause.'

'You've spent every minute following the child. It is time to take action. We have protocol, brother Azrael.'

'This prey is special. She will not repent her sins.'

'Brother,' the other man pulled his hood down. 'Please. You must come with me.'

Azrael rose and turned to him. 'Why?' he seethed accusingly. 'You think I've become obsessed? Is that it? You think my judgement is clouded?' The other did not reply. Azrael took a slow step forward.

'Azrael- Kakuta- please…'

In a single, sweeping thrust, Azrael plunged the blade into his chest with a dull slicing sound. His limbs froze, his face looking down and paling in horror as the front of his robe dampened in the spreading red. He took one ragged breath as he staggered back to the wet sound of the knife scraping out against blood-dampened flesh.

'I am Azrael,' Azrael snarled, 'I am the angel of death, and I will bring justice.'

The man reached the edge of the building and fell. One more unworthy soul rooted out and cast into the depths of hell, and the devil child would follow.

Azrael returned his gaze to the apartment, and the vengeance that was his by right.

23

Aleera woke slowly and blinked in the glare of the sunlight. The thick fog that had previously kept her asleep refused to dissipate, and her eyes ached. The first thing she thought was that today was the day.

She turned over in bed. Getting up and facing the day was far from the most attractive of prospects, but she wasn't going to lie there all day. Going was the right thing to do; what Michael would want her to do.

She'd been hurt. The realisation had come to her a few times, and always seemed somehow alien. She'd been hurt by losing someone for the first time, and she just didn't know a word to describe the twisting knot of emotion. God, she really had cared about him, and she'd realised it far too late.

Climbing out of bed, she stripped off and entered the shower, letting the cold water wash the rest of the fog from her head. A single tear was undetectable in the running water. Once dried, she checked her bedside clock to ensure that she still had plenty of time. Michael's funeral was at four. She dressed in a T-shirt and jeans and laid a black, formal dress-suit out on the bed with matching gloves, shoes, and a hat and face veil, all with slow and mournful simplicity. She hadn't expected to wear them again this soon.

What had happened? She never even thought about something like this, about how things between her and Michael and Sara might be different than she'd always thought. Was she that self-absorbed, that inhuman?

She made herself a breakfast of cereal. It was hard to feel like cooking. She'd done it to enjoy herself, or for her friends, or Lilith, or to celebrate something. She didn't presently have much to celebrate. Even the honey in her fridge sat undisturbed. While eating, she made her way into the living room and half-heartedly glanced out the window.

She dropped the cereal and ran to the door.

Humans seemed to be drawn to disaster, be it electing incompetent governments or getting as close as they possibly to could to something, that, by all logic, they claimed to find horrific. She could even hear people muttering about how "awful" the situation was. Still, she had her reasons to be there: namely because the murder scene was on the roof of the apartment building adjacent to her own.

The mass was gathered like a flock of vultures at the edge of the perimeter of yellow police tape. Figures in white ducked in and out to make reports. Aleera squeezed her way through the pack, trying to catch a glimpse to confirm or deny the possibility that was clawing at her mind.

'Aleera.' The firm voice cut sharply through the low buzz of the crowd. Its source was a familiar shape in a navy-blue suit, spots of grey at the temples of his dark hair.

'Khazahn,' Aleera addressed him curtly. Well, he had plenty of nerve, one had to concede that. 'What are you doing here?'

'Chara's protective detail,' Khazahn replied grimly.

'What about them?'

Khazahn pointed to the two shapes on the ground covered by white tarps. 'That's them.'

Ah. All questions more-or-less answered, then, once the merciless logic train finished its route. Logic might be more interpretable, but it could be at least as much of a bitch as emotion ever was.

To her left, Harry and Tomoko emerged from the gathering of forensics. Thanks to the coveralls, goggles and surgical masks they were wearing, Aleera could only identify them upon hearing their voices.

'Stab wounds to the hearts of both victims,' Tomoko reported methodically, 'but it looks like that was just to incapacitate them; the cause of death is more likely to be having their throats slit. The bodies are in the same condition as the others.'

'Different M.O. this time, though,' Harry pointed out. 'A lot quicker. Think it's another of those psychos?'

Khazahn shook his head. 'Doubtful; from what we gleamed, it looks like Azrael's the only one with anything enchanted. Keep me informed,' he instructed as he stepped over to another figure, likely another disguised Guild soldier.

'You Ok?' Harry asked of Aleera.

'As well as can be expected,' Aleera replied.

Harry shuffled awkwardly. 'I'm just going to call ahead to HQ before we move the bodies,' he said as he walked away, 'probably take a while though.' Because the bodies were in public, most likely.

Standard procedure was to take advantage of the usual CSI cover to get that done.

'Jesus, this is a nightmare,' Tomoko muttered as she glanced back at the crime scene. 'Two corpses in black body armour, helmets and cloaks in broad daylight. I do *not* envy the cover-up boys. Did Khazahn tell you about the other one?'

'Other one?'

'One of those cult lunatics. We found the body on the other side of your building, lying in a dumpster. The initial analysis matches the stab wounds from the other victims- only this one hasn't been burned.'

'He killed one of the cult?' Aleera parroted. Wow, now this was unexpected. It seemed that it wasn't just Chara who had lost control, cold logic declared for her. No need to be emotional and think that Azrael held some kind of loyalty in the face of the evidence. He was a psychopath, as driven by the dark things inside him as she was, and if he was anything like her, he had a very low tolerance for frustration.

Were they that alike? The thought was a sudden and painful electric shock. Was that why she'd been so able to think as he thought; to work out his means and motives?

'Looks like it,' Tomoko answered her. 'Anyway, I should go. Catch you later.'

'"Catch you later"?' Aleera repeated, one eyebrow raised. She might not have known Tomoko for two weeks yet, but being nicely detached helped with noticing a change in someone's behaviour. As Tomoko left, she noticed how quickly she was in close proximity to Harry. Well, well. Being detached also made it easy to forget how much other people might have happening to them at the same time.

'I thought you'd be here right now,' a more familiar voice called to her. This time it was Jake emerging from the crowd. Immediately, their prior conversation came flooding back to her.

'How did it go?' she asked urgently.

'Got called here first,' Jake admitted guiltily. 'I'm on my way to deal with it right now. What'd you find out?'

'Two Guild soldiers and a cultist,' Aleera reported. 'Seems you were right about Chara not being in charge.'

'Think it's a message?'

Aleera pursed her lips dreadfully. 'Two. He's telling Chara he can't manipulate him. And he's telling me,' she bit her bottom lip, 'I'm not safe.' Well, when Azrael left a message, it wasn't a note on the door.

'You are,' Jake promised.

'No offence, but I'll feel a lot safer when nobody's trying to kill me,' Aleera answered.

'Aleera! Jake!' Both turned to see Khazahn approaching, either Harry or Tomoko (Aleera couldn't tell) on one side.

'We've got a problem,' Harry-so it was him- said. 'Another kidnapping.'

Aleera felt her stomach contract like she'd been punched. 'Sara,' she whispered, her voice carrying more horror than she ever thought it could.

'No, but it's hardly a mercy. Our victim is Chloe Mcrae: ten years of age-'

'How old?' Aleera interrupted. Any remaining fear was quickly submerged in rage. A child? A *child*? He kidnapped a *child*? And what he would do to that child... she found herself retching as she remembered her worst childhood memories and how Azrael would recreate them.

'Ten,' Harry said disgustedly. 'Caucasian. Lives about a block from here. Demon mother, human father. Reported missing this morning.'

'The child,' Aleera breathed. Oh God, how could she have been so moronic? She'd heard Azrael and the others talking about the "devil child" and just assumed it was her they were talking about.

'Well, the good news, if you can call it that,' Khazahn stated, 'is that Chara can't get away with letting this slide; if a child ends up dead, the High Council will throw him in a cell so fast that it'll make his head spin.'

'Chara couldn't stop this guy if he wanted to,' Jake replied sharply, while sending a cold glare suggesting that Khazahn was far from being in a position to talk about the morality of letting things happen.

Jake turned suddenly as someone tapped him on the shoulder, having just emerged from the gaggle of spectators. 'We've got company,' Katya warned, pointing across the rooftop. Everyone looked at once, and Aleera and Jake were the first ones to mouth "shit".

'What's he doing here?' Jake whispered.

'Here's here because two Guild Soldiers were found dead on a rooftop,' Khazahn answered matter-of-factly, 'and I should warn you: he wants you and Katya arrested.'

'Yeah, I know,' Jake said dismissively.

'I'll talk to him,' Khazahn offered.

'Me too,' Jake's visage was like an iron mask.

'You won't be able to talk him out of it,' Khazahn warned.

'I know,' Jake said, breathless. 'I just want to yell at him for a while.'

'Then I'm coming too,' Aleera spoke up with hate dripping from every word.

'Is that a wise idea?' Khazahn pointed out.

'Does it matter?' Jake shrugged, 'Chara's on his last legs.'

Khazahn, allowing his expression to give an outward display of conflict just this once, led them past the rest of the still-gathering spectators and toward the man who surveyed them with cold grey eyes.

'I've been informed of the developments,' Chara declared before anyone had a chance to speak. 'A full enquiry will be underway by this evening.'

'Inquiry?' Khazahn regarded him worriedly, 'into what?'

'The homicide committed here,' Chara replied with the same glance he would probably use on someone who didn't know the solution to two-plus-two.

'What's there to inquire about?' Khazahn pressed. 'We can see what happened here.'

'I am referring to the *other* homicide,' Chara replied. 'With such a different *Modus Operandi*, one can never be sure.'

'Who else is it going to be?' Jake demanded.

'There are always suspects,' Chara answered in the shrewdest of voices, turning his grey eyes on Aleera.

'Excuse me?' Aleera demanded.

'You can't be serious,' Katya stared.

'Every possibility has to be considered,' Chara replied without looking at her. 'After all, if someone so close to the case has a potential motivation, it is our duty to investigate.'

'No.' Jake stepped forward. 'No. There's no way you'll make this stick, Chara. Not in a million years.'

'My young friend,' Chara said, turning to him, 'I assure you that I am not the only one who has been watching for any sign of criminal behaviour on Ms. Maheste's part.' Aleera's eyes narrowed as the tone of "we-can't-wait-to-throw-her-in-a-padded-cell" sank in.

'You'll never even get this to a tribunal,' Khazahn glared.

'I'll remind you to mind you how address your superiors, Sergeant,' Chara snapped at him to fall back into line. The slightest pigmentation rose in his cheeks as his loyal sergeant actually dared to stand up to him. 'And for your information, this investigation remains at Division level.'

'You can forget it, Chara,' Jake seethed as he stepped right up to him, 'I know. It's over. You're finished.' He made sure that his mouth shaped every word perfectly.

'And what do you intend to do?' Chara sneered. He leaned forward and said, quietly, 'you and your pet cat are out of your league. You are a freelancer and a repeated past suspect with a sentence currently hanging over your head. Face the facts... you can't *touch* me.' He stepped back and glanced mockingly at Aleera. 'Like father, like daughter,' he scoffed. 'That's what they'll be hearing. And believe me, they say it for themselves enough.'

Oh, Chara, that silly bastard, he'd gone and said the "F"-word.

'Aleera!' Jake snapped, blocking her with one hand as he waved the other with a quiet '*Tyasans*.'

'You *bastard*,' Aleera seethed, protocol and restraint forgotten as the wings erupted from her back, the claws extended and her eyes flooded with blood-red. Oh God, she just wanted to tear his hide clean off. 'You piece of *filth*! Do you even know what you've done? Is there any part in that sick little mind of yours that realises how deep a grave you've dug for yourself? Seven people have died in nine days because of you! And then- to think you can just throw this at me and get away with it?' She stepped back and glared at him with all the contempt and hate in the world. 'You think you're untouchable, and I promise you: you are going to pay for what you've done.'

All present fell silent. Even Jake stepped back.

The scary part was that Aleera hadn't even raised her voice.

She allowed herself to enjoy the sight of Chara composing himself as quickly as possible, straightening his suit. 'Threatening a Guild officer?' he said with the face and expression of a child trying not to cry, 'we'll see how that turns out, won't we? Then again- that was always the first resort of your kind.'

He turned, walking away and through the door that led down into the building, while Aleera calmed herself with deep breaths and fought the urge to unleash herself and cut Chara to pieces right then and there.

'Let it go,' Jake advised quietly. 'He'll get what's coming to him. I promise.'

Aleera gave a long, heavy sigh. 'Thanks,' she finally said. In retrospect, there was no telling how much worse she could have made her situation by adding assault on the Head of the Eighth Division to the matter. She turned away, wings and claws receding as the remains of her shirt fell from her body. 'I need to go and change,' she said quietly, and then left without another word.

As Aleera left, Khazahn took a long, slow glance at the bodies, then back to Jake, whose fist was taught around his old coin. 'I didn't-' he started.

'You could have brought Chara down whenever you wanted,' Jake interrupted with a voice that carried pure hate. 'Siding with me and Aleera now isn't going to absolve you.' He walked away without looking at him. 'I have nothing to say to you.' He walked away, pocketing the coin and left Khazahn standing alone on the emptying rooftop.

Jake gave three sharp knocks on the door of the apartment. Katya and Aleera stood next to him, Aleera anxiously running a hand through her hair. From within, there were sounds of movement as someone made their way, apparently somewhat awkwardly, toward the door.

'You don't have to be here,' Katya said gently to Aleera.

'I do,' Aleera insisted. She was finding this child, come hell or high water. All of this was happening because of her, however much she wished she could distance herself from it, and she was damned if she was going to have a child's blood on her hands.

The door swung open, dragging across an old, rough carpet. On the threshold was an elderly woman, her worn features looking at the three of them with cautious curiosity in her faded blue eyes, narrowed in a touch of suspicion. Thin, bony fingers that seemed to be made entirely out of knuckles tightened around a battered wooden cane.

'Yes?' She asked finally asked, looking from Jake to Aleera to Katya and back to Jake again, her hands tightening further around the cane..

'Mrs. Mcrae,' Jake addressed her, holding up a small, silver Guild emblem in his hand, 'We're from the Guild,' he elaborated as reassuringly as he could.

'What's your name?' The woman asked, evidently not entirely convinced and clearly ready to step back inside. Her voice carried a thick Irish accent.

'Jake Connolly. This is Aleera and Katya.'

The woman softened. 'Yes, I was told you were young,' she nodded, relieved. 'Can't be too careful nowadays. Come in,' she gestured, stepping back and allowing them inside.

The apartment was old, and somewhat on the stuffy side, with a great many old black-and-white pictures on the walls and surfaces of an old cupboard and a bookshelf next to the television. The living room was furnished with a thick carpet, an old sheepskin rug and a two-seater sofa.

'I don't suppose you have any news?' Mrs. Mcrae asked hopefully, her eyes wider now and her fingers relaxed on the old cane. Aleera realised that she looked so much more… *frail*. She hadn't even noticed that the old woman was at least half-a-foot shorter than her.

'We're just here to ask some questions,' Jake explained.

'People have been doing that all morning,' Mrs. Mcrae sighed in heavy defeat. Suddenly she was even shorter. 'Asking me where she went to school, when I saw her last, who her friends were…'

'I understand how you feel,' Jake told her sympathetically with a soft tone that suggested that every word of that was accurate, pulling the old coin out of his pocket and turning it over. 'We needed to ask about… well, about her parents.' Apparently he knew this would by a touchy subject.

'My daughter,' Mrs. Mcrae said distantly, 'Janet. She was a lovely girl, God rest her soul.'

'Do you mind if we ask what happened?' Jake hesitated to ask.

'A car accident,' Mrs. Mcrae explained with the sadness that only a parent who had lost a child could know. 'Chloe was only seven, the poor girl. That's why I take care of her, you see. Such a sweet little girl. She was going to the park,' she wavered and then sniffed into a handkerchief. 'I'm sorry,' she sobbed into the fabric. 'If I'd gone with her…'

'It's OK," Aleera said reassuringly, feeling herself fill with determination that she was going to find this girl and unflinchingly make Azrael pay for what he had done.

'What about her father?' Katya asked.

'I can't say much about him, I'm afraid. Bit of a shock, though, when I found about that half of what you read in storybooks is walking around working the nine-to-five. A little after they were married, he started showing his true colours. Janet never told me about what he did, the poor thing was so scared she didn't even want to tell the police. I saw the bruises, though. And poor Chloe, she was so afraid…' She shook her head bitterly. 'Then one day, he went for Chloe, and that was it. They were divorced and he was arrested. Beastly man,' she muttered.

'Has Chloe had any contact with him since then?' Jake inquired.

'No, her father won't be seeing anyone where he is. He got into a fight in prison, you see.'

'I see,' Aleera nodded slowly.

'Why are you asking about her father, though?' Mrs. Mcrae asked worriedly and with a note of knowledge. She was old, not naïve. 'Is this because he was…?'

'We have reason to suspect that this is linked to Chloe's father being a demon,' Jake admitted sensitively.

'I thought so,' Mrs. Mcrae sighed. 'Will you…'

'We'll find her,' Aleera promised. 'I swear.'

'Had Chloe been talking to anyone strange lately?' Jake pressed with all the implication of the world that this question was *very* important.

'Not that I could tell you. She spent most of her time here or at her friend's home, and she just lives across the street. Every Tuesday and Thursday she goes to her dance class. Either that, or she goes to the park and school. I don't even have the internet, so she hasn't been getting involved in any of those things you hear about.'

'Right. There's just one more thing I have to ask you,' Jake continued, 'have you seen this man lately?" Katya handed him a piece of paper, which he proceeded to show to Mrs. Mcrae. It was a photograph of Azrael's face, shaved head, beard, eyes slightly close together and high cheekbones. 'He's around six-foot-four, quite well-built,' Jake prompted.

Mrs. Mcrae thought back. 'Yes,' she finally answered, "the refrigerator repairman.' Seeing the inquisitive looks from Jake and Aleera, she elaborated. 'There was a problem with it last week. He came from the company and fixed it. Is he…?'

'We believe so.' Jake answered, holding the coin still. 'Thank you, Mrs. Mcrae.'

'We'll find your granddaughter,' Aleera promised as she and Jake stood up. She left out the part about what she intended to do to her kidnapper.

'Thank you,' Mrs. Mcrae sniffed into the handkerchief. 'Lord,' she sobbed, doubling over. All Aleera could do was kneel next to her and comfort her- to her, a rather alien practice altogether. This woman was the type of parent she'd never had. She didn't deserve to be put through this. 'Please,' she sniffed, 'I lost my daughter- I don't want to bury my granddaughter as well…'

'You won't,' Aleera said fiercely. 'I swear it.'

Mrs. Mcrae nodded, sniffed, whispered 'thank you' and stood up.

'Why do you young people do this?' She asked, not demandingly but out of some strange gregariousness that Aleera was unable to identify. 'Things like this happening, it's no life for people so young.'

'Circumstances,' Jake answered ambiguously.

'Or are you really that young?' Mrs. Mcrae asked cryptically, moving forward and pointing to her faded blue eyes. 'You're young, true, but your eyes… they tell a different story. You've been around for longer than it looks. Seen more than you'd think.' For a long moment, she stared intensely at him like a particularly confusing puzzle.

'That's a long story,' Jake replied quickly and breathlessly as if the words were an intake of air after being underwater.

'What about you?' Mrs. Mcrae asked of Aleera. 'A pretty young girl like you, you shouldn't have to deal with this sort of thing.'

'Like Jake said,' Aleera said honestly, 'circumstances. We'll see ourselves out.'

Once the three were safely outside, Katya finally piped up with 'what do you mean by "Circumstances"?', tilting her head sideways, both to try and press her friend for information, and taking the opportunity to distract Aleera from her evident guilt.

'Like I said: long story,' Jake shrugged, idly rolling the old coin across his fingers.

'And that thing about the eyes?'

'Can we focus?' Jake shrugged off the question, taking a few strides ahead.

'So he doesn't tell you any more than me, huh?' Aleera asked of Katya. She probably shouldn't be so relaxed at such a time, but really, it was either this or curling into a sobbing ball.

'Tell me about it,' Katya sighed, shaking her head slightly and biting her tongue to keep from saying anything else.

Aleera looked ahead and lost herself in thought. She would find this girl no matter what she had to do.

And she had a rather good idea of where to start.

Let the games begin.

In all the excitement of the past few days, it was forgivable to forget the existence of the four Sword of Heaven members arrested after the otherwise-failed raid on the factory. Of course, clearly not everyone had forgotten about them, as they had clearly been fed during their stay and were alive and well.

According to Harry, they were in fact awaiting trial. They'd each confessed to their intentions of, bluntly, killing as many "wretched devils" as they could get their hands on. Apparently Azrael had the most understanding of self-preservation out of the entire cult.

After having to promise Jake- repeatedly- that she wasn't going to do anything unduly violent, she'd been allowed in the room along with one of the cultists. Jake would enter in five minutes. More than enough time.

She shoved the greasy, bald, pasty little man with extremely bad teeth and altogether too many tattoos into the rickety wooden chair.

'Ok,' she started, not bothering to sit down as her wings extended (she'd been sure to wear one of her tops with a low back) along with the claws, 'I'm going to ask you a question. You're going to tell me the truth, and if you don't I will make you hurt until you do.' That was, if she felt like stopping. If they were willing to do this to a child, then she saw no reason not to keep going. 'Now: where is Chloe Mcrae?'

The cultist sneered. 'No idea what you're talking about.'

'You know,' Aleera mentioned offhand, 'I used to have a girlfriend whose eyes turned to the left like that when she lied.'

The cultist sneered. Oh, thank you. Now she had an excuse. Much obliged.

She backhanded him across the face with the blunt edges of a set of claws; far better, and slightly harder, than any brass knuckle.

'Where has Azrael taken Chloe Mcrae?'

The zealot glared up and spat at her.

'Wrong answer.' Now, this was not something she was fond of doing, but a child's life was in danger and, by all previous accounts, there was less than a day in which to find her. Desperate times and all that. So she pulled back her foot and delivered a sweeping kick into his most intimately masculine body part. 'Where are they?'

He looked back and broke into a smile of yellow, rotten teeth. 'You stupid whore,' he snickered. 'You wretched little…'

Aleera pulled him up, retracting the claws of one hand and punched him in the face. He was laughing! *Laughing* while a child was going to be put through hell and murdered.

It dawned on her that, technically, she had only promised not to kill Azrael. And here was a subject who was simply begging for the attentions of a good set of claws.

'She's a child,' she hissed as she threw him into the opposite wall with an audible 'thud', a raging river of red surging through her every vein as that dark little thing inside reminded her of that laugh and what would happen to the child and egged her on and laughed and screamed and… 'a child! She is ten years old!'

'And I don't even know who she is,' the man giggled, spitting out a mouthful of blood.

'Remember what I said would happen if you lied?' Aleera hissed as she picked up one of his hands and pushed the little finger back until it snapped and he yelped like a wounded terrier.

'I don't need to lie,' the cultist cackled. 'The truth is what will break the devil, and the truth is that none of us even know whom the Angel of Death targets.'

'That lying thing again?' Another finger, another yelp. 'I'm going to break something else once I'm done with these, just to let you know.'

'We were never told any target other than you,' he chuckled; face red with pain, 'in case of this ever happening. We don't know who he targets or where he takes them.' He broke into his biggest, bloodiest grimace. 'I couldn't tell you where Azrael was if I wanted to.'

Aleera stepped back. She could feel her skin drain of colour at the unthinkable thought. Indignant, frustrated fury welled up and screamed to be let out. She didn't know, she had no idea, he was gone, lost, *she couldn't stop him…*

'*No!*' She screamed and delivered a final kick to his stomach, listening to the blow knock the wind out of him. Then she turned, stormed to the door and slammed it shut behind her.

As soon as she was out, she felt herself grow flustered and embarrassed. She'd lost it again. Low tolerance for frustration reigns supreme, right up there with Azrael.

'Aleera?' Jake was approaching from another door. 'Harry checked on Pentagram; it's still under airtight guard. They're not there.'

Aleera cursed under her breath. She'd known that one to be a long shot at best. She bit her lip as hopelessness started to dawn on her, her mind racing for a solution and finding nothing. She was off her game again, she knew it, and it was going to cost someone else their life.

'Look,' Jake started anxiously, 'we'll take it from here. You've got… you know.'

Of course. Not that she was looking forward to putting her friend in the ground, but his murderer owed it to him to at least be present.

'How's she doing?' Katya asked as Jake shut the door behind him, looking up from a magazine that she'd somehow managed to locate amongst the clutter.

'About as well as you can expect,' Jake replied, breezing into the living room. 'But in lighter news: done it.'

'Finally,' Katya sighed, sitting up. 'You're sure?'

'Well, the High Chancellor wasn't thrilled to see me burst into a meeting waving a file, but I managed to get her to listen. Handed the papers to the Head of the Guild myself.'

'So Chara…?'

'Probably behind a heavy door by now. Which just leaves…' his face fell. 'The big problem.'

Katya bit her lip. 'Yeah.'

'And looking back,' Jake said regretfully as he started to fiddle with the old coin, 'we really haven't done enough about him.'

Katya gave him a look that passed clear through incredulity and came out the other side as a sort of bizarre amusement. 'You don't stop beating yourself up, do you?'

'Guess not,' Jake said breathlessly. 'I just-'

'I know, I know,' Katya insisted, 'you feel responsible for the girl, I get that, but you can't be everywhere. With Chara blocking everything we tried, it's impressive that you managed anything, and *wake up,*

Jake, you just cracked a magical conspiracy, for Christ's sake. Give yourself some credit, boy.'

Jake gave a quiet chortle and broke into a smile. 'Couldn't have done it without you, kitkat.'

'What I'm here for,' Katya winked and grinned. 'That and lecturing you on being a complete self-kidney-puncher.'

That was when the knock came. Anything involving the Guild, much like with the police, had that unmistakably sharp edge.

'I swear to God,' Jake grumbled as he approached the door and pulled it open, 'if this is Khazahn, I am going to take that staff and shove it up his-'

'Jake Connolly?' one of the two men in creaseless police uniforms asked. The badge he was holding up was a silver Guild emblem. 'We're going to have to ask you to come with us.'

Jake looked at him, then at the other, then back again.

'Chara sent you, huh?'

'You are under arrest for illegally withdrawing classified information from the Archives of the Eighth Division of the Guild of Guardians.'

Jake clicked his tongue and looked from one of them to the other.

'You're not the only two here, are you?'

The one who had spoken looked somewhat nonplussed. 'No,' the other said uneasily.

'Hmm. Just asking,' Jake drummed his fingers idly on the doorframe, flashing a knowing smile back at Katya, 'I expect there's an illusion spell being generated, so that even if you deactivate your own cloaks, all anyone will see is two ordinary cops. And, of course, a suppression field so that I don't blast my way out of here.'

The two nodded, unable to explain their growing feelings of unease.

'Interesting thing,' Jake pointed out sagely, 'suppression fields: they don't affect enchanted objects. Hence, you having them to maintain your cloaks, and of course that's why Guild staffs will still be working. And,' he reached his hand behind the open door, 'if I just reach into my Uncle-Santa-Jim'll-Fix-It-Magic-Box,' his hand wrapped around a large wooden stick, the top third of which was stylishly carved into a spiral, 'you will find something I keep for just these occasions- can't teleport over long distances with it, but still: *Appiras*.'

The air shuddered, pulled back-and-forth, and Jake was at the other end of the corridor as the door into his apartment slammed shut, a faint glow around the frame indicating that the protective seal was activated and they wouldn't be getting in to Katya anytime soon.

One of the soldiers shouted something about "suspect mobile" as Jake, affecting something of a pole vault with the aid of the stick, flipped himself over the banister of the staircase to cut off a few vital seconds, ducking as a bolt of force collided with the wall above him. Flipping himself over the banister to clear another floor, he ran into the adjacent corridor to the front of the elevator shaft and slammed the button as he heard the soldiers' footsteps bypass the floor completely. 'No sign!' a soldier shouted. 'Check the elevator!' a third yelled.

When the elevator completed its descend with a shrill "ding", no less than seven Guild soldiers had their buzzing staffs trained on the grated metal of the door. It opened slowly, with a rusty creak.

Jake shot across the other end of the corridor and inwardly laughed that it had actually worked. He threw open the fire-exit doors…

…and was struck across the chest, flipping him backwards as if he'd run into a very hard metal clothesline and sending him falling to the floor. A thick, black boot stepped down on the stick even as he gripped it, and eight buzzing staffs were subsequently pointed at his head.

'So much as think about casting a spell,' one of the soldiers growled from beneath his mask, 'and we will blow your damn head off.'

Jake looked around and weighed his options. Oh, please. As if he even needed to say it; just by thinking it, he could smash the staffs to pieces and have all eight of them strewn across the scenery. On the other hand, that certainly wouldn't help his current legal standing, and in that sense wouldn't be overly conducive to helping anyone.

And, of course, Katya knew the plan for these situations. The "escape attempt" had been for entertainment, more than anything else.

He relaxed his grip on the stick.

'Alright,' he shrugged, 'I give up.'

24

Aleera had never seen so many lilies in one place. It looked like a wrinkled, stained white blanket draped over the upturned earth in front of the cold slate headstone.

The funeral had been over for almost a half-hour. She actually hadn't burst into flame at any point while in the church. Probably not the most appropriate thing to be thinking at the time, but it beat contemplating the fact that someone she loved was in the ground. It hadn't been overly different from what she expected: the priest had done his best to soothe people he didn't know with sweet nothings that didn't numb the pain one bit. Something about being God's plan. That hadn't been pleasant to listen to; what Azrael would have called it.

This wasn't right. It happened in inner-cities every day; people younger than Michael were knifed or shot walking home, but that didn't make it right. It shouldn't happen. Michael shouldn't have been dead, and that was the most sickening thought. He should have still been there. A cold piece of meat that no longer even looked like him shouldn't have been packed into a wooden box with six feet of dirt on top of it.

She stared down at the fresh gravestone that sat amongst worn, moss-coated peers. The fresh, crisp inscription read: *Michael Prince, Beloved Son, Taken From Us, Aged 17*.

And that was where he was, and where he would remain forever. He was *dead*. The awful notion had finally sunk in at some point during the service. What they'd had, and what they could have had, ended in a second and saw a good person, a friend, turned into a pile of cooling flesh, life and soul cast away as though it had never been there. He was dead. Gone. Forever. She would never see him again. Ever.

He was in a better place, the priest had told them all. Somewhere better.

Was this one that hard to top? Part of her asked.

At least it was better, another part said.

If it was, another said.

Was it? Another asked.

Was there one? Another asked.

It was the last one that made her not-quite-shiver as she stared down at the gravestone.

Was he really somewhere better? Somewhere good and shining and beautiful, looking down at what was left behind? Or was he just lying in a wooden box in the dirt?

What if..., she thought without wanting to, what if he wasn't? What if he was just... dead? Gone? Nothing? Just dark and... and nothingness? Lying there in the dark forever without knowing, without being able to know, just complete and total nothing where a mind and a life should be? No dark to see, no wooden box to feel, not even anything left to comprehend the darkness, nothing, nothing at all, nothing?

Then one day, that would be her, in nothing and nothingness. Too much nothing to even care that it was nothing, just... nothing. Gone. Dead. Nothing. That would be her, or Sara, or Katya, or Jake.

It was worth it, Michael had said. He'd said it was worth it to be with her. It wasn't. Nothing could be worth this.

She heard wary footsteps on the gravel path. A cursory glance included the old priest, white hair on the sides of his head and a chasuble draped over his white robe. He looked at her with uncertain caution as his hands moved slowly to the crucifix around his neck, lips slightly parted as he struggled for something to say. He knew. People didn't have that look without knowing.

'Yeah,' she said quietly. 'I didn't think I'd be too welcome.'

The priest released the crucifix. 'Were you a friend?'

Aleera blinked. It was an unexpected question; she'd expected something more along the lines of "how dare you profane this place with your presence". Past experience and all that. 'Yes,' she said.

The priest looked sorrowfully at her, apparently caught between his duty, what the bible said about being a demon- "don't do it" was in there somewhere, if she recalled- and knowing that what he was looking at was no dark metaphysical spectre, but a teenage girl who was going through hell.

'I was about to go anyway,' Aleera said, sparing him the trouble of deciding. 'Just saying goodbye.'

'It's quite alright,' the priest said in a voice that was somehow very reassuring. So this was what a man of God actually looked like. 'I know you're not here to hurt anyone.'

Aleera looked down at the fresh headstone. 'It's not something I have to work hard at,' she said bitterly. The priest remained sympathetically silent before turning back to the church, and as he did,

Aleera saw another black-dressed female figure walking determinedly up the path. If nothing else, she knew when she'd worn out her welcome, so she stepped back and walked away from the grave.

'Aleera?'

The voice was soft, mournful and... something else. The woman's voice was different, not angry and hateful and vengeful, but with the sorrow and grief that only someone who lost someone so truly precious to them could ever understand. But it was also a different kind of sorrow, a tone of hesitation and anxiety that Aleera had rarely heard.

'I'm just here to say goodbye,' Aleera pointed out, not looking up, in the thin hope that her words would help to avoid what she was sure would follow.

'Actually,' Michael's mother started awkwardly, 'I wanted to apologise.'

This time, Aleera looked up, with a slight frown of surprise.

'I came to... to apologise about what I said,' the woman explained hesitantly.

'Oh,' Aleera realised with unintentional bluntness, thinking back to the angry, hurled shouts she'd just recalled, so different from the shaken, grieving woman standing in front of her now. Her eyes lidded in shame, just a little. 'Mrs. Prince... you don't have to...'

'No, I-I do,' She insisted awkwardly and shamefully, 'and please, call me Mary. What I said to you at the hospital, it was...' She paused, seeming to swallow a lump in her throat as she searched for the words. 'It was wrong of me.'

'It's alright,' Aleera said quickly.

She didn't want to hear this, not now. She didn't want to hear an awkward apology from a woman who had lost her son because of her. To hear her say it wasn't her fault- when she knew, when they *both* knew, that she was. She couldn't deal with that, and somehow it felt as though if she could just stop the poor woman from saying it, she wouldn't have to feel the guilt that would come with it.

She was wrong. The gnawing guilt was already working its way through her stomach. That pit was wide open again.

'Please,' Mary insisted, 'you had enough to deal with. I was just angry, and...'

"You were right", Aleera wanted to say, but the words wouldn't come, only a stillness and dryness in her mouth.

'But that's no excuse,' Mary finished, turning to her son's grave as a few strands of her tightly-tied hair hung unintentionally loose. 'I'm so sorry- for that, and... for this.'

Aleera still said nothing, staring down at the freshly chiselled headstone again as the lily rolled over in a calm breeze. She knew she should have said something, but what was there to say? What was there to do, other than look at the stone?

'I... If you don't mind my asking,' Mary said, this time even more hesitantly, 'about you and Michael.'

Aleera still didn't answer, but it felt like a knife was twisting inside her.

'No... we... we weren't.' She managed to force the words out through her choking mouth, but failed to disguise the note of regret they carried. It wouldn't be politic to add that in another day or two, they would have been.

'You know,' Mary gave a long, slow sigh as she tenderly rested a hand on top of the headstone, 'I never did forgive him.' Aleera looked up, surprised. 'Dhitao,' the woman explained, 'Michael's father. It all seems so stupid, looking back now.'

'Do you mind if I ask what happened?' Aleera asked tenderly.

'He was always good to Michael,' Mary explained distantly. 'But he and I... we never really saw eye-to-eye. We had very different ideas about what would be best for him. We got divorced when Michael was six, and... well, we never really spoke much after that. Not until recently, at least.'

Aleera happened to glance up and spot the tall, bald African man who walked away from the church. He'd been at the grave just before her, she realised.

'It all just seems so petty now,' Mary sniffed, 'so foolish.' Her voice broke down into a soft whimper. Aleera put a comforting arm around the crying woman as she went on: 'I forgot. I forgot what I always told Michael myself... never hate. Dislike if you really must, but never hate, not over something like that. Because...' She wiped away a tear, 'Well, none of it really matters in the end, does it?'

'I guess not,' Aleera admitted distantly as she looked down at the headstone.

Mary turned away from the grave and walked back towards the church, her head hung low. 'He was so young...' Aleera heard her sob quietly.

Aleera lingered next to the headstone for a short while, placing one black-gloved hand on top of it. 'I'm sorry,' she whispered.

'Touching.'

No. Here. Now. That voice. *Him*. He wouldn't, even him, not if he thought he was a man of God. Yet there he was, leaning on one of the headstones.

'Leave,' Aleera ordered flatly, feeling her eyes change colour. 'Now.'

Azrael ignored her and stepped forward. 'This is hallowed ground,' he snarled like a guard dog. 'A funeral, no less. You don't belong here.'

'I am in no mood for this,' Aleera scowled as Azrael stood parallel on the other side of the headstone. It was true; already her fingers were flexing of their own accord.

He's standing right in front of you, part of her screamed.

Too many people, said another.

But he's right there!

No. Not now. She'd promised Sara.

But he was right there.

No. Stop it.

She could end it right here, right now. Take off the glove and just stab him. Right there. Between the eyes. He was less than a foot away.

Stop it.

Easy target.

Stop!

Kill him.

Enough!

'I just told you,' she said, fighting to keep herself under control, 'leave. I am not dealing with you today.'

'That isn't your decision,' Azrael spat as though she'd just committed some foul effrontery. 'You don't get to make that decision. You don't decide! *I* will kill *you*, and that is how it goes!' Didn't like being stood up to, did he?

She wasn't giving him the time of day, she realised, and that angered him. Made him feel beneath her notice. Small. Powerless. That evil part of her was giggling like a ten-year-old in a toy store.

'You weren't invited to the funeral,' she said levelly. 'Go.' She turned away from the headstone. She heard Azrael follow.

'Don't you walk away!' Azrael shouted. He made to grab her and she dodged. 'You *dare*? You dare toy with me after everything I did to purge this world of you?'

'Oh, get over yourself. By this time tomorrow, you'll be locked up in a very uncomfortable cell, and I won't even have to look at you again.' She glanced back at Azrael and smirked. Well, it was fun, finally having the upper hand in this game. 'Chara's probably been brought down and exposed by now.'

'Chara?' Azrael scoffed. 'He was a puppet. A tool that forgot his place.'

'A tool who put your glorified lynch-mob back together, knows all about it, and by now probably lost all of that information to the High Council.' She saw Azrael's face drop. 'Now stay away from me,' she glared warningly, '*forever*. Unless you can avoid the Guild for long enough.'

'The devil's Guild have no authority over me,' Azrael grimaced. 'We know them as well as they know us, and they've no jurisdiction over human crime.'

'They do if a human's been killing people with an enchanted pendant.'

This was it, she realised. She felt almost giddy.

Check.

'They were demons,' Azrael snarled. 'They deserved all I did and more!'

Kill him. He was begging for it. Kill him!

No.

Find out first.

'Chloe Mcrae,' Aleera said sharply. 'Where is she?'

Azrael's mouth curved into a grin. 'Well,' he smirked, 'it seems I do have one last ace.'

An ace? It was a child.

Kill him. Just kill him right now.

Will you shut up and let me think, she screamed to her herself.

An ace. A piece of value. Still of value, and therefore still alive. Still time.

'Tell me where she is.'

Azrael grinned. 'The hunt continues.'

Kill him. Just do it!

'Ok,' she said quickly, aware of her own fast breathing as her eyes flushed bright red, quickly pulling off her gloves and letting the claws extend, 'continue it. Finish it. Right now.'

'On hallowed ground? No.' Azrael stepped back. 'The girl will die. And I promise… your suffering is nowhere near over. You will beg for death, demon, and then you will know the torments of hell.'

Oh, to hell with it.

She leapt at him, claws extended and screaming to sink into something warm. In a heartbeat, she was upon him- and in that heartbeat, Azrael raised one hand and announced '*Blaish.*'

The air shuddered. It twisted and hardened into what looked like a transparent mass of gelatine before herself and Azrael's outstretched palm, and, when struck, felt like a brick wall. Aleera slumped to the ground as gravity took over, wincing at the sharp pain in her right shoulder even as the barrier dissolved.

'Don't worry,' Azrael chuckled, 'you'll get your chance. *Appiras.*' The air shook, and he was gone.

The stone doors grated sideways as Khazahn gave a sharp nod to the Guild soldier seated behind the desk and jerked his thumb towards the door in a clear instruction. The soldier hurriedly did as told, running out and shutting the door behind him.

The holding area was filled with long shadows from the barred windows in the cell, sending grids of light across the floor and onto the wall below, like shafts of light pouring through the small, round windows in the stone doors that led into the cells. Khazahn stopped at the heavy door in front of him, knocking on it twice before the figure sat on the bench at the back of the cell looked up at him, continually turning over an old coin.

'Go ahead,' Jake said bitterly as he glared at the hole in the door. 'Tell me how right you were.'

'Knock it off, Jake,' Khazahn shrugged off the comment as he placed both hands on the door to look in at him. 'You got yourself into this.'

'How long do you think I'm going to stay in here?' Jake quizzed knowingly.

'You don't get it, do you, Jake?' Khazahn sighed angrily, his jaw set between his mask. 'This isn't just a matter of something happening and you playing the knight in shining armour and stepping in.'

'Heard this already,' Jake reminded him.

'Chara's desperate,' Khazahn lectured. 'He has been ever since he figured out you were poking your nose around. Do you think he'd have pressed charges otherwise? Detained Makian? Confined Aleera? He was on the edge as it was.'

Jake looked up.

'Why do I have this strange, completely-unfamiliar feeling that you've got a point?'

'You overplayed your hand,' Khazahn insisted, 'both of you. Chara tried to manipulate Azrael, and... well, look what happened.'

'I should have gone to the Council straight away,' Jake admitted hesitantly.

'You didn't because you tried to stop Azrael at the hospital.'

'And inside of a day, you let him escape,' Jake said icily.

'You just don't get it, do you?' Khazahn shouted, slamming his fist on the door. 'You might not understand or care, Jake, but actions have consequences! You can't just go throwing accusations against the head of the Eighth Division!'

'And that justifies all this?' Jake yelled back. 'People have died, Khazahn, because there's a psychotic killer on the loose and Chara's stopped anybody doing a damn thing to catch him.'

'I couldn't go against him!'

'Yes you could!' Jake shouted. 'You could just go to the High Council with this and have him thrown in jail for life.'

'And myself and a dozen others for being accomplices.'

Jake froze.

'I knew it,' he said with venom that Khazahn had never seen in him before. 'You were just trying to save your own hide, weren't you?' He shook in place, hands gripping tight on the bench beneath him as his eyes blazed with silent fury. He trembled, taking a deep, ragged breath as he obviously struggled to contain his anger. 'Get out of my sight,' he snarled.

Khazahn gave no reply. Instead, he turned away from the door, and Jake sat still angrily as he heard the stone door open and close. He stood up, hands on his head, exhaled slowly, then, with an angry shout, turned round and punched the wall.

'Did that help?' A familiar female voice chimed from the other side of the door.

'No.'

'Did that hurt?'

'Yes.' Jake winced and rubbed his fist.

The door slid open behind him, and there was Katya, one hand on her hip and leaning against the doorway.

'You could've just flattened him with the door,' She suggested.

'I'd have to disrupt the suppression field,' Jake explained, flexing his neck from the effort he'd been keeping up throughout his and Khazahn's conversation, 'just letting you get in takes a lot of doing. It's professional stuff.'

'Not professional enough,' Katya said sagely, pointing to Jake's wrists.

'Yeah,' Jake mused, 'I've been thinking about that too.' He gave another bemused glance at his wrists. Nothing unusual about them, save for the fact that there were no handcuffs on them to keep his magic in check. They had the suppression field, but the handcuffs were normal procedure as well. Strange.

After returning to her apartment, Aleera changed back into a T-shirt and jeans and sharply pulled out the black ribbon that had kept her hair back. Her dark eyes looked like sunken pits thanks to the smudged mascara. She ran some water in the sink, splashed it over her face and removed the last of it with some make-up remover. Then she leaned on the sink and stared vacantly at her expression for a few minutes.

That was it, then. Over. Done. Carrying with it a dull, aching finality. And it would be over. She would find Azrael and drag him into a cell herself if she had to.

And it wouldn't help.

If it came to it, even if she wasn't going to kill him, she would still beat him within an inch of his life.

And it wouldn't help.

It would be over.

And it wouldn't help.

Nothing would help. Michael was dead and nothing would help. Nothing would change that. He was dead, and-

And she'd loved him. She'd realised it all of two days before he was burned to death.

She stepped back, sat down, slumped against the bathroom walls and held her head in her hands. Maybe a normal person would have cried. Maybe a normal person would have realised what there was between herself and Michael before something like this happened.

She was sick of this. If this was the cost of it, she was well and truly sick of being an evil, twisted thing by the circumstances of her birth. She was done with it. She-

Her cell phone rang in the bedroom. She took it as a saving grace, pried herself away from that train of thought, entered the room and saw who was calling. She answered all the more quickly.

'Jake?'

'Quick update: Chara's busted,' Jake said quickly. 'You Ok?'

'Yeah,' Aleera lied. 'Is Makian still-'

'Working on that. Just checking on you.' Checking on her. He sounded like a father. There she went again. 'How's Sara?'

'Not exactly happy, but then again it was a funeral. I didn't go to the wake.'

'Why's that?'

'I doubt they'd be happy to see me,' Aleera sighed. 'Besides, guess who turned up.'

There was silence from the other end of the line. The heavy kind of silence that meant Jake absolutely dreaded the next sound. 'Everybody's fine,' Aleera reassured him quickly. 'He just left the-' she stopped in mid-sentence.

'Aleera?'

Her mind started to tick. He threatened her and left straight away, and she'd just left Sara and Michael's family at the wake with no idea of it? Oh, Aleera, you stupid, stupid girl!

'I'll call you back,' she said before hanging up. She shot the apartment, pulled the door open and slammed it shut behind her. Then it was down the stairs and out into the blinding light street in a blink.

Nothing to her right. How could she have been so stupid? She didn't realise it even after Azrael showed up to threaten her again. She and Sara were both right there, right in the open. *God*, how stupid could she be? And what was going to happen now? Stupid, stupid, stupid!

She should have killed Azrael when she had the chance.

Stop that!

Well, she should have.

Her cell phone rang. It dawned on her that she'd been in such a hurry that she never actually put it down. It was Sara calling.

'Sara,' she gasped as she answered it. Calm down. No need to worry her.

'Aleera? Where are you?' Sara asked.

'In the street,' Aleera answered dumbly, caught somewhat off-guard. 'Are you at the wake?'

'Yeah, did you go home or something?'

'Just to change,' Aleera half-lied, 'are you still at the wake?'

'Yeah, are you coming?' and yet Aleera had told her she was just going to change. Sara really did know her well.

'Sure.'

'Tell you what, why don't I come to you?'

'I can be there in a minute-'

'Relax; I'll be right there.' Sara hung up.

For the hundredth time, Makian put down his copy of the *Sports Illustrated* swimsuit issue, sat up on the side of the bed and surveyed his empty quarters. It had all the essentials: food, toilet, even TV access that was paid for by putting money into a slot. A lot of soldiers lived on-premises for various reasons. Having been evicted from two apartments in a row was Makian's. Unfortunately, after two days with nothing to do but watch *Star Trek* re-runs and make use of magazines, it got entirely too cramped.

Oh, that and pray that Jake succeeded in- well- in whatever the hell he was doing, because that was the only way he'd be leaving the room without an accompanying court-martial. That would mean a trial in front of the Head of the Guild, and the entire High Council really hated D-Unit- mainly because of Jake, although credit had to be given to their association with Kudra's daughter.

The door suddenly clicked and slid open. One of the two uniformed guards stationed outside as standard procedure entered and said 'You're free to go.'

Makian blinked uncertainly. 'Come again?'

Katya's head poked in through the doorway. 'Can Makian come out and play?' she grinned.

'Kat, please tell me your roomie managed to fix this shit,' Makian said urgently, grabbing his jacket.

'Oh, please,' came a chuckle from outside. Jake stepped round the doorway, flipping the old coin and catching it in his hand. 'Show a little faith.' He pocketed the coin. 'Come on,' he said seriously, 'we've got things to do.'

As soon as she let Sara into the apartment and closed the door behind them both, Aleera could see that something was... not wrong, but not quite right either. She'd hardly said a word on the way, and her eyes were lidded, she kept avoiding looking at her and seemed hesitant to say anything at all. It was one of those moments when it actually *didn't* pay to be as detached as she was.

Worst of all, she thought with a stab of guilt, she'd been so focused on her own guilt, on blaming herself for what had happened that she hadn't stopped to think about how Sara was taking what had happened. Maybe she was really that self-centred. Or just that much of a bitch.

'Do you want to talk about it?' she forced herself to ask.

'Do you?'

'You do,' Aleera said as they both sat down. She'd been focused on her own problems enough; she was due to make time for a friend. Besides, any distraction she could get, she'd take. Better than thinking about Michael, or about the child...

No. Jake was going to find her.

And if he doesn't?

Don't *you* start, she mentally snapped at herself.

Sara tensed, curled her legs up and wrapped her arms round them. Her eyes blurred and seemed to have lost some of that shine. 'I miss him,' she said quietly. It dawned on Aleera that, in all the time they'd known each other, she'd never really noticed how withdrawn Sara was. She always knew she was quiet, a little timid, but she'd never even seen her cry, not until Michael. Maybe that was why they got on so well.

And she'd never quite realised how much she'd cared about Sara, and why those shining blue eyes had always softened her. She reached out and wiped away one of Sara's tears for her.

'Me too,' she said gently.

Sara sniffed and smiled. 'I understand,' she said, adding 'about the wake' when Aleera looked slightly confused. 'I know you guys were... close... so it's alright if you just wanted to be alone for a while.'

Yes, that was the reason. Not because of Azrael, or her own guilt, just that she wanted to be alone for a while-

'Yeah,' she said before anything could slip out. 'How was everybody?'

'As you'd expect, I guess,' Sara sighed.

'You didn't have to leave.'

'It's alright. Besides, I guess I'm doing more good convincing you.'

'Of what?' Now Aleera truly was perplexed.

'You know what.'

Oh, that. Yes, she knew. It would have been nice to pretend that wasn't it, or that it wasn't why she left the wake, but Sara knew her entirely too well for that. Hence coming here. That was something Sara would do. It was something a real friend, a good person, would do. Whichever way she looked at it, the world would do well with more people like Sara Lammbe.

'I'm sorry,' Sara said quickly, 'I shouldn't have said that-'

'It's fine,' Aleera insisted. It would be nice to drop the subject right then, and however much she would have liked to, something still tied her to it and forced her to see its conclusion.

Sara bit her bottom lip. Her hand was around the silver crucifix again. She was going to say it, Aleera realised. She was going- oh, please, don't- 'It wasn't your fault, Aleera.'

Aleera couldn't seem to muster the willpower to say anything, so her eyes did it for her.

'Look at me,' Sara said gently, placing a hand on Aleera's shoulder. She fixed Aleera's dark eyes with her own sparkling ones. 'I don't blame you,' she whispered.

'I know,' Aleera said quickly as the pit in her stomach expanded.

'But you think I should, don't you?'

Now that really did catch Aleera off guard. It had been a long time since anyone had ever figured her out quite like that. It was almost unnerving, although… well, it certainly helped to open things out.

'Aleera,' Sara said gently. She leaned forward and gently stroked Aleera's shoulder. 'If I blamed you,' she said when they were only inches apart, 'if any part of me actually thought that you were responsible for what happened,' she closed the distance, 'I wouldn't do this.' Then Sara's lips pressed against Aleera's, softly and gently and with a quiet, loving sigh.

A great many parts of Aleera were telling her to stop this, that it wasn't right, that she'd only sorted this whole mess out a few days ago, and that if she was going to take advantage of the pheromones and let this happen, she might as well go the whole nine yards and slip someone rohypnol. Unfortunately, they ended up in a stalemate with the parts of her that, as much as she was a demon, she was a succubus, to whit, a thrice-damned sex demon, and at that, a very stressed one that hadn't gotten laid in entirely too long.

Mercifully, she was spared the trouble when Sara's eyes opened with the realisation of what she was doing. Aleera became aware of how fast her heart was beating, the way her cheeks burned, and how shallow her breath had become.

'Sorry,' Sara squeaked, covering her mouth, 'oh my God, Aleera, I'm so sorry, I didn't- I never-'

'It's alright,' Aleera said quickly. In a heartbeat, she was whisked from confusion into feeling about as much of a sick, twisted monster than she ever had.

'I didn't mean to- I-' Sara stammered on.

'Sara, stop, *please*,' Aleera insisted, without even knowing why her voice became suddenly so desperate. 'Just calm down, okay?'

Sara almost looked like she was choking. 'I'm so sorry,' she gasped, 'I didn't mean for that to happen, I swear...'

'It wasn't your fault,' Aleera said, taking hold of Sara's shoulders. 'It's just-' just her. Her and what she was, poisoning someone else. 'I'm sorry, Sara,' she sighed, 'I never wanted anything like this to happen.'

Sara breathed deeply. 'I should go,' she said quickly.

'You don't have to.'

'Aleera,' Sara blurted out, 'I- you don't know-' she shook, fresh tears leaking from her eyes. 'God, I don't even like girls. I don't even like to think about it,' she sobbed as all that confusion and unwanted desire started pouring out and Aleera took hold of her gently, 'just you, and it's just because of...' she sniffed.

'It's Ok,' Aleera whispered. 'It's Ok. It's not because of you. Like I said, I can't- Sara, I wish I could stop it, but there's nothing I can do.'

Sara stepped back and wiped her eyes. She took a ragged breath.

'I...' she said between quick breaths, 'I just don't know what to do. I should- I should just go...'

'If you want to,' Aleera said quietly as the air grew heavy, 'but- I think we really should straighten this out.'

'That's the problem,' Sara sniffed, 'Aleera, when I'm around you, I just can't stop feeling- this- and I can't just leave you now, after everything that's happened, and now it just explodes like this, right now of all times, and… and I just feel so…'

'Confused,' Aleera said gently. Sara nodded slowly.

Aleera let out a long, heavy sigh. The fact had finally crept up on her that she had no idea what to do, and that she wasn't sure why she'd ever thought that explaining the pheromones would help solve the problem.

'I'm sorry,' was the only thing she could think of to say.

'It's not your fault,' Sara said automatically.

'It's somebody's.'

Neither of them said anything for a moment. There was nothing to be said. It was Aleera who finally broke the silence.

'This would really be awkward if we'd stayed at the wake, wouldn't it?'

A second passed, and then Aleera and Sara both burst into a fit of laughter. It was about all they could do, and it seemed to warrant an outburst of hysterics given the context. Plus, it would help put things into a better perspective.

'I love you,' Sara said through the settling giggles, 'you know that? Not that way, but I do; I really, really do.'

'Ok,' Aleera smiled back. 'Why don't I get us something to drink?'

From that moment on, any number of things could have happened. Everything could have actually been good. Maybe perfect.

Instead, that was when it happened. It would be the last time she would laugh like that for some time.

There was a sharp, hard knock at the door, fast and urgent and without a trace of menace. It was hard for anything to have any at such a time.

'Well, we could have done with that five minutes ago, couldn't we?' Aleera commented, earning another giggle from Sara. In retrospect, Aleera had actually laughed herself. Imagine that. Her, laughing. And making a joke. Two in a row. Wow.

She opened the door. Jake stood there, looking hurried and out of breath.

'Aleera, we've got a problem,' he said quickly, 'can we talk?'

'Sure, come in,' Aleera said reflexively, stepping back to let him in the door. He almost hesitated. Most people wouldn't notice, but something in Aleera's brain picked up on it.

Jake spotted Sara as he entered. Something seemed to tug at the edge of his mouth. 'Are you both Ok?' he asked breathlessly.

'Yeah,' Sara replied, 'why?'

'Azrael turned up at Michael's funeral,' Jake replied.

Aleera immediately stopped. Her heart caught in her throat and that pit of dread opened.

'What?' Sara's eyes almost doubled in size.

'Relax; he can't get in. I put a protective seal on this place years back. Nobody who wants to harm her can get in without being invited.'

'So what's this about?' Sara asked.

Aleera's heart started to pound. Blood rushed in her ears. She felt the colour drain from her cheeks as the horror of the realisation set in.

'Jake,' she said levelly, 'how did you know he was at the funeral?'

Jake turned to her.

He grinned. He grinned the grin of a cat in front of a cornered mouse. Aleera felt herself freeze with the nightmare of what she'd just done.

'*Sure, come in.*' Oh, you stupid, *stupid* girl!

The image of Jake vanished, a flowing white robe folding around him as he grew taller and wrapped his hand around a dagger, the illusion spell fading instantly.

Azrael's hands pulled the hood up over his head.

'Thanks for the invitation.'

25

As she stood frozen, watching the dagger turn in Azrael's hand, something in Aleera's head finally had the good sense to scream "hit him!"

'*Whoahn*!' She thrust both palms forward and poured every last ounce of desperation she had into the word. Azrael was hurled clear across the room and into the bookcase with the sound of wood splintering and book after book falling onto his prone body.

The slayer was forgotten immediately as Aleera turned to Sara. 'Are you alright?' she asked urgently.

Sara nodded uneasily. 'Yeah,' she gasped. 'I'm fine, it's-' she looked over to the heap on the other side of the room. 'Oh, God...' she wrapped her fingers around the cross.

Then Azrael was suddenly on his feet, a mass of whirling cloak and glinting dagger.

'Still some fight in you,' he grinned, wiping a trickle of blood from his mouth. 'But you needn't worry; this...' he turned the dagger over in his hand, 'is not meant for you. Not tonight.' He turned his dark eyes on Sara and tightened his grip on the blade.

Aleera stepped forward, eyes red and wings erupting from her back in a shower of falling fabrics. She let the claws slip out and flexed them in front of herself. This was it. No killing, she would remember that, but now desperation had led him to make his mistake. Now, the claws could have their fun.

And yet there was no joy to be found in this. No thrill, no excitement. Not if Sara was there. That made all the difference.

'Don't you touch her,' she hissed as she shifted her weight into the stance she'd learned years back.

'I told you before, demon,' Azrael growled, 'you've no right to choose. This is holy work, and you will not interfere! *ThuraiShiahl*!'

'*Blaish*'!

There wasn't enough distance for the attack to be fully blocked. The force that made it through the still-forming shield struck Aleera, shaking her to the bone as her senses reeled in confusion. Then Azrael was upon her, her back and head striking the floor as Azrael's fingers tightened round her neck, his raving, foaming face snarling above hers as he pressed against her windpipe. She felt herself gag, her vision starting to blur. It would be useless to grab at him; there was nothing hard to grab hold of... so it was damn lucky that her fingers ended in something even better.

Azrael roared in pain as the claws slashed through the flesh of his arm, releasing his grip as Aleera pulled back one leg and drove it into his stomach. He howled and raised his fist-

'*Get away from her!*'

The shaking wave of red-tinted air struck him with impossible force, the edges of his cloak disintegrating and his gauntlets cracking as he was lifted from the floor and into the bookcase behind him, wood splintering before him even as everything else gave way before the force of the wave, the plaster of the walls bending and buckling, the television and the table smashing as the sheer force of desperation and fear and rage tore through everything in the room.

Sara stood there, in the middle of it all, the wooden floor torn and splintered, the walls scarred and everything in the path of her fury devastated, shaking and breathing in ragged gasps, wide-eyed with the fear and shock that came as the after-effect of her sudden burst of rage and power.

Aleera had only seen that done once before, when she was eleven years old, when she'd lashed out with sheer power and rage and thrown her father- Kudra, the most horrific demon war-criminal in history- away from her with enough force to knock him unconscious.

'Sara...' She said quietly, rising to her feet, her expression a picture of shock and awe.

'Was...' Sara asked shakily, 'Was that me...?'

Sara fell forward slightly, Aleera catching her to help her balance. Sara's face was pale, her eyes frozen for just a moment.

'Oh my God,' Sara asked after a long moment her eyes suddenly full of fear and guilt. 'W-what have I...?' Part of Aleera almost laughed. Selflessness incarnate.

'He's not dead,' She reassured her, before it finally clicked. 'We need to call Jake.'

She stepped away, reaching into her pocket for the Call Stone.

Then, it happened.

Azrael's voice suddenly shouted '*ThuraiShiahl*,' and the sudden force struck her in the back, her world spinning as she fell through the air, lurching back and forth as she struck the floor. She felt her ribs crack, sending jabs of pain through her side, everything drowned out for a moment by the ringing in her ears.

She didn't hear the sickening, wet, tearing sound.

Her eyes turned up, then widened in unspeakable dread as the colour drained from her face.

'*NO!!!*' Her desperate scream hung in the air, echoing as she froze, her mind a mass of horror in its purest form.

Sara's face was blank, frozen in empty shock, her eyes fading. Her limbs hung limp and lifeless. Something about her was almost unnaturally serene, frozen in the sudden, total realisation that brought with it some kind of impossible acceptance that couldn't be comprehended outside of exactly what was happening.

The cracked metal of the gauntlet covering Azrael's hand was wrapped round the handle of the dagger.

Its blade was buried in Sara's chest.

With another low, slicing sound, Azrael pulled out the blade. Sara fell back, and the "thud" with which she hit the floor was hollow, empty, and inescapably final.

Aleera felt her heart stop. The bile rose in her throat. Her eyes blurred with tears from something beyond thought, beyond what could ever be described. She couldn't think, react or move through the quagmire of awfulness.

Then, with a sudden, total surge of rage, she did. With a cry of "*ThuraiFwaiyal!*" the air between her and Azrael shimmered, dancing with sparks of fire that gathered into a searing, flaming mass and struck the figure of white in the side, consuming him and carrying him into and through the shattered plaster wall in a shower of burning splinters and a bursting cloud of smoke.

She was next to Sara in an instant, kneeling by her side and unable to do anything but stare in horror at the raw, red wound and the dark, soaked patch that spread across her chest.

'L… leera…' Sara gasped, her chest rising and falling shakily as she took a sudden, sharp breath, a faint trickle of blood leaking from the side of her mouth.

'It's OK,' Aleera said desperately, her hands on either side of Sara's head. Do something, her mind screamed at her, think, it's what you're good at, step back and think. 'I'll call…' She went to pull the cell phone from her pocket, only to realise that it wasn't there. Instead, there was a crushed phone on the other side of the room.

'…'s ok…' Sara whispered almost inaudibly.

Aleera urgently placed both her hands on top of the wound with a cry of '*Xiaol*', sparks of blue light dancing uselessly across the wound.

'...can't...' Sara gasped through ragged breaths. '...A... Aleera...'

'You'll be alright,' Aleera insisted, her eyes beginning to streak with tears. This couldn't be happening, not again, it couldn't... 'I...'

'Aleera...' Sara repeated. 'Th... it... wasn'... y...'

'*Xiaol*!' Aleera half-shouted, half-sobbed. Again the sparks just sank into the red flesh. It was too late. A healing spell could fix a cut, or a bruise, maybe a broken bone at a stretch, but not this, not a stab through the heart, not something...

Something fatal...

Oh, please, God, no...

No, it *couldn't* be. There had to be something, this couldn't happen!

Wait... she reached into her pocket, wrapped her hand around something... then felt a sharp, stabbing pain in her hand. When she pulled it back out, it was smeared red, the fragments of the vial that had contained the dragon blood splintered in her palm.

No... no, no, no...

'Come on,' Aleera begged, thick tears streaming over her face. 'You'll be alright, Sara, I promise, just...'

'N...' Sara moved her head gently, a trickle of blood leaking from her mouth. '..leera... mnot gonna...'

'Yes you are,' Aleera almost shouted, 'We just have to get you out of here, and...'

'Aleera...' Sara managed to say through a mouthful of blood. ''s ok...'

'*Please!*' Aleera sobbed, hunched over Sara as the tears flowed, 'Please, Sara, you can't...'

'Go...' Sara managed to say, 'B'for... h- comes b-'

'I'm not leaving you!' Aleera cried, 'I can't...'

'Aleera...' Sara said again, taking hold of her hand. 'It's ok... it's ok...' she coughed, another spurt of blood between her lips. '...go...'

'Don't be stupid,' Aleera insisted, desperately holding back her tears. 'Come on, you'll be fine... Sara...' she whimpered gently, knowing that she wasn't, but with something, some last false hope, forcing her to say it anyway, 'Please... please, God, no...' She leaned over her, her tears streaming down her face. 'Don't go,' she sobbed, suddenly as weak as she had ever been. 'Please, Sara, don't go,' she trailed off into a splutter of tears.

'It's ok,' Sara said again as her eyes glossed over. 'I... I L...'

Sobbing quietly, Aleera leaned further down and, stroking Sara's cheek, planted her lips softly on her forehead. Resting her forehead against Sara's, she sobbed quietly as the flames crackled around her.

When she sat back up, the shining softness in Sara's eyes were gone, replaced by a glossed-over emptiness as the last breath left her body.

Aleera reached up with one hand, tenderly pulling her eyelids down and leaving her to rest on the floor, her face calm and serene.

'I love you,' She whispered through her tears.

'Very good,' she heard Azrael's voice grate out of sight, 'now you see. This is what you bring. Now you can't deny it. Now you must repent, now that you've seen her die in front of you.' His footsteps approached slowly and deliberately. 'Now you will repent, and you will accept your eternal punishment.' He kneeled down next to her. 'They all did. The girl will. You will.'

Aleera felt herself rush with rage. She felt burning, hateful tears pour from her eyes.

And then, the pit inside her swallowed everything.

And then, the thing inside her woke up.

And then, for the first time since before she could remember, there was no conflict, no doubt, no detachment, logic or reasoning.

The world slipped away into a shade of grey, and she was awake, thinking clearly and coldly, all that rage and hatred, not left to flurries of shouting and violence, and instead focused like a laser.

And her target had been stupid enough to walk within two feet of her.

She lashed out even as Azrael whirled to the side, slicing through the fabric of his cloak. As the dagger swung for her, she grabbed the arm, pulling it back and grinning at the disgusting "pop" as his elbow dislocated. Pushing his head down, she raised her elbow and jabbed it downwards in-between his shoulder blades.

She didn't think, because she couldn't. She didn't hesitate, because she couldn't. She didn't stop, because she refused to. She wanted him *dead*. For the second time in her life, she wanted to kill someone. She wanted nothing more than to see the blood spill from him.

Without another word, she lifted one clawed hand and struck downwards with it.

Azrael lashed out with one foot, kicking her in the side. Aleera gave a vicious, painful snarl as she felt the sharp stab of another stabbing rib. Something in the back of her bloodlust-fuelled mind took note of the fact that she hadn't healed herself. Just one more reason to rip him apart.

Azrael pulled back one metal-covered fist, his face contorted in a snarl of rage beneath his hood. He punched her in the face. Hard. Her nose broke. Thick, warm, salty blood spurted over her top lip.

She barely felt the blow. One clawed hand lashed out on its own, ripping through skin and flesh with the most satisfying 'slice' of ripping flesh, and the most gratifyingly inhuman shout of pain from Azrael as he fell back, clutching his face with one hand as the gaps between his fingers filled with blood.

Azrael wavered, his face in his hands and the dagger dropped to the floor. Without a moment's consideration, she retracted the claws of one hand and delivered a sharp, solid punch to his face, watching as he collapsed to the floor.

The next second, Aleera's hand was on his neck, the other pulled back as its claws dripped with blood and thirsted for more. The deep, pouring gashes on Azrael's face begged for the cut. But before she could strike, Azrael's foot had struck her in the knee like a sledgehammer. She fell back; felt his weight upon her, pushing her to the floor, saw the glint of light on the dagger. With one hand she lashed out, Azrael rolling to the side to avoid the strike.

'Now...' Azrael spat out a mouthful of blood, his sick grin made all the more so by the smears of blood over his face as the ripped flesh folded and creased, 'now you are ready. What 'good' you professed to have is gone. Now is just the evil. The rage. Just the...'

'Oh. Shut. *UP!*' Aleera shouted. '*Sliahozai*!' The shower of burning sparks shot forth as Azrael thrust the dagger forward with a command of '*ThuraiSola*!'

As soon as the light struck her, it burned. Aleera felt herself howl in pain, doubling over as her skin lied to her and told her it was on fire, the pain consuming every inch of her. Her blood boiled, her lungs stopped, her brain burned with white-hot pain.

Then, it was gone, and Azrael stood over her. She couldn't move for her own trembling, her limbs felt like dead weights...

'Light Magic,' Azrael sneered. 'The light itself pains you devils.'

The pain of the dagger cutting into her skin was almost... mundane. Just one more thread laid into a pattern of hurt from her skin, her arms, face, her ribs, and now from her waist, where the blade had cut through her hip in a deep, damp cut.

For a moment, she thought she was dead, thought she could see the world slipping away into blackness, until she heard him speak, muffled by the splitting ring in her ears.

'Burn, demon,' Azrael commanded, "burn here... and burn in hell! *ThraioFhieh!*'

The air around Azrael was suddenly hot, impossible hot, a burning wave washing over her and the entire room. The air shimmered and shook before being consumed in rolling orange and black, burning through and catching on everything around them. The spell ceased, and everything around them was a wall of fire.

Aleera recovered almost too suddenly giving a sharp gasp as the stinging abruptly stopped, replaced by a dull, numb shaking that, if the numbing fear and adrenaline were gone and she could think clearly, she might have realised to be the shock setting in.

The heat of the flames licked painfully at her skin, the air around her clogged with smoke as she let out a cough. She bit her lip and pushed herself up, forcing her way through the jabs of pain from her side. Just barely visible through the smoke and fire was the outline of Sara's body. As soon as she laid eyes on it, she felt herself grow cold with hate and hot with anger again. The pain no longer mattered, the flames no longer mattered.

All that mattered to her, at that moment, was that she had just lost someone she loved. And when she got hold of the one responsible, she would make him pay. It was all she wanted, just to see his blood. The rage was not mindless, but cold and hateful. Part of her was sickened. But the part that demanded vengeance was bigger.

She let her fingertips glide over her wound as she whispered '*Xiaol*.' The sting was sudden and sharp as the wound shrank and healed. It was still painful, and would need attention again later, but hopefully she could at least deal with most of the pain from it. With a strike of winding realisation she realised how drained she suddenly felt, how much energy healing spells required. Adding that to the spells she and Azrael had thrown at each other... she was out.

She had to get out of there, she told herself. She was weakened, she was out of magic, and most notably, the apartment was *on fire*.

No, she told herself firmly. The bastard that cut Sara down in front of her had just set fire to her home. She was not going to run away from him. This was going to end.

There. The sound of movement, breathing, tension, like a snake about to bite. She turned sharply, her claws extending, and found herself face-to-face with nothing more than a wall. He was toying with her; letting her heal for sport, for the sake of the hunt; to make her feel that he was the good guy. The smoke parted behind her, dark orange light glinting off the polished surface of Azrael's dagger in the corner of her eye. Aleera spun round, and as the blade swung towards her, her mind screamed to a stop. Without thinking, she lashed out, the claws of her right hand meeting the blade as it scraped to a stop in their grip, the other swinging for Azrael's chest and being caught in a solid grip.

The blade stopped an inch from her face, its tip bearing a tiny drop of blood, either hers or Sara's. For a second, she couldn't think, couldn't react at all, couldn't do anything except glare all her hatred at Azrael, who stared back with his own. Staring into his eyes, that pure, mindless, total, burning hate welled up again.

She would never be sure why, but her mind suddenly raced back over the past week; finding the first body, being stalked, being threatened in the street, being confined to her own home, finding the dead, completely innocent, mutilated victims, Michael being attacked, finding his body in the hospital bed, the conspiracy, the lies, losing Michael, losing Sara and now this...

The rage was all she needed.

She swung her right hand to one side, sending Azrael's blade twirling through the air. As she pulled her hand back to strike, Azrael's free hand went to her forearm, his fingers wrapping tightly around it.

'Enough, demon,' Azrael snarled, '*EiahFhieh!*'

Dark fire. It dawned on Aleera with sudden, awful realisation exactly what manner of dark magic had killed Michael and the other victims of Azrael... and what was about to be done to her. As soon as Azrael had spoken, there was suddenly a fierce heat from his palms, spreading into her arms and through her body with burning, fiery waves of pain. She bit her lip, clenching her teeth just like all the others, like Michael and that demon in the park and like all the thousands of others at her father's hands. She felt herself fall to her knees as the spell set to work, knowing that ay any second the runes would start to form on her face...

No. No, not like this. Not on her knees, in her home, not at the hands of someone who invaded her life and took what she cared about most from her. Not as long as there was breath in her body.

With a raging, inhuman shout, she lashed out, pushing her right hand forward, breaking through Azrael's grip and sinking her claws into his shoulder. Azrael fell back in shock, the heat going with him and the slayer gave a monstrous howl of pain that was music to Aleera's ears, all the while the claws sinking through skin and flesh and bone.

Aleera pulled out the claws, now soaked in blood, as the dark red stain spread across Azrael's cloak, grabbed him by the shoulder and threw him to the floor.

'*Appiras!*' Even through Aleera's shout of protest, he was gone in a fold of air, enveloped by emptiness and leaving Aleera standing alone, falling to her knees in pain and exhaustion as the choking stench of the smoke enveloped her.

26

Aleera choked in the thick grasp of the smoke, ignoring the constant wail of fire alarms and panicked shouts as the building emptied itself. All she could hear was the hollow, empty sound from the implosion of air as Azrael escaped and took her vengeance with him.

So find him again.

She couldn't.

Yes, she could! She'd figured out where Michael was, and she could figure out where Azrael was.

And what would be the point? Michael was dead. Sara was dead. Another few hours and an innocent ten-year-old child would be dead.

Not if she stopped it, came the reply. Not if she tracked Azrael down and did what she had to do.

She just needed something, some kind of stimulus that would drag her mind out of this numbness.

The door was kicked inward with the sound of burning, splintering wood. Something that sounded like Makian cursed over the flames. 'Aleera!' Jake yelled into the fire, 'Jesus- *Zialahk*!' The air became impossibly cold and harsh, more so after the heat, then took on the faintest hint of blue as the flames dwindled and died to reveal the ashen, scorched apartment and a remaining thick haze of smoke.

That would do.

'Aleera!' Katya shouted as the three ran up to her. 'Oh my God, are you-'

Aleera coughed. As it happened, she hadn't been thinking much about the smoke, which she thought was permissible under exceptional circumstances such as these.

Jake was the first to catch sight of the body. 'Get her outside,' he said quickly.

'I'll be fine,' Aleera said coldly. All eyes turned to her. Her friend was dead; maybe she should have broken down into tears. Instead, she was calm, level, numb, and thinking clearly for the first time. The thing inside her was awake now, truly awake, and it bayed for blood.

Unfortunately, as demonstrated when she took a step and nearly collapsed, her body wasn't quite so up for a fight.

'Come on,' Jake said, holding her up. 'You're drained,' he realised as he saw how pale she suddenly was, 'let's get her out.'

She half-walked and was half-carried down the stairs and out into the street. Fire engines and police cars were already present, all either relieved that the fire seemed to have remained confined to one room, or confused as to how it had suddenly died down.

'Here,' Jake said as they ducked under the police tape, making sure to keep the illusion spell maintained. They sat Aleera down on the bench opposite the apartment building, while thick smoke still billowed from her windows.

Jake sat next to her, placing one hand on her chest. He closed his eyes, and the point of contact seemed to take on a faint glow. Aleera took a sharp, stabbing breath, and for a second every nerve felt like it was on fire. Her lungs seemed to empty and fill at the same time. Then, just as suddenly, the aching numbness was gone, replaced with all the raw hate that had been stirred inside her.

Makian stared at them, bug-eyed. 'That was *not* what I think it was,' he shook his head, 'no way. That was a-'

'Magic transfer,' Jake answered simply, 'now did you call Khazahn?'

'Tried to,' Makian shrugged.

'What happened to the dragon blood?' Jake asked.

'Broken,' Aleera wheezed, and then the memory of how she'd found out shot back to her. 'Sara,' she realised in a whisper. 'Jake, she was-'

'I know,' Jake said gently. 'I'm sorry.'

'Where's Azrael?' Aleera demanded without another thought. Grief could come later, even if she had to force it back with everything she had.

'We'll find him. Here.' Jake handed her another small, red vial.

'Jake, seriously,' Katya stared, 'where do you get this stuff?'

'That's dragon blood?' Makian squeaked. 'You have dragon blood?' Jake shrugged affirmatively. 'Well fuck me...' he breathed as Aleera swallowed some of the red liquid. Too much of the stuff, she knew, could do a lot of damage.

'What about the girl?' Aleera coughed.

Jake regarded her in a moment of dumbfounded silence. 'You're not going anywhere,' he ordered.

'Tell me,' Aleera answered sharply.

'Aleera, you are staying here,' Jake near-shouted.

'You gave me a transfer, didn't you?'

'To keep you out of a coma; maybe enough for one spell at the outside.'

'No,' Aleera declared, rising to her feet, 'there's a ten-year-old girl somewhere who's been kidnapped by that lunatic, and it's because of me.'

'Aleera!' Jake shouted as he stood up to face her, 'you can barely stand! There's no way in hell you're going after him!'

'You're not stopping me,' Aleera said flatly as she pushed past him.

'Try me,' Jake warned.

'*Don't* get in my way, Jake Connolly,' Aleera turned back to him with fire in her eyes, 'this is my fight. I don't care if it's my fault, not anymore. I am going to find Chloe Mcrae, I am going to find Azrael, and nobody else is going to die because of me. *Not one more!*'

'Aleera!' Jake grabbed hold of her arm.

Without any command from Aleera, the thing inside her lashed out at its nearest target. She spun round and struck Jake in the face. His grip relaxed and he reeled backwards as Katya caught him. Aleera spread her wings, and with a shout of '*Tyasans*' she took the air and vanished from sight.

Aleera covered quite some distance before the realisation finally started to dawn that Jake had been right. She had no idea of where to look for Azrael or the child. After leaving, she'd gone some distance on her wings, then finally landed on a rooftop and stopped as she finally began to think rationally. The knowledge that she didn't know where to look was the second thing she realised. The first, equally discomforting, was that when and if she found him, she was indeed in no condition to do anything to him.

There were no longer any actual wounds on her, but she was nevertheless entirely drained. Barely a drop of magic remained, definitely not enough to use any sort of spell without leaving her comatose. And the workings of magic demanded that the energy come from somewhere, and the spell used to cloak her when she flew off had pushed her own reserves past their breaking point- the fact that she'd even managed it for as long as she did was nothing short of a miracle. She felt exhausted, her limbs seemed to be made of rubber, and her entire body felt abnormally heavy.

She took it to be a small blessing, therefore, that at least her brain still seemed to be in working order, and it had some good news, however little, to impart to her. However much of her own energy she had used, she could take some comfort in the fact that she had forced Azrael to use just as much. To add to that, a spell as demanding as teleportation, added to the wound she dealt him, doubtless hadn't rendered his condition much better than hers. So, it was time to put said brain to use.

Where would he go? She thought to herself. She cast her memory back, over everything he'd done so far- the burned bodies, those four women, Michael, Sara, and it all turned up a frustrating lack of revelation- until the two links between all of them came back to her. One, she knew, was her, the cause of this and the hands that would soon bear the blood of that child if she didn't do something now. The other, she forced herself to press on rationally, was *him*. All of this was done as *he* would have done it.

She'd been told about what was happening right from the start. The message left with the first body, the confrontations, the threats, and the death themselves, all a message. And with that knowledge, her mind raced back to finding Michael's body at Pentagram. Why take him there, knowing that the place was bound to be searched? The answer was almost maddeningly obvious: *because* it would be searched. Aleera was meant to find Michael. After all, what was the point of sending a message unless its recipient was certain to get it?

And then came another moment of epiphany. The knowledge that wherever he had taken the child, he would want her to be there, to let her see him hammering the last nail into the coffin.

That was why he killed Sara as he did, Aleera realised in shock. So differently done from the others- why not just grab her and teleport them both out? He wanted her to see what he was doing to the child. He wanted her to figure this out and follow him.

It was a leap in logic, she knew, and a long shot at best. But that dark thing was in the driver's seat now, and somehow part of her was so completely certain that she could do nothing else but obey it and be certain that she knew where they were.

27

The rusted gate of the old factory hung open on creaking hinges, the sound of a slow wind whistling through the cracked walls and broken windows. Somewhere out of sight, the sound of waves lapping against the dock and the mournful calls of seagulls echoed to Aleera, a few of the birds perched on the roof to look down upon the solitary, dark figure with warning black eyes.

Aleera silently stepped through the gate, taking a short moment to steady herself. Slowly, she crept forward with quiet steps and blazing red eyes. Every step seemed somehow slow, and her surroundings now resembled something from a Hammer horror film, compete with the front door of the factory banging on its frame and the hushed, suffocated silence that hung in the air.

Through the door, the way into the factory floor was just as empty, just as silent. Still particles of dust were suspending in the air in thick beams of light. And there was the floor itself, dark and filled with…

With…

Aleera gagged at the sickening stench of rotting meat. There were twelve of the corpses, spread out over the factory floor in thick puddles of congealed blood, their faces red and carved, and each clad in blood-soaked robe that, prior to its new coating, she suspected would have been white.

So. Aleera had experienced a little bit of instability, maybe more so over the past ten or so days, but maybe this was what real evil looked like, raw, uncut and allowed to run free. And with that dark thing inside her finally loose, the playing field was finally level.

For a moment, somewhere in the tense anticipation, it dawned on Aleera that she may well have been wrong. It had been almost a day since the child disappeared and there was every possibility that… no. No, she would have no more blood on her hands, especially a child. That frightened little girl would not suffer that fate. She wouldn't have it.

Then, there it was; that sudden movement through the window above, the dark shape against the light of the cloak moving out of the frame of the window.

Aleera cleared the factory floor in seconds, swinging herself round a corner to race up the stairs, her heartbeat pounding as she forced her legs to keep moving despite the tiredness and dizziness and the dry, crackly layers of blood on her waist and forehead. She reached the door to the office and threw it open, bursting into the office and looking around. There was no Azrael, only another open door still swinging on its old hinges, the creaking the only sound besides…

Besides the quiet, shaking, wet sound of muffled sobs that, she suddenly realised, was that of a crying ten-year-old girl.

She kneeled beside the crates, down next to the child crouched in the corner with her arms wrapped around her knees, her red cheeks covered in streaming, frightened tears and her dark hair hanging messily around her, some of it stuck to her face in salty wet layers.

'Chloe,' Aleera whispered gently, causing the child to look at her with another quiet spasm of tears. 'It's alright,' she told her gently, reaching one hand out, speaking impressively soothingly considering the state she was in, 'I'm not going to hurt you, I'm going to take you home, OK?' The girl nodded, quivering slightly with the look of a helpless, innocent little girl who didn't know what was going on.

In the midst of another series of infantile sobs, Chloe managed to blurt out 'don't let him come back,' before another wave of tears covered her face.

That dark part of Aleera came to the realisation that this was what Azrael's victims would have been like, all shaking and crying and pleas for mercy. And that same part of her realised who else she had seen like this, so young, so scared, so broken; that quiet, dark-eyed little girl from all those years ago who had shared the name Aleera and who had suffered so at the hands of a twisted madman. With that came the disgusting, horrible realisation of why Michael, unlike Chloe, had been burned in the day he had been missing, and the thought of exactly what Azrael had done to those women, and to this frightened little girl, in that first awful day. And it gave rise to a fury the likes of which she'd never felt before.

'Come on, now,' Aleera whispered, 'let's get you out of…'

She never finished that sentence. Before she could, a hand pulled her back by the hair, and a strong arm wrapped around her throat to drag her away from Chloe and send her falling back into the wall with an inhuman howl of protest.

'So you came,' Azrael spat. Aleera looked up just in time to see him pull the hood back up over the flapping cuts and the blood that covered his face and stained the shoulder of his cloak dark red. 'Just as you came for the boy. You're intelligent, I'll grant that.' He moved above her, plunging down one fist. Aleera wrapped her hands round his wrist, tiredness and horror forgotten and kicked out, striking Azrael in the stomach as he fell back. A second later, and she was upon him, bringing her fists down onto him again and again as Azrael roared and struggled.

The dagger's blade cut through the flesh of her arm, the pain driving out Aleera's wings and claws as she wrapped her hands around Azrael's throat, hissing with anticipation as the claws pressed against the skin. She pulled him up, then pushed him down and listened to the sound of his skull striking the hard floor.

Then her world exploded in pain as something struck her hard and fast, and she doubled over, hands on the back of her head as the room tumbled over itself in a stabbing whirlwind. Everything faded and darkened, her ears rang, and the blood pounded in her ears. She couldn't be sure how long it lasted, but then the room was back, minus Azrael and whatever had hit her and…

Chloe, she realised as she rose to her feet, ignoring the stinging pain in the back of her head and the dampness she seemed to feel in her hair. Down there, beyond the window, the white shape of Azrael's cloak moved through the darkness, just cumbersome enough to tell that there was something roughly the size and shape of a ten-year-old girl under his arm, and almost at the door. 'Oh, no you don't,' she hissed.

She could get down the stairs, but that would take too long. She would loose track of them. That only left one option that she could think of.

She stepped back, spread her wings and took a running jump straight into the window, arms folded in front of her. She heard the dusty glass smash, and winced as the shards cut into her arms. Then, expertly, the wings did their job and carried her across the floor and to the door Azrael had used. Everything blurred past her, the pain in the back of her head acting as a thick wall of gelatine that she struggled to push herself through with every step. Her clever stunt with the window hadn't helped things either. Finally, she was outside, the air suddenly bitingly cold and the sound of the waves deafening. She stepped forward over surf-soaked concrete and found herself struggling to stand on the pier as the waves lashed against it, roaring as they rose and hissing as they splashed, the seagulls circling overhead with mocking cries.

'Don't take another step,' Azrael hissed, his hood falling from his face as the cuts on his face flapped with every word. One arm was wrapped around Chloe, holding her to him by the neck as she wheezed and cried with big, fear-filled eyes that were locked onto the gleaming, blood-soaked blade that the other arm held to her throat. 'Come further, and she dies,' Azrael finished.

'Let her go,' Aleera ordered, taking another shaky step forward and letting her wings fold out to their full length. 'She's a child!'

'A child raised in sin,' Azrael spat blood. 'Your kind's as bad as ours ever was; they raise their daughters to be every bit as full of sin and hate. Now we can prune the weed before it sprouts. The best chance to do God's work.'

'She's done nothing!' Aleera shouted, 'You're calling yourself a man of God, and you're holding a knife to an innocent girl's throat!'

'One more black soul in hell,' Azrael grimaced. 'Now get back!' he commanded, pressing the knife to the girl's throat.

Aleera pointed one set of claws towards him, their tips dancing with weak sparks of magic.

'You have nothing left, demon,' Azrael chuckled, his words gurgling in another mouthful of blood that poured over his chin. 'Stay right where you are, or I'll slit her throat!'

'But you won't,' Aleera said with an unearthly calm, 'because I've got just enough left in my body for one last spell, and if you kill that little girl, I'll use it, even if it kills me. So you just think this through, *very* carefully,' she hissed savagely, 'because you've managed one thing, I'll give you that; you took away two of the people I loved the most, and one of them was one of *very* few people who could probably talk me out of what I'm thinking of doing right now. So if you murder that little girl in cold blood, then *there will be nothing to stop me from blowing your fucking brains out!*'

Snarling, Azrael pulled back the blade, tightened his grip, and tensed his arm...

'*No!*' Aleera grabbed hold of his arm, propelled forward by her wings, carrying Azrael back as Chloe screamed and fell to the soaked wood of the pier.

Now, every fibre of her being screamed at her. Kill him. Take your revenge. Cut him down.

Well, it did sound tempting. She wrapped one hand around his slipper, blood-coated neck and squeezed, blood covering her fingers. She felt herself grin.

Kill him.

End it.

Do it.

She raised one clawed hand.

He killed all those people.

Tear out his throat!

He killed Michael.

With your teeth!

He killed Sara.

Then the memory of Sara, and those shining blue eyes, and that promise, came back to her, and brought with it all the silent vows to herself that she would never be as her father had dictated, and even as the thing inside howled its protests, Aleera was back in charge, and moving the claws down was impossible.

Aleera took a deep, shaking breath. The waves crashed louder in the silence, and around them everything was somehow darker in the light of the moon.. What felt like an eternity slipped past in a moment as parts of her warred for authority. Slowly, fighting every urge in her body, she stood up, lowered her claws and stepped back.

The daughter of Kudra, who had lost so much, and known so much pain and loss and grief in a handful of days, stepped back from the man she hated with every fibre of her being, lowered her claws, and with her dark eyes softening, looked at her enemy and silently offered him mercy. And even as she backed away, every inch of her wanted to sink her vanishing claws into his flesh, to feel hot blood on her skin, but she wouldn't. She would not be like her father.

Chloe Mcrae, her face half-covered in tears, stepped out from besides one of the old oil drums that littered the end of the pier. Aleera turned to look at her, and the child tried to speak, but whatever words she would have said caught in her throat.

'It's Ok,' Aleera said gently, 'come on. Let's get you back to your grandma.'

Azrael rose behind her and whipped the dagger from his belt, fixing his gaze squarely on Aleera's back. 'May God have mercy on your soul,' he snarled, 'though the path you chose to follow leads not to him. *HuoohlShiahl!*'

Azrael carried himself forward with a rush of wind, the dagger gleaming as he moved with impossible speed.

Chloe screamed.

Aleera turned.

Without her even thinking, the dark thing lashed out on purest, darkest instinct. She shouted a spell she'd never even heard and lashed out with one hand.

'*EiahShliahsh!*'

Azrael jerked to a stop as the claws cut through his cloak, not even touching the skin as Aleera's vision blurred, all red and hate and bloodlust.

Aleera took two deep, gasping breaths, her chest rising and falling and splattered with blood as her world reeled into a sudden, lurching stop.

The flailing cloak fell.

The claws completed their ark, their edges dancing with dark light, light that could only come from darkness, sparking and crackling and vanishing into nothingness.

Aleera's blood-red eyes darkened, blackening in their moment of hate.

Then Azrael was standing still, shock and sudden fear in his eyes mixing with a strange knowledge, a touch of what could only be victory. With their last moment, the edges of the valleys of blood on his face twisted and folded over each other as his mouth turned into a grin of bloodstained teeth, bloodshot eyes dilating.

Aleera felt herself tremble with the awful realisation of what she had done, as the red lines began to appear, forming from nowhere on Azrael's skin alongside the ones that already marred Azrael's face, more and more pools of blood spreading beneath his cloak. His face became calm, almost ethereally serene, as his fingers relaxed and his dagger fell to the floor, its blade and handle smeared with blood. Trails of blood leaked from his eyes and nose, as his figure beneath the cloak became a streaked shape of red.

'I knew it,' Azrael's blood-soaked face whispered.

'May God have mercy on your soul,' Aleera whispered for reasons she would never know, 'though the path you chose to follow leads not to him.'

Azrael fell, his white cloak flailing around him and falling to the cold, hard wood of the pier, the shroud of cloth soaking up the dark red pool of blood that began to spread beneath him.

Checkmate.

And Azrael died.

Aleera felt every deep breath burn the back of her throat. She watched every inch of the fabric slowly fill with red as, somewhere beyond her knowledge, the gulls gave a mocking cry for the passing of a black soul.

She shook and looked down at her blood-caked claws, hot and full and pouring.

She'd killed him.

She grinned.

She'd killed him.

Oh, and it had felt *good*. It was a rush like she'd never imagined. Beating up street thugs couldn't compare to this. Now she was unleashed. She was free. It was like nothing she'd ever felt, and it made her beg for more like some sick, black drug coursing through her veins. She'd taken his life and ended it with nothing but a spell and a few inches of keratin. All of Azrael's life, experience, hatred, it all passed away in an instant by her hand, and turned him from a living, breathing thing into a piece of bloody meat. And that... that was like being God. It was like being beyond rules and laws and...

And promises?

The fires of obsession died down, rationality returned and that promise echoed back to her.

She'd killed him. She'd murdered someone.

What had she done?

A man's life was splattered all over her hands, her face and her body, so hot and filthy that she just wanted to cry and scream and make it go away...

And every bit as much, she wanted to do it all over again.

Azrael's empty eyes start up at her from their pool of blood, the disgusting smell of the burning cuts in Azrael's blood-soaked flesh wafting up to her.

Dark magic, some faint part of her realised, unheard. She'd killed him with dark magic. She'd never used it before, never learned it... and yet, there it had been, when there was nothing else left, that darkness inside that lashed out and saved her and cut him down.

She took a deep, calming breath to quiet the inner storm as the dark thing inside her remained quiet and satisfied.

Then her shoulder exploded in pain. A bolt of pure, shimmering force struck it, and the tired joint twisted and buckled. She let loose a primal howl as the impact pushed her forward, falling headfirst onto the soaked, blooded wood and tasting thick, salty blood in her mouth for the hundredth time.

A million things rushed into her mind at once. She'd been upon Azrael inside. He'd been within her grasp. He couldn't have struck her.

Someone else had. Someone else had been in there.

The thick, blurry shape came into view as she turned her head up. Things came into focus one-by-one. First the human shape, then the still-humming Guild staff held with its pronged end facing her, then the white lab coat shrouding the figure, then finally the curly-brown hair and green eyes of… of…

No…

'Harry?'

28

Harry stepped forward, every footstep echoing on the soaked wood, keeping the staff trained on Aleera. All Aleera could do was feel herself go weak in a moment of surprise and uncomprehending fear at the sheer impossibility of what was before her.

'Just stay still,' Harry said shakily. His eyes darted from side-to-side and the staff wavered in his hands. 'I can at least promise you that it won't take long.'

Most people would have frozen. Maybe panicked. Maybe given up right then and there. Instead, Aleera noticed that there was blood on his face. That meant he would have to have been somewhere where there was a plentiful supply of it.

Her thoughts turned back to the bodies inside. He'd been there the entire time. He'd escaped. No, not while the rest of them were cut to pieces. He'd been spared. And there would have to be a reason.

Because he was needed.

Because someone was needed to hold onto the girl.

As soon as she remembered one more thing, it clicked. There was no moment of "Harry wouldn't do such a thing", because... well, she didn't know him that well, and this was another moment when it really helped to be a little distant. She remembered every important piece of evidence, every clue and hint that turned up. The cause of death that had cemented Azrael's message, locating Sword of Heaven, every little twist and turn; Harry had been the one who told them about all of it. As if he knew what to look for and where to look for it every single time.

After all, who sends a message without being sure that it will get through? Nobody said that there was only one wolf in the fold.

'Funny, though,' Harry trembled, 'I'd have thought you'd caught on. I even warned Azrael and Chara that somebody might think something was suspicious. I said I might be a little too helpful.'

He was stalling, Aleera realised. He'd seen Azrael butcher those others, he'd seen the bodies he left behind, and he didn't have it in him to add another corpse to the list. 'I can do one last thing, though,' he stammered, 'I'll write up the report on this; tell them the truth. All of it.'

The staff clicked. The end buzzed with power.

'I just want to tell you,' Harry shuddered, 'I don't take any pleasure in doing this.' He raised the waving weapon. 'I'm sorry, Aleera. Profoundly.'

'Harry, it's over,' Aleera spat through a mouthful of blood, one hand still nursing her broken shoulder. 'Sword of Heaven's gone. Azrael's dead. Chara will be out of a job by this time tomorrow.'

'Oh, but I'm not a member,' Harry rambled. 'This just has to be seen through to its course. I'm sorry, Aleera. You don't deserve this,' he tightened his grip, 'none of them did. Honestly, I wish he'd just finished it. Then we could have shut them down and- and just gotten on with things. None of this was meant to happen.'

Then we could have shut them down?

Aleera felt every part of herself ice over. She retched.

'Chara just did this,' she whispered hoarsely, 'to kill me?'

'Like I said,' Harry licked his chapped lips, 'you don't deserve this. You're like- no offence, but- you're like a rabid dog. Nothing you did, just... born that way. You just...' he trembled slightly, '...need to be put down.'

Born that way. People came out with the most interesting things at times like this.

'This is because of my father,' she breathed, 'like everything else that's happened. Isn't it?'

Harry swallowed a lump in his throat. 'Yes,' he said shamefully. 'I'm sorry, Aleera, but you, your father, all the psyche reports...' the power built up to its full charge on the end of the staff, 'it's just not a chance we can afford to take.' The staff hummed. That much power, that wasn't to incapacitate the target. It was a killing shot. 'Like I said... I truly am sorry. Despite everything- even if you're a fucked-up little bisexual killing machine- somehow, you're a lovely girl. And I'm sorry.'

What happened next was a blur.

The air buzzed. Aleera closed her eyes involuntarily. The wall of force smashed into Harry like a runaway car, lifting him from the ground as his shot sailed harmlessly into the air. Harry hit the ground hard, and the staff slipped from his grip.

'Put your hands on your head!' One of the five black-cloaked Guild soldiers ordered. 'Now.'

Harry scrambled for the staff, but when he reached it, there was a foot in a white sneaker rested on it. Jake raised his eyebrows and kicked the weapon back toward the soldiers.

Tomoko stepped past the line of soldiers, stopping as something caught in her throat. Her mouth hung slightly open, and her eyes dampened.

'Hands on your head, doc, and stand up,' Jake scowled.

Harry stifled a sob and stood up shakily, moving towards the assembled soldiers on their instruction. Jake forgot him immediately, racing across the pier back to Aleera.

Aleera's eyes lidded as her limbs relaxed and a long, slow sigh escaped her. A weight rose from her shoulders, leaving her as light as the cold night air. Suddenly, she felt all the more drained, and the wind was somehow cooling and relaxing as it blew strands of hair across her hot, sticky, bloodstained face. It was over now, and as she opened her eyes again, she felt cold, and empty, and very, very tired.

In a second, Jake and Katya were knelt next to her, urgently saying things that didn't register as she found the strength to push herself up, her world stinging with pain again from the back of her head.

'Easy,' Katya advised as Aleera managed to sit up, 'Come on now.'

'Hold still,' Jake instructed as he waved one hand over her. '*Xiaol.*' There was another sharp, stabbing sting, jabbing into her shoulder and the back of her head, and she gritted her teeth as skin and muscle sewed itself back together, and finally Aleera let out another sigh as the pain escaped her and the drained, heavy feeling that filled her body started to slip away.

She sat bolt upright at the sound of a scream from the other end of the pier. Harry, in a whirl of motion, pulled out what had been the nearest thing to him: Chloe Mcrae had been crouched behind an oil drum crying.

'Harry!' Tomoko shouted over the immediate buzzing of the soldiers' staffs, 'Harry, please, don't!'

'Guess we won't be going for that dinner date,' Harry chuckled weakly. 'Now do as I say,' he wrapped a hand around the child's throat, 'or she dies.'

Aleera pushed herself up to her knees, narrowing her red eyes.

'Shoot her,' Harry indicated to Aleera, 'or I snap her neck.'

Aleera felt her stomach tie itself in knots as each one of the soldiers showed just that one hint of conflict.

'They won't choose you,' Harry shook, 'none of them will. They can't wait for an excuse. They live to get rid of people like you. They won't choose you,' the faintest smile tugged at his lips, 'would you?' He turned back to the soldiers. 'Anyone comes near me,' he warned, 'and the kid dies!'

Aleera didn't bother panicking. She didn't bother worrying. Instead, she muttered, 'I am not putting up with that crap again,' grabbed hold of the lid of a drum that had been knocked off at some point, and threw it with practiced precision. It hit its mark on the back of Harry's neck, Chloe fell forwards, and Harry collapsed. Before he could even try to get up, five staffs were pointing at his head.

Aleera released a stifled breath and collapsed onto her hands and knees. She pulled some blood-caked hair from her face. It was only then that she realised what a mess she was.

'Nice,' Katya sighed.

Jake glanced up. A frown of concern took over his face. 'Be right back,' he said hastily, getting up and walking urgently away.

'I thought he'd be madder than that,' Aleera breathed.

'Oh, he will be,' Katya smiled.

Behind them, Jake turned to look down at Azrael's unmoving, blood-soaked form, and allowed one hand to hover in the air above it, closing his eyes and letting his magic call out to that which surrounded the body. He knew exactly what to find.

His hand was suddenly cold, a chill that cut through the flesh to the bone and crept up with arm with silent whispers of death. It was deadly, dark, and unmistakable. Dark magic.

Hesitating for a moment, he lowered his hand back to his side.

Aleera had never used dark magic before. As far as he was aware, she didn't even know any. She'd refused her father's teachings on the subject, never studied anything of its techniques or roots, yet there was no question that Azrael had died by her hand, and that the deed had been done by black magic.

This was what he, more than anyone else, had always feared. The reason the Guild insisted on monitoring Aleera. They would want to know about this. And once they found out... Jake shuddered at the thought.

Raising his hand again, he gave a quiet whisper of "*WhoahnEiah.*" His eyes closed, he felt the chill of the dark magic slip away, cast away from the body by the spell, taking with it the intangible evidence that any such magic had been used. Then, kneeling down and letting his fingers glide over the dead face with a whisper of "*Xiaol*," he watched with a mix of satisfaction, mischievous glee and a stab of guilt as the smaller cuts on Azrael's face shrank and vanished, leaving only the deep marks made by Aleera's claws.

There. No aura of dark magic, no dark-magic-induced injuries. Nothing to imply the use of such power. The Guild would definitely not be hearing of it.

'Jake,' Makian called as he walked away from the body, 'you see this shit?'

'We've got our killer,' Jake said bitterly, turning away as his hands clenched into fists. 'Just not in time,' he added with total disappointment.

'I'm sorry, man,' Makian said distantly, not looking Jake in the eye and casting just one regretful glance in Aleera's direction. 'I mean, if you hadn't gone and gotten me out… we should've thought of that.'

'We couldn't have known he'd get into Aleera's apartment like that,' Jake muttered. 'There's no way we could have expected this to happen when it did.'

'I called Khazahn,' Makian brought up in an effort to change the subject. 'Chara can't keep his ass covered after this.'

'Aleera killed someone,' Jake said with an echo of dread. 'Even if it was a psycho-killer fanatic, it's all Chara needs.'

'But you busted the guy, right?'

Jake nodded slowly, then glanced back at the body one more time. 'Anything clever to say?' he muttered.

Makian shook his head slowly. 'Not now.'

Jake's expression didn't change. 'We failed her, Makian,' he said with undisguised guilt and anger. 'We utterly, utterly failed her.'

Not so far away, Katya helped Aleera move to lean against the old drums. 'Where's the girl?' Aleera asked groggily. She felt more tired than she ever had before, every part of her felt heavy and empty as she prepared to push herself up again. Before she did, however, she turned her eyes up as they shifted back to brown and her wings and claws were pulled back into her form. Standing there on the pier, her arms down by her sides and her eyes, surrounded by dried tears, staring unblinkingly at her, was Chloe. 'Hi,' Aleera smiled weakly, coughing as she stood. Before she got halfway, however, Chloe reached her and wrapped her arms around her, sniffling quietly.

'It's alright,' Aleera whispered. 'You're Ok, Chloe. It's over,' she breathed quietly, closing her eyes as she held onto the child and stroked her hair soothingly. 'It's over.'

Aleera leaned back against the wall as the Guild soldiers moved back-and-forth around them. Katya stood next to her as Aleera took another sip of water that flooded her dried mouth, ignoring the cold of the night air.

'How's the shoulder?' Katya asked.

'Not bad, considering,' Aleera answered, flexing it stiffly. Jake had done a fine job with the healing spell. 'Head's still splitting, though.'

It was over, though, and she knew it at last. Azrael was dead and Sword of Heaven with him. Just not soon enough; Sara, Michael, they were both gone. Both lost to her, she realised as she choked back another wave of tears. The grief would have to wait for now.

On the other side of the assemblage of Guild Soldiers, there was the one thing that made it bearable. Little Chloe, shaken but unharmed, collapsed into her grandmother's arms as the old woman cried joyful tears and held her granddaughter to her.

Looking up, Mrs. Mcrae turned to Aleera with tear-filled eyes, and silently mouthed 'thank you'.

'She'll be fine,' Katya reassured her.

In that sense, Aleera mused, taking another sip of water, but the physical damage Azrael might have done wouldn't be the end of it. Through everything, she'd caught the look in Chloe's eyes, the fear and the hate that she'd been forced to push back, so much like that frightened little girl from so very long ago. She was a child who had been through and witnessed the unspeakable, and Aleera knew only too well what that could do. She found herself silently praying, bringing to mind the image of Sara's dangling crucifix, that little Chloe would be alright, that she would be able to move on from the horrors she had seen. And with that feeling came the realisation of why, whenever Aleera was angry or vengeful, Sara would hold onto that silver cross.

'So what happened after I left?' Aleera finally asked, returning to the conversation at last and feeling the colour start to slowly return to her cheeks.

'Jake was fine after a second; he was pretty upset,; Katya recalled, 'Khazahn and Tomoko showed up, we all put our heads together and figured out where to look, then Khazahn got called about something before we could get here.'

'So, I was right; Jake's mad,' Aleera observed with an exhausted smile.

'And a little impressed that you managed to figure out what it took the five of us to work out,' Katya commented.

'So where's Khazahn?'

'No idea. He said he'd send some backup, which at least…' Katya nodded to the ever-growing number of soldiers.

Not far away from them, a pair of Guild soldiers held Harry between them, his wrists bound together by metal handcuffs behind his back as he briefly glared over at Aleera, his dark green eyes filled with cold contempt. Tomoko watched from nearby, anxiously fumbling with a lock of hair as she looked down away from him.

'I'll be back in a minute,' Aleera told Katya as she stood up, walking over towards Tomoko. The doctor looked up sharply, turning her almond eyes to Aleera as she completely turned away from Harry and the soldiers arresting him.

'How are you?' Tomoko asked awkwardly.

'I've been better. What about you?'

Tomoko sighed and glanced anxiously over at Harry. 'Not my best idea for a relationship,' she said stoically.

'Been there,' Aleera sighed. It was strange, but conversation actually seemed to suddenly be easier for her. Maybe she should spend more time utterly exhausted. She took a slow sip of water. 'I'm sorry.'

'Don't be,' Tomoko said, forcing herself to be as brisk as possible, 'I'm fine. Really. He was just…' she stifled what looked suspiciously like an urge to cry, 'just some lunatic.' She turned away sharply and walked back to the pier. Grief was a personal thing, Aleera recalled, and there were few kinds of it worse than knowing someone you once thought to be good and decent to be capable of something like that.

The buzz of conversation silenced itself abruptly as Khazahn in his typical business-suit disguise and five other Guild soldiers, their disguises vanishing around them, strode towards the pier, their footsteps echoing in its quiet emptiness and their staffs buzzing to life.

From a conversation with Mrs. Mcrae, Jake took one look at the soldiers, and then marched angrily up to Khazahn. 'Don't you dare!' he snapped commandingly, his open jacket rising on a breeze that didn't exist and his fingertips dancing with energy.

'I've got my orders,' Khazahn replied with neither conviction nor enthusiasm.

'Back off,' Katya hissed savagely, standing between Khazahn and Aleera, her golden eyes narrowing and her catlike ears standing straight.

'That will be all,' an unmistakably conceited voice interrupted as its owner pushed through the crowd. "You are all hereby under arrest," Chara declared, straightening his suit and fighting to contain his vindication, 'three counts of illegally obtaining information from the archives of the Guild of Guardians,' he looked around Jake, Katya and Makian, 'one count of freeing an incarcerated suspect,' to Katya, 'one count of insubordination,' to Makian. 'You all understand, of course, that these are *very* serious charges.'

'You just don't get it, do you?' Jake demanded. 'You won't make anything stick. Not after all of this. You're finished, Chara; you might as well have put your own head in the noose.' Chara either didn't hear or ignored him.

'And of course…' Chara continued, turning to Aleera, 'at least nine counts of murder of the first degree.'

'*What*?' Aleera shouted, realising that she hadn't said much of anything, 'You…!'

Jake held one palm up, shimmering red light dancing to fill his entire hand as he brandished the sizzling, red-hot spell at Chara. 'Don't even try it,' he seethed.

'You'll never pin it on her!' Khazahn snapped from beside Chara, 'they'll see right through you.'

'Be *quiet*, sergeant!' Chara barked, his face flushed red and shaking with barely-contained indignation, 'that's an order! So help me, this has not happened for nothing, and I will see that little witch behind bars for the rest of her life!'

Then Chara fell silent. Something unnerved him, far more than anything else. It was Jake. He didn't appear angry, betrayed or outraged. He was smiling.

'You should really think about whose company you're in before saying that,' he advised.

Chara, his face ashen, turned to the man who had appeared behind him. He trembled as the man, whose shoulder-patch was pure white, removed his helmet to revealed the chiselled, forty-year-old face beneath, a full black beard and faded blue eyes staring intently at Chara.

Besides the man, a woman who looked to be around thirty and of Asian descent, clad in a form-fitting black dress with a gold dragon down the seam on one side, stepped forward. Chara looked about ready to faint.

'Aleera,' Jake couldn't help grinning, 'allow me to introduce General Daeiol, the Head of the Guild, and to his right, head of the High Council, High Chancellor, Lady Tamara.'

Neither of the two new arrivals made any action, until Lady Tamara finally spoke. 'This morning,' she said, 'a mutual acquaintance of ours burst into the High Council's meeting room and, before being ejected by security, handed us some very interesting information. General, if you would?'

'Commander Chara,' Daeiol said in a deep, cutting voice, 'by the power vested in me as head of the Guild of Guardians, for gross misconduct, you are hereby stripped of your rank as Commander and commission in the Guild of Guardians, and all rights and privileges thereof. Sergeant, would you do the honours?'

'Gladly,' Khazahn declared. 'Mohan Chara, you are under arrest for multiple charges of manslaughter and corruption. You have the right to an attorney. You have the right to remain silent; anything you choose to say can and will be given in evidence.' He moved to attach the handcuffs to Chara's wrists.

'Get your hands off of me!' Chara roared, thrashing his arms and pulling away.

'It's over, Chara,' Khazahn shouted. 'Face it.'

'You unbelievable idiots,' Chara shouted, 'do you even know what you're doing? Do you even know what that girl is?'

'I'm a demon,' Aleera replied levelly, 'I'm the daughter of the worst warlord that our society has ever known.' She glared at Chara through blood-red eyes. 'And right now, it's a hell of a lot better than being you.'

'No,' Chara seethed, '*No!*'

He grabbed the staff of the nearest Guild soldier and, as it hummed with energy, turned it towards Aleera...

In a split-second, Jake grabbed hold of the staff, Chara lurching back and loosening his grip in a moment of surprise. The weapon swung in Jake's hands, pulling back before lashing out and striking

Chara in the stomach as he doubled over in pain, grunting as the air was forced out of him and Jake swung the staff in an arc, slamming it down on his head with a metal 'thud'. Chara fell, hit the floor, and passed out with a final pathetic, humiliated groan. 'He had a weapon,' he shrugged as he idly dropped the staff on top of Chara's prone body, 'self-defence.'

Two soldiers pulled Chara to his feet, locking the handcuffs around his wrists. The ensuing hum of talk died down as Daeiol stepped forward.

'I really cannot tell,' he said grimly, 'who it is that I am most disgusted with. Him for causing all of this,' he gestured to Chara, 'you for allowing it,' Khazahn, 'you for your holier-than-thou attitude,' Jake, 'or myself, for having any of you in my organisation.' The air became heavy with silence. 'This entire affair has been shaming,' Daeiol said quietly. Without another word, he turned away.

'By the way, Mister Connolly,' Lady Tamara said to Jake as she turned away, 'all charges have been dropped. Consider yourself in good fortune.' If she came with subtitles, they would have read "don't let me catch you doing something like this again".

'So,' Makian piped up awkwardly, 'that's it?'

Aleera watched, motionless, as Chara was carried away.

'Yeah. Just like that.'

29

It had been two weeks, and among other things, Aleera's suspension was over. The usual clamour sounded around Aleera as a mass of bodies and faces started shoving their ways to lockers, classrooms, or in a few cases outside to see how stoned they could get before they had to get to class. Like an ant's nest they scurried away until only a few remained.

Aleera closed her locker half-heartedly, her usual frustration and that self-nagging touch of contempt gone and replaced by pure emptiness, a numb tiredness that seemed to fill all of her. Her body seemed to move autonomously; at least, until something knocked into her, and the stack of books she was carrying fell to the floor. Muttering something under her breath, she bent down to pick them up, and came face-to-face with Gregory Smith.

'What do you want?' she asked icily. She wasn't in the mood to be civil. She hadn't been for a while. It was therefore a mild surprise when he handed the dropped books to her. 'Thanks,' she said, a little dumbly, as she took them.

'Um,' Gregory started awkwardly, ' I'm really sorry about Ryan being... well, a complete hole.' Well, Aleera might have used slightly stronger language, although hearing this sudden apology was also quite surprising. She realised that she hadn't seen hide nor hair of Ryan Shane since her return to school. 'He kinda got suspended for it when the PTA complained or something.'

'Did he now?' Aleera asked disinterestedly. Ryan Shane wasn't her favourite topic of conversation.

'Look,' Gregory began, 'he's not really a bad guy, y'know?'

'Yes he is.'

'He just- I dunno- wait, what?'

'Yes he is,' Aleera said fiercely, as the last near-month boiled up inside her. 'He *is* a bad person. I've seen bad people, and Ryan Shane is a bad person. And the world- not just the schools, but the whole world- is full of people like him, and because nobody ever raises a hand to him, because nobody gets in his way, he's going to go out there into the world thinking that's how people are supposed to act.' She turned past him and walked down the corridor.

'Am I one of them?' Gregory asked. She stopped and turned round. 'I mean, I- I kinda hang out with him, so does- does that make me one?'

Aleera seriously considered this. 'Yes,' she said levelly, 'yes you are, because you let him get away with it. You let him treat you like something he stepped on, and that's the worst part, because Gregory, you, honestly, are ten times the person he is ever going to be. But if people who can stop bad people don't do anything, then that's all the bad people need.'

She walked away without another word, and left Gregory alone with his thoughts.

Aleera turned round slowly, briefly studying herself before she finished dressing. A dull patch of greyish skin now adorned her left shoulder, and across her left hip there was a thin scar like a piece of string. The skin seemed to have tightened around both scars. After taking a short moment to run one fingertip across the second scar, she slipped on the black dress, glancing at her reflection again as she held the veil between gloved hands. The scar on her forehead seemed almost unnoticeable by comparison.

The black shoes still rested at the foot of the bed as she turned her dark eyes, again tipped with mascara, down to the veil. This was it, then; and then back to the temporary quarters at the Guild until her old place was more than a charred wreck. She was only even in the hotel room thanks to her visitor.

A knock came from the door. 'You decent in there?' The female voice called.

'Yeah,' Aleera said quietly, partly turning round as the door opened, and in strode a slightly taller young woman of nineteen years, her long, silky black hair highlighted with streaks of pure gold that framed her strikingly features and flawless complexion, and a dark shirt and form-fitting jeans adorning her perfectly shaped body.

'I'll need to get to the airport soon,' Lilith said slightly guiltily, 'are you gonna be Ok?'

'Yeah, I'll be fine,' Aleera replied distantly. 'Thanks for coming, though.'

'You just have to call, you know that,' Lilith smiled warmly, pulling her younger sister into a soft hug. 'I missed you, you know.'

'I know,' Aleera sighed, a silent tear running down from her eyes. She didn't bother to stop it. Lilith was the one person she could never be embarrassed to cry around. ;I'll visit sometime, OK?' Even as she tried to talk, her voice wavered and her eyes crumpled into sunken wet pools.

'Hey, hey,' Lilith said warmly, stroking her sibling's hair fondly, 'it's alright.' Aleera shook quietly, crying into her shoulder. 'Come on now, it's alright.' Aleera's crying continued for another second before she stepped back, wiping her eyes. 'I'm sorry,' Lilith sighed, 'I shouldn't have moved. I shouldn't have just left you. I'm sorry.'

'I'll have to sort that mascara out before I go,' Aleera blurted out through her tears, forcing a laugh.

Lilith looked at her sister softly and sympathetically, stroking her hair again. 'You loved her, didn't you?' she asked tenderly.

'And Michael,' Aleera sniffed quietly. She might as well admit it now. No point hiding it from either of them anymore. 'I didn't know what I was going to do about it, and... and then this happened,' she sobbed.

'There, there,' Lilith whispered, giving her sister a soft kiss on the forehead. 'Do you want me to stay a little longer?' She offered.

'I'll be alright,' Aleera answered quietly, 'thanks for coming, though. I needed some company.' She wiped her eyes again.

'Any time,' Lilith promised. 'I've always got time for my baby sister.' Aleera allowed herself a small smile. Even now, Lilith always insisted on calling her by that old name. 'You know,' Lilith brought up softly, 'there's one thing I've been meaning to mention since I got here. I could- I've been thinking of it, so if you like- I could always come back to New York.'

Aleera was about to give an automatic reply, but then caught herself as a different, truer answer crept up on her. She smiled. 'I'd like that.'

From a distance, Jake watched Aleera approach the headstone from the dispersing attendants of the funeral with mournful sympathy tinged with troubling thoughts. Worries of dark magic still forced their way into his mind, swimming around his brain and biting at his thoughts as he tapped the old coin against the tree.

'How is she?' A voice asked from his side. Jake looked up darkly as Khazahn strode forward into the shade of the tree that he stood under.

'I don't think she'll be in a mood to talk to you,' Jake replied. 'For that matter, neither am I.'

'You're still upset.'

'Don't you dare tell me I, or Aleera, should *ever* forgive you.' Jake said viciously. 'Not after what you did. You're no better than Chara, Khazahn.' He finally spat, folding his fingers around the coin.

Khazahn turned away, casting a distant gaze over the headstones.

'I did what had to be done." He answered. 'Anyway, you'll probably be happy to know that Chara won't be bothering you again; by the time Daeiol's done with him, he'll be stacking shelves for a living. And the High Council is personally going to disband Sword of Heaven.'

'I guess that's good,' Jake said harshly, 'anything else?'

'We won't be seeing Harry again,' Khazahn informed him. 'I haven't seen Tomoko in a few days. I think she took it rather hard. The idea that one of our own could have been…'

'Well that's rich, coming from you,' Jake cut in. Khazahn didn't reply. 'I take it you've got your own ass covered, then,' he observed flatly, 'you must have known we'd start looking.'

'Of course I did,' Khazahn chuckled. 'Didn't you ever think that part of this whole thing didn't quite make sense?' And with that sentence something in Jake's mind clicked.

'The documents.' Jake nodded slowly. 'I never really figured out… why would Chara make documents on something like that?' Truth be told, he had thought of several explanations: Because he thought he was untouchable. To use as blackmail in case Sword of Heaven ever got too overconfident. But nothing quite seemed to make sense. Chara was a lot of things, but 'idiot' didn't make the cut. Jake could at least admit that.

'He wouldn't.' Khazahn answered simply. 'He was a madman, not an idiot.'

'You.,' Jake realised with a quiet gasp and a burst of surprise, 'you made a record of it.'

'And stored it in the archives,' Khazahn affirmed, "there to be found.'

'Clever.' Jake admitted with a slow nod. 'You planned it. Ever since you didn't show up to meet me…' Another mental click, 'You never had anything to tell me. You just wanted to make me curious.' That sly dog, he chuckled.

'Did you really think I'd let Chara get away with it?' Khazahn shrugged.

'You did.' Jake answered flatly, clearly to Khazahn's surprise. 'What?' he demanded angrily, 'you think this absolves you? Letting people die for your own ends is alright as long as you're doing it to get at someone worse?' He shouted.

'I never planned for that to happen,' Khazahn snapped back.

'It still did. At any moment when this was happening, you could have just gone to Daeiol with what you knew.'

'And get myself fired in the process?'

Jake just stood and glared at him.

'At least you finally said it for yourself,' he said darkly, returning the coin to his pocket. 'You betrayed all of us, Khazahn. Eight people- *eight* people- died just because you were too much of a coward to go around the paperwork or lose your job.' As he turned away, he looked at Khazahn with a mix of anger and utter contempt that said without words that he would never, *ever*, forgive him. 'I have nothing else to say to you.'

Khazahn turned and walked away himself, crumpling dead leaves underfoot. Then, after a second, he stopped, and slowly turned around.

'Give her a message from me,' he requested solemnly.

'What?'

'Tell her to enjoy herself while she can,' Khazahn said quietly, 'because in three months, she's theirs.'

Jake froze. His fists clenched.

'This isn't my decision,' Khazahn said, 'as far as the High Council's concerned; this mess just proves what we've always been worried about. The day Aleera turns eighteen; it's her choice between a Guild job and an eight-by-ten cell.'

Jake shook, his eyes burning holes in the back of Khazahn's head.

'This won't be the last,' Khazahn called back as he walked away. 'For her. Looking like that, associating with you, being *his* daughter… that's courting trouble from all angles. Do you ever think about that?'

'I do,' Jake answered, without turning around.

'And then?'

'And then," Jake had to fight to stop himself from smirking, 'I feel a great swell of pity for whatever poor idiot goes after that girl looking for trouble.'

Jake turned and walked away.

Even more lilies.

Sara Lammbe, the freshly chiselled letters read. Again the priest had soothed the mourners with sweet nothings to try and mask the tragedy as the coffin was lowered into the ground and thick, damp dirt shovelled onto it, and again she had stayed behind in the black dress, not to say goodbye, but to say how sorry she was.

That last, awful image was how Sara ended up, her eyes glossed over and her mouth full of blood as the tried to say her last words.

Aleera knew what those words would have been; the same thing she had said herself there at the end, the same thing she would have said to Michael if she had only been there at his last moment. And she meant those words. She truly did. So did Sara, and that was the worst part of all.

She wiped away another tear, allowing herself one more quiet sigh that was somehow tempered by the knowledge that, for better or worse, it was over. All of it.

She heard the footsteps approach behind her. "Skipping the wake again?" Jake asked.

'I just felt like going home.' Aleera said simply.

'Haven't seen you in a week.' Jake grabbed a thread of conversation from thin air. 'How're you holding up?'

'Not too bad, considering. Did you talk to Khazahn?'

'Sword of Heaven's going to be disbanded.'

Aleera nodded dimly, arms folded.

'I don't suppose telling you it's not your fault would do any good?'

Aleera's eyes lidded.

Jake sighed, glancing over as Khazahn left the cemetery.

'Aleera,' he asked, 'do you know why Chara did all of this?'

'Because of me?'

'Yes,' Jake said bluntly. 'Because you were raised by the worst madman that draconic society has ever known, and that is a risk beyond risks. And even discounting that, with everything that's happened to you in your life,' he said honestly, 'you would be entirely within your rights to go right off the deep end. From their standpoint, they needed to be ready in case that ever happened, because it looked to them like they were witnessing the beginnings of the next Kudra.'

Aleera nodded slowly and bitterly.

'But,' Jake went on, 'and here's the thing: they weren't. You didn't. You didn't kill anyone, Aleera, and I don't want you to ever forget that. It was Azrael that killed them- him, and him alone. Do you understand me?'

Aleera looked up at him, and the reason why she kept thinking of Jake as some kind of twisted father came back to her. It was because the idea wasn't twisted in the least.

'You saved a child's life, Aleera. You stopped him.'

'By killing him,' Aleera reminded him, 'with Dark Magic.'

'That doesn't make you like Kudra.'

'Then what does?'

'*You*,' Jake said with raw, pure honesty. 'Who your parents were doesn't matter. What happened to you doesn't matter. The only thing that matters is what *you* do. It's a choice that you make, your decision, because it's your life and what you do with it is up to nobody but you. And you...' he let out a slight chuckle, 'Well, just look at you. Your parents, your life, and then... you. Like this, after where you came from and what you've been through. Even now. God...' he looked her in the eye, 'You amaze even me just by being *you*.'

Aleera felt herself smile. She couldn't help it.

'Thanks, Jake.'

'No problem,' Jake smiled. 'So what now?'

Aleera shrugged. 'College,' she hazarded, 'get a job. I always wanted to open a restaurant somewhere.'

'Not a bad idea,' Jake beamed.

They both stepped back towards the church, Aleera glancing at Jake with a curiosity that had forced its way into her mind more than once, and which, reflecting on the cause of everything that had happened, she couldn't help asking.

'What are you, Jake?' She finally asked. Jake turned to look at her inquisitively. 'Really. What are you? You're not human. You're not Draconic. You're not a demon. You have access to dragon blood, and there haven't been any dragons for centuries. So what are you?'

Jake clicked his tongue, glancing over the cemetery as he removed the old coin from his pocket and flipped it over. 'You really want to know?'

'Yeah.' Aleera nodded.

'You'd never believe it.'

'Try me.'

Jake shook his head, stopped, and turned to her.

'OK,' he finally said, turning to her and taking a deep breath as if there were some inaudible drum role around them, as Aleera looked on in wide-eyed anticipation. And finally, he answered: 'I am...' he paused for a second, 'the only one there is.'

Aleera stopped, watching him with a perplexed face. 'What the hell does that mean?' She finally asked.

'Unique,' Jake grinned. 'Or as Katya puts it, bizarre.' He flipped the old coin.

'You're never going to tell any of us, are you?'

'No,' Jake answered more seriously. 'No, I'm not.'

'Why?'

'Because,' Jake answered definitely, taking a deep breath, 'I wouldn't wish it on my worst enemy.'

With that, he put the coin in his pocket, turned and walked back to the church, disappearing behind the heavy wooden door as Aleera watched, shaking her head in open confusion.

Jake was right, Aleera finally decided as they re-entered the church. But what she'd realised was that all the talk about 'good' and 'evil' always left out one thing that was at once small and so very vast: and that was the space in-between.

There was black and white, but then there was everything else, everything in-between. Nobody, none of the people around her in the street, none of them at school, was either of those things. And neither, she had finally realised, was she.

No, a shade of grey, a melting pot of both, a mix of her past, her blood and her own... soul? What else could it be? She'd never really thought about herself as having one of those. Almost strange to think about, really. Nice, though.

So how light, or how dark, was her shade of grey?

Whatever it is, came the answer. Where she came from didn't make a blind bit of difference, and her life was entirely at her discretion. It was something she should have realised sooner, and her single greatest regret was that she hadn't done so in time, and she would never know how things with Michael or Sara could have been. It wasn't a mistake she would make again.

She wouldn't be the monster that her father, or Azrael, or the world, wanted her to be. When the world told her what she was meant to be, it was up to her to plant her feet firmly on the ground and say: no, *this* is what I am.

And there was that word, that name, neither black nor white, waiting for her to change its shade of grey.

Aleera.

She turned to the church, to the wake, and to her life.

DRACONIC TRANSLATIONS

A list of translations of the examples of the now-unspoken Draconic language used in this novel.

<u>Draconic</u>   <u>English</u>

Appiras .... **Transport**
Blaish ....**Shell**
Eiah ....**Dark**
Fhieh ....**Fire**
Fhoa ....**Pull**
ThurraiFwaiyal...**Burning Wave**
Hthwail-Yiens ....**Third Eye**
Phoux ....**False**
Shliahsh...**Cut**
Sliahozai ....**Sting**
Sola ....**Light**
Thraio ....**Cast**
ThuraiShiahl ....**Wave of Force (basic offensive spell)**
Tyasans ....**Disappear**
Whoahn ....**Away**
Xiaol ....**Heal**
Zialahk ....**Cold**

Aleera will return in

Without Rules

Book 2 of the *Aleera* series